SO-BTE-859

Praise for
Their Wildest Dreams

"Like a demonic alchemist, Peter Abrahams has thrown several unstable compounds into his cauldron and is waiting to see how big the explosion will be."
—*Baton Rouge Advocate*

"Abrahams is once again at the top of his game in this wildly inventive, captivating caper. . . . This novel's multiple plot threads and unlikely assortment of characters carom off each other like so many carnival bumper cars."
—*Publishers Weekly*

"Surprise is a key ingredient for Abrahams. . . . His engaging characters—and their unpredictable journeys—keep the pages turning."
—*Kirkus Reviews*

"Abrahams excels at weaving his characters into a very intricate puzzle . . . the web of lies and deceit turns into the biggest mystery of all."
—*Romantic Times*

"*Their Wildest Dreams* takes [Abrahams] into another realm. . . . The book is hypnotic."
—*The Globe and Mail* (Toronto)

By Peter Abrahams

THE FURY OF RACHEL MONETTE
TONGUES OF FIRE
RED MESSAGE
HARD RAIN
PRESSURE DROP
REVOLUTION #9
THE FAN
LIGHTS OUT
A PERFECT CRIME
CRYING WOLF
LAST OF THE DIXIE HEROES
THE TUTOR
THEIR WILDEST DREAMS

Books published by The Random House Publishing Group
are available at quantity discounts on bulk purchases for
premium, educational, fund-raising, and special sales use.
For details, please call 1-800-733-3000.

THEIR WILDEST DREAMS

A NOVEL

PETER ABRAHAMS

BALLANTINE BOOKS • NEW YORK

Sale of this book without a front cover may be unauthorized. If this book is coverless, it may have been reported to the publisher as "unsold or destroyed" and neither the author nor the publisher may have received payment for it.

Their Wildest Dreams is a work of fiction. Names, characters, places, and incidents are the products of the author's imagination or are used fictitiously. Any resemblance to actual events, locales, or persons, living or dead, is entirely coincidental.

A Ballantine Book
Published by The Random House Publishing Group

Copyright © 2003 by Pas de Deux

All rights reserved under International and Pan-American Copyright Conventions. Published in the United States by Ballantine Books, an imprint of The Random House Publishing Group, a division of Random House, Inc., New York, and simultaneously in Canada by Random House of Canada Limited, Toronto.

Ballantine and colophon are registered trademarks of Random House, Inc.

www.ballantinebooks.com

ISBN 0-345-43942-2

Manufactured in the United States of America

OPM 9 8 7 6 5 4 3 2 1

First Edition: August 2003
First Mass Market Edition: November 2004

To Ann and Catherine

Acknowledgments

Many thanks to Niki Cohen and David Weisberg

In a way I knew less than before, as something written in a foreign language extends the range of your ignorance.

ROSS MACDONALD, *The Ivory Grin*

One

Mackie dreaded the mail. That was new, one of many new things in her life, none good. Lying in bed on a Saturday morning, clinging to sleep although she wasn't tired—this greediness for sleep also new—she heard the mail truck turning into Buena Vida Circle. The sound of its motor—part truck, part toy—grew louder, every little throb and rattle distinct in the desert air. Then came a squeak of brakes, followed by a pause in which she thought she heard mail thumping into the boxes at the foot of the circle; too far away to hear that, of course, had to be her imagination, if not playing tricks on her then anticipating that tricks were going to be played.

Two drivers shared the mail route—a man and a woman, both with sun-worn faces and long gray ponytails. The man always tapped the horn as he drove off. Like that: *toot toot*. People were friendly out West, as everyone said, and that toot-toot had sounded so optimistic in the beginning, back in the ground-breaking days. Now it made her heart race, like the opposite of a defibrillator. A wireless fibrillator: there was an idea. Niche-marketed to sadists and torturers it might bail them out, they being Lianne and her. Kevin would have to do his own bailing. Mackie got up, put on sweats, went outside.

A tangerine tree grew in her front yard. Each house in Buena Vida Estates—nine in all, arrayed like jewels around the circle, as the architect had put it; crammed, as

Mackie had said the first time she'd seen the plans, drawing one of those looks from Kevin—had a tangerine tree. Cost: $850 apiece. "Maybe this is a place we could cut back," Mackie had said. But Kevin wouldn't hear of it. Tangerines went with *estates* and the Santa Fe–style beams poking through the adobe walls and the heavy Spanish dark oak front doors, the whole concept they were selling, even if there was barely enough room to plant them. Mackie picked two bright orange beauties as she went by—pretty close to stealing from the bank.

She opened her mailbox, number four. Number four Buena Vida Circle—in her name alone now—was the original model home. And the nicest: she'd even loved it for a while, despite all the shortcuts and compromises she knew were part of it, from the foundation up. At the same time, she'd known it wasn't a permanent home, just the last and biggest sale, leading to a move even higher up. Now, no longer loving it, even closer to hate at times, Mackie wanted to hold on to this house forever.

Surprise: just one little envelope in the box, not the dammed-up cascade of overdue bills, lawyers' letters, and collection agency threats so often waiting to spring. Mackie plucked it out, one of those letters that still came addressed to her as Mrs. Kevin Larkin, even though the divorce was six months old and she'd gone back to her maiden name. A little distracted by that, she didn't notice at first that it came from the IRS.

The IRS. They never had any correspondence with the IRS; everything went through the accountant, Mr. Fertig, a careful old guy with lots of starch in his short-sleeve white shirts and neat little knots in his striped ties. Then she remembered Kevin saying something about a refund this year. Wouldn't that be something, a check he didn't get his hands on first? Mackie opened the envelope: no check. Kevin didn't slip up on things like that. She scanned the page inside, thick with type, waiting for the meaning to jump out at her. It did not. She had to read it three times, her eyes all of a sudden wild to speed ahead, faster than her mind could follow, before she understood that she owed the IRS $101,961.

Impossible. Mackie knew there were lots of people who didn't fear the IRS, but she wasn't one of them. She always made sure that Mr. Fertig had the two returns, their joint personal and the Buena Vida Development Company corporate, ready a month before filing date. It had to be a mistake. Her mind knew that, but the signal didn't get passed along to her hands, too unsteady to fold the letter and stick it back in the envelope.

She walked back toward her front door, the nine houses of Buena Vida Estates fanning out around her, the canyon rising into the Foothills beyond them, the mountains standing in the middle distance, cloudless sky above. Mountains on all sides, the first thing she'd noticed when they'd moved here, back when Kevin was still teaching tennis and Buena Vida Estates wasn't even a dream, at least not in her mind; mountains the first thing and still the best, the air a close second. She'd hiked in those mountains now, even in the heat of the summer, learned a bit about them. They weren't as green as they appeared from down here in the foothills, for example. Green came from the accumulated effect of the saguaros, like pixels, individually invisible at this distance, living up high at their own slow pace, blind to the million-dollar views of the city down below. Hiking up there, it was impossible, at least for Mackie, not to feel them doing something like thinking. Only recently was she starting to understand what was on whatever they had for minds: nothing human can make a lasting impression in this landscape.

Mackie went inside. Lianne was in the kitchen, hanging up the phone. That meant they still had service and the last check had cleared; this immediate reaction another one of those new things, not good.

"Morning, hon," Mackie said.

"Hi, Mom," said Lianne.

Who was on the phone? Mackie kept that remark, a mother's natural remark, inside. Teenagers needed space. But she couldn't help being curious because Lianne didn't have many friends. No fault of her own: she was a great kid. Going over all the good things about Lianne in her mind was one of Mackie's secret pleasures. But there'd been so many changes. First the move from back East, Lianne in the middle of sixth grade at the time. Then a few years later, when the development got going and the bank loans came through, they'd put her in private school, which was what everybody did, the kind of everybody they'd been getting to know. Now she went to Kolb High.

"Straight off the tree," said Mackie, handing Lianne a tangerine.

"Thanks." Lianne loved them.

They ate the tangerines—sweet, juicy, perfect. True luxury: $850 divided by two.

"That was Dad," Lianne said.

"Oh?"

"He's on his way over."

Saturday was Kevin's day with Lianne. That was the agreement. But he hadn't shown up the past three Saturdays, hadn't even bothered to call.

"What's the plan?" Mackie said.

Lianne shrugged. She was tearing the tangerine rind into tiny bits.

You don't have to go, Mackie thought. But unfair to say. A girl needs a father. She said: "Better get ready."

Lianne rose, pushed herself up from the table, really, like a nine-to-fiver off to work. Maybe divorce was like that for kids, an adult job suddenly handed to them, a hard one, sometimes a backbreaker.

Lianne was still in the shower when Kevin knocked on the front door. Mackie knew that knock—three taps, very quick, almost urgent. She knew every little thing about him. The big things were where she'd slipped up.

Mackie opened the door. "Oh, hi," he said, as though this were some nice surprise. "Lianne all set?"

"Not quite," Mackie said, moving aside. He came in, glancing at the mops and brooms by the door, went into the kitchen. Mackie checked his car out in the street before closing the door, in case he somehow had a new one, which would mean another big slipup on her part. But it was the same car he'd been driving since a week or two after the bank shut them down, yes, a BMW and, yes, a convertible, but this one twenty years old; and no graduate of the Yale School of Architecture waiting in the passenger seat, tapping her suntanned foot.

Kevin was leaning against the counter. Mackie sometimes still forgot how good-looking he was. From certain angles, like this one, he even appeared strong and resolute.

"Coffee brewing, by any chance?" he said.

"No."

Mackie handed him the letter.

"What's this?" he said.

"You tell me."

Kevin read the letter. She watched his eyes, beautiful deep brown eyes, like Lianne's although not so intelligent, one of Mackie's postdivorce realizations about him, and like all of them far too late. Did a little tremor cross their dark surface as he read, last faint wavelet from some deep disturbance? If so, it was gone in a flash.

"Must be some mistake," he said, handing the letter back. "I wouldn't worry about it."

"You're sure?"

"As I can be, under the circumstances."

"What does that mean?"

"It is addressed to you, after all," he said.

"What are you saying?"

"Just that I'm no longer privy to your finances."

Privy. Something about that word made her want to hit him in the mouth.

"What?" he said. "What?"

Privy. It meant free to root around. He'd rooted around in her finances, all right, to the tune of sixty thousand dollars, her inheritance and the foundation of the whole Buena Vida plan, the sixty grand turning into the down payment for the land less than a month after she got it, the land becoming the collateral for architectural, planning, and construction cost of the houses; a logical plan with millions in profits the inevitable result, golden, visible, almost tangible. *Leverage* was the magic word. They'd leveraged her father's heart attack.

But Mackie hadn't said no, had been caught up in the dream herself. Even now she wasn't sure how crazy it was. Who could have foretold all the bad things, the economy going one way, mortgage rates the other, and those last five houses sitting empty, month after month, no one even coming to look at them? "Unreal," as Jenna had said more than once, shaking her curls.

Jenna was the architect. Paid in full, Kevin had been scrupulous about that. She'd done a beautiful job, wedging those houses—clones, but all slightly unique, as though they'd been to different plastic surgeons or tailors—around Buena Vida Circle. Kevin had learned a lot from her, as he'd pointed out when Mackie questioned the size of Jenna's bills. And in the master bedroom of the model house, he'd taught Mackie some of those lessons. At first, she'd assumed he'd suddenly taken to reading *Maxim* or one of those magazines: *how to drive women wild.* What other source could there be of this newfound expertise? All of a sudden he had the touch, after years of not having it, of being just slightly off. Now he was dead-on, and with new themes and variations every time, rooting around inside her and, yes, driving her wild.

Mackie had figured it out eventually.

"Just tell me one thing," she said. Didn't *privy* also mean outhouse? Something right about that, although Mackie couldn't have said why.

"What's that?" Kevin said. He was leaning back slightly against the counter, wary, as though sensing an impending punch in the mouth, although of course there'd never been any of that.

"Tell me there are no more time bombs," Mackie said.

"Time bombs?"

"Financial time bombs you've left behind."

"How could there be?"

"That's not an answer."

"Then no. No time bombs."

"Not even one or two that could never possibly go off in a million years?"

He laughed, the kind of laugh that said, *What a character.*

"Think."

"Your tone could be a little more civil."

She didn't change it. "Think."

He thought. "Not a one," he said. "We're in a bomb-free zone." But she saw that fucking tremor in his eyes again.

"What's funny?" said Lianne, coming into the room with her overnight bag.

They turned to her. "Hey," said Kevin, crossing the room, giving her a big hug. "Who's getting better-looking every day?"

The top part of Lianne's face, from the eyes up, poked over his shoulder. Her gaze was on Mackie. "What were you laughing about?" she said.

"Mom—your mom and I were just shooting the breeze," said Kevin.

"About what?" Lianne said.

"Nothing important," said Kevin.

Lianne stepped out of Kevin's embrace, came over to give Mackie a quick kiss. "See you tomorrow, Mom."

"Have fun," Mackie said.

"Do our best," said Kevin, although she hadn't been talking to him.

Then they were out the door. Mackie watched them get into the car. Kevin said something that made himself laugh. Lianne put on sunglasses. They drove off, a little too fast, which was how Kevin drove, leaving an oily cloud hanging in the air. The desert wind swept it away.

Mackie tried Mr. Fertig's office, picturing him hard at work on a Saturday, tax time only a couple months away. But no. She left a message on his voice mail, brisk and untroubled, "Helen MacIsaac here, Mr. Fertig. Got a quick question, if you could get back to me."

Mackie went into the bathroom. It had his-and-her sinks, a vanity mirror surrounded with lightbulbs, and a round whirlpool bath where she and Kevin had played once or twice. A tiny spider ran down the drain.

Mackie brushed her teeth, pulled back her hair, and wound it into a tight bun, then stuck in her turquoise and silver comb, a gift to herself the day she arrived in Tucson, all about a new future and her belonging in it. Now she was a lot smarter and it was just a comb, but a nice one. Mackie gathered up her stuff—mops, broom, vacuum, cleansers, dustpan, toilet brush—and left for work.

Two

"Where are we going?" Lianne said. Her dad had an apartment over a video store on Stone Avenue, down in the Mexican part, but they weren't headed that way, which was fine with her as it was such a pit.

"A little surprise," said Kevin, raising his voice over the wind. It streamed through his hair like in a commercial for perfect male hair. She was the envy of all the other kids when it came to how young her dad looked, which wasn't worth thinking about for more than twenty seconds, and no one did.

"Like what?" Lianne said.

"Hardly be a surprise if I told you," said Kevin, "now would it?"

Mom and Dad were just full of surprises. For example, this hint of a Western cadence that was creeping into his speech, like he came from deep cowboy roots: why did that have to happen? Nothing stayed the same. Safe behind her bronzed Revos, slipped down her shirt at a Sunglass Hut, Lianne closed her eyes.

The ride got bumpy and she woke up. They were on a dirt road out in the desert, crossing one of those washes. A faded sign read COLDWATER WASH, but like almost all the washes, arroyos, and even the goddamn rivers out here, it was dry. Trees grew along the banks, sharing in the joke. Lianne wished she'd brought one of those tangerines. Ever since they'd moved West, she'd been thirsty all the time; not hungry, just thirsty.

"Where are we?" she said.

"Almost there," said Kevin.

Lianne pictured an endless tail of dust rising behind them. She looked back and saw it was there.

They mounted a rise, rounded a bend with steep hills on either side, crossed a gray-green valley full of cacti, mesquite, palo verde, none of which she was sure about when it came to matching the name to the thing. Some buildings dwarfed by rocky outcrops sat at the other end.

"Feast your eyes," said Kevin.

"On what?"

"Our new home," Kevin said. "Leastwise mine, and yours too, every Saturday and alternating holidays."

Leastwise? Was he trying to be funny? She glanced over, saw no clue. Then came a sign arching over the road, the letters branded in: OCOTILLO RANCH.

"You're living on a ranch?" Lianne said.

"Living and working," said Kevin, as pavement began and took them past stables, corrals, and outbuildings to a big lodge, much bigger than it had appeared from the valley entrance, with a long shaded porch and a stone fountain out front. Kevin switched off the engine. It was quiet, just the fountain splashing softly and a horse neighing somewhere out of sight.

"What kind of work?" Lianne said.

He turned to her. "Where'd you learn to ask all these questions?" he said, and added a big smile.

Was that some sort of jab at Mom? Lianne didn't think of her mother as much of a questioner, at least not until recently. She said nothing.

"Hop out," said Kevin, "and I'll show you."

Lianne didn't move. "Is Jenna here?"

Kevin stopped smiling. He licked his lips. "This thing,"

he said, "was never about her. I thought I'd got that across."

"Thing?" said Lianne.

"Divorce. People grow apart. That's the unfortunate truth. But I'm still your dad and always will be. Do you understand?"

What was to understand? Dads and their offspring, it happened all the time: pop pop pop.

He patted her knee. "Everything's going to be fine," he said. "And she's not here. Not here and won't be."

"You mean you've grown apart from her too?" Lianne said.

"If you want to put it that way, yes."

That was fast, Lianne thought. Did it mean that maybe there was a chance Mom and Dad might grow back together? "What were you and Mom laughing about back in the kitchen?" she said.

He thought back. Whenever he was thinking hard like that, he didn't look quite so young. "I guess that was just me laughing by myself, baby," he said.

Lianne got out of the car. She felt the wind, blowing out of the north; not that she was good at directions, just assumed it was north from the chill it gave her. They climbed the steps to the front door, dark, massive, and scarred, although the brass studs were polished bright.

"See this?" said Kevin, pointing out something in the wood.

She saw an arrowhead stuck in at an angle.

"Apaches," he said.

"They didn't like the food?" Lianne said.

"For Christ's sake, Lianne, this was in the eighteen somethings." He opened the door. "Very funny," he added as they went in.

"What's funny?" said a man coming the other way, a young man in tight jeans, cowboy boots, spurs.

"Jimmy," said Kevin. "How're you doin'? This is my daughter, Lianne. Say hi to Jimmy Marz. He's the head wrangler."

"Hi," said Lianne.

"Assistant," said Jimmy. There was just a tiny still moment while he looked at her. She looked back, undetectable behind her Revos. "Nice to meet you," said Jimmy. "What was funny?"

"Just a little joke Lianne made about the food," said Kevin.

"The food at Ocotillo?" said Jimmy. "What's the joke? It's the best in southern Arizona."

Lianne laughed, not knowing why. It was funny somehow—arrowhead, gourmet cooking, assistant wranglers. Jimmy laughed too. Small teeth, but white and even, in a suntanned face; pink tongue. "Here for the weekend?" he said.

"Overnight," said Lianne.

"At college somewhere?"

"Still in high school," said Lianne.

"Cool," said Jimmy. "See you at suppertime." He went out with a jingle-jangle of spurs that should have sounded silly, but didn't.

Lianne and her dad crossed the room, a big room with a high ceiling, stone fireplaces at either end, terra-cotta floor with scattered Indian rugs, little groups of heavy leather furniture, and flowers everywhere. On the far side stood a hotel-style front desk, suitcases lined up beside it. Behind the desk, an old man sat staring at a computer screen.

"Frozen again," he said.

"Let me have a look," said Kevin, going behind the desk. "My daughter, Lianne. Mr. Croft, owner of the Ocotillo Ranch and all you can see for miles and miles."

"Me and Western Savings," said Mr. Croft, raising his eyes from the screen. Tired old eyes, half-shut from the heavy lids, but they brightened a little when they saw Lianne. "My, my," he said.

"There you go, Mr. Croft," said Kevin, tapping at the keyboard. "All set." A hand of solitaire popped up on the screen. "And I should have those estimates for you tomorrow."

"Mr. Efficiency," said the old man. "Your father's a breath of fresh air around here, I can tell you. Had lunch yet, young lady?"

"No," said Lianne.

"Well then, take her on over to the buffet, Kevin, and get her fed," said Mr. Croft.

"I'm not really hungry," said Lianne.

"On my tab," said Mr. Croft. "Number one."

The dining room had a view of the swimming pool, bluer than any she'd ever seen, for some reason, and three horse trails leading up into the hills, each trailhead marked with a giant saguaro. They helped themselves to lunch—eighteen-ounce T-bone and fries for Kevin, fruit salad and coffee for Lianne—and took a table by the picture window.

"Quite a guy, Mr. Croft," said Kevin.

Lianne ate a cherry. "What estimates?" she said.

"Estimates?" said Kevin, dipping a forkful of fries in ketchup.

"That you're going to have by tomorrow."

"Right," said Kevin. He raised his hand and a waiter came over. "How about one of those prickly pear margaritas, Ramon?"

"Certainly," said Ramon. "And another for the lady?"

Lianne glanced at her dad.

"Specialty of the house," said Ramon.

"Okay," said Kevin. "As long as it's mostly virgin, Ramon."

"Mostly virgin," said Ramon, moving toward the bar.

Lianne tried a cantaloupe ball, biting it in half, leaving the rest uneaten.

"These estimates," Kevin said, "are what my new job's about."

"Which is?"

"Hard to put into words. The leisure business in general, I guess you could say."

"You're working for Mr. Croft?"

"Officially, no. Not yet. We're still in the exploratory phase." He leaned forward. "But just between you and me, this is the beginning of something good."

"Like what?"

"Bringing Ocotillo Ranch into the twenty-first century. No more, no less."

Her dad's face was glowing. Lianne could feel his enthusiasm, like a warm front pressing against her. "What does that mean?" she said.

"Look around," Kevin said. "What do you see?"

Lianne looked around. "It's one of those dude ranches, right?"

"We don't say dude ranches anymore. *Dude*'s kind of changed a bit, the meaning. They're guest ranches now. But basically, you're right. It's a place where city people can come for the Old West experience. And this is one of the best, in terms of the existing infrastructure and real estate. The problem is the riding, the horses, the desert, all that's not enough anymore. Mr. Croft knows that. He just needs someone to help him get started."

"Doing what?"

Ramon arrived with two big glasses of peach-colored liquid, thick and frothy.

"Here's to Ocotillo Ranch," her dad said.

Lianne took a sip, a sip that turned into more of a drink. Prickly pear and lots, lots more, not virginal at all: the Old West experience. She took off her Revos.

"Good, huh?" said Kevin.

She nodded.

"And good for you too, that prickly pear juice. Grown and pressed right here on the property."

Lianne had some more. "Doing what, Dad? What are you going to be doing?"

He smiled at her, a loving smile. She realized she'd called him Dad. "I'm in charge," he said, "or soon will be, of the first phase in the redevelopment of the ranch."

"Which is?"

"I'll put it in three words," he said, chewing on a bite of steak; a juicy one because a little leaked out of the corner of his lip. "Golf. Tennis. Spa." He cut another piece. "Leaving out the later phases, condos and such, for now, since our discussions haven't reached that stage. Phase one is tennis. The estimates are for eight lighted DecoTurf courts that'll go right about there."

"Where the eucalyptuses are?"

"They'll have to come down."

She took another drink. "So you'll be teaching tennis again?"

A rider came over the ridge on the middle trail, easy and relaxed in the saddle, followed by about a dozen more, not as easy and relaxed, but looking richer somehow, even though everyone was dressed the same in jeans and denim shirts. Maybe it was their cowboy hats, all crisp and clean, except for the lead rider, his hat dusty and stained.

"I'm going to tell you something important," Kevin said. *Uh-oh. Mood change.*

"What?"

"Regarding that remark you made, teaching tennis again."

"A question," said Lianne, "not a remark."

"It doesn't matter. Listen up."

She felt the temptation, even at her age, to cover her ears. He held up his knife. "When life knocks you down, you have to get right back up. If you do it quick enough no one even notices."

But what if you knock yourself down, Dad?

"What's funny?"

"Nothing," Lianne said.

"Your mother has exactly the same—" He stopped himself. "The point I'm making is that you have to develop people skills in this life. Real estate companies, vacation companies, they all come and go, but people will always be around. Do you understand what I'm saying?"

"People will always be around."

"And therefore?"

The riders came down the hill, smiling and talking, probably wondering what was for lunch. Another rider galloped into view from off to the right, rode up to meet them, a FedEx package under his arm. A hatless rider, this one, and she recognized him: Jimmy Marz. Some expression she'd heard about being one with the horse? Lianne understood it now.

"And therefore?" her father repeated.

"And therefore you have to make them like you."

Kevin sat back. "Well, I wouldn't put it quite so bluntly. But yes."

Suddenly Lianne began to understand the divorce much better. Her father sold himself. Her mother didn't.

A woman on a white horse took the FedEx package from Jimmy Marz and said something that made him laugh. Lianne finished her drink. Nothing virginal about it. She caught Ramon's eye.

Three

It wasn't just that you learned a lot about people by cleaning up their shit. Mackie had expected that. But why was all of it nothing you wanted to know? Didn't anyone leave a few good things about themselves lying around, didn't anyone have secrets of the admirable kind?

Take, for example, the Thorsens at 7 Buena Vida Circle. The Thorsens had actually begun negotiating for number seven while Mackie and Kevin still owned the Buena Vida Development Company, or BV Devco as he always called it, the name itself almost magic on his tongue, like *presto* or *shazam*. Presto, shazam, and suddenly after five whole months without a single showing, up drove the Thorsens, out for a Sunday spin. In less than an hour they'd made a full-price offer.

Too late: by the time of the closing, the bank owned BV Devco, shutting them down the day before. If only that check from the Thorsens—$247,900, the exact number branded in Mackie's permanent memory—had gone to them, if only they could have hung on a little longer, wasn't it possible that when number three . . . She stopped right there. That was a bad tendency of hers—looking back led nowhere useful. Remembering that exact number, or how she and Kevin had hugged each other after the Thorsens left, how he'd lifted her and spun her around, that whole wonderful high that came with last-second victory: how could that be useful? Kevin forgot the past completely and at once. And his present was just the launching pad to the future, where he did most of his living, as she'd come to learn. The crazy thing was she'd had lots of fun living in that future of his too, while it lasted. Now he was probably working on another one.

Mackie returned to this little problem of the Thorsens' bedding. Saturdays—when she also cleaned for the Herrods at number two and for friends of the Herrods around the corner on Tanque Verde, as well as dusting and vacuuming the two still unsold houses, six and eight—was the day for changing the Thorsens' sheets. Mrs. Thorsen knew that; she'd laid out the schedule. So why had they left behind under twisted sheets this little three-tailed whiplike thing?

Mackie picked up the whiplike thing, tiny, more of a toy, really, and read the logo on the handle: EROTIBOUTIQUE, the letters bent into the outline of a couple having sex. She flicked it lightly at the back of her hand. It stung. What was she supposed to do with it? Mrs. Thorsen was one of those a-place-for-everything-and-everything-in-its-place people. Where was the place for this, Martha Stewart? Under the bed? Under a pillow? On top of a pillow? None of them right, all too intimate or knowing. Mackie laid it on the bedside table for now, beside the framed photo of the Thorsens' grandchildren in front of a Christmas tree, and therefore not right either—and stripped the bed.

Mackie threw the sheets and pillowcases into the washer, made the bed with fresh bedding from the linen closet, vacuumed the house from top to bottom, scrubbed the shower stalls and sinks and toilets, mopped the bathroom floor—Mr. Thorsen was one of those hairy guys, shed lots of silvery hair, curly and brittle. She had the music cranked up high—today she'd brought Paquito D'Rivera, with those congas, mesmerizing, irresistible— and in no time she was done. Maybe not no time, but done, and there was her pay envelope, fifty dollars inside, on the kitchen table.

Mackie took it, packed up her stuff, and moved on to the Herrods': two hours, another $50. Then the Herrods' friends on Tanque Verde, messy friends who didn't seem to know the purpose of a toilet brush, but liked having the baseboards scrubbed every week: three hours, $75.

You could make good money cleaning houses, better than working in an office, for which Mackie wasn't trained, or teaching dance, for which she was. Needing money was her life right now, the plain truth. Christ, that sixty grand, so hard not to think about. Without any lever-aging, that sixty grand, her share of her father's house in Albany, could have been her future, more than enough to start her own dance studio. She'd even found a space, over a gym on Park, near the U of A. Kevin had had other ideas. *You can open a whole chain after we're done with Buena Vida.* And he would run through the numbers, punching them on the calculator, always reaching that huge climax of really big ones, the last three properties turning into pure profit, thanks to the way Jenna had fit nine houses on the space for six. The beauty part, as Kevin liked to say.

But a whole chain of dance studios had never occurred to Mackie. Her dream had always been owning just the one. She'd given a lot of thought to the name. Some studio owners used their own—Angie Garcia's Dance Academy, for example, where Mackie had taught until the develop-ment got going and Kevin needed her. But for her own place, Mackie wanted a name that said something, maybe the most important thing, about what dance meant to her. The name she'd finally settled on—Into the Mystic School of Dance—wasn't even original—she'd had no luck com-ing up with anything original—but it put in words that feeling of being inside the music, like one of the instru-ments, only silent.

By the time Mackie drove back into Buena Vida Circle, the sun was low in the sky, the mountains red and gold. Once a week she cleaned six and eight; in return, the bank reduced the monthly mortgage on number four by $500, just enough to allow her to hold on to the house, if things stayed the way they were.

Mackie parked in the driveway of number six, used her key to enter the side door, the vacuum cleaner hose getting caught and almost tripping her as she went in. "Shit," she said, and only then saw the four people in the kitchen: a man opening the ice cube drawer—fridge from Amana, one of seven at $1,590; a woman gazing into the cabinet over the sink—laminates, but good ones, Mackie had spent days finding them, averaging $6,700 per kitchen; another woman wearing a Century 21 button; and Carole from the bank. They all turned to her. Had she missed their cars parked out front, her eyes on those mountains? That would be her.

"Ah," said the Century 21 woman to her customers. "The help."

The customers made friendly little waves.

"Mind coming back in a bit?" said Carole. Mackie liked Carole. Carole had sold her bosses on the idea of separating number four from the bank's takeover and then made the numbers work.

"Sure," said Mackie. "I'll do eight first."

"We've got a showing going on there too," Carole said.

"Oh," said Mackie. A silent moment or two went by. It struck her that they'd been discussing the history of BV Devco; perhaps she'd even interrupted it. Mackie backed out of the house.

Darkness lay on Buena Vida Estates now, but above, the sky was pink and the rocky crests of the mountains on fire. Fire glowed on the windows of the cars in front of numbers six and eight. Mackie went home.

She turned on a light or two, not many; electricity bills

were high and the air-conditioning season hadn't even started. The answering machine was flashing. Mackie hit *play*. Mr. Fertig. "Funny you've got a question for me. I've got one for you too." Mackie tried his office and home numbers, reached machines at both places, left her name.

She was hungry. Had she eaten anything since that tangerine? She found herself sitting down to think about it. Her favorite chair, severe-looking but very comfortable, chosen by Jenna during the furnishing of the model home, stood in a corner of the family room and had a view of the Catalinas. Darkness was flowing up their slopes now, swallowing up the red and gold foot by foot. Mackie watched night taking over; then closed her eyes, just for a moment. Sleep was out of the question: six and eight were waiting. Plus she never went to sleep without saying a few words. Not a prayer, exactly, because she didn't believe anyone out there was listening: this was more of a wish list, almost certainly useless. Lately she'd pretty much pared the list down to two items. One: Make me a little stronger. Two: Keep an eye out for Lianne. She didn't say them now because she wasn't going to sleep. Just because her eyes were closed didn't mean she was sleeping.

Lianne smelled smoke. She opened her eyes, saw stars through a window, many more than usual and much brighter, remembered at that moment she wasn't in her bed at 4 Buena Vida Circle, but in her sleeping bag on the couch in the living room of her father's place at Ocotillo Ranch. What did he call it? A *casita*. There were four or five of them, little adobe cabins for the staff on a hill near the nature trail.

Lianne got up, opened the window. A campfire burned down by the corrals, human shadows moving around it. And maybe a guitar was playing too. She leaned out the window, was sniffing in that peppery mesquite smoke, when she heard a voice close by, close and sudden enough to startle her; her father's voice. ". . . even crazier, if you know what I mean," he was saying. Lianne jumped back inside the sleeping bag.

The front door opened, too dark to see, but Lianne heard its creak. Then, softly, he said: "Lianne?"

Lianne was silent.

"Shh," he said.

Then came another voice: "I'm shhing as hard as I can." And a giggle. A woman's voice, but not Jenna's.

"Shh," he said again.

Two dark forms crossed the room, slow and quiet, passing within a few feet of her head. Lianne could hear them breathing. The bedroom door closed with a little click.

Lianne lay still. In a little while, she began hearing more sounds, predictable ones. She got up, got dressed, all in silence, and climbed out the window.

Lianne walked down toward the campfire, a breeze, faint but cold in her face, the hard ground crunching under her feet. Six people sat around the fire but none of them—four men and two women, one strumming a guitar—heard her. She stood just beyond the reach of the firelight—like one of those long-ago Apaches, she thought, part of the land. The woman with the guitar was singing. *"Why can't I free your doubtful mind, and melt your cold cold heart?"* The others—she recognized only the lead rider from that afternoon and Jimmy Marz—were drinking beer and passing around a joint. A nice little scene, Lianne thought, rustic but fun. She stepped into the light.

The music stopped. Everyone looked up at her. The expressions on their faces all changed to two basic types, one for the men, another for the women.

"Hey," said Jimmy Marz.

"Just out for a walk," said Lianne. An inane kind of remark, but no one seemed to notice.

"Cool," said Jimmy Marz. "Everybody, this is Kevin's daughter."

"That's easy to see," said the woman with the guitar.

"Lianne, right?" said Jimmy Marz.

"Right," said Lianne.

"Have a seat," he said.

She sat on a rock, warm from the fire.

"This here's . . ." And he introduced them all, a string of names, Lianne catching the lead rider's—Rags—and the guitar player's—Nadine.

"First time at Ocotillo?" said Rags; there were lots of silvery hairs in his mustache, tipped orange by the firelight.

Lianne nodded.

"How do you like it so far?" said Nadine, passing her the joint.

"I don't know much about ranches," Lianne said, taking it. She didn't really want to smoke. Smoking weed with adults, even though most of these adults didn't seem what you could call old—how weird would that be? Putting it like that, on the other hand, made it more like an experiment, part of growing up. *Talked myself into it,* Lianne thought, and took a big hit, passing the joint to Rags. "But the sky's nice," she added.

"We got sky," said Nadine.

"I'm so sick of it," said the other woman. "We should have gone into town."

"And done what?" said one of the men.

"Anything. That blues bar on Speedway."

"Full of tourists," said Nadine. "I can play some blues if you like."

No one said whether they would or not. Nadine took out a slide, stuck it on the baby finger of her left hand, played some blues. She was pretty good. Every time the word *ramblin'* came around, she made a high whining sound with the slide. She had thick, square-ended fingers with chipped nails and rings on almost every one.

Someone handed Lianne a beer. She didn't like the taste of beer, but what the hell.

I've got ramblin', ramblin' on my mind.

"Your dad's a resort developer?" said Rags.

"I guess," said Lianne. The music faded, although Nadine still played. Lianne grew more conscious of Jimmy and Rags on either side of her, and the warm stone beneath.

"Any particular resorts he's worked on?" said Rags.

"Hey," said Jimmy. "Don't pester the lady."

The lady. That was kind of dorky. But nice too. Jimmy handed her the joint. She took another hit. The moon popped up, over the sharp black edge of some distant peak. Had she ever seen the moon quite like this? Nope.

"Like horses?" said Jimmy.

"Not really."

"Done much riding?"

"A little." She'd gone on some of the Pusch Peak trails with friends from Fenster, back in her private school days; correction: acquaintances from Fenster.

Jimmy nodded. The fire glowed orange on his profile, redder along his cheekbone and jawline. "I've got an idea," he said.

"What?" said the woman who wanted to go into town.

"Full moon," Jimmy said. "How about a little ride?"

"Christ sake," said the woman. "I was out all day. Won't be able to close my legs for a week as it is."

"What's new?" said Nadine.

"Anybody?" said Jimmy. "Just up the canyon, far as the mine, say."

They all shook their heads. Jimmy turned to Lianne.

"What mine?" she said.

"Old gold mine, over toward the Ruby Road."

Lianne was starting to like all this, slide guitar, gold mine, Ruby Road. "Why not?" she said.

"Any other takers?" said Jimmy.

She liked that word too, *takers*. There were no other.

Jimmy rose, lowered his hand to help her up. She got up on her own.

"I'm not much of a rider," she said.

"Don't have to be for this," Jimmy said. "It's cake."

Cake was good too. *Slide, gold, ruby, takers, cake.*

Jimmy saddled two horses, led them out of the barn.

"This here's Bonnie," he said. "Gentlest animal on the ranch. The thing about mounting a horse," he began, but she was already up, foot in the stirrup and leg over in one easy motion. "Hey," he said. "You're a pro."

Far from it, but right now it all seemed so easy for some reason. "Try to keep up," Lianne said.

Jimmy laughed, mounted his horse, a huge black thing. Lianne felt Bonnie shifting under her, maybe worried about something, like going out at night. Lianne squeezed her legs and Bonnie relaxed. She was starting to like horses.

"Just stay beside me," Jimmy said. "Bonnie'll do all the work." He made a little click with the side of his tongue— Lianne could tell from the sound—and they were off, walking at first, then trotting. Lianne felt Bonnie's rhythm, slid back and forth with it. She'd taken enough dance, God knew, to have a little rhythm.

"What's his name, your horse?" she said.

"Clyde," said Jimmy.

They rode around the back side of the stables, came in sight of the campfire a few hundred yards to their right, the people now shadows again. Bonnie thought of going that way, but Lianne gave a little tug on the left rein, and Bonnie got in line behind Clyde, following him up past the three trailheads, their tall saguaros silver in the moonlight.

Jimmy turned in his saddle. "So far so good?" he said, his little white teeth shining, and the white of his eyes too.

"No complaints."

"Gets a little steep in here."

She caught up with him. A dark mass sloped up on their right. She smelled leather, polished and sweated on over and over by horses and people, and something else, a spice maybe, the kind Mom sprinkled in the spaghetti sauce.

"All set?" Jimmy said.

"Say the word."

Jimmy made that click again, headed straight up the dark slope. Bonnie went in tandem, as though that click had been for her too. Lianne leaned forward a little, helping Bonnie up, but Bonnie didn't need it. Lianne could feel the shifting of muscles, smooth and heavy, beneath her. They reached the top of the rise, halted.

The moon was higher now, and very bright, everything more like a black-and-white movie than the night. Ahead lay a wide canyon with complicated arrangements of hills on either side, almost green in the moonlight. A sharply angled rocky outcrop, silver on the side, black in front, rose in the distance.

"The mine's up there," Jimmy said, following her gaze. "But if you've had enough . . ."

Lianne was about to say, *Don't say that again, this is fun,* when something stopped her. A sound, very close, like one of those marimbas. No, not marimbas, more like a rattle. The next moment, Bonnie bolted up beneath her, hooves clawing the sky. Lianne grabbed the pommel with both hands. Then she was in midair, but her feet still somehow in the stirrups, and she came back down hard in the saddle, clutching at the pommel again as Bonnie sprang ahead, flying down the back side of the slope and into the canyon.

Lianne clung on with her legs, found the reins, jerked them back with all her strength. "Bonnie, Bonnie." Bonnie took no notice, just galloped faster and faster, her strength now jerky, frantic. This was speed beyond anything Lianne had felt, wild, out of control, deadly.

"I could die." She grabbed Bonnie's mane and yanked it

again and again. Bonnie surged forward. Lianne dug her hands into Bonnie's neck. Bonnie's pulse roared in there. *Fucking bitch, you're going to kill me.*

The speed, the noise, the pounding: it was going to end in something horrible. That was Lianne's last thought before Bonnie threw her and bashed her brains out. But in that moment after thinking stopped, Jimmy suddenly flew up beside her. He leaned down from the saddle, got an arm around her waist.

"Let go," he said.

Lianne let go. He lifted her off Bonnie like nothing, swung her over the empty space between the horses—the stony ground flashing by—and onto his saddle, facing him. Now she was going faster than ever, but there was nothing jerky about it. She was just floating, floating in Jimmy's lap, way up in space somewhere.

"Hold on," he said. She put her hands around his neck. He reached across, took Bonnie's rein. "Now, now," he said, not loud, the vibrations of the words right in Lianne's ear. Bonnie pulled up right away.

The horses came to a stop, shuffling around a little, their steam rising in the night. Lianne thought she could feel them forgetting the whole thing already. She looked into Jimmy's eyes. There was really nowhere else to look, their faces about six inches apart.

"You all right?" he said.

"Better than that," said Lianne.

"Yeah?"

"Yeah," she said, leaned forward those six inches and kissed him on the lips. On the lips, but no tongue or anything like that. Still no thinking: she'd had her last thought.

Then there was tongue. He tasted good: no surprise there, those little white teeth, so clean.

Clyde began to move, at a walk, up the canyon. Jimmy moved with him, so easily, the easy movement passing right through to her. Even though the reins were loose,

Jimmy's arms around her now, she felt his complete control. Bonnie followed, making a snuffling sound.

Horse smells were stronger now, and so were their own. Her shirt opened up, his too, a cowboy shirt with those funny slanted pockets. Jimmy moving underneath her, Clyde beneath them both; all that power and the moon above: there was no stopping this. Somewhere along the way, Lianne unzipped Jimmy's jeans, freed him up.

"Let's get down," he said.

"What for?" said Lianne, and then did something that amazed him, although it really wasn't much—all those dance classes had made her supple. Lianne rolled back, up onto Clyde's neck, snapped off her own jeans. Then she rolled back onto him, or almost. Jimmy got his hands under her, shifted her a little. She saw amazement in his eyes, had no doubt of that.

Be gentle, she thought, this is my first time. But she didn't speak. Who would believe it? Clyde moved on up the canyon, a little faster now, his huge muscles rippling.

Four

Mackie awoke, the phone ringing beside her. Milky early-morning light came through the window. She was still in the chair, Jenna's chair, angular but comfortable; a destabilizing image of Kevin and Jenna in this same chair rose in her mind. Could that have happened? Had there ever been an opportunity? Lots, probably. She pushed herself up from the thing—in what way was divorce final?—and picked up the phone.

"This is Marge Thorsen."

"Yes, Mrs. Thorsen?"

Pause. "We won't be needing you anymore."

"You're moving?" Mackie said.

"Whatever gave you that idea? I take it we're all paid up."

"Is there something about the quality of the work? Because I—"

"We won't be needing your services, that's all."

At that moment, Mackie remembered the stupid whip, toy, whatever it was, that she'd left temporarily on the bedside table, beside the photo of the grandchildren—and that goddamn Christmas tree!—and forgotten. It must have looked so judgmental, exactly the kind of statement Jerry Falwell would have made if he were a cleaning lady. Mackie was trying to find the lighthearted remark that would make everything right, maybe something having to do with Jerry Falwell—although, come to think of it,

didn't the Thorsens go to church every Sunday?—when
Mrs. Thorsen said good-bye.

Fifty dollars, twice a week, now subtracted. Mackie
couldn't afford subtraction. She gathered her stuff—mops,
broom, vacuum, cleansers, dustpan, toilet brush—and left
for work.

Mackie cleaned number eight first. They'd come so
close to selling number eight, three offers the day it went
on the market, bang bang bang, all within 10 percent of
asking price. That had given Kevin the idea they'd priced
them all too low; he upped the other houses ten to fifteen
thousand dollars apiece and sent back the three offers
without budging. *A bidding war! This is it, baby.* One
woman had even pleaded on the phone—it was the house
of her dreams but they couldn't afford a penny more, oh,
please—but Kevin had been firm. This was around the
time his sexual prowess was at its height.

The buyers went away and no others had appeared since.
Months later Kevin had talked Mackie into calling the
pleading buyer—*I'd do it myself but this needs a woman's
touch*—to ask if the offer still stood, making a plea of her
own; spurned with relish.

Mackie walked over to number six, the Thorsens driving
past at that moment in their Sunday best, eyes straight
ahead. One of yesterday's visitors had used the downstairs
bathroom, blocking the toilet, as she found out when she
tried to flush it. Mopping up the mess, Mackie tried to picture Jerry Falwell in cleaning-lady garb and found she easily could. She went home for the plunger. The phone was
ringing.

"This is Carole. Just wanted to give you a quick heads-
up."

"About what?"

"Offers came in."

"Offers?"

"On six and eight. From yesterday's showings. Good offers, Mackie. I'm sure the bank will accept them."

"Meaning?"

"Meaning I'll be by to pick up the keys tomorrow."

"You're changing the locks?" Mackie didn't get it.

"Is there something wrong with them?" Carole said.

"No."

"Then why would we do that? It's just that you won't be needing the keys."

"But how can I—"

"Mackie."

She started to get it. "I'm not taking care of the houses anymore?"

"Basically."

And got a little more. "So the five hundred dollars you've been deducting from the mortgage?"

"Will start appearing on your next bill," Carole said.

Oh, God.

"Although that's not really the problem," Carole added.

Mackie sat down. "What is?"

"Simply that unless your financials have changed, the bank can't allow you to maintain a mortgage at the new level."

"Are you saying I'll lose the house?" Mackie realized she was still holding the plunger, let it go.

"Not in so many words. But unless your financials have changed . . ."

Financials. The meaning of the word wouldn't come. "I don't understand."

"Are you earning more money than last year?"

"You know the answer to that."

"Then can you pay off some of the principal?"

"How much?"

"I don't have the figures here. But probably something in the nature of fifteen or twenty thousand."

Giant numbers, as big at that moment as any end-of-the-rainbow numbers Kevin had ever crunched. "There must be another way."

Pause. "Can I venture a comment here, Mackie?"

"What?"

"At the risk of . . ."

Mackie waited.

"Maybe you should just let it go," Carole said.

Mackie didn't get that either. "The toilet's blocked in number eight," she said, and hung up.

Needing money was her life. That meant she had to be doing something to earn it every second, yet ahead lay this long Sunday with nothing money-making scheduled. Who wanted the cleaning lady around on Sunday? Mackie called Angie Garcia.

"Do you still have classes Sunday afternoons?"

"Lyrical and jazz," Angie said.

"Do you need anyone?"

"Thinking of getting back into it?"

"Today."

"Today?" Angie said.

"And maybe Sundays in general."

"You know how small those Sunday classes are. I teach them myself."

"So you don't need anyone?"

"Not on Sundays. But I'd love to have you back, Mackie. What other times would be good for you?"

"Night," Mackie said; after she'd finished cleaning houses, put something on the table for Lianne, just been there. "Late at night."

"Late at night?" There was a silence. Then Angie said, "Things aren't any better?"

"No."

"Worse?"

Mackie was silent. After a few moments, Angie said: "I never told you about Panky's."

"What's that?"

"This was about ten years ago, after *my* divorce. Maybe divorce leads down this trail in the dance community."

"What trail?"

"I needed money too then, back when I was still in Denver. Panky's was a gentleman's club off Larimer Square."

"A strip club?"

"Exactly."

"You were a stripper?" Angie was in her forties, had three kids, and a second husband who worked for the V.A.

"For six months. I made fifty grand, Mackie, the money that got me back on my feet."

"I couldn't do that," Mackie said.

"That's what I thought too," said Angie. "You never know."

"Out of the question."

"You'd be really good, actually."

"What does that mean?"

"First of all, you're a great dancer. Second, the way you look, wholesome, all-American."

"That's how I look?"

"To them, it would be. The guys at the tip rail."

The tip rail. "Never," Mackie said. She almost added a cliché that would have been pretty silly in her case: *I'd scrub toilets first.*

The door opened and Lianne came in. "Hi, Mom."

"Hi, honey. Have a good time?"

"It was okay."

Through the window, Mackie caught a glimpse of the old BMW vanishing around the corner. Was Kevin wearing a cowboy hat?

"What did you do?"

"Nothing much."

"I hope you didn't just hang around that apartment the whole time."

"No."

"You look tired," Mackie said. There were gray imprints under Lianne's eyes, and she'd broken out a little on her chin. "Feeling okay?"

"I feel great." Lianne went by her, trailing a faint smoky smell, entered her room, and closed the door. *Please don't smoke,* Mackie thought. *Anything but that.* And then suddenly she was really angry about it. She was picking up the phone to call Kevin—*Are you letting her smoke now?*—when it rang.

"Lianne there?" said a boy; a deep-voiced boy.

"Can I tell her who's calling?"

"Got it," Lianne said on her bedroom phone.

Mackie hung up.

Boys didn't call often, and when they did Lianne usually got rid of them quickly. Mackie made coffee, then walked down the hall, not stopping outside Lianne's door, not even slowing down, but she couldn't help it if she heard Lianne talking. Not the words, just the fact of talking. *This might be good.* Mackie gathered her supplies and cleaned her own house from top to bottom. She forgot about money for an hour, maybe more.

Lianne came out of her room, wrapped in a towel. "There was a call for you," she said.

"Who was it?"

"Mr. Fertig."

No ring; he must have come through on call-waiting. "You should have told me."

"It was only a few minutes ago. I said you'd call back—he's at his office."

Mackie let it go. "Who were you talking to?"

"Nobody," Lianne said. "Just a school thing." She turned toward the bathroom.

"How did you get that?" Mackie said.

"Get what?"

"That bruise on your shoulder."

Lianne tilted her shoulder up and forward, twisted her head around to look, the pose, and her daughter, so beautiful Mackie caught herself holding her breath.

"Must have bumped into something," Lianne said. "It's nothing." She went into the bathroom. The shower started running.

Mackie called Mr. Fertig. "I got this strange letter from the IRS," she told him, "claiming I owe this crazy amount of money."

"How much?"

She read him the amount.

"Who is it addressed to?"

"Me."

"You and Kevin or just you?"

"Just me."

"Who signed it?"

Mackie read the name at the bottom. "S. Menendez."

"Tell you what," said Mr. Fertig. "You busy right now?"

"No."

"Then how about coming down to the office? And bring the letter."

"Is something wrong?"

"I'll be here till noon," Mr. Fertig said.

Mr. Fertig's office stood between a Mexican restaurant and a Kinko's. He saw her through the plate-glass window and waved her in.

"Doughnut?" he said.

"No, thanks."

"Coffee?"

"I've had some."

"Have some more. This is really good. My wife makes it."

Mr. Fertig filled two china cups from an expensive-looking silver thermos. His desk was tidy, papers arranged in neat squares, the doughnuts—chocolate and mocha—in a little wicker basket.

"Tell me if that isn't great coffee," he said.

"It is."

He gazed at her over the rim of his cup. "How are things?"

Mr. Fertig was old enough to be her father. That probably had something to do with the sudden upwelling inside her, an upwelling that was going to lead to a long cry, wretched and purposeless. She might even feel better when it was over, but that wouldn't mean anything, just a weird physiological offshoot of crying. Mackie mastered the up-welling, capped it, handed him the letter. "You tell me," she said.

Mr. Fertig read the letter. She could feel him reading, a contagious intensity that seemed to sharpen her vision, the tiny red veins in his cheeks, the slight tremor in his fine hands, the heft of his wedding band, all heightened in her consciousness. He looked up.

"Were you aware that Kevin is no longer my client?" he said.

"No."

"As of about six months ago," he said. "Would that have been after the finalization of your divorce?"

"Yes."

"Around that time, Kevin informed me of his desire to declare bankruptcy. I thought the step unnecessary. After the bank assumed ownership of BV Devco, your remaining debts were supportable, in my judgment. Bankruptcy is rarely as inconsequential as people make out these days, and I told him so. He fired me soon after."

"I don't see where this is going, Mr. Fertig."

"I'm trying to find out if it was intentional," he said.

"If what was?"

"I called Sharon Menendez at home while you were on the way over."

"The IRS agent?"

"She's a friend."

"You have IRS friends?"

"Like any good accountant."

"Then you told her it was a mistake?"

Mr. Fertig opened a file that read BV DEVCO on the front, handed her a sheet of paper. "Recognize this?"

"The K-one statements from three years ago."

"Check number three, fifth line."

"Planning and design, one hundred thirty-six thousand, four hundred ninety-two dollars."

"Paid to?"

"The architect. Jenna Bennet and Associates."

"Does the figure seem accurate?"

"I'd have to check the bills," Mackie said, "but yes."

"Were any other firms involved in planning and design?"

"No."

"So the full amount went to Jenna Bennet and Associates?"

"Yes. Is there a problem?"

"A discrepancy," said Mr. Fertig. "The corresponding corporate return for Jenna Bennet and Associates shows a net payment of only forty-seven thousand, four hundred ninety-two dollars."

"I don't understand."

"The effect was to pad the expenses of BV Devco by the difference, eighty-nine thousand dollars. Since BV Devco showed a loss that year and would have even at the lower figure, the purpose isn't immediately clear."

"Isn't it?" Mackie said. "Jenna Bennet ends up paying less tax."

"My first reaction too. Then Sharon brought up the photocopied checks."

"What photocopied checks?"

"Provided to the IRS by Jenna Bennet during their audit of her firm, which was how the discrepancy came to light. One shows a payment from BV Devco to JBA for one hundred thirty-six thousand, four hundred ninety-two dollars, as per your return. The other shows a payment for consulting services from JBA to Kevin Larkin in the amount of eighty-nine thousand dollars."

Mackie was lost.

"Eighty-nine thousand dollars which should have been reported as income on the personal return and was not."

"Has this got anything to do with me?" Mackie said.

"The joint personal return," said Mr. Fertig.

"He and Jenna had a joint personal return?"

Mr. Fertig gave her a long look. When he spoke, his voice was gentle. She started to get scared. "Your joint personal return," he said. "Yours and Kevin's."

"I still don't see."

"Were you aware your ex-husband had an account with the Phoenix Savings branch at Plaza Palomino?"

"No."

"Where the check was cashed. The eighty-nine-thousand-dollar check."

"Where are you going with this?" said Mackie. Kevin had screwed up somehow; no surprise. "We're divorced, as you know."

"It's a question of sequence," said Mr. Fertig, "in this case, three events in unfortunate order."

"Talk in plain English."

"Simply this: The filing of the incorrect personal return, bearing your signature, one, precedes the divorce, two."

Not plain enough, but now she knew what scared her: "Are you saying the IRS is right?"

"More or less. Their figure includes penalties and interest, probably negotiable to an extent. The actual tax due would have been about half that."

"It's Kevin's problem, not mine."

Mr. Fertig shook his head, almost imperceptibly, as though unwilling to offend her. "And three," he said, "the court's acceptance of your ex-husband's chapter eleven petition precedes this IRS finding by almost two months."

"So?"

"Sorry if I haven't been clear," said Mr. Fertig, bowing his head a little, as though ashamed. "The point is the IRS is entitled to come after you for the money, and they are."

Mackie understood what that sentence meant. The problem was it didn't match her understanding of certain basic things, like justice and America. She tightened her grip on the arms of her chair. "That can't happen."

"It does, everyday. They choose the most promising target."

"But it's wrong," Mackie said.

"That's always been my feeling."

Mackie saw a way out. It was obvious. She got to her feet, felt light-headed, almost staggered. "I'm going to fix this right now."

"Some water, maybe?" said Mr. Fertig.

"Just tell me one more thing. You work with money all the time."

"I work with numbers," said Mr. Fertig. "But try me."

"Why?" said Mackie. "Why did he do it?"

"In a larger sense, I can't say," said Mr. Fertig. "But the effect was to divert the construction loans to personal use without the bank knowing."

"He was undermining his own fucking dream," Mackie said.

"That's one way of putting it," said Mr. Fertig. "Any idea what happened to the money?"

"That's what I'm going to find out."

"We can hope," said Mr. Fertig.

* * *

Mackie drove to Kevin's crummy apartment on Stone Avenue, jumped out of the car, jabbed her finger at the door buzzer next to the video store, kept it there. In five or ten seconds, she heard footsteps coming down the stairs. The door opened.

"You—" she said, but it was a tiny dark-skinned woman, Guatemalan, maybe, not Kevin.

"*Sí?*" she said.

"Where's Kevin?"

"No *inglés.*"

"Kevin. *Dónde está* Kevin Larkin?" Mackie gazed past the woman, up the stairs to the walkup. Three or four little children appeared, gazed back down.

"Kevin Larkin?" said the woman, and made a universal gesture of ignorance with her open hands.

Mackie banged open the door at number four, Buena Vida Circle. "Lianne?" She hurried through the house; not in the kitchen, family room, living room. "Where are you?" She banged open Lianne's door too, forgetting all about the sanctity of teenage privacy.

Lianne was in bed, talking on the phone. ". . . not soon enough," she was saying; and looked up in surprise.

"Why didn't you tell me?" Mackie said.

"Got to go," Lianne said, hanging up. "What the hell, Mom?"

"Don't you talk to me like that. Why didn't you tell me?"

"Tell you what?"

"That that son-of-a-bitch your father"—she just couldn't help it—"has moved."

"Hey! I was going to. I didn't get a chance."

"Where is he?"

Lianne sat up, pulling the covers to her chin. "Ocotillo Ranch. What's with you, Mom?"

"Where's that?"

"I'm not exactly sure."

"What do mean? Were you with him yesterday?"

"Yes. I just didn't pay attention on the drive, that's all. Somewhere south, I think."

Mackie gazed at her daughter. Nothing added up. "Don't hide things from me," she said. "Not things I should know."

"I wasn't," Lianne said.

Mackie went out, closed the door, not hard. From the kitchen, she called Kevin's cell.

"Hello," he said; a big hello, energetic, sunny.

"You'd better have that money," she said. She heard her own voice, low and venomous, hardly her voice at all.

"What money?" he said.

"You'll have to sound more surprised than that to fool me now," Mackie said. "Mr. Fertig told me everything."

"About what? He's kind of a bit past it in the accounting world."

"Because he's honest? You told me there were no more time bombs."

"I wouldn't call this a time bomb."

"That's because you're taking care of it."

"Of what?"

"The hundred grand you owe the IRS."

"Even if I wanted to, I couldn't. Haven't got a dime."

"What about your secret little account at Phoenix Savings?"

"Empty. Closed."

"And all the other secret little accounts you've got."

"You're letting your imagination run away on you, Mackie."

"Don't call me that."

"What?"

"Don't call me anything. Where's the eighty-nine grand you defrauded from the bank?"

"Where did that figure come from?"

"If you don't tell me, I'll send them after you."

"Who?"

"The bank."

He laughed. "Why would they do that? They've already got the houses."

His laughter maddened her; she raised her voice high above it. "Where is the money?"

"Gone."

"Gone where?"

"Nowhere special. Pissed it away."

"On Jenna?"

"Some, maybe. In fact, this little financial arrangement was kind of the beginning of the end for us."

Hot rage, a jet of it, spurted up from somewhere deep in Mackie's chest. She fought to control it, fought to control her voice. "Do you want me to fix you up with someone new?" she said.

He was silent. Had she reached him at last, down to some remaining good part? Or had he fooled her—or she fooled herself—about that as well, the good in him, from the start?

"You've got to lighten up a bit," he said. "Why don't you move into an apartment someplace and go chapter eleven too?"

There was her answer: she knew nothing. He'd made her do a lot of things; she wouldn't do this. Mackie hung up. Not long after that, she got in the car and drove to Angie's studio.

Five

Snow fell all day and night, covering the mountain like a shroud. Hazelton had to dig his way to the front door of the cabin. He knocked on it.

"Max?" said a voice within. Myra. "Is that you?"

"Yeah," said Hazelton. He fingered the Glock compact .45 in the pocket of his parka and pushed the door open.

Myra stood in front of the fire, dressed in a bra, a thong, and sheepskin slippers from L.L. Bean. There was blood on her right forearm and down her left leg. That was bad. So were her wide-open eyes, too wide-open. And then there was the poker. Sticking out of the sink.

"Where's Freddy?" Hazelton said.

"I don't know what happened, Max. The power's been out and everything's so mixed up since Willie went away."

"Death row is a little more than going away," Hazelton said.

Nicholas Loeb, author of the Timothy Bolt novels—*White Out, The Whites of Her Eyes, White Midnight*—read over the above passage, the beginning of chapter ten of his next book, as yet untitled. He liked the shroud bit, prefiguring what Hazelton was going to find inside the cabin. Not Hazelton, of course: when Loeb came to the final revision, he did a universal find/replace, changing Max Hazelton to Timothy Bolt throughout. After *White Out*, he'd found he could no longer write the character under that

name, had lost his feel for him totally, this despite the
months of agonizing over the name in the first place, and
the initial feeling of triumph when the sensitive prename
had fused with the macho surname. Halfway through *The
Whites of Her Eyes*, he'd even asked his editor at the time
about changing it.

"A little unusual in a series," his editor had said, "changing the name of the main character."

"What about if Bolt himself decides he can't stand the
name anymore and changes it in front of a judge?"

His editor had taken another call. Later, when the editor
lost his job after a merger or takeover or whatever it was,
Loeb had been about to float the name-change idea at the
getting-to-know-each-other lunch with his new editor,
Lucy Pearlstein, when she'd said, even before the arrival
of the mineral water: "You're so good with names."

Shroud was good, but would everyone get the connection? He moved the cursor, typed *funeral* in front of it.
What else? Gun, blood, poker, all in place. His readers
needed them, the way dope fiends needed their fix. Or,
more accurately, the readers he was hoping to attract. The
truth was that after a promising sell-through with *White
Out* and a decent follow-up with *The Whites of Her Eyes*,
sales of *White Midnight* had been disappointing. Loeb was
quoting in his mind now from *Publishers Weekly*. He
rooted around in his desk drawer, the top one where he
kept important things—passport, car title, apartment lease,
divorce decree—and found a crumpled pack of Camels
with two bent cigarettes inside. Loeb hadn't smoked in a
week, was well on his way to quitting. He lit one up, inhaled deeply.

Of course, that was only the opinion of *Publishers
Weekly*. Disappointing to whom? Lucy Pearlstein had
never used the word, and neither had Harry Pond, his
agent. Lucy had said sales were "absolutely market appropriate," and Harry had said, "Steady-eddie." Loeb took an-

other drag. So everything was cool. Timothy Bolt, Max Hazelton, whoever he was, was a great concept; agent, editor, publisher all in agreement about that. No one had done a skiing private eye before, and when Loeb thought of making him a veteran of the Tenth Mountain Division, thereby laying the foundation for his outdoors and weapons expertise at a stroke, everything clicked into place like the words and music of a Puccini aria. And if not that, at least a saleable commodity, although deep down Loeb knew he harbored Puccini dreams.

He went back over the passage once more, deleted *funeral*, moved the cursor down to the waiting open space. Outside the window of his Brooklyn Heights apartment—fifth-floor walkup, one bedroom, partial river view, $2600—snow was falling, real snow, white, white, white. He didn't see it.

"You don't know anything about Willie," Myra said.

"Just what I learned from his confession on Court TV," said Max.

A pretty funny line, right? But Loeb suddenly realized that other line—*Death row is a little more than going away*—could be sharper. A lot sharper. He stopped right there. He'd done a breakfast with another writer once—more successful, if you wanted to go by sales—who'd told the audience that he never went on to the next sentence before he was totally satisfied with the one before. Loeb, riffling through a copy of this perfectionist's book while waiting his turn at the podium, had soon found the flaw in that: The guy was easily satisfied. But the idea had stuck. It was all about building on solid foundations.

You call death row going away?

That's what it is to you, going away?

It's like a sabbatical to you?

A vacation?

A cruise?

Where do you go away after chopping up your wife and

*burying the pieces in half the states of the old Confeder-
acy?*

*Going away? Euphemisms will be the death of you,
Myra.*

Loeb deleted them all. He waited for an idea. The cursor,
blinking patiently, waited with him. He had all those giga-
bytes on his side, but nothing came. After a while, he tried
forcing his mind, commanding it to think, think. He even
spoke the word aloud, a momentary interruption of the silence in his apartment. Nothing.

Time passed. Loeb gave in to the temptation he'd been
fighting all morning, went on-line, clicked over to Ama-
zon.com, checked on how *White Midnight* was doing. A
sickening number awaited him, the worst yet, huge, incomprehensible. Were there even that many titles in the
whole history of the written word, from Aristotle to
Grisham? And what was this? He'd lost a star. That meant
there was a new reader review. He scrolled down, found it.
One star. Someone calling herself Jersey Jane ("see more
about me") had given him one lousy star, the lowest possible rating. Loeb, his heart suddenly racing, read her review.

> *For a series that started off with lots of promise, this
> one went into the Dumpster PDQ. The idea here is ac-
> tually pretty good, all about a plot to dope Olympic ski
> racers without their knowledge, and the PI, Timothy
> Bolt, can be funny, but there are too many unbeleiv-
> able coincidences. And the women are even more un-
> believable. Has Loeb ever met a real woman? Avoid
> like the plague.*

Loeb clicked on the *close* button, made it go away. How
great, the Internet, like magic. Any idiot—this one
couldn't even spell *unbelievable,* at least the first time—

could rise up from some corner of the world and stab you in the back.

He gazed at the blinking cursor. Sometimes, if he gazed long enough, he got the impression that all the right words were already there, just beneath the surface of the screen, and his job was to overprint them exactly, thus making them visible, a kind of kindergarten art project, like tracing. Some of those sometimes, that line of thinking even got him going again. Especially if the right music was playing: he clicked on the sound. Lately, "When Rita Leaves" by Delbert McClinton was the right music, over and over. Yes. Loeb began to get the feeling. Maybe the problem wasn't in the death row remark itself, maybe—

The phone. He picked it up. "Yes?" he said, cleared his throat and tried again. When was the last time he'd spoken to anyone but himself?

"Not interrupting anything?" said Harry Pond.

"Like what?"

"Whatever writers do on a snowy day."

Loeb looked out the window, saw the snow. "Just working on the book," he said.

"How's it going?"

"Good."

"Got a title yet?"

Loeb didn't want to say no. He picked the best from the reject list. "How's *White Heat*?"

"Hey," said Harry. "Not bad." And Loeb knew he hated it. "I spoke to Lucy, by the way," he continued. "About the contract situation."

"Yes?" said Loeb, leaning forward a little. Harry had decided to go for a three-book deal on the new contract, giving Loeb the security to really develop the series. He and Harry hadn't actually discussed any numbers, but they kept bobbing up in Loeb's mind anyway, big ones.

"They've decided to give it a little space," Harry said.

"Space?"

"You know," said Harry. "Time."

Time and space. "What are you saying, Harry?"

"To let things shake out."

"What things? Shake out how?"

"You don't know how shitty everything is out there, Nick. This country is fucking mindless and getting more mindless by the minute."

"I don't understand."

"You don't? No one reads. Bottom line."

"What's that got to do with me?"

"No one reading? You're a writer, Nick. It's like if you're a whore and the whole rest of the world were eunuchs."

"Business is bad, is that what you're saying?" Loeb said. At the same time, almost without thinking, he jotted *whore/eunuch* on the pad by the phone, for possible future use.

"Worse than I've ever seen it," said Harry. Loeb heard phones ringing in Harry's office, could picture Harry holding up two fingers to some assistant, or possibly one. "That's why they want a little space on this. Especially after the slight dip with *White Midnight*."

Loeb waited. Someone in the background at Harry's office spoke the word *Spielberg*.

"So, that all right with you?" said Harry. "Giving them some space for now?"

"You can't be saying they don't want another contract?"

"No, no, no," said Harry. "Where did you get that idea? Of course they want another contract. Just not now."

"When?"

"After they see how the new one—what is it, *White . . .*"

"Heat."

"It's growing on me. How *White Heat* does."

"But I'm not even finished, Harry. It won't be published for year and a half."

"Exactly. Time. Space."

"But I need a new contract before that," Loeb said. "The advance."

Harry was silent.

"Did you tell them that thing about giving me the security to develop the series?"

"My very first point." Phones kept ringing. "Got to run."

"Wait, Harry. Maybe we should move."

"Move?"

"To Bantam, say. What was the name of that editor who's a big Bolt fan?"

"This isn't a good time for moving," Harry said. "Just write, Nick. You're still a fine writer. I'll take care of things on this end."

"But—"

But he needed that advance, not right away, maybe, but in three months, six at the most. And then came an even scarier thought, one never before considered: What if this was the beginning of the end of his career? He was thirty-six years old.

Loeb went into his kitchen—a tiny squeezed-in space with the ceiling sloping down over the sink—heated some coffee, drank it standing. Writing—his writing, at least—came from a single slow-throbbing pulse somewhere deep in his mind, a pulse now overwhelmed by a chaos of firing neurons all over the place. He thought of going for a run, remembered it was snowing.

Loeb got down on the floor, did twenty push-ups, thirty crunches, twenty more push-ups. His head cleared. He went back to the desk, sat in front of the monitor, watched the blinking cursor. Neurons started firing, first in ones and twos, then multitudes: advance, contract, space, time, Spielberg, Bantam, eunuchs, whores. He got up, put on his coat, walked down the five flights and into the street.

Verlaine's was the closest bar, just around the corner, but Loeb's feet were wet by the time he got there. He'd forgotten boots; in fact, was wearing slippers. The jukebox was

playing Hank Williams and there were only two people inside, that asshole bartender with all the piercings and opin-
ions, and V, a woman from the neighborhood who wrote
poetry for an S&M Web site.

"Hi, Nick," she said, looking up from something she was
writing. No danger of her showing it to him, though: he
was a sellout in her eyes, also a no-talent by virtue of the
fact he was published by a commercial house.

Nick waved, sat several stools away, as far as he could
without being rude. Where was he? Right, the problem
wasn't with the death row line, and therefore—

"What'll it be?" said the bartender.

Normally, Nick wouldn't have even been here at this
hour, and he never had a drink before five. So an espresso,
like V was having, was the obvious choice. But he'd just
had coffee, and any more would wash away all hope of
shutting down those neurons.

"Got any of that cabernet?" he said. "The one from Ar-
gentina."

"The pinot's better," said the bartender.

Loeb drank the pinot.

"Up to the elbows in another mystery?" V said.

Up to the elbows. He didn't want to think about what she
was writing. "I see them more as crime novels," said Loeb,
"but yes."

"What's this one about?" said the bartender.

"Too early to say." Always the best answer, sparing
everyone a plot summary.

"Meaning," said the bartender, "you don't know what
it's about yet?"

"No," said V. "He doesn't want to jinx it by speaking too
soon."

"Which is it?" said the bartender.

"A bit of both, I guess," Loeb said. "I'll have another."

The bartender poured another. "Ever read that guy—?"
he said, naming a best-selling private-eye writer whose

prose reminded Loeb of oatmeal left overnight in the pot. "He's the bomb."

It was getting dark when Loeb went back to his place with V, and most of the snow was melting, everything foggy and reeking. He knew as soon as he sniffed the air that he didn't want to be doing this. On the other hand, he'd never been to bed with an S&M poet before.

Twenty minutes later he had. Right the first time.

V didn't hang around. No hard feelings. No feelings of any kind. In Harry's whore/eunuch Manichean universe, he and V were both whores. Loeb helped himself to some of his own cabernet, returned to the computer. All on their own, his fingers started tapping away, until in moments, there he was, back at the Amazon.com *White Midnight* page. He scrolled down to Jersey Jane's one-star review, read it again.

Bitch, he thought, or maybe said aloud. And that stupidly perky "see more about me." He took a big swallow of wine and clicked on the link.

Six

"Even Swan Lake is about sex," Angie said.

"Sublimation makes all the difference," said Mackie.

They stood in Angie's studio, in tights, leotards, bare feet, leaning on the barre, surrounded on three sides by their mirrored selves. Photographs of Angie's dancers and instructors, going back for years, covered the fourth wall, with a few of Angie mixed in, going back even further to her chorus girl days on Broadway. Mackie's favorite showed Angie and Donna McKechnie backstage, McKechnie laughing at something Angie had just said, both of them looking exhausted.

"Besides," said Angie, "there's plenty of sublimation in stripping."

"Naked sublimation?" Mackie said.

"I never thought of it as naked. All that bare skin was just another costume."

"That's where the tease part comes in?"

"Bull's-eye," Angie said. "This is going to be a snap."

"I don't think so."

"At least doable," Angie said, and gave Mackie's shoulder a squeeze. Angie was one of those optimists who spread cheer, as opposed to Kevin, for example, whose optimism ended up being contagious in the worst way.

"Fifty grand?" Mackie said.

"In sixth months. Not counting customer gifts."

"What kind of gifts?"

"Cashable ones, like jewelry."

"For which they expected—?"

"I don't know what they expected," Angie said. "They got nada."

Mackie liked the look that came into Angie's eyes at that moment, tough, hard, confident. "Doable will be fine," she said. "Where do we start?"

"Clothes, first," said Angie.

"For stripping?"

"Square one. You'll need a getup or two, maybe more, depending how it goes."

"What kind of getup?"

Angie looked her up and down, a quick, cool evaluation. "How about a minidress?" she said. "I've got a sparkly black one somewhere around here. You'll have to come up with panties and bra to match, plus a couple of G-strings— they stay on in Arizona, as long as there's drinking. As for shoes—what size are you?"

"Seven."

"I'll see what's in storage from the *Cabaret* production." Angie did the choreography for the Southern Arizona Players. "Didn't we use stilettos? A lot of the girls wear platform mules, Lucite de rigueur, but stilettos are easier on the feet, believe it or not."

"How about sneakers?" Mackie said, feeling a little giddy all of a sudden. "For those who like the athletic, out-doorsy type?"

"This is an indoorsy job," Angie said. "And sneakers don't get your butt up to that level where it has to be."

The giddiness passed.

"Plus a wig, of course," Angie said.

"A wig?"

"Essential," said Angie, "for the customers and for you. They want something exotic—that's right there in the job description—and while you've got beautiful hair, nicely cut, there's nothing exotic about it."

"Not so beautiful," Mackie said, "and mouse brown besides."

"That's what I'm saying," said Angie. "You'll appreciate the wig, I promise you."

"Why?"

"Because it's a big part of the character. No one even recognizes you. You can walk by some guy on the street whose eyes were six inches from your nipples the night before and he won't even blink."

Six inches. "If I try this," said Mackie, "it won't be where anyone can recognize me."

"We're back to hypothetical?" Angie said.

Except for the numbers, mortgage payment, equity shortfall, IRS bill, all the other bills: they were real. "What kind of wig?" Mackie said.

Angie squinted at her, tilted her head. "Huge," she said. "Huge and red."

"With my complexion?"

"Exotic," said Angie. "Bear that in mind. Let's try some moves. No point calling them steps, this isn't at that level."

She went to the CD player, popped something in. Sound flowed from the multiple speakers, rich, clear, live; Angie had excellent sound.

We were born before the wind
Also younger than the—

"Something else," Mackie said.

"I thought you liked Van the Man," Angie said.

"Not for this," Mackie said. "How about 'Like a Virgin'?"

Angie laughed. "You got it."

"Like a Virgin" started up. Angie didn't move a muscle, but Mackie could see the music entering her body. A middle-aged body, now, of no particular distinction, plus a thickening face and graying hair, but all that became invisible when music played.

"The first thing you've got to know," Angie said, taking

one step forward and then pirouetting, so easy, an inside turn with her arms rising as part of the same movement, framing her head in a perfect oval, "is that there's no such thing as unsubtle in the stripping business. You can't be obvious enough." Coming out of the pirouette, she raised her right leg to the side, then in a smooth curve up over her head, comma-shaped foot pointing at the ceiling; and at that moment, she thrust her crotch right at Mackie. "Now you," she said.

Mackie waited for the beat, stepped forward, pirouetted, raised her leg in those two separate motions, copied the routine right down to that crotch thrust on *virgin*.

"You're good," Angie said.

Not that good, not in Angie's league. "Head wasn't right," Mackie said.

"Head?" said Angie. "What's that got to do with anything? You're going to be rich."

They worked up a simple routine. "You need three numbers," Angie said. "Dress comes off in the first, top's off by the end of the second, everything else in the third. I suggest two up-tempos bracketing something slow."

They picked "Are You That Somebody," by Aaliyah, "When Rita Leaves," by Delbert McClinton, and "Honky Tonk Woman," by the Stones. "This way you can throw in most of the floor work during number two while you've still got something on," Angie said, "saving the pole for the end."

"Floor work? The pole?"

"I can show you the floor work," Angie said. "The pole we'll just have to fake."

Angie showed her the floor work, demonstrated some pole moves around an imaginary pole.

"Tell me about the fifty grand again," Mackie said, down on the floor, on her hands and knees.

"In six months. Without table dancing, lap dancing, friction, any of that."

"Friction?"

"Stick to stage dancing would be my advice," Angie said. "At least until you get comfortable."

"Did you get comfortable?"

"Not completely."

"Which is a good thing, right?"

Angie gazed at her. "How much money do you need? I could—"

"You couldn't," Mackie said.

"So we're beyond hypothetical again?"

Angie watched her. *Make a decision.* At that moment, Mackie was struck by a thought that seemed important, even revelatory: This might be more than just her only option, might also be the right thing to do. Didn't the hero always face some ordeal, some seemingly insurmountable challenge, then prove himself by surviving, overcoming, triumphing? Not that there was anything heroic about her, but at least she could be the main character in her own story. There had to be a challenge, even an ordeal. "I want to take a little control here," she said.

Angie nodded. "Then let's use what you've got," she said. They shook hands.

"Bringing us to another problem," Mackie said.

"What's that?"

"How much weight do I have to lose?"

"None."

"I've put on ten pounds since I worked here."

"Doesn't show," said Angie. "And even if it did, it wouldn't matter. You've got a great body, and that little bit extra—in your case it really is a little—is what men want. They're hard-wired for that little bit extra. Please, sir, give me more—that's them. They're hard-wired for everything. Don't you know that by now?"

Mackie had lots of evidence to back that up, years of it. "There must be more to it than that," she said.

"Maybe on Planet Feminina," Angie said. "Not here."

Were women soft-wired, incompletely wired, hard-wired in some flexible way? There were very few strip clubs where men danced naked for women. Why was that? Mackie had loved Kevin's naked body, in fact still shied from the memory of it.

"I'm going to need another name," she said.

"Very important. No one ever has to know your real name. Got anything in mind?"

"What were you?"

"Aurora," Angie said.

"I like that."

Angie shook her head. "Too hard to pronounce. I ended up being Rory."

"Sky?" said Mackie.

"Nope."

"Star? With two *r*s?"

"Nope."

"Three?"

"How about Red?" said Angie. "To match the hair-piece?"

"Doesn't it come on too strong?"

"That's what's good about it," said Angie. "Red. We're building a dream here. Let's give it some edge." That was Angie, the artistic side of her. There was edge in Angie's dancing, and in her choreography too, even the dances she did for the Beginners One recital. Mackie had never been sure what the parents thought, but the kids—the girls—loved it.

"Red it is," Mackie said.

"That leaves the audition. No need to call. Most places you can just walk in—early afternoon is good."

"Tomorrow," Mackie said. Delay wouldn't help.

"Where are you going to try first?" Angie said. "I've heard the Empress is all right."

"Where's that?"

"On Speedway."

"Didn't I say not here?" Mackie said. "Not in Tucson."

"Phoenix, then?" said Angie. "The commute will kill you, all that traffic."

And too far from Lianne. "There must be somewhere closer."

They went into Angie's office. Angie got on the computer. "Isn't the Internet something?" she said. "Here's a Web site where customers rate all the strip clubs west of the Mississippi." Angie scrolled down. There were hundreds. "How does this sound? Buckaroo's. Five stars. The latest review, from some guy calling himself Big Bad Tex—"

"Jesus."

" '—a real fun place and the girls rock. Even the margaritas aren't bad. Highly recommended. Plenty of free parking.' "

"Where is it?" Mackie said.

"Agua Fría." Down on the Mexican border. "You can be there in forty-five minutes."

Doable. "Buckaroo's," Mackie said. "Could be worse."

"Like the Busy Beaver," said Angie. "Tell me about it."

Seven

Name: Mary Jane Krupsha
Nickname: Jersey Jane
E-mail: jjkrup@aol.com
About Me: I'm an avid, avid reader. I read in all
genres—historical, mystery, romance, thriller, gothic,
etc. I found that if I stick to just one all the books
start sounding the same. I like characters that are
real, especially women, and I'm a sucker for scenes
of people eating, especially in bistros. I also do a lot
of painting—check out my stuff on eBay (E-mail me
for more info). My goal is to review a book a week for
the rest of my life. When I was in high school I took
the Evelyn Wood speed-reading course. Smartest
thing I ever did. I read The Corrections—what a
great book!—in forty-five minutes.

Nick Loeb poured himself another cabernet, reread Jersey Jane's autobiographical sketch several times. It maddened him in many ways, and the more he read it, the madder he got. He downed the glass, refilled it, took a sip, a slug, whatever it was, and then his finger was on the mouse and click: he'd hit Jersey Jane's E-mail address.

Under subject, he typed: *your review.*

In the space for the message, he typed: *I read the stupd thing.*

He felt a little better, avenged somewhat, even though

he had no intention of sending it. Perhaps he could think
of another cutting line or two, feel better still. Trying to
come up with one, at the same time reaching for the bottle,
he noticed that he'd written *stupd* instead of *stupid*, jabbed
the baby finger of his bottle hand at the *delete* key on the
fly, missed slightly, and zap: the E-mail message was on
its way.

Had that really happened? Yes: there in the mailbox was
the *S* for sent. Was there some way to intercept it, turn it
around, yank it back like a bad dog on a leash, or possibly
blow all its component electrons to smithereens as they
barreled down a wire, or barreled down whatever the wireless kind used? Word had an *undo* button, but this wasn't
Word, was an E-mail something or other, linked to Ama-
zon and God knows where else. Loeb was hunting for the
manual, had just knocked over the box containing all the
drafts of *The Whites of Her Eyes*, a blizzard of disorder,
when his computer beeped, that beep it made to announce
the arrival of E-mail. *Thank God,* he thought, a miracle,
his E-mail bouncing back, rejected for technical reasons by
some switch, server, electron monitor.

But no. He opened the E-mail.

> *Dear Mr. Loeb,*
> *Stupid how?*
> *Best wishes,*
> *Mary Jane Krupsha*

How to respond? Perhaps a nonresponse was best.
Wasn't it Evelyn Waugh, speaking of Evelyn W.'s, who'd
said, "Never apologize, never explain"? Would Waugh
have wasted even a second batting around E-mail with a
reader? Loeb tried to picture Waugh in front of a computer—suit tweed, face pink, eyes pissed-off blue—but
the image stayed blurry; there would be no more Evelyn
Waughs. Waugh was probably not the best model when it

came to dealing with readers. Wasn't it clear from the novels, *A Handful of Dust* especially, that he despised his readers, one and all? Loeb kind of liked his own readers, those he'd met at signings, talks, book fairs. The books always meant something to them, even if he hadn't intended whatever it was. Why else would they come?

He typed: *Waugh would never respond.* And hit *send.* And thought: *Did I do that?*

The reply came back. *He was colder than you. Stupid how?*

Remembering *Misery*, Stephen King's *Misery*, Loeb shut off the computer, had one more glass of wine, to guarantee sleep, thus drinking to promote good health, and went to bed, all limbs intact. But sleep didn't come. Neurons fired up as never before, destroying any peace of mind like a swampful of cicadas. Cicadas. He was in a bad way, thinking of cicadas. Loeb had a strict rule that called for the immediate abandonment of any book that even mentioned the sound of cicadas.

Stupid how? He'd gotten off to such a promising start. Max Hazelton—Timothy Bolt—was "a great character" (*People* Page-turner of the week). There was plenty of action, always a slam-bang climax on some towering peak, the snow turning slowly red. The avalanche in *White Midnight*, for example, sweeping Bolt and Streiber, locked in combat, over a cliff in the Bugaboos. Anything wrong with that? Or what about—

The phone rang. At this hour? He realized at that moment he had no idea of the hour. "Hello?" he said.

"Mr. Loeb?"

"Yes?"

"This is Mary Jane Krupsha. I thought maybe your computer was down."

"It's not. How did you get my number?"

"From the Mystery Writers of America directory."

"Are you a member?"

"No."

"Then how did you get the directory?"

"It's not a state secret, Mr. Loeb. You're not a CIA operative. You're a mystery writer, although you probably prefer the term crime fiction. Stupid how?"

"Look, Ms. . . ."

"Krupsha."

"Ms. Krupsha. I'm sorry if I offended you. It was all a mistake, that E-mail should never have gone out. You've got a right to any opinion you want."

"But you disagree with it?"

"What I think doesn't matter."

"But I want to know."

"Why?"

"Because of my responsibility to get it right."

"I don't follow."

"I'm a reviewer, Mr. Loeb."

A reviewer? You're not a reviewer. You're just another fucking busybody living on the Web. One more glass of cabernet and he might have said it. That would have been bad: he realized she'd had the grace not mention his misspelling of stupid.

"So," she said, "stupd (sic) how?"

"I'm hanging up now, Ms. Krupsha. Please don't call again."

Loeb hung up. He lay in bed, eyes wide open. He knew what was going to happen next, and it was worse than *Misery.* Mary Jane Krupsha was about to murder him digitally, panning him from one end of the Internet to the other. There was nothing he could do about it. And she'd probably borrowed all his books from the library, doing her best to keep sales flat.

Loeb heard a boat horn on the river. Would it be nice to have someone with him now? Yes. Anyone, even V? No. He thought about his ex-wife, now married to an optometrist upstate, raising a family at last. The writing thing had driven her crazy.

He lay in the dark, his digital recorder beside him. From time to time an idea cut through the turmoil in his mind. "Myra, blue dress from chapter one, maybe she . . ." And later: " 'You like barbecue?' Willie said." Still later: "What if Freddy adds a little something to the recipe? Such as . . ."

That talking in the night: one of the things that had driven her crazy, no improvement on his previous method, pen, pad, click of the pencil-light switch. "When," she'd wanted to know, with increasing frequency, "can there be just the two of us, instead of you, me, and that thing inside your head?" She'd wanted kids too, not at first, when they'd shared a common dream of travel, adventure, excitement. What had he yelled at her toward the end, something ludicrous, humiliating to contemplate still? *The books are my children.* Come meet the kids—White Out, The Whites of Her Eyes, White Midnight. And we're thinking of calling the next one White Heat, unless I miscarry. If she were back with him now, was there a way to delete all that, revise their marriage? Loeb had an idea, spoke into the recorder. "Max hides the cartridge in plain sight, maybe—yes!—in the eye of the avant-garde sculpture from chapter eight. And if—"

He heard a knock at the door. How was that possible? He checked the time: late, late, late. No one could get in the downstairs door without a key, and he hadn't given one to anybody. That meant someone from the building, or—was it possible his ex-wife still had a key, had been thinking about him too? Loeb got up, found boxers and a sweatshirt in a pile on the floor, pulled them on, went to the door.

"Who's there?" he said.

"Me." A woman.

A woman, and the voice seemed familiar, but he

couldn't quite place it. Certainly not his ex-wife. Not V, not the publicist from Penguin he'd dated a couple of times that fall.

"I don't recognize your voice."

"But we were just talking."

"I haven't been talking to—Ms. Krupsha?"

"I actually don't pronounce it that way, but not to worry."

"How did you—" But of course, the directory. He would resign from MWA first thing in the morning. "You'd better go now."

"But we haven't resolved this."

"Resolved what?"

"This issue about your book *White Midnight*. I reread it on the way over so I'd be prepared."

"In fifteen minutes? Less?"

Silence. Then she laughed. She had a nice laugh, completely unexpected given the harshness of her speaking voice, even a bit infectious. "Oh, the Evelyn Wood thing," she said. "I exaggerate that a little, kind of like fishermen."

Silence.

"So," she said. "Here I am."

"Uninvited," said Loeb. "In the middle of the night."

"I took a taxi. From Piscataway."

"Then you're very rich or very crazy."

Pause. "Are you afraid of me?"

He said nothing.

"I'm thinking," she said, "what would Timothy Bolt do in your place?"

"Timothy Bolt"—even speaking the name was painful—"is an imaginary character."

"Don't all characters have something of the author in their souls? I assumed there was a lot of you in Timothy Bolt."

Not in Timothy Bolt, but in Max Hazelton—yes, goddamn it, and the best part; it had to be. Loeb opened the door. He was struck by a powerful olfactory force, a gale scented with perfume, cigarette smoke, garlic.

"You're bigger than I thought," Mary Jane Krupsha said. "And not as sensitive-looking as your picture."

"They have a lens for that," said Loeb.

Mary Jane Krupsha laughed her unrestrained laugh. She was overweight enough to jiggle slightly, and she did. Had he had expectations about her size, she would have exceeded them too, reminding him slightly of a female shot-putter who'd lived in his college dorm. Mary Jane Krupsha wasn't as good-looking as the shot-putter. She had a plain face, the kind that used to be called mannish, huge red-framed glasses, and a massive semiglobe of frizzy hair. Behind the glasses her eyes were subjecting him to a careful examination.

"You don't use a pseudonym or anything, do you?" she said.

"No one changes their name to Loeb," he said.

She laughed again. "That's just the kind of thing Timothy Bolt would say." Laughter and voice, both loud: he glanced down the hall.

"You might as well come in."

"Why, thank you."

"For a few minutes."

"That's all I can spare anyway," said Mary Jane Krupsha. "It's getting late."

They sat in Loeb's living room/dining room/office, Mary Jane Krupsha on the corduroy couch that had once been in his parents' den, Loeb in the matching chair. He pulled an afghan over his bare legs.

"Is this where you work?" she said.

"Yes."

"Not many books around."

"To avoid the temptation of reading."

"I hear you." She nodded to herself, as though they'd

reached some level of commonality. "So," she said, light-ing up a cigarette, dropping the match in an almost empty sushi carton that happened to be on the side table, "stupid how?"

Loeb's little brother Mikey had been like that when they were kids: just wouldn't stop.

"What are you smiling about?" said Mary Jane Krupsha.

Now he was a partner at a big Wall Street law firm, spe-cializing in something Loeb didn't understand and making millions, literal millions. "All right, Ms. Krupsha," Loeb said, "let's start with these unbelievable coincidences."

"You can call me Mary Jane."

He nodded.

"Can I call you Nicholas?"

"I guess."

"Or would you prefer Nick? Nicky, maybe?"

"Let's stick with Nicholas."

She squirmed on the couch, like a happy kid. "You could be really good, Nicholas. Please don't forget that, no mat-ter what comes next."

He pulled the afghan tighter around his legs.

Mary Jane riffled through her copy of *White Midnight*, the pages festooned with Post-it notes. "Here, for example, where Bolt and Sergeant Falco find the syringes in Ingrid's ski pole. Why would Streiber pick that for a hiding place?"

"Why not?"

"Because he's smarter than that. He's got the FBI and everybody else thinking that the Allgoods are behind the whole thing. Besides, it's not really a question of hiding the syringes—he wants to get rid of them. Why not bury them in the foundation of the new ski jump? In fact, that's what I thought you were setting up with the first ski jump scene, besides that love interest thing with Rena."

For a moment, Loeb couldn't remember who Rena was. Then she came back to him, and with her a faint and con-fused memory that he had indeed been setting it up that

way in the very beginning, had forgotten somewhere along
the way. Thus, he suddenly realized, losing that nighttime
scene up on the ninety-meter jump that he'd planned for
right before the climax but had never written because it no
longer made sense.

"Or," said Mary Jane, turning to another page, "how
about in chapter twenty-six where Sergeant Falco gets
trapped in the warming hut?"

"What's wrong with that?"

"And this leads us into another area of weakness,
Nicholas, kind of related—police procedure. Mystery
readers are sticklers for police procedure. They know all
about it from TV."

"I don't watch TV."

"Oh, boy." Mary Jane, down to the butt of her cigarette
now, lit another right off it, dumping all the debris in the
sushi carton. "You see, Nicholas," she began, taking a deep
drag and blowing clouds of smoke out her nose like some
dragon, "it's like making love to a woman."

"What is?"

"Writing. You've got to warm them up slowly and carefully, until the heat gets so intense that the slightest little
spark . . . Follow me so far? You have to make them yours,
is what I'm saying. Putty. But if you do the writing equiv-
alent of taking them out of the moment—and it doesn't
have to be a big thing like calling out some other woman's
name, it can be something small, like touching where they
don't like to be touched, or some grunt you do—and just
like that the fire's out." She gazed at him, her eyes tiny behind those huge glasses. "When you get really good," she
said, "you can even make them like being touched where
they don't like to be touched."

"Got another one of those?" he said. She tossed him her
cigarettes. He lit up.

"So when Sergeant Falco goes up the trail to the warming hut without calling for backup, you turn off every

reader who knows anything about police procedure, and no matter how good the rescue scene that comes after is—and yours is pretty good, Bolt out there on that cable, you can do action—they're reading with cold eyes."

Reading with cold eyes: he wanted to write it down.

She flipped through the book. "I've noted other police procedure errors—pages eight, twenty-one, twenty-two, sixty-eight, seventy, eighty-six, eighty-seven, eighty-eight, eighty—"

"Bolt's not a cop, for Christ's sake," said Loeb.

"He's a licensed PI," said Mary Jane, "which means he's got to know procedure. Doesn't have to follow it— except when he's with Sergeant Falco, a relationship that works very well by the way, although I think that note of mutual distrust could be even stronger—but he's got to follow it." She glanced around. "Talking is thirsty work," she said.

Loeb poured cabernet.

"Not bad," said Mary Jane, "although I generally prefer merlot. Answer me a question—are you really in your heart of hearts interested in police procedure?"

"Sure."

"Since you're not, you're going to have to approach it like a job. That and plotting through the coincidences. You've got to improve your plotting. But you're luckier than most writers—those are two areas you can fix through sheer work."

"What do you mean approach it as a job?" said Loeb.

"Pretend you'll get fired if you don't do it."

They've decided to give it a little space. He wouldn't have to pretend very hard.

"A little more?" he said.

"Why, thank you." She took a ladylike sip. That was the way she drank, ladylike sips but frequent. "You're good, you know, Nicholas—dialogue, atmosphere, humor, story ideas, all very nice. And the ski scenes are better than that. How come you know so much about skiing?"

"I skied in college."

"Yeah?"

"Without distinction," said Loeb. "I barely made the team."

"Ever win a race?"

"Once." He remembered that wild Saturday at Stowe, blizzard blowing forty miles an hour, all the good skiers going too fast to even see the number-six gate. "Pure luck," he said. "But if you like the skiing so much, and if the dialogue, atmosphere, humor, and ideas are acceptable, isn't 'avoid like the plague' a little strong?"

"That's just reviewer talk," said Mary Jane. "Got to make a name for yourself somehow. Don't pay any attention."

"But—"

"This is what I want you to pay attention to," she said, leaning forward suddenly, voice rising. Wine slopped from her glass onto the rug, Persian, slightly valuable, unusually light-colored. "Women," she said.

"Women?"

"You can't do them at all. If you really want to get good, really want fame and fortune, you've got to learn how to do women."

"No one's ever mentioned that before," Loeb said. "And I get complimentary mail from women about Athena." Athena was Bolt's on-again off-again girlfriend.

"That's because of her name and the fact she's part black. Women readers fill in the rest themselves. They've pretty much given up on finding male writers who can write real women."

Loeb was wide-awake now. Had he ever had a conversation this substantial about his work? No—not with Harry, Lucy, his old editor, or anyone else. Mary Jane Krupsha— fingerprints on her glasses, cigarette ash in her hair—knew

more about writing than anyone he'd ever met. "To tell you
the truth," he said, "maybe just four or five letters on that
subject."

"Oh, I knew that," said Mary Jane, waving off the qual-
ification; more wine spilling.

"Freshen your drink?"

"Why, thank you."

He went over to pour it, holding the afghan around him
with one hand. She held out the glass, her eyes meeting
his, trying to communicate something although he had no
idea what.

"Want to continue this in bed?" she said at last; her
voice lacking for the first time its harshness, and the au-
thority too.

"How can I answer that?" said Loeb. "I don't know
women."

Her former voice returned. "This has nothing to do with
knowing women. I asked what you wanted." She put her
hand on his wrist, seized it really, almost knocking the
afghan loose. Her hand was hot, close to feverish.

"Then, no," Loeb said; although without that V episode,
would he have been so sure?

"I don't really want to either," said Mary Jane, letting
go. "You'd probably fuck it up, just like the books."

They both laughed, long and loud. Mary Jane took out
her cigarettes, lit another. He saw the tremor in her hands
and felt bad.

"Maybe if we knew each other bet—" he began.

"Timothy Bolt would never say that," she said, angry
now.

Loeb sat at the other end of the couch. "He wouldn't
sleep with a stranger either," he said.

"Fair enough," she said. "Is there an Athena in your
life?"

"No."

She thought about that, smoke rising around her.

"Tell me about your writing," he said.

"I don't write. I paint. I thought you read my bio." She gave him one of those careful looks. "Do you have memory problems, Nick?"

"I forget."

He expected that laugh of hers, but it didn't come. "Memory problems are bad for writers. Maybe you should cut back on the booze."

"I don't have a booze problem."

"Course not. I couldn't help you there, anyway. And I can't help you when it comes to doing women—that'll have to come from life. But police procedure's easy." She stabbed her cigarette, half smoked, into her wineglass, half full. "All you've got to do is follow some cop around for a few weeks. I could give my ex-husband a call."

"He's a cop?"

"Plainclothes. Nineteen years with the NYPD and now he's out in Arizona."

Why not? It would be a lot easier than actually writing. "That sounds good," Loeb said.

Mary Jane closed her copy of *White Midnight* and rose. "Clay Krupsha," she said. "I'll call him in the morning. He's captain of detectives."

"Where?"

"Agua Fría, down on the border. This is the best time of year."

Eight

Homework all done?" Mackie said.

"Uh-huh," said Lianne.

Lianne sat at the kitchen table, dressed for school—jeans and a sleeveless T-shirt that just reached belt-level, conforming to the rules—and gazing into the steam rising off her coffee. Mackie stood by the toaster, waiting for it to pop.

"What was it?" Mackie said.

"Huh?"

"Your homework."

"English, mostly."

"Like?"

"Questions about this book we're reading."

"What book?"

Lianne opened her binder, took out a paperback, read the title aloud: *"Lord of the Flies."*

The toast popped. "I remember that one," Mackie said. "What do you think of it?" She buttered the toast, brought it to the table, sat down.

"I don't know," Lianne said. She spread jam on her slice, spread it thickly, which was unusual, and ate it all in three bites, even more unusual.

"Wasn't it hard to believe how mean those kids were?" Mackie said.

"Any more toast, Mom?"

"Have mine."

"I don't want to take yours."

"I'll make some more."

"Sure?"

"Sure." Mackie slid her toast across the table, returned to the toaster, stuck in the end piece, all that remained of the loaf.

"And an egg, maybe?" Lianne said.

"An egg?" When had Lianne last had an egg?

"Scrambled, if that's okay."

Mackie scrambled an egg, leaving four more and not much else in the fridge, slid it off the pan onto Lianne's plate. "Didn't you find them a little too mean?"

Lianne shrugged.

"About it being believable, and all," Mackie said.

"What I didn't believe," said Lianne, the inside of her mouth yellow with egg, "was how they talked. Kids don't talk like that."

"Aren't they supposed to be English?" Mackie said.

"Oh." Lianne rose, took her dishes to the sink, picked up her binder, kissed Mackie on the cheek. "See you tonight, Mom."

"Got your key?" said Mackie, the smell of Lianne's perfume—Jean-Claude Gauthier, her stocking present Christmas morning—mingling with the eggy smell, somehow reminding Mackie of the breast-feeding days. "I may be a little late."

"How come?"

"New customers, farther away," Mackie said, both elements literally true.

Lianne turned at the door. "Everything okay, Mom? All the money stuff?"

"We're hanging in."

"See you tonight."

"Love you."

"Love you too."

Lianne went out, walking down Buena Vida Circle toward the corner where the school bus stopped. The bus drove up just at she got there, the door opening.

Lianne didn't get on. "Got a ride coming," she said. The door closed; the bus drove off. Lianne tilted her face to the sun, not hot at this time of year, just nice and warm.

A motorcycle glided up a few minutes later. Jimmy Marz, hair all over the place from the wind, lowered one foot to the pavement, gave the motor a little vroom-vroom.

"Hop on," he said.

"Got a helmet for me, Jimmy?" said Lianne.

"What for? We're not leaving the state."

"Don't you need a helmet till you're eighteen?"

Jimmy's eyes got wide. "How old are you?"

"I'll be eighteen in May."

His mouth made an O and he breathed out some air, relieved. "I guess it's okay, then."

"To not wear a helmet?"

"Just hop on," he said. "Nothing's going to happen to you."

Lianne got on. He wheeled into a U-turn, real quick, taking her breath away, and headed south. Same as with the horses, he had complete control, like the bike was bolted to a moving ramp.

Jimmy turned back. There was a diamond in one earlobe; had he been wearing it Saturday night? "What day in May?" he said.

"The ninth. Why?"

"None of your business," he said.

She gave him a little squeeze.

Mackie drove into Agua Fría. She'd passed through once or twice before, on the way to Mexico with Kevin, but never stopped. No one she knew actually stopped in Agua Fría. It was a small city, or a maybe a big town, built on a rising slope; half a city or town, more accurately: the other half tumbled down the far side of the slope, over in Mexico. A high steel wall, corrugated and rusty, separated the two halves, except at the center where the border post was. Mackie drove down Oro, the main drag, turned left on Pershing, the last street before the crossing. On her right stood a chain-link fence guarding a strip of desiccated, debris-strewn land grading up to the steel wall; a white SUV with BORDER PATROL on the side idled in the empty space. On Mackie's left stretched a long row of businesses: clothing store, shoe store, bar, notary, restaurant, bar, souvenirs, bar, parking lot, Buckaroo's. Buckaroo's had a towering sign with two red nipples in the Os. She sped up, drove quickly by. Pershing came to an end in front of another chain-link fence. There was nowhere to go but left. Mackie turned left, drove a few hundred feet before there was nowhere to go again but left. She followed a street full of potholes, came back to Oro.

Mackie paused. One more left meant south, back around the block to Buckaroo's. Right meant north and home. She could just walk away from all those debts, let it go, the house and everything. But the house was home. She owed Lianne a home. It was also her inheritance, financed by the sixty grand that came from the sale of her own childhood home. Lose all that without a fight? It seemed so disrespectful. Suppose she were a performance artist, or even an avant-garde dancer with some cutting-edge company: no one would think twice about her taking off her clothes, would probably admire her for it. So, no big deal, and therefore turning right would be weak, even cowardly. Mackie went left.

She drove down Pershing again, this time turning into the parking lot beside Buckaroo's. A sign in two languages read: PARKING FOR BUCKAROO'S CUSTOMERS ONLY. ALL OTHERS WON'T BE HAPPY. The lot was empty. Mackie parked, checked her face in the mirror, locked the car, and walked around to the front door.

Buckaroo's had a big, heavy door, painted from top to

bottom with a lengthwise flag of the United States, the stars in the left top corner. Mackie tried the handle; locked. She knocked on the door. Early afternoon was best, Angie had said. She checked her watch—twelve fifteen—and knocked again.

The door opened.

A woman looked out. She had a mop in her hand, the same green-handled kind from Wal-Mart that Mackie used. *"Sí?"* she said.

"Audition," Mackie said; could barely get the word out, for some reason.

"No speak," the woman said.

"I'd like to audition."

The woman closed the door.

Mackie stood on the threshold of Buckaroo's. The world wasn't eager to see her naked. It was almost funny.

The door opened. Another woman looked out, this one older, maybe sixty, with a pile of upswept platinum hair on her head, one eye made-up, the other, almost lashless and browless, not. "We don't open till one weekdays."

"I don't want to come in," Mackie said, appalled that she might be considered a customer. "That is, I do. For an audition."

The woman looked her up and down. Mackie, dressed in khaki slacks and a blue shirt, felt naked already under the scrutiny of those two very different eyes.

"One thing we don't have to worry about," the woman said, "you're over eighteen."

"Way over," Mackie said.

Now the woman checked her face, the only part she'd scanted the first time. "Way over isn't usually a selling point in this business. Done much dancing?"

"Oh, yes."

"We're short, right now."

"I see."

"We're always short."

"Oh."

"Tell you what. No one does any hiring but the boss. I'll check if he's in." She closed the door.

Mackie waited. A copper-skinned family walked by, husband and wife very small, the noses of all the children runny, eagerness in none of their steps.

The door opened. "What's your name again?" the woman said.

"Red."

The woman glanced at Mackie's hair.

"On account of the wig in here," Mackie said, holding up her dance bag.

"I'm the manager," said the woman. "Call me Verna."

"Nice to meet you, Verna."

"Got your music?"

"On tape, if that's all right."

"Tape, CD, CD-ROM, DVD, we can handle anything. Come on in."

Mackie entered Buckaroo's. It was dark and empty inside, but she could make out a long bar to the left, lots of tables in the middle, something soft, curtains maybe, along the far wall, and to the right a stage, footlights off, with a runway sticking into the room like a long tongue. That image popped into her mind immediately and of its own volition.

"Hey, Dane," Verna called. "You around?"

A voice came over the speakers. "Yup."

"This way," said Verna, giving Mackie's arm a nudge in the right direction. They walked past the stage and partway around it to a glassed-in booth. A light went on inside, revealing a bony man, head bald and lumpy in front, long-haired in back, sitting at a control panel and eating a sandwich; white bread, peanut butter, Marshmallow Fluff. "Dane," said Verna, "Red."

"Hi," Mackie said.

Dane waved, his mouth full, a little glob of Marshmallow Fluff stuck in a loose strand of hair.

"Red's auditioning," Verna said. "Give Dane your music."

Mackie handed the tape over the top of the booth. Dane checked the label she'd written. "Delbert McClinton, cool," he said. "He was in here around Thanksgiving."

"Dressing room's this way," said Verna, leading Mackie past the booth, backstage, then up a short flight of dark stairs. There was no door to the dressing room. Verna went in, flicked on the lights.

"Anywhere you like, for now," Verna said. She handed Mackie a key. "Valuables in a locker, if you want to see them again. When you come back down, just keep going under the tinsel arch and onto the stage. Five minutes."

Verna went down the stairs.

Mackie sat on a stool in front of the makeup mirror. The makeup mirror lined two walls of the dressing room, with a formica countertop at the bottom and a row of bright little bulbs on top. Someone had stuck a photo of a baby between the mirror and the frame in front of Mackie; the baby brandished a silver rattle and had one tooth.

She opened her dance bag, took out the makeup kit, started with eyeliner, but her hands were too unsteady, and she gave up. In the end, she could manage only the lipstick, a red she thought would go well with the wig. She took off her clothes, all except the G-string she'd worn underneath, and got into the costume: ivory-colored satin panties and bra from Victoria's Secret, a birthday present from Kevin she'd worn once, finding out about Jenna a week or so after; Angie's sparkly black minidress; silver stilettos from the *Cabaret* production; and the red wig, which she now saw didn't match the lipstick at all, made both reds ridiculous, hair like a fire truck, mouth like rust. She checked herself in the mirror: looked terrible, had never looked worse.

"Hey, Red," Verna called from somewhere below.

Mackie glanced around, actually thinking there might be some escape route. Not even a window: the only way out of the dressing room was down those stairs. She dabbed deodorant under her arms, sweat flowing visibly now, and started down, wobbly in the stilettos. Her foot touched the stage, not a bad stage—some dancer's part of her record-ing that information automatically—springy but firm. She stepped under the tinsel arch, at that moment remembering the locker key, still in her hand. What was she supposed to do with it? She put it in the only safe place as the footlights flashed on and Aaliyah's "Are You That Somebody" started up, the volume high and pounding.

Mackie gazed into the darkness. At first, blinded by the footlights, she could make out nothing in the room. Then her eyes adjusted and she saw Verna and a man sitting at a table in the middle. The table and their torsos were lost in darkness, and the two faces only foreheads, noses and shadow, but their hair—his the same platinum color as hers, cut very short—captured any light escaping from the stage.

Mackie didn't move. This was the moment for saying, *Not a good idea, thanks for your time.* And then what? The ride home, nothing accomplished, no better off than be-fore, but weaker. Angie had said there were two hundred and fifty thousand exotic dancers in the country now. Was she better than all of them when it came to morals? Or just worse when it came to nerve? She picked up the beat, took one step forward, just the way they'd rehearsed, into the inside turn, arms rising in an oval, came out of it with her right leg rising high, and then, timing the move exactly to that weird high-pitched sound on "Are You That Some-body"—almost a baby's cry—she thrust her crotch at her little audience, the key falling to the stage. The shadows on their faces changed shape.

She danced. There were lots of sexy moves in dancing; Angie was right about that. Mackie just made them all more obvious. *You can't be obvious enough.* The minidress came off at the end of the first number, sliding unzipped down her body as they'd rehearsed; then came Delbert McClinton, floor work, slow and languorous but never stopping, serving the music but in a single-minded way, as though it were about one thing and one thing only, and suddenly she was into it—not turned on, or anything stupid like that—but into the performance. Those shimmies—top off, wearing only the G-string—the spreading, the grinding: nothing but choreography from an old routine, an old, old routine, and primitive, but it worked. And the pole— "Honky-Tonk Woman" now—wrapping her legs around it as though it were an irresistible object of desire, bending way back, that red hair trailing on the stage: anyone not getting this yet? It was really kind of funny. Mackie realized she was actually smiling to herself as the Stones' drummer, that Charlie guy with the sweet face, brought the song to a rattling stop; she herself vibrating to that rattle and falling still.

Then, through the silence, came applause, not from Verna and the man at the table in the middle of the room, motionless, but from others, men, four or five of them, sitting here and there. When had they come in? How had she missed them? Mackie backed into the darkness behind the tinsel arch.

A couple of the men rose and approached the stage. One motioned for her to come closer.

"What do you want?" Mackie said.

"What do I want?" he said. "Just to show my appreciation." He held up a bill.

"That was just an audition," Mackie said.

"You passed, to my way of thinkin'."

Mackie came to the edge of the stage, wearing only the G-string, arms crossed over her breasts.

"What's your name?" said the man.

Mackie came close to blurting her real name, first, last, middle. "Red," she said.

"Name's Bub," said the man. "I'm a regular here and let me tell you I'm going to be a lot more regular, with you around."

"That's very nice, Bub, but—"

Bub leaned forward, stuck the bill inside the strap of her G-string, against her hip. Mackie was so surprised she wasn't sure the slight scratch she felt was the edge of the bill or his fingernail.

The second man stepped up, stuck money in the other side, eyes, slightly crossed, on her butt.

"Red?" Verna called. "Got a moment?"

Mackie turned, picked up the minidress, slipped it on. The money stayed where it was, unexamined. *Never open the envelope like that in front of Auntie Ruth again, Helen—it's rude.* She hopped down off the stage, went to Verna's table.

"Sit down," Verna said, both eyes made up now, and heavily.

Mackie sat.

"This is Mr. Samsonov," Verna said.

"Nice to meet you," Mackie said. Mr. Samsonov nodded, the muscles in the sides of his neck standing out like cables.

"Mr. Samsonov's the boss," Verna said.

"CEO," said Mr. Samsonov. "Plus managing partner and one hundred percent owner of common and preferred shares."

"He does all the hiring and firing," said Verna.

"You are hired," said Mr. Samsonov.

"Thank you. I—"

"Tell her the rules," said Mr. Samsonov.

"No sex with the customers," said Verna. "Sex and you're fired. Understood?"

"Yes."

"What about the problem of—what is this idiom, again?" said Mr. Samsonov.

"Hand jobs?" said Verna.

"I will write it down." Mr. Samsonov opened a leather-bound notebook. Mackie saw two columns, one in English, the other in the Russian alphabet, the name of which she'd forgotten. "It is here that I am enriching my vocabulary," he said, writing some Russian word and beside it *hands job*.

"It's singular," Mackie said.

He looked up, his eyes, unblinking and almost colorless, on her.

"Hand job," Mackie said; probably saying it out loud for the first time in her life.

"Ah," he said, making the correction. "I am loving this expression, hand job. I am loving all things American. You have noticed the front door?"

"Yes."

"We are very patriotic here. That is another rule. Go on with the rules, Verna."

"The problem with hand jobs," said Verna, "is that some of our former girls didn't realize they counted as sex. You don't look like the kind of girl who would make a mistake like that."

"No."

"We have table dancing, lap dancing, and friction, but they're not compulsory," said Verna. "Dane signs off on all the music. No rap, no heavy metal. Drugs and you're gone. Drinking and you're gone. G-string comes off and you're gone. Got it?"

"Got it."

"I do the schedule—two shifts, early and late, open every day. We expect six shifts a week, minimum."

"Early would be best."

"No guarantees," said Verna.

"That is life," said Mr. Samsonov. "American life. No guarantees, but the moon is the limit."

"Agreed?" said Verna.

"Agreed."

"Any reason you can't start now?"

"Today?"

Verna checked her gold watch, thick and diamond-studded. "Showtime in ten minutes."

"I guess that'd be all right," Mackie said.

Verna held out her hand. "Stage fee's twenty bucks."

"I'm sorry?"

"Each shift."

"Like golf," said Mr. Samsonov. "Greening fee first, then play ball."

"I don't have any money on me," Mackie said.

Verna laughed, a high-pitched sound quickly cut off, but Mr. Samsonov laughed and laughed, deep and booming, a sound like Henry Kissinger on laughing gas. "I am liking this girl," he said.

Mackie reached up inside the minidress, under the straps of the G-string, pulled out the money: three bills—a hundred and two fifties.

"This is the girl that goes with the flag," Mr. Samsonov said, as Verna changed the fifty from a huge roll she kept somewhere down her front. "The All-American girl."

Mackie made $943 that afternoon, two one hundreds, three fifties, nine twenties, seventeen tens, twenty-eight fives, one two, and one hundred and one ones. She changed it to a money order at a bank Verna recommended a few blocks up Oro: Patriot Frontier Savings and Loan. While the teller counted out the bills, Mackie overheard two tiny old ladies talking in the line behind her. "Waitressing must be good these days," one said.

Lianne was doing her homework at the kitchen table as Mackie walked in, a few minutes after seven.

"Sorry I'm a bit late, sweetheart," Mackie said. "Have you eaten?"

"No."

"Good. I've got a treat."

"What's that?"

"Thai."

"Thai?"

"I thought we'd try something new."

They tried Thai food, both of them for the first time, and liked it a lot. "Was it expensive, Mom?"

"Don't worry about that," said Mackie, sitting back in her chair; her muscles a little sore, but not nearly as sore as they were after cleaning for Mrs. Thorsen. "How was your day?"

"Not bad," Lianne said. "And yours?"

Nine

What's your old man all about?" said Jimmy Marz.

"How do you mean?" said Lianne. She ran her finger over Jimmy's nipple and it got all stiff. What were men doing with nipples anyway?

"Besides the tennis," said Jimmy. "I know that part. Rags played him a couple days ago. Rags was on the team up at State for a year or so, but he didn't take a game off your old man."

"He's good at tennis," Lianne said. "He taught Jenna how to play."

"Who's Jenna?"

"Nobody."

They lay on the bottom bunk of the bed in this place she went with Jimmy. Lianne wasn't sure where it was, somewhere on the edge of Ocotillo Ranch, far from the lodge and the casitas. The dirt road ended miles away; Jimmy drove his motorcycle on a faint track across the desert after that. Lianne liked the view she had lying right there, through the open window: a two-humped mountain that kept changing color as the sun moved across the sky.

"Can we climb up there, Jimmy?"

"That's Mexico."

"So?"

"One day, maybe," Jimmy said. "What's with your old man—the golf course, condos, all that shit?"

"I guess he's got ambitions," Lianne said.

"Me too," said Jimmy. "But why fuck up the ranch?"

She rolled on top of him. "What kind of ambitions have you got, Jimmy?"

"This is my ambition," he said, rolling her back over like she was nothing, him on top now.

When she looked out the window again, the mountain was glowing. "What else?" she said.

"You know," he said. "Money."

"What would you do with it?"

"Shit. What wouldn't I do with it?"

"Be specific."

"You're funny, you know that? The way you talk. I bet you get good grades in school."

"They're okay."

"Straight A's, right?"

"Pretty much."

"Got a boyfriend there?"

"You know I don't." She had a thought. "What about you?"

"What about me?"

"Got a girlfriend somewhere?"

"Sure do."

"Nadine?"

He laughed. "Maybe you're not so smart. The girlfriend I'm talking about's stark naked right now."

"Yeah?"

"Down in the South End bunkhouse. And she tastes like honey from the bee."

Lianne had a feeling at that moment unlike any she had ever known. Pure happiness: it was real. She made a buzzing sound.

He laughed, shivering at the same time; she felt that shiver down his spine. "You're going to kill me," he said.

A little later, she said, "Still alive?"

"Barely."

It was the warmest day in a while. They had the door

open now for the breeze. Lianne saw a little dust cloud in the distance. It got bigger.

"I think someone's coming," she said.

Jimmy opened his eyes. "Get dressed," he said.

"Think it's my father?" Lianne said.

"Not from that direction," said Jimmy.

"If it is, I'll just tell him."

"Bad idea," said Jimmy. "Anyways it's not him. The city people don't know this place." Jimmy was dressed now, standing on the porch, his back to her. She could picture its contours right through the cotton of his shirt. "Got any ID on you?" he said.

"No. What for?"

He turned to her. "I guess it doesn't matter. Nobody's going to take you for Mexican."

Lianne zipped up her jeans, went out on the porch. An open-topped Jeep or dune buggy came over a rise, swerved around a cactus, one of those organ pipes, a kind she'd seen only once or twice, and skidded to a stop a few yards away.

"Try taking it easier on the ecosystem," Jimmy said.

The driver got out, a tall bony guy, bald in front, long stringy hair in back; but any man would look bad next to Jimmy. He had a bandanna over the lower part of his face, like an old-time movie outlaw. "Sorry, Jimmy," he said, pulling it down and coughing once or twice. "Didn't know you'd be here."

"Even when no one's watching," Jimmy said. "That's the test."

"Won't happen again," said the man. "What I meant was I didn't want to disturb anybody." His eyes shifted to Lianne.

"You're not," Jimmy said. "Lianne, this is Dane. Dane, Lianne."

"Hi," Lianne said.

"Howdy," said Dane.

He went to the back of the Jeep, unloaded a bottle of

water, the big kind that goes on coolers, and carried it up to the porch. "All right to put this inside?" he said.

"Against the back wall," Jimmy said.

Dane carried it in, went back for more bottles, half a dozen in all. After that, he rested a moment on the porch, mopping his head with the bandanna and scanning the sky. It was empty, clear blue and nothing but. "You from around here?" he said to Lianne.

There was nowhere around here for her to be from, Lianne thought. She said: "Tucson."

"Yeah? What part?"

"Foothills."

"Nice." He stepped off the porch, walked to the Jeep, opened the door. "Got a second, Jimmy?"

Jimmy went over to the Jeep. Lianne backed into the bunkhouse, acting polite. Acting polite, but she had a good view of Dane holding out an envelope.

Jimmy said, "What's this?"

Dane answered in a low voice. Lianne's hearing was sharp. "A little payment," he said.

"We're all square, far as the money," Jimmy said.

"Call it a bonus," said Dane.

Jimmy shook his head.

"The boss wants you to have it," Dane said. "Buy something for the kid."

I look like a kid to him? Lianne thought.

Jimmy took the envelope.

Dane turned the key, drove off, not slow.

"The fuckin' ecosystem," Jimmy yelled after him.

The Jeep vanished in a dust cloud.

Jimmy came inside.

"Who's that?" Lianne said.

"Dane."

"But who is he?"

"Just some asshole. The desert is fragile."

"How do you know him?"

"From way back. We kind of grew up together, at least in the same town."

"What town?"

"Arivaca."

"I've never been there," Lianne said. "I'd like to see it."

"Nothing to see," Jimmy said. "We'd better get going."

"But it's not late."

Jimmy gazed at the two-humped mountain. "Late enough," he said. "And I got work to do."

They mounted the motorcycle, rode off in a different direction than Dane had taken. Lianne tried to figure out the directions. They were going northeast, she thought, meaning Dane had been headed southeast, or just plain east. But how it would all look on a map was hazy to her; she wasn't good with maps.

She leaned forward, gave the edge of Jimmy's ear, the one with the diamond, a little lick. "You'll have to show me where we are on a map sometime."

"Sometime," he said. They were going slow and it was easy to hear; Jimmy drove slow in the desert and stuck to the hardest ground whenever the track disappeared.

"Is all that water for the horses?" she said.

"Sure," Jimmy said. "And the mules."

"There are mules on the ranch?"

"Of course."

"Which is the one that can't have babies, donkeys or mules?"

"Mules, for Christ's sake. What do they teach you in school?"

"How to get pissed off."

Jimmy laughed. "You're something," he said.

They bumped up onto the beginning of the dirt road, mountains rising on their left, the sun about a finger-width above the crests. Their shadows—hers, Jimmy's, the bike's—stretched far to the right, enormous, racing them across the desert.

"So Dane works for some kind of water company, is that it?"

"No more questions."

"Why?"

Jimmy laughed, shook his head. "That's another one right there."

"I think I figured it out," Lianne said.

"Figured what out?"

"What's bothering you."

"Nothing's bothering me."

"You can make good money at the water company, right?" said Lianne. "But you don't want to give up all this."

"All what?"

"The wrangling life."

"The wrangling life? Know how stupid that sounds?"

Lianne let go of him, stopped holding on.

"What the fuck?" said Jimmy, and brought the bike to a stop. He got off, kicked down the stand, faced her. "What's with you?"

"The way you said that."

"What way?"

She gazed at him. He was beautiful. Maybe he really didn't understand.

"All right," he said. "I'm sorry. The tone, and all. Of course you're not stupid. Anyone can see that. But don't ever do that again, letting go."

The sun sank below the mountain crest, darkening the desert although the sky remained bright. The tone and all—he got it. Jimmy understood her. Who else was on that list? Lianne couldn't name one other person for sure. "I don't care whether you've got money," she said.

"Easy for you to say," said Jimmy. "With that house in the Foothills."

"You think we're rich?"

"Well?"

Lianne got angry. "You know what my mother does for a living these days?"

He shrugged.

"Cleans houses," Lianne said. "Scrubs toilets. Picks up people's shit. Last night she didn't come home till eight o'clock."

"I don't get it."

"And she never complains," Lianne said, her voice rising. "So we're not fucking rich."

"Hey," said Jimmy, putting his arms around her. "You're upset."

Lianne cried a bit, managed to keep the sounds inside, but couldn't stop a few tears from getting out. They dampened Jimmy's shirt, right around those funny slanted pockets.

"What's wrong?" he said.

"Nothing."

He patted her back. "I don't get what happened, your mom cleaning houses."

"Things went wrong."

"The divorce, you mean?"

"And the bank coming in."

"What's the story, exactly?"

"They had a development going, my dad and my mom. It's complicated."

"A development?" said Jimmy. "Like condos and golf?"

"Another kind."

He kissed the top of her head, then made a little involuntary sound, as though he'd just smelled a nice flower. "Your mom sounds like a stand-up kind of person."

Lianne nodded. "You should meet her."

"Maybe not a good idea."

"Why not?"

"She might not understand about the age difference."

"It's only ten years, Jimmy."

"Twelve."

"So? And if it doesn't bother us, why should it bother anyone else?"

Lianne raised her head from his chest, looked up at him, caught a little quiver in his eyes, like pain. She must have looked a mess.

"Let's think about it, meeting your mom," he said. "We've got time."

Yes, they had time. A wonderful thought, and it made a lot of sense, out there in the huge desert space. She'd hold on to that one.

"Better go to school tomorrow," Jimmy said.

"Okay."

A big bird flew high overhead, wings outlined in gold. Jimmy's eyes followed it.

"Gray hawk," he said. "Don't see those very often."

"Is it a good sign?" said Lianne.

"Must be."

The gray hawk made a long, slow circle, all alone up there.

"What you don't understand," Jimmy said, "is money buys security. And after that, why, say you have a dream. You can get started on that."

"You've got a dream, Jimmy?"

"I wouldn't say dream. But owning a big spread . . ." He went silent.

"Like Ocotillo?" Lianne said.

"Wouldn't have to be that big," said Jimmy. "Running it right's what's important."

The gray hawk glided down, out of the bright sky and into the evening shadow below. It flapped its wings once or twice as it passed over them, dark wings now, making a very clear sound in all that quiet, like muffled drums.

Ten

Turbo was the bouncer. He stood about five feet, five inches, shorter than any of the dancers, looked fit but not particularly muscular; could have been taken for some kind of dancer himself. Turbo spent most of his time at the end of the bar, reading Mr. Samsonov's books on how to be successful in business, eyes intense behind black-framed glasses, the Buddy Holly kind.

"You might see Turbo in action today," said Zazee, coming up the stairs from the stage and sitting on the dressing-room stool next to Mackie. Zazee was billed as the French bombshell, although she came from Lubbock, Texas, Hispanic on both sides.

"Why do you think that?" said Mackie.

Zazee reached for a Diet Coke, her implanted breasts following her movement, a little late in a way that reminded Mackie of the seventh dwarf, although there was nothing dwarfish about Zazee's breasts. They actually stirred the air in the room; Mackie could feel the breeze. "The Mavericks are in the building," Zazee said.

"Who are the Mavericks?" said Mackie.

Zazee tilted back her head, took a long guzzle. "Skinhead bikers," she said. "The kind with attitude."

"Lots of them?" said Mackie, wondering what other type of skinhead biker there might be.

"I don't know. Five or six."

"How's Turbo going to handle so many?"

"It never gets that far," Zazee said.

"What do you mean?"

"You'll see."

Cocoa entered, pulling a wad of bills from the tiny crotch of her G-string. "You're up, sugar," she said to Mackie. Mackie shook out the curls of the red wig, straightened the black minidress, strapped on the silver stilettos, started down.

Dane's announcer voice, modeled on Don Pardo, came through the sound system. "And now, ladies and gentlemen, if any, are you ready for something really special? Buckaroo's is proud to present, dancing under exclusive contract, the smoothest mover west of the Mississippi. Let's hear it for the beautiful and talented, and this time we really mean it—Red!"

Up rose the first notes of "Are You That Somebody"—Mackie wasn't bored with the song at all, was liking it more and more—and she danced through the tinsel arch and into her number. Applause, lots of it. Friday afternoon and the place was packed. She spotted regulars here and there—the skinny guy with the Dali mustache, the businessmen from the Mexican side, the old couple who drank white wine, and Bub, front and center, bills already in his fist, couldn't wait to give them to her.

Mackie shimmied onto the runway. If you knew anything about dance, this kind of dancing was easy. At the end of week one, Mackie was already finding she could think about other things at the same time. Mostly, she thought about money. Hard not to, the way it was falling at her feet that very moment. Mackie suspected that the other dancers did a lot of thinking about money too, just the way the men watching must be thinking mostly about sex. She'd made almost $3,000 in four days, $2,623 to be exact, and that was after paying Verna the stage fees and tipping Dane, Turbo, and the bartenders.

"When Rita Leaves." Mackie got down, rolled slowly over, went into the floor work, felt money sliding down her flank right away, under the G-string strap. She'd gone to the bank that morning, handed Carole a check for $2,000, a check and a thin story about a consulting job for some relative back East. Carole wanted to see some paperwork, but there would be no foreclosure for now. She'd also called Mr. Fertig and told him to make the best deal he could with the IRS, work out some installment plan. This was going to be all right. She could breathe again, real breaths. She—

Mackie felt a hand on her breast. A hand shooting out from the crowd at the tip rail, and not just on her breast but grabbing it, taking it: a big moist squeezing hand, squeezing hard enough to hurt. She cried out, snapped around, found herself eye-to-eye with a huge shaved-head, tattooed freak in a leather jacket, piercings all over his face. *The Mavericks are in the building.*

"You like?" he said.

Mackie punched him in the face. He didn't let go, smiled, in fact. Then another hand reached in, Turbo's hand, Turbo's finely shaped finger, almost delicate, sliding right up one of the Maverick's nostrils, and after that came spouting blood and a brief glimpse of a face, minus half the nose.

The biker screamed, staggered back. Other bikers came charging, jumped on Turbo. They all fell to the floor, Turbo on the bottom. The music stopped, and right after that Mackie heard a loud crack, followed by another scream, this one terrifying. The bikers scrambled up, all but one; Turbo rose slowly, brushing something off his sleeve. Somehow his glasses were still on, undamaged. The biker on the floor lay twisted in agony.

Verna came up, a shotgun in her hand, a gold-nugget bracelet clinking on her wrist. "What's going on?"

"Dislocated hip," Turbo said. "Like Bo Jackson."

"Who's he?" Verna said.

Turbo looked shocked. "Bo Jackson? He could have been one of the all-time greats."

Verna made a little motion with the shotgun. "Git."

The upright Mavericks, except for the one with the hole in his face, gazed down at the one on the floor. "What about him?"

"You're bikers, for fuck sake," said Verna. "If you don't have painkillers, who does?"

Zazee and Cocoa came onto the runway, led Mackie backstage.

"You all right, Red?" said Bub at the rail, tears in his eyes. "You all right?" He thrust money at Mackie. Zazee took it without even a glance, backhand, as they went by.

They sat in the dressing room, the dancers—Zazee, Cocoa, Aria, Sola, Shasta—huddled around Mackie, patting her on the back, stroking her knee; the knee-stroking mostly on Sola's part. After a minute or two, Janet, one of the bartenders, came up, handed Mackie a glass.

"What's this?" Mackie said.

"Stoli," said Janet. Janet was prettier than any of the dancers, a real beauty, and had a great body too, but the burn scars down her front, the result of a childhood accident in the kitchen of her father's diner in Fort Collins, kept her off the stage.

Mackie wasn't much of a drinker.

"Go on," said Janet. "Mr. Samsonov sent it personally."

Mackie took a little sip.

"Fuckin' knock it back," said Shasta.

Mackie knocked it back. She felt good for a moment, warm inside; then she wanted to cry.

"And he'd like to see you in his office," Janet said. "When you're ready."

"I'm getting fired?"

"For having your tit grabbed?" said Shasta. "Don't work that way."

"I hope it doesn't hurt too much," said Sola.

Mackie got dressed, in real clothes, not her costume. "All set," she said, and followed Janet downstairs. On the way down, she heard Sola saying, "It hurts more when they're real," and Zazee replying, "Who can remember?"

Janet turned right at the bottom of the stairs, led Mackie past the back of Dane's booth—music throbbing again, "Maniac," which meant Sola was up—then through a door where Mackie had never been, and down more stairs, lots of them. At the bottom, they followed a hallway with cinderblock walls and a cement floor to a heavy steel door at the end.

Mr. Samsonov's voice came over a speaker. "Waltz right in," he said, the *w* more like a *v*. Janet opened the door for her. Mackie went in.

Mr. Samsonov rose from behind his desk, a huge wooden desk, dark and gleaming. "How are you?" he said. "I am concerned, horribly."

"I'm all right," Mackie said.

"Thank God. You are a trouper. Please accept my apologies."

"You have nothing to apologize for."

Mr. Samsonov shook his head, a very slight movement that at the same time sent a completely unyielding signal. "Turbo was too slow in the reacting. He will be spoken to."

"Please don't," Mackie said. "I thought he was—" What did she think? *Superb, magnificent, a real gentleman?* None seemed right. "—a fine deterrent."

Mr. Samsonov's eyebrows—platinum like his hair—rose in two sharp little Vs. "Ah," he said. He came out from behind the desk, a very big man in snakeskin cowboy boots and matching belt with a diamond-studded buckle, tight jeans, and a Buckaroo's T-shirt, with those nipples in the Os. "Sit down," he said, "by all means."

Mackie looked around. There was nowhere to sit but Mr. Samsonov's executive chair or the couch, long, wide, white leather. She sat at one end of it.

"You've got a nice office," Mackie said. In fact, she'd never been in one so opulent: Persian rug, paneled walls, chandelier; all opulent, except for the steel door she'd entered, and its duplicate on the other side of the room. Framed celebrity photos, all signed, hung on the walls. From where she sat, Mackie could read Waylon Jennings's inscription: "To my good pal Buck Samsonov—thanks for one <u>fuck</u> of a night."

"Much obliged," said Mr. Samsonov, "although of course this is just one of my offices." He opened the freezer door of a huge built-in fridge—Sub-Zero, Mackie recognized it from the Buena Vida appliance phase—and took out four or five frosted bottles and two shot glasses. "Now for a drink."

"I just—"

"Choose from Stoli, Grey Goose, Finlandia, Ketel One, Absolut."

"They're all vodka?"

"Certainly."

"Stoli," she said, since she'd just had one.

"Me too," he said, putting the other bottles back in the freezer. "We are like peas in the pods."

Mackie noticed a bank of black-and-white monitors on one wall, saw shots of the stage—Cocoa on the runway now, doing that backing up wiggling to the edge thing she did, and there was Bub, his image sharp and clear, leaning into the picture with a rolled-up bill between his lips; shots too of the bar, the floor, the dressing room, the front door, the parking lot, the employee lot. And other places she didn't recognize: one might have been the border crossing from a high angle; another seemed to be a corridor, long and shadowy, with crude wooden beams and naked bulbs dangling from above into the grainy distance; a third was a stage with a dancing stripper, but it had to be some other club, one without a tinsel arch or runway. And with different rules: the dancer was completely naked and a customer was up on stage with her, his face in her crotch.

Mr. Samsonov, bottle and glasses in hand, sat on the couch a couple feet away, hooking a mirror-topped table closer with his foot. He poured, handed Mackie a shot glass, set the bottle on the table.

"Here's to a long and mutual arrangement," he said.

"Thank you, Mr. Samsonov."

He downed his in one gulp. Mackie did the same.

"And everybody calls me Buck," he said. "See?" He twisted around, showed her the diamond-studded belt buckle, the diamonds, she now saw, spelling *Buck*.

Mackie had heard no one call him Buck. "It doesn't sound very Russian," she said.

"Are we now going to introduce for discussion the matter of real names?" He turned to her, those eyes of his not too dissimilar in color from the vodka in one of the other bottles, the one with the hint of yellow.

Mackie laughed. "Touché," she said.

"Touché," said Samsonov. "I love this word." He wrote it in his notebook. "I love all these American words." He leafed through the book, reading a few: "Brownnose, poltroon, cancer stick, dickhead, sleazeball, trailer trash, filibuster. What a language!" He refilled their glasses.

"Is cakewalk in there?" Mackie said.

He went still. "It is meaning what I think?" he said.

"Yes."

He wrote it down, closed the book. "You will be a big help to me." He shifted an inch or two closer on the couch.

"Cheers." He downed his drink.

Mackie took a sip.

"Down the hatch," he said. "Already in my book, this downing the hatch."

Mackie gulped it down.

"You speak of deterrence," he said. "Did you know I am a veteran of the Cold War?"

"No."

"The tail end. Is that correct, tail end?"

"Yes."

"The tail end, in Afghanistan." He filled their glasses again. "I am so glad it is over. We are such a good match, America and Russia. Like lovers from the start."

He gazed at her. Mackie looked away. On the monitor with the shot of the corridor, all grainy shadows, a thick-bodied man in a too-tight suit, back to the camera, walked beneath one of the hanging bulbs, his bristly hair in close-up for an instant.

"Let me show you my proudest possession," Samsonov said, opening his wallet, spilling platinum and gold credit cards on the mirror-topped table. He poked through them, plucked out an ID card, handed it to her.

"What's this?" she said.

"You don't know what is a green card?" he said.

"I know what it is," said Mackie. His first name was Yevgeni. "I've just never seen one."

He gave her a long look. "Sometimes I am thinking Americans don't deserve the greatness of their country. Do you know the story of J. P. Morgan?"

"Kind of."

"That is greatness." He raised his glass. "J. P. Morgan, John D. Rockefeller, Andrew Carnegie, Cornelius Vander-bilt."

"I've really had enough, Mr. Samsonov."

"They are the standard," he said. "Here is to the Wild West. Drink."

What the hell. She drank. Stoli. A cute name. Stoli felt surprisingly good going down this time; her muscles relaxed, and the pain in her breast faded away. Weren't there occupational hazards in every job?

"I will tell you something," said Samsonov. "But first, to

make a solemn promise: You will never be the subject of violation again. No one touches my girls."

"I appreciate it," said Mackie. "But I'm my own girl."

Samsonov laughed, that deep, rumbling laugh. "My very point, what I was about to say. Your own girl—so American. Marketing perfection: you, my all-American girl. They will come in droves to see you. Droves. And what is the best part?"

"I don't really consider my—"

"The other girls are not even the slightest bit of jealousy. And why is that?"

"They have no reason to—"

"Because you are . . . what is the word I look for?"

"Supplying them with crank?" Mackie said; a crazy reply, perhaps Stoli-induced, that came looping out of her mouth unbidden.

Samsonov sat back. "This is a joke, right?" A new look appeared in his eyes, one that made her a little uneasy.

"Right."

"Did not Verna make the rules clear as crystals?"

"She did. A joke. Sorry."

He nodded. The disturbing look faded. "But I now have the word for you," he said. "Wholesome. Everyone likes you because you are wholesome."

"Thank you." Wholesome, all-American: Angie's prediction coming true.

"This is your image," said Samsonov. "Like Betty Crocker. And therefore?"

"Ease up on the jokes?" said Mackie.

"We have understanding," Samsonov said. "You and I."

Eleven

"I don't get it," said Harry Pond. "Is there skiing in this Agua place?"

"No."

"Then how's it going to help?"

"I'm approaching this as a job," Loeb said.

"Come again?"

Plotting; police procedure; doing women: his assignment. "It's complicated," Loeb said.

"Not too complicated, I hope," said Harry, "with the manuscript being due in six weeks."

Six weeks was out of the question, of course, but Loeb wasn't worried. In the publishing business, time was flexible, six weeks just a way of saying in the not-too-distant future. Loeb had never met a deadline exactly, and hardly anyone else did either, as Harry knew: almost unprofessional of him to bring it up. Loeb thought for the first time of switching agents. "You know how soft those deadlines are," he said.

"They're getting harder," said Harry. "One of my other authors had a book canceled last week for coming in two months late."

"Canceled?"

"And they want the advance back."

"That's barbaric," Loeb said.

"So my advice—" At that moment, the announcement about switching off all electronic devices came over the cabin speakers, and Loeb missed Harry's advice.

"What was that, Harry?"

". . . them any excuses," Harry was saying, "so do your-self a big favor."

"How?"

"By getting it in on time."

"What do you mean by on time?" Loeb said. "You can't be—"

"If you don't mind, sir," said the flight attendant.

Loeb switched off the phone.

Six weeks, and he wasn't even halfway done, hadn't even figured out how Myra switched the bodies, or even more important, in terms of any psychological truth the story might have, why Willie let her do it. At cruising altitude, Loeb opened his laptop.

"Death row is a little more than going away." He couldn't get past it. Six weeks to go, and he was stuck on that maddening bit of dialogue, not glaringly wrong, just wrong enough. He decided to try something he'd never done before, leaving the chapter unfinished and going on to the next one, violating the creed of solid foundations.

And what was the next chapter, number eleven, about, anyway? He could think of three ways to go. When he'd written *White Out*, he had trouble coming up with one. Did that mean he was getting better or worse?

One: a flashback to Willie's barbecue, Willie setting the pink Caddy on fire by accident, and starting all the trouble. Two: follow Bolt on his search for Freddy, deep into the Maine woods to the old hippie cabin on the lake. Three: Bolt tries to find out why Athena's been acting so strange, realizes she's been hiding something, maybe something Sergeant Falco told her.

Loeb gazed out the window, into the blue, and had a sudden vision of Mary Jane Krupsha's face out there, lips moving, sound off. He chose option two.

Hazelton came into the clearing. He studied the cabin. It had duct tape on some of the windows and a faded peace

*sign painted on the door. Hazelton had seen cabins like
this before. What bothered him about this one was that no
smoke was coming out of the chimney. It was twenty below.
He crossed the clearing, took off his snowshoes, knocked
on the door. It swung slowly open on its own. Hazelton
reached inside his—*

Loeb grew aware of his seatmate in 14B, who was reading along as he wrote. He took his hands off the keys.

"Hey," said the man. "Is that supposed to be a story or
something?"

"Something."

"Who's this Hazelton guy?"

"A private detective."

"Yeah? You write mysteries?"

"Yes."

"Ever published any?"

"Three, in fact."

"You're kidding? I read a ton of mysteries. What's your
name?"

Loeb told him.

"Doesn't ring a bell." The man chewed a smoked al-
mond, licked his fingers, dipped them back in the foil bag.
"You use a pseudonym?"

"No."

"Almonds?"

"No, thanks."

"What are some of the titles?"

Loeb named them.

"They all have white in them?"

"You know," said Loeb, "like *A Is for Alibi, B Is for*
whatever it was."

"That's not the same as white in all of them."

"Maybe not."

"Ever get one made into a movie?"

"No." Harry hadn't even had a nibble; maybe his con-
tacts out there weren't as good as he said.

"Bet that would make a big difference, huh?"

"Probably," Loeb said. "What line of work are you in?"

"Sand and gravel," said the man. "So this Hazelton guy's the PI?"

"Except he's called Bolt in the actual books."

The man gave him a quick sideways glance, as though Loeb might be putting him on. Then his gaze slid back to the screen.

"So what happens next?"

Loeb gazed at it too. He'd forgotten completely.

"He reaches for a gun, right?" said the sand-and-gravel man. "And inside the cabin is all blood and gore, and the dead body of the key witness. Then maybe he hears a noise in the cellar."

Loeb's fingers moved to the keyboard. The sand-and-gravel-man in 14B was right: something like that had been about to happen. But not now. If he was ever going to be any good, in the eyes of Mary Jane Krupsha if no one else, this scene would have to turn out differently.

Hazelton reached inside his parka for the Glock, then took a cautious step inside.

Someone was in there, hurriedly packing a backpack, but who? It came to him, all at once and with a force that was almost physical.

A woman with her back to him was throwing things in a backpack. She turned at the sound of his footstep. Athena.

Athena. My God. Why hadn't he thought of this before? Much more than option three, much more than one of their little spats, soon patched up: This was the beginning of the end for Athena. He would write her out of the series, and in a way that left Timothy Bolt—yes, suddenly he found himself back to thinking of the character as Bolt, everything snapping into place, as though some master chiropractor of narrative had adjusted his brain—in a way that left Timothy Bolt unable ever to be happy again, not way down deep. My God. Was this what Mary Jane

had meant about working on plot? He changed *throwing*
to *jamming*.

"What kind of name is Athena?" said the sand-and-
gravel man.

Loeb rented a car at the Tucson airport; not any car, but
a pickup, a spur-of-the-moment decision that felt right,
plus they were offering a deal. He locked his luggage in
the covered bed and drove south. Someplace new; deep-
blue, late-afternoon sky; desert: he liked Arizona right
away. Was there anything to stop him from moving out
here, freshening up his life and work at the same time?
Nothing. Loeb felt light, free, full of potential energy,
imagining a future of pickup trucks, a new accent inflect-
ing his speech, shotgun ownership. Anything was possible.
That thought didn't vanish until he crossed the Agua Fría
town line. What was the name of the town in Hammett's
Red Harvest? It would come to him.

The police station stood a few blocks from the border—
Loeb could see the lineups as he parked in the McDonald's
lot next door. In the banged-up car next to his, a man was
shouting into a cell phone in Spanish, the backseat full of
yellow sombreros with little red balls dangling from the
rims. Loeb locked his car and went into the station.

"Detective Krupsha, please," said Loeb to the uniformed
officer behind the counter. "Nick Loeb."

The officer pressed a button. "A Nick Loeb here to see
you," she said into her microphone. A tinny reply leaked
from her headphones. "Come on in," she said. Loeb went
through a half door at the end of the counter. "Third left,
second right."

Loeb walked through the station. He'd never been in a
police station before, but this one resembled Sergeant
Falco's pretty closely. Maybe police station architects got
their ideas from reading mysteries, in which case further

research was unnecessary: all he had to do to stay on the
cutting edge was write whatever came to mind.

CLAYTON KRUPSHA, CAPTAIN OF DETECTIVES. Loeb
knocked on the door.

"Yup," called a voice.

Loeb went in.

Clayton Krupsha, on the phone, pointed to a chair. Loeb
sat. Krupsha reminded him right away of Sergeant Falco,
except everything in the real man was exaggerated: the
thickness, the heaviness of the face, the seams cut into it,
the bristliness of the bristly graying hair, the too-tightness
of the too-tight suit.

"Some nurse, it musta been," Krupsha said. He listened.
"Doing her fuckin' duty, how the hell would I know?" He
said good-bye, hung up, gazed across the desk. "You the
author?"

"Right. Nick Loeb. I really appreciate—"

"Never met an author before. Reporters, yeah. But no
authors. I hope there's a difference."

"In my case, fiction only, a big difference," Loeb said.
"Did your, did Mary Jane explain the reason I—"

"What's the connection?" Krupsha said.

"Connection?"

"Between you two."

"No connection, really, except through literature, if you
want to put it that way." Krupsha's lips, quite purple,
turned down. "Mary Jane has read my books—here, by the
way, with my compliments—" He placed a copy of *White
Midnight* on the desk. "—and she made some excellent
suggestions."

"I'll bet," said Krupsha. He picked up the book, looked
at the front, turned it over, looked at the back. "You know
this guy from the *Chicago Tribune*?"

"The reviewer? No."

"He just said that on his own?"

Loeb nodded. He tried to picture the Krupsha marriage. Only the divorce was clear.

Krupsha leafed through the book. "What's it about?"

"It's the third in a series," Loeb said, "about a private detective named Timothy Bolt who specializes in skiing and back-country cases."

"Skiing cases?" said Krupsha.

"But Mary Jane thought the books could be improved if I had better knowledge of police procedure, which is why I'm very grateful—"

Krupsha held up his hand, not particularly long, but wide and thick, the pinkie ring dug deep into his flesh. "Let's get one thing straight from the get-go," he said. "You dickin' her?"

Loeb sat back in his chair. "What difference would it make?"

The skin on Krupsha's face seemed to tighten, making him look younger for a moment. Then he smiled, the kind of smile that doesn't include teeth. "Right you are," he said. "How about signing the book?"

"My pleasure," said Loeb. He rose, took out his pen, opened *White Midnight* to the title page. "Anything special you'd like me to put?"

"You're the author."

"How about 'To Detective Krupsha, thanks for showing me the ropes'?"

"Hell," said Krupsha, "you can call me Clay."

Loeb inscribed *White Midnight* to Clay. Krupsha read it over. "Shit, that's a first," he said. He turned the page. "What's this?"

"An epigraph."

Krupsha read it aloud. " 'For winter's rains and ruins are over, And all the season of snows and sins.' " He gave Loeb a suspicious look.

"It's meant to comment on the story," Loeb said. "Maybe even sum it up a little."

"Who's this Swinburne?"

"A poet."

"You know him?"

"No."

Krupsha closed the book. "So you want to tail me around."

"As unobtrusively as possible," Loeb said.

"Guy like you in a town like this, going to be obtrusive." He rose, pushing himself up from the desk, his forearms like pier supports. "Might as well get started," he said.

Krupsha led him out the back way to the parking lot.

"You rent a car?" he said.

"Yes."

"Where is it?"

"McDonald's."

"Should be safe enough," said Krupsha. "For now."

They got into Krupsha's unmarked car, a green Crown Vic with a cracked taillight and a hanging muffler. Krupsha wheeled out of the lot, turning into the street without a look left or right.

"See that guy?" he said.

"Yes."

"Illegal."

"How do you know?"

"Shit. How do I know."

They drove past the man, copper-skinned like most of the people on the street, wearing a baseball cap, toothpick in his mouth.

"He looks like everybody else," Loeb said.

"You got it."

Loeb glanced at Krupsha's immobile profile, decided he was making a joke. A voice came over the radio. "Dispatch. Gunshots vicinity Pedras and Delina Road."

"Fuckin' Conklin," said Krupsha.

"Who's Conklin?"

"Old bird, takes potshots at wetbacks runnin' through his backyard. Or anything he thinks is wetbacks."

Loeb took another look at the people on the street.

"Car three," said another voice, cutting through static. "On Pedras now."

"Dispatch. You want backup?"

"For Conklin?" said the man in car three.

Krupsha turned onto a road that climbed a hill, the houses so close on either side that Loeb could see the bruises on a bunch of bananas in someone's kitchen, and ended in a circle before a low building marked BAJA MEDICAL CENTER. Krupsha parked in front of the emergency entrance. They went inside.

"Where you got Lonnie Mendez?" Krupsha asked the desk nurse.

"Two-oh-nine."

They rode the elevator to the second floor. "Any bikers in your stories?" Krupsha said.

"No," said Loeb. But why not? How about bikers trying to take over some little family-run ski place in New Hampshire? "Not yet."

The door to 209 was open. In one bed lay an emaciated old man on oxygen, in the other, a young big one with lots of tattoos on his uncovered torso and his leg in a sling.

Krupsha stood over him. "How ya doin', Lonnie?"

"Decent."

"Dislocated hip?" said Krupsha.

"It's back in now."

"Same what happened to Bo Jackson," Krupsha said.

"Everybody's tellin' me that," said Lonnie.

"He never ran good again," said Krupsha. "Say hi to my buddy, the author."

Lonnie's eyes shifted toward Loeb, back to Krupsha. He said nothing.

"Hi," Loeb said, trying not to be too obvious about gazing at the tattoos. Lonnie was like a big breathing comic book, of the sado-porno Japanese type.

"So how'd it happen?" said Krupsha.

"I didn't file no complaint," Lonnie said.

"Someone else musta called in," Krupsha said. "Happens from time to time in the wide world of crime."

"What crime?" said Lonnie. "I fell off my goddamn bike."

Krupsha nodded. "What're you ridin' these days?"

"Harley Sportster."

"The little one or the twelve hundred?"

"Fuck," said Lonnie. "What do you think?"

Krupsha laid his hand on Lonnie's leg, the one in the sling, not heavily. Loeb could see Lonnie trying not to wince, almost successfully. "How'd it happen?" Krupsha said.

"Hit an oil slick."

"That'll do it," said Krupsha. "Whereabouts was this?"

"Old Sonoita Highway."

"What were you doin' up there?"

"Ridin'."

Krupsha thought for a moment, tapping his thick fingers on Lonnie's leg. "Nice scenery, Old Sonoita Highway," he said. Lonnie watched Krupsha's tapping fingers. "How'd the bike make out?"

"All right."

"You're lucky."

"You call this lucky?"

"Coulda been worse. A lot worse. Like if there happened to be a next time, for example. You got a will?"

"A will?"

"For who gets the bike when you're gone."

Lonnie wrinkled his forehead; his eyelid piercings clicked against each other.

"It's never too soon," Krupsha said. He took his hand off Lonnie's leg, turned to Loeb. "Got any questions?"

"Me?"

"Why not? Lonnie don't mind. Tell him you don't mind, Lonnie."

Lonnie's gaze went to Loeb again. *Venomous, hateful, murderous:* they all fit the expression in Lonnie's eyes. "I don't mind," he said.

Loeb asked the second question that came to mind. "How bad did it hurt?"

"Fuck," said Lonnie. "What do you think?"

Loeb offered to take Krupsha to dinner. Krupsha chose the McDonald's, ordered a Big Mac, fries, and a Coke, supersizing everything. Loeb had a fish sandwich and orange juice.

"There's something I don't understand about Lonnie," he said.

"Scum of the earth," said Krupsha, pouring more ketchup on his fries. "What's to understand?"

"This Old Sonoita Highway—is it paved?"

"Yeah. So what?"

"He fell on it with enough force to dislocate his hip," Loeb said, "but there's not a mark on him."

Krupsha paused, mouth open, full of sawed-off fries and ketchup. At that moment, Loeb remembered the name of the town in *Red Harvest*—Poisonville.

"Like I said, Nick," Krupsha said, "—okay I call you Nick, now that we're getting to know each other?"

"Sure."

"Then like I said, Nick—he was lucky."

Twelve

Saturday morning.

"I could stay and help you," Lianne said.

"Help me what?" said Mackie.

"With the cleaning. Whatever."

"You're an angel." Mom gave her a hug. "But I don't need help. And this is the time to be with your father."

"Sure?"

"Sure."

Lianne didn't make the offer again, had no idea what she would have done if her mom had said yes; must have known deep down she wouldn't, and now felt bad. But just for a moment: she hadn't seen Jimmy in a week; and he'd called only once, after she'd left about a million messages on his cell.

Lianne opened the front door. Kevin was waiting in his car.

"Is that a cowboy hat?" her mom said.

"Oh my God," said Lianne.

Her mom gave Kevin a wave, closed the door. Lianne got in the car.

"What's up with your mom these days?" Kevin said, driving out of Buena Vida Circle. Fresh air hit her as they picked up speed, full of flower smells. Headed for the ranch, top down, weather getting warmer, the mountains impossibly close, the whole world sharp and clear: Lianne was psyched right away.

"Up with her how?" she said.

"I don't know," said Kevin. "She's looking good, that's all. Seems kind of relaxed."

What fucking business was it of his how Mom looked? Lianne switched on the radio, punched the stations till she found a song she liked—"Are You That Somebody"—and ramped up the volume. Any second, he'd say, "Mind turning that down?"

But he didn't, was actually tapping his fingers to the beat on the steering wheel. "You like this?" she said.

"Like what?"

"The song."

"Oh. It's all right." He glanced at her from behind his shades, new ones, and very cool for a dad. "Might have some good news today," he said.

"Like what?"

"Phase one."

"What's that?"

"Gee, Lianne, I told you all this stuff."

"The golf course?"

"The golf course, the tennis complex, the boutiques, the croquet. Mr. Croft met with some investors from Houston yesterday."

"Croquet?"

"Not part of phase one, of course, but yeah, an authentic croquet pitch—with proper leveling, drainage, and sod. Guess what that costs."

Lianne shrugged.

"Go on, guess."

"Eight thousand dollars."

"Jesus, Lianne, you've got to start learning how the real world works, honey. A hundred and fifty grand, minimum. There's not another one in the whole state."

They were out of town now, in one of those empty stretches that led to the mountains, Ocotillo on the other side. Way off the road, Lianne spotted a dry wash, not the wash itself, but the cluster of palo verde and mesquite that marked it, as Jimmy had shown her. "What's wrong with the ranch the way it is?" she said.

"The way it is?" said Kevin. "It's nothing, the way it is, just some horses and cowboy druggies hanging on long after the last roundup. Bottom line—it's boring. I've tried to make Mr. Croft see that, in a nice way, of course. That's a good lesson for you, Lianne, in case you ever get involved in business. Don't criticize what's there, especially with one of these old-school ranchers like Mr. Croft. Instead talk about untapped potential. Identify related areas and blaze away. That's how I got through to him. Look at Disney. They wrote the book."

"Hey! Did you see that?" Lianne said.

"What?"

"Javelinas chewing on that cactus."

"Missed it."

He glanced at his phone, checked for messages.

"Why do you call them druggies?" Lianne said.

"The wranglers? Look at them."

They drove in silence for a while.

"Thought about what you're going to do?" he said.

"When?"

"After you graduate. How're you doing in school, anyway? Still good?"

"Yeah."

"You're a smart girl. But it takes more than that. There's book smart and there's street smart. Me, I wasn't at my best with the books. But when it comes to pulling together something like Ocotillo, that's a different story." He gave her a smile. "Let's say you could have a car for your birthday, hypothetically now. What kind would it be?"

"You mean it, Dad?"

"Sure I mean it. Hypothetically."

"You know what I'd really like? Not a car at all."

"No?"

"A motorcycle."

"A motorcycle?"

"Of my own."

"What do you mean—of your own?"

"A motorcycle, that's all. It wouldn't have to be a big one."

"Think your mother would go for that?"

"Probably not."

He thought for a moment. "Of course, you could always keep it at the ranch. That way she wouldn't worry."

"You mean not tell her?"

"Unless she asks. Can't lie to your mother."

Lianne felt a little guilty for a moment, which was kind of crazy since nothing had even happened yet. On the other hand, she was going on eighteen. How old was Jimmy when he got his first bike? Did anybody give him permission?

"Any particular bike caught your fancy yet?"

"There's a little blue Honda," Lianne said. "Just a two-fifty."

Kevin laughed. "Sounds cute. What's the model?"

"I can find out."

"You do that."

Lianne smiled. The day got even more beautiful. They drove through the Ocotillo gate, parked by the lodge. Lianne looked around for Jimmy, didn't see him. Kevin rubbed his hands together as they got out of the car.

They went inside. The dining room was empty, except for Jimmy, Mr. Croft, and Rags, sitting at a table in a pool of sunlight, drinking coffee from steaming mugs. In their faded clothes, and the light all fuzzy, they could have been from long ago. Lianne followed her father to their table.

"Hi, gang," Kevin said, taking a seat. "Man, does that coffee smell good."

"Care to sit down, young lady?" said Mr. Croft.

Lianne sat.

"Hi," said Jimmy. "Coffee?" He filled her mug, and Kevin's.

Rags rose. "See y'all later."

After he left, Mr. Croft said, "When you've finished, Kevin, why don't we step out on the balcony?"

"All set," said Kevin, taking a quick sip and standing up, coffee slopping over the rim.

Mr. Croft got up, his back not quite straight until he'd taken a few steps, and opened the sliding door to the balcony overlooking the pool. Kevin followed him outside. "Mind closing that?" said Mr. Croft. Kevin closed the door. He and Mr. Croft leaned on the rail. Kevin said something and laughed, no sound penetrating the glass. Mr. Croft wiped his hands on the sides of his pants.

"I didn't hear much from you this week," Lianne said.

"I know," said Jimmy, his eyes on the balcony. Kevin pointed out something in the distance, made a sweeping motion with his arm. Mr. Croft plucked a dead leaf off a potted plant.

"Is something wrong?" Lianne said.

Jimmy didn't answer. On the balcony, Mr. Croft said something and Kevin's arm came slowly down.

"What?" Lianne said. "What's wrong? Look at me."

"Not so loud." Jimmy looked at her. Something in his eyes changed, changed just from seeing her.

"Then what is it?"

"Nothing. I wasn't here, that's all."

"Where were you?"

His eyes shifted, watched the steam rising off his coffee. "Phoenix."

"Doing what?"

"Nothing much."

"You've got a girlfriend there, don't you?" Lianne didn't raise her voice, but she had to know. "Look at me."

He looked at her. "There's no other girlfriend. I told you. I swear."

"Then what? There's something."

"You're too smart for me."

"Just say it."

He bit his lip, the most beautiful lip in the world.

"Oh my God." What had the guy from the water company, Dane, said? *Buy something for the kid.* And she'd taken that *kid* for herself. "You're married."

"I'm not."

"Divorced?"

Jimmy nodded, kind of ashamed. Lianne glanced at his ring finger, checking for an untanned circle where a ring might usually be—a trick recalled from a movie—saw none.

"And there's a kid, or more than one," she said.

"Just one. He took sick a little. I had to go on up."

"Is he okay?"

"Now he is. They thought it was leukemia there for a while, but it's not. Something treatable, long as we can afford the treatment."

"We?"

"Me and my ex-wife."

"You fuck her?"

"Huh?"

"You fuck her, your ex-wife, while you were up in Phoenix?"

Jimmy eyed her, then smiled, showing those white teeth, small and even. "Just the once," he said. "After a few drinks, when we got the word it wasn't leukemia."

Lianne stared at him. Then she laughed, couldn't help it. Jimmy laughed too. They were still laughing when a crashing sound came from the balcony.

Lianne turned to look, aware that Jimmy was on his feet already. Out on the balcony, Mr. Croft's open hands were raised in a calming gesture, Kevin was poking his finger in Mr. Croft's face, and the potted plant was gone.

"Hey," Jimmy yelled, real loud.

Kevin wheeled at the sound, strode to the door, banged it open, right off the rails, and stormed inside.

"Easy, Kevin," Jimmy said. Rags appeared at the dining-room entrance, a lasso over his shoulder.

"Easy?" said Kevin. "Fuck you. That gutless son-of-a-bitch's been stringing me along the whole fucking time."

"Language," said Jimmy.

Her father's face went bright red. "I'll give you language." He flipped the table, old and heavy, halfway across the room—mugs, plates, silverware flying all over the place, coffee spilling on Lianne. Jimmy and Rags moved in on Kevin. He balled his hands into fists. "You losers," he said. "Just try."

"Let him go peaceful," said Mr. Croft from the doorway, shaking visibly, face pale, a little spit at the corner of his mouth.

"Go peaceful, man," Jimmy said. Rags had the lasso in his hands.

Kevin's chest heaved. "You're not worth it," he said. "Come on, Lianne. We're going."

"Where?" Lianne said.

"What the hell are you talking about, where? You're coming with me."

"I don't want to."

"I'm not asking. I'm telling."

Lianne shook her head.

His voice rose, like some furious being of its own. "Obey me, you little whore. Think I don't know what's going on? I'm responsible for you."

"No," Lianne said, and started to cry, nothing she could do about it.

"That's enough right there," Jimmy said.

Kevin's eyes, wild, went to Jimmy, Rags, the lasso, back to Lianne. "No mystery where that disloyalty gene comes from," he said. Then he barged through the space between Jimmy and Rags, neither of them giving an inch, and out of the room, bumping into some guests on their way in for lunch.

Mr. Croft came inside, put his arm around Lianne; he was still shaking but now she was too, even harder. He led her into the empty bar, sat her in a chair by the fireplace, left her alone with Jimmy. They just sat there. Lianne settled down, at least on the surface.

"What's his name?" she said after a while.

"James, like me. But we call him Jamie."

Lianne nodded.

Ramon came in with his prickly pear margaritas, tiny flowers floating on top.

Saturday afternoon. Mackie drove down to Agua Fría. She was dancing Saturday nights now, the biggest night of the week and the only one when Lianne wasn't home. She'd made $1,021 the previous Saturday, paid the mortgage on time, and at least something on all the outstanding bills—phone, electric, credit card, property tax, car. Mr. Fertig had talked the IRS down to sixty grand, was now negotiating the monthly payment amount. Mackie felt good; this was working. She parked in the employee lot behind Buckaroo's, had a quick drink from the bottle of Stoli in the glove box—one of those flat little bottles—and got out of the car.

On the far side of the fence behind Buckaroo's sat four or five dwellings, old and decayed. As Mackie watched, a bulldozer rumbled up to one of them and knocked it down. The back door of the club opened and Samsonov hurried out, a roll of blueprints under his arm and a yellow hard hat on his head.

"Hi, there," he said. "I am almost missing this."

"What's going on?"

"I am building on my land," he said. "Perhaps you didn't know it was mine."

"I didn't."

"And the tenants. Do you know how hard they are to get rid of in America? This was a complete surprise to me. Is it simply a matter of saying go, *andale*? So far from that you would not believe. Therefore, what is the meaning of landlord? In the end, I had to sweet-talk them, Turbo and I, before they would leave. It took a week, for Pete's sake."

Another house folded up on itself and subsided, making a faint sound, like the splitting of a balsa-wood wing on a toy plane.

"What are you building?"

"Ha," he said, unrolling the blueprints. "Feast with the eyes."

Mackie could make no sense of the plans, had never seen anything like them. "What is it?" she said.

"A waterslide, of course," said Samsonov. "What kind of citizen are you? And here"—turning the pages—"is for the minigolf, kiddie rides, tropical lagoon. These, for Wild Western show, authentic gold-panning experience and food court come later. I am buying up the neighborhood, Red, lock and stock." He flipped back to the waterslide. "Did you notice how high at the top?" he said.

"It looks high."

"Fifty meters! Will be the tallest man-made structure south of Tucson. Think of the view from the top."

Mackie gazed over the roof of Buckaroo's, took in the bare hill, the Border Patrol SUV, the corrugated steel wall. From behind came the balsa sound of another house going down. She felt his hand on her shoulder.

"You are different from the other girls," he said.

She looked up at him. The sun, behind his head, blinded her.

"There will be places for smart people in this organization," he said. "Opportunities for advancement. Benefits, health plan, four-oh-one K, and Keogh. Is it too much to think, one day, stock options?"

Samsonov paused. This was a question she was meant

to answer. She'd heard questions like it before, from Kevin, when he rose into what she now thought of as one of his fugue states. But there were differences between Kevin and Samsonov. Even without his hand on her shoulder she could have felt them; they radiated off his body. She shied away from the expression that entered her mind, but that didn't stop it from making an impression: He had the balls to do it.

"No, it's not too much," Mackie said, same as she'd said to Kevin, almost to the end. "Can I ask you a question?"

"Anything."

"Were you rich when you came here?"

Samsonov laughed that deep laugh, like a rumble underground. "I came with nothing, not a single kopek. All I had was this"—holding up his hands—"this"—tapping his head—"and this"—grabbing his crotch.

"I should have known," Mackie said.

"No apologies necessary," said Samsonov, putting his hand back on her shoulder. "We understand each other very well already. You know how I am conceiving of you?"

"How?"

"My little America." He removed his hand. "Go dance."

Mackie danced a little wildly that night, almost out of control once or twice. Not getting turned on, nothing real like that, what men would probably do if they were strippers: but turning on the men by the tip rail, deliberately and knowingly, gauging their basest fantasies from the expressions in their drunken eyes and pitching her act one notch lower. She collected $300 from Bub alone.

"Felt the power tonight, dint ya?" said Sola, counting their money in the dressing room.

To be free and clear, to settle all her debts, to own number four Buena Vida Circle outright, to open her own dance studio: all possible. She just had to keep it up.

"Productive night?" said Turbo, as he walked her to her car, part of his job after the late shift.

"Hanging in," said Mackie. "I never thanked you for the other night."

"But you've been tipping me pretty good."

"Not the same," said Mackie.

He nodded. "That's exactly what Jack Welch says. About motivating people."

"You were motivated that night."

"I'm always motivated," Turbo said, checking his watch. "What Mr. Samsonov says, I do. You're smart, you'll do the same."

"Why?"

"Because anyone in on the ground floor's going to he rich."

Mackie drove away. She passed a Border Patrol checkpoint, and a second one with lights flashing and a tired old truck pulled over. After that there was hardly any traffic. She reached into the glove box for the Stoli.

When Lianne and Jimmy reached the bunkhouse, sunset lighting up the desert like she'd never seen, Dane was carrying the water bottles outside, lining them up on the porch.

"Didn't know you'd be along," he said. "I can put 'em a little ways over there if you want."

"Do that," said Jimmy.

Dane moved the bottles to the base of a barrel cactus nearby, the kind Lianne now knew pointed south, toward the two-humped mountain. He stepped into his Jeep. "We've got a proposal you might be interested in, Jimmy, you want to give us a call."

"What kind of proposal?" said Jimmy.

"Lucrative." Dane turned the key.

"Drive nice this time."

Dane drove nice.

"Who's we?" Lianne said.

"Dane's got some friends. Went his own way, if you like."

"He's not with the water company, is he?"

Jimmy shook his head.

"What kind of friends?"

"Not your kind. You hungry?"

"Yes, but—"

He put his finger on her lips. "Just relax."

There was a fire pit out back.

"Want to get me some of that mesquite?" Jimmy said.

Lianne opened the wood box, saw split logs on one side, a small steel trunk on the other, the top fastened down with a combination lock. "What's in here?"

Jimmy came over, spun the dial, opened the steel trunk. "Dynamite," he said.

"What's it for?"

"Blasting for gold," Jimmy said.

"There's gold around here?"

"Not so far," said Jimmy. "But there's lots of stories." He reached into the box. "This here's the charge," he said. "This here's the detonator. Hook it up like so, and then"—fishing around in the bottom of the trunk—"you just hit this remote."

"Show me," Lianne said.

They walked up a rocky outcrop a few hundred yards away. "I've actually tried here once or twice, based on the geology," Jimmy said. "See all those fragments?"

"Yes."

"That little crevice is a good spot," Jimmy said. "Stick this in."

Lianne stuck it in.

"Now come on over here."

They lay flat behind a little rise.

"Point like this," said Jimmy.

She pointed the remote.

"Hit the button."

She hit the button.

Kaboom. Broken rock went pinging off this and that; dust rose in a little cloud.

"Fun, huh?" said Jimmy.

"But is there any gold?"

"Let's see."

They went to look, everything very quiet after the boom, some big rocks freshly broken, glistening inside.

"Zip," said Jimmy.

He built a big fire with the mesquite logs, a fire that smelled lovely, smelled a little lovelier when he lit up a joint. Lianne sat on an Indian blanket. Jimmy unloaded supplies from the saddlebags—two big T-bones, a huge red tomato, a case of beer.

Jimmy grilled the steaks over the fire. He cut the tomato in sections, sprinkled on salt, fed them to her out of his hand. "Not much of an eater, are you?" he said.

"I'm going to be."

The sun went down. The sky turned purple and orange, flaming here and there. Deep blue took over from the east and the stars came out, first one by one, then by the billions. Lianne ate the best meal of her life. They sat by the fire, the Indian blanket over their shoulders.

"You all right?" Jimmy said.

"Kaboom," Lianne said.

He laughed. "Let's go to bed."

They went inside. Jimmy brought the motorcycle in too, locked the door. They went to bed. Then came the sex part, more kaboom, the best of all.

"How old is he?" Lianne said. "Little Jamie?"

But Jimmy was already asleep.

* * *

Lianne awoke sometime later. She heard voices outside, voices, footsteps, gurgling sounds.

"Jimmy," she said, low and in his ear. "Someone's out there."

His eyes snapped open. She felt him listening. "It's okay. Go to sleep." He closed his eyes.

Lianne could pick out some of the words they were saying outside: *estrellas, mañana, peligroso.* She got up, moved silently to the front window.

The night was full of shadowy people, thirty or forty of them, burdened with ill-shaped luggage, clustered around the barrel cactus. Starlight gleamed on water bottles, flowing ropes of water, tin canteens. A flashlight shone on a mother with a baby at her breast, the beam then swinging onto the face of a man standing off to the side. He shielded himself with his hand, but not before she got a good look at him. Not big or powerful, wearing geeky black-rimmed glasses: Lianne would never have taken him for a boss or leader. So she was surprised that when he said *"Andale,"* the flashlight went off at once, the others all stopped whatever they were doing and straggled away in the opposite direction of the two-humped mountain, north. Footsteps faded out somewhere behind the bunkhouse.

The man in the glasses moved off the other way. Headlights blinked in the southern distance. He changed course slightly, headed in their direction. Lianne lost sight of him a few minutes later. She waited for the headlights to blink again, but they didn't. The desert was still.

Thirteen

Day starts like this," said Clay Krupsha, dipping a chocolate Danish in his coffee. "First, I check the computer log from yesterday, see if maybe something's actually been solved. It happens. Come around so's you can see."

Loeb walked around Krupsha's desk. He saw a column of about a dozen numbers on the screen.

"We go by year, month, day, then the order they came in the particular day," said Krupsha. "That's the numbering system. Course when we talk about them they've got a name, most always the victim's. Let's click on this," he said, moving the cursor to a case that was a few months old, if Loeb understood the system correctly. "The Whiskers case, I call this one."

"Whiskers being the name of the victim," Loeb said.

"Most definitely."

A report popped up on the screen, entered by F. Nuñez. "One of the detectives," said Krupsha. "I got four under me in all. Go on, read it."

Loeb read. F. Nuñez had written a summary of his interview with Flora Gutierrez, formerly of 14 Frontera Street, where the crime had taken place, now living at Kemp's Mobile Home Village on the Arivaca road. *Followed up on information that Gutierrez's former boyfriend Harvey Dunn told associates she owed him $700. Gutierrez said she paid him back a long time ago, but can't remember when. She also said they get along just fine, and besides he* *liked Whiskers. Gutierrez had no information on Dunn's current whereabouts.*

"What do you make of it?" said Krupsha.

"Whiskers is a cat?" Loeb said.

"Was," said Krupsha. "Someone nailed him or her to a tree back of Gutierrez's place on Frontera Street." He looked at Loeb, eyebrows raised, waiting for some reaction.

"And you suspect this Dunn character?" Loeb said, keeping his revulsion out of it.

"Be nice. He's scum of the earth."

"In what way?"

"Put it like this," said Krupsha. "How many shits do you take in a year? Say three fifty? Times ten is thirty-five hundred in ten years, in fifty years be"—punching numbers on a calculator—"seventeen thousand, five hundred, give or take. Telling me you're gonna have to check in the toilet after the seventeen thousand, five hundred and first, to see what happened?"

"Meaning?"

"Meaning? Christ. Meaning I been doing this for fuckin' ever."

For the first time, Loeb began to believe in the possibility of the Krupshas' marriage. "So where do you go from here?" he said.

"Come again?"

"On the Whiskers case."

Krupsha dipped some more of his Danish in the coffee, bit off a chunk, talked around it. "Got any ideas?"

"What about questioning Dunn?"

Krupsha waved that away with the remains of the Danish. "What else?"

"Maybe see if there's any record of a seven hundred dollar payment from Gutierrez to Dunn."

"Like maybe he gave her a receipt?" Krupsha said. "In

triplicate? Hey, no offense, I'm just havin' a little fun. Read the first chapter of your book, by the way."

"Yeah?"

"Yeah." Krupsha finished the Danish, slurped down some coffee.

When Loeb tired of waiting for Krupsha to say more, to say anything, about *White Midnight*, he said: "Have you considered motive? Why someone would do a thing like that?"

"Your point?"

"Whoever did it was aiming at Gutierrez or at Whiskers, right? If it was Whiskers, then you're looking for some sicko. Maybe the ASPCA has a list of them."

"Not a bad idea," Krupsha said. He picked up his phone. "Frankie, on the Whiskers thing, you ever look into animal torturers and such?" He listened. "Can't hurt," he said, and hung up. "There you go, Nick. A working lesson. We may end up owing you one."

Loeb felt a crazy little flush of pride, a physical sensation that not even a good review—even a really good one, like the *Chicago Tribune*'s—had given him.

A uniformed man leaned into the doorway.

"Be right there," Krupsha said. He rose. "How about you come back after lunch, Nick. Hook you up with Frankie Nuñez, you can crack the Whiskers case together."

"And maybe I could see the write-ups on the Mendez case at the same time," Loeb said.

"Mendez case?"

"Lonnie Mendez," Loeb said. "With the dislocated hip. I thought reading them might be useful since I saw the interview."

Krupsha paused. "There is no Mendez case. Didn't I explain that, back at the clinic? Got to have evidence of a crime before we open a file. Falling off your bike don't count. Clear on that?"

Loeb nodded.

"Good. Don't want any slipups in your next book now, do we?"

"No."

"Got a name for it?"

"I was thinking *White Heat.*"

"Wasn't that a Vanessa del Rio movie?" said Krupsha.

"Who's Vanessa del Rio?"

Krupsha looked shocked. "One of the biggest porn stars that ever walked the earth. You might want to come down from that ivory tower, time to time."

Out in the lobby, Loeb plugged in his laptop, sent an E-mail to Mary Jane: *Thanks for setting this up. Ever heard of Vanessa del Rio?*

A reply came back right away: *Sure. Clay and I used to rent her movies. But that's not what I meant by learning how to do women. Keeping your eye on the ball, Nicky?*

Loeb went to Google, typed in *Vanessa del Rio*, got 15,600 hits. He typed in his own name and got 212, but a lot of them were for another Nicholas Loeb, who built microscopes to order.

Eye on the ball: maybe not, but he was learning a lot, could feel some empty well in his consciousness filling up. And Krupsha was right: it was all about climbing down from the ivory tower and, to pile one cliché on top of another, getting his hands dirty.

Frankie Nuñez ate something bad at lunch—the uniformed cops thought it was the crab-and-onion burrito, the detectives favored the fudge walnut cheesecake—and booked off sick. Loeb found himself driving northwest on the Arivaca road anyway; a two-lane blacktop that wound through silvery-gray hills, towering red outcrops rising here and there, and even a roadrunner crossing his path: smaller than he'd expected from the cartoons, but he recognized it right away. He tried to think of a way to maneuver Timothy Bolt into the desert, was getting nowhere when blue lights flashed in his rearview mirror and the Border Patrol pulled him over.

Two agents in green uniforms approached, one coming to his window, the other standing by the back of the truck, hand on the butt of his gun.

"I don't have my passport on me," Loeb said, wondering how else to prove his American-ness. Perhaps he could say something about the Federalist Papers, subject of his senior thesis at Middlebury.

The agent smiled. "Need you to open up the back," she said.

Nick got out, unlocked the bed cover. Had illegal aliens somehow gotten in there during the night? Did the Border Patrol already know? He raised the cover. Unoccupied.

"Beautiful," said the agent. "Enjoy your stay."

Loeb drove on, unable to remember a single goddamn thing about the Federalist Papers.

He almost missed the sign for Kemp's Mobile Home Village, standing alone on the empty roadside, but so faded he could hardly read it. Loeb took the next left, followed a dirt road for about half a mile, came to a small grove of trees, low and dusty, with ten or twelve trailers parked here and there, none together. He got out of the pickup—the sun warm today, almost hot for the first time—and knocked on the door of the trailer with OFFICE spray-painted on the side.

A screen door with holes in it, like cigarette burns: smells came through, not good. A woman appeared, her face familiar from dustbowl photographs.

"I'm looking for Flora Gutierrez," Loeb said.

The woman gazed out, at him or possibly through. He was about to repeat the question when she said, "Way at the back."

Loeb craned to see. "The farthest one, with the yellow?"

"What I said," said the woman, withdrawing into the shadows.

Loeb walked to the back of Kemp's Mobile Home Village, the earth crunching under his feet in a way that reminded him of old Western soundtracks, and knocked on the door of the trailer with the yellow stripes.

" 'Round here," called a woman.

Loeb circled the trailer. From that side there was a nice view of a red-rock mountain with a great slabby head shape at one end, like an Indian lying down, watching. The woman sat in a lawn chair, dressed in a frayed bathrobe and carpet slippers, reading a paperback.

"Flora Gutierrez?" he said.

"Who wants to know?"

Loeb was about to give his name when he noticed the cover of her book: *The Whites of Her Eyes.* A first, and one he'd anticipated for a long time: to come upon someone actually reading one of his books. Why now? There was a God, all right—no accretion of evolutionary mix-and-match could ever culminate in a moment like this.

"Hazelton," said Loeb. "Max Hazelton. I'm with the ASPCA."

"What's that?"

Couldn't this, his very first reader-in-the-wild, have been a little more informed? "American," he said. American something. "Society. Society for the Prevention of Cruelty to Animals."

"I got no animals."

And if not informed, was grammatical asking too much? The reader he'd fantasized would have freely offered the opinion, for example, that Loeb's influences were not John D. MacDonald and Robert B. Parker, but Graham Greene and Dostoyevsky. "That's why I'm here," Loeb said. "It's about Whiskers."

Flora Gutierrez closed the book. There on the back was his face, the horrible photograph that emphasized its asymmetries, since replaced by the one Mary Jane found sensitive. "I didn't file no complaint," she said.

A line he'd heard recently, but where? "We got a call from the police in Agua Fría."

"I didn't complain to them neither," she said.

"Someone must have," Loeb said. "That's not really my department." What fun to say that! How tempting to repeat it! But Flora Gutierrez was chewing her gum at him aggressively, and he was getting nowhere. All at once it hit him: This was about knowing women. He bit his lip—a gesture he could have smacked himself for making, aware even at that moment of its probable inspiration, the former free-world leader known for his knowing of women—and said: "Tell me a little about Whiskers."

Flora Gutierrez took out her gum, stuck it on the book cover for later, not quite touching the photo, or at least the part where he was. "You mean what he was like?" she asked, her voice now soft.

Loeb nodded.

"He was the cutest little thing," she said. "Wanna see his picture?"

He nodded again. She reached into the pocket of her robe, handed him a framed photograph of a cat. Loeb examined it. "He does look cute."

"Thank you." There were tears in her eyes.

"Which is why we'd like to"—Loeb deleted *nail* at the last possible instant—"bring the culprit to justice."

"Ain't no justice," said Flora Gutierrez, a few tears spilling over. She reached for Whiskers, slid him back in her pocket.

A crazy thing happened at that moment: Loeb felt like crying too. He cleared his throat, rose, gazed at the lying-down-Indian mountain, realized that many of the mountains he'd seen here looked like that; giant lying-down Indians all over the land. "How about I drive you to fourteen Frontera Street and we'll take a look around," he said.

"Fourteen Frontera Street?"

He turned to her. "Where you used to live," he said. "The scene of the crime."

"I ain't ever goin' back there," she said, her voice hardening fast.

"It might help."

"Who you kidding?"

"Why do you say that?"

Flora Gutierrez was silent for a few moments. Scraps of toilet paper blew across the desert. "You ever seen Ultimate Fighting?" she said.

"Never heard of it."

"On pay-per-view. You don't get cable?"

Not the time for his line about not watching TV. "What's this got to do with anything?"

"Nothin'," she said.

"Is there some connection to Harvey Dunn?"

"Keep Harvey out of this," she said. "He's a red herring."

"What do you mean?"

"You don't know 'red herring'?"

"I do," said Loeb. *Although I never resort to that kind of shit.* "But what's the 'this' you're keeping him out of?"

She rose. "Nothin', like I said. And now I'm runnin' late. Nice chatting." She waited for him to go, turning her body slightly to point the way. Their eyes met.

So, how's the book? Loeb wanted to ask that question, might never have another chance, but he kept it in. "Goodbye."

"Bye," said Flora Gutierrez, sticking the gum wad back in her mouth. Her eyes went suddenly to the photograph. Loeb walked away.

Frontera Street ran east off Oro, the main drag, a block from the border. As Loeb walked along, past number twenty, past eighteen, he could see, over the rooftops to his right, a bare brown slope rising toward a tall corrugated steel wall, Mexico invisible on the other side. A nice image: weren't there lots of illegal aliens doing the dirty work at Aspen and Vail? Maybe Timothy Bolt could get a call from—

What was this? A number sixteen, but no fourteen, not another house all the way to the end of the block, bounded on the far side by a narrow street and a chain-link fence. And no trees either: not Whiskers's or any other. All the trees lay on the ground, getting pushed toward Frontera Street by two bulldozers. Men in hard hats were digging trenches, clearing brush, taking measurements. Loeb watched them work for a while. They all had tattoos. He remembered where he'd heard *I didn't file no complaint* the time before Flora Gutierrez said it: inside Baja Medical Center, from Lonnie Mendez.

A tall man in a hard hat, blueprints under his arm, came over to where Loeb stood. "Looking for something?" he said. Russian accent: Loeb had heard many just like it in Brooklyn.

"Number fourteen," he said.

"Too late," said the tall man. "Redevelopment has begun."

"What kind of redevelopment?"

"I am building a theme park."

"What's the theme?"

"Excellent question. You are an intelligent man. The theme it is possible to put in one word—pleasure." The tall man smiled. "And your interest in number fourteen?" he said.

"It's about a cat."

"A cat?"

"I'm with the ASPCA."

"Wonderful organization. America at her best. I make donation every year."

"We're grateful," Loeb said, smooth as Timothy Bolt in one of those chapters that really came together.

"But now I will deliver a small joke," said the tall man. "Of cats I know nothing, but if you are interested in pussy you have come to the right place."

"I don't get it."

The tall man pointed to a sign rising over an adjacent building: BUCKAROO'S, with nipples in the Os. "Now are you getting it?" he said.

"Yes."

"Visit anytime. Animal lovers welcome always. Here is my card, presentation of which entitles to one free drink, champagne included."

"Thanks," Loeb said, checking the card, "Mr. Samsonov."

"Everyone calls me Buck, please. And you, if I have the honor?"

Loeb gave his name. They shook hands. Buck Samsonov's hand was huge, full of bone-crushing power, unreleased but not hidden.

Fourteen

Sunday night, after ten, Lianne still not home, Kevin not answering his phone. Mackie poured herself a little glass of Stoli, no more than a few drops, really, and sat on her front steps, leaning against one of Jenna's fluted columns, $387 apiece, excluding the painter. Two walkers appeared under the street lamp by the mailboxes; the Thorsens, out for a stroll, arm in arm. Furtive glances from both of them: they must have thought she'd be long gone by now.

"Lovely night," Mackie said, resisting the temptation to raise her glass.

"Isn't it?" said Mrs. Thorsen. They moved into the shadows.

Mackie tried Kevin again. "Hi! This is Kevin! I can't come to the phone right now, but if—"

Mackie took a sip, gazed into the sky, watched the lights of a plane gliding through the stars. A feeling unfelt for a long time came over her, the desire for male company. Not Kevin, of course, not anyone she knew: a new man, reasonably attractive, reasonably intelligent, reasonable.

Out in the darkness, someone was humming. Mackie didn't recognize the tune, but the hummer had a pretty voice, much too pretty to be Mrs. Thorsen's. Then Lianne walked into the glow of the street lamp, came up the flagstone path to the house, quick and light, backpack slung over one shoulder. Had Mackie ever heard her humming before?

"Hi, Mom. What are you doing out here?"

Humming, and more beautiful all the time. "Waiting for you," Mackie said. "Where's your father?"

Lianne made a sweeping gesture behind her.

"Why didn't he drop you off in front of the house?"

"You know Dad," Lianne said. "Always in a hurry." Lianne sat down beside her.

"How are things at the ranch?" Mackie said.

Lianne shrugged.

"What are the people like?"

"You know."

"I don't."

"Nice."

"Your father gets along with them?"

"Pretty much."

They sat in silence for a minute or two; a lovely minute or two, worry-free. Mackie leaned against the column like it was all hers.

"Any homework?" she said.

"Just the *Lord of the Flies* essay and I finished it in study," Lianne said. "You were right about how mean they were, Mom. But if they were nicer, then what's the story? Just another desert island adventure with dorky boys."

Mackie glanced at her daughter, this smart daughter of hers; she was gazing at the sky. "What are you thinking?" Mackie said.

"Just how incredible the stars are," Lianne said. "Did you know that all the ones we see are in the Milky Way?"

"I didn't."

"We're in the Milky Way, Mom. Living right in the middle of it. You knew that, right?"

"Of course," said Mackie. "Think I'm dumb?"

"Never," said Lianne draping her arm over Mackie's shoulders, pulling her close.

"In fact, I remember when it happened," Mackie said.

Lianne laughed. They were going to be all right, the two of them; Mackie knew it. "What's that you're drinking?" Lianne said.

"Just water."

After lunch on Monday, Lianne went to the nurse. Mrs. Feldman, thank God: the good nurse.

"What's wrong, dear?"

"Not feeling too well."

"How?"

"My period, one of those bad ones."

"Like to lie down for a while?"

Lianne glanced at the shabby old couch in Mrs. Feldman's office. "Maybe just go home."

Mrs. Feldman checked her card. "Should I call your mom to come get you?"

"She's working. You'll never reach her. I can get home all right."

Mrs. Feldman wrote out the slip. It was two point three miles from Kolb High to Buena Vida Circle; Kevin had measured it on the odometer. Except for the first hundred yards or so, in sight of the school, Lianne ran the whole way.

Mom was gone; she'd left a note on the kitchen table, under a tangerine. *Home by 7. I'll bring dinner. Love, Mom.* Lianne made sure the front door was unlocked, went to her bedroom, took off her clothes, got in bed, started reading about Reconstruction for tomorrow's test. She'd gotten to the Ku Klux Klan when she heard the bike. The words in her textbook swam around after that.

Jimmy came into her room, his face reddened from the ride, his smile extra-white. "Nice room," he said.

"Thanks."

"Nice house. A little too nice for the likes of me."

"Stop talking silly," Lianne said.

He stopped talking silly, got undressed. Lianne watched him. This was really happening, in her bedroom and therefore in her life. Jimmy, this man with the beautiful smile, who understood her and got a funny little stunned expression in his eyes when he looked at her sometimes, who had that hard-on right now she couldn't wait to get hold of, was in her life. Her stuffed animals gazed down from the shelves.

"What's so funny?" Jimmy said.

"I'm just happy."

He climbed in beside her, his head on her pillow.

"You gelled your hair," she said.

"For you city folks."

Lianne laughed, rolled on top of him. A shaft of light coming through the curtains shone right on his face. She could see little lines around his eyes: crow's feet? Was that the name? And three horizontal lines across his forehead, but faint; she wouldn't have noticed them at all if it hadn't been for the windburn.

"What're you staring at?" he said.

"You," said Lianne, running her hands through his gelled hair. Was that where his hairline really was, back there? "You're beautiful."

"No," he said. "But you are."

Lianne reached down between them, a little gel on her hand, and took him. Surprise. He'd gone a little soft.

Lianne kissed him. She tried a few things. His eyes closed. Could you look unhappy with your eyes closed? All of a sudden, Jimmy did.

"Jimmy?"

"What?"

"Look at me."

He opened his eyes. Unhappy, or worried, or something wrong, no doubt about it.

"What's wrong?"

"Nothing."

"Tell me."

"I said nothing's wrong."

He was soft now, completely. "I don't believe you."

"I'm not a fucking porn star," Jimmy said.

Lianne rolled off him. She sat up, raising the sheet to her collarbone. He blinked, a slow blink she took for an apology, even if he didn't know he was making it.

"Is it little Jamie?" she said. "A turn for the worse?"

He shook his head, made a tiny snorting sound, almost a laugh. "Don't quit, do you?" he said. "It's not the kid. He's fine."

"Then what?"

She gazed right in his eyes. The momentarily stunned look happened.

"Cough it up," she said.

Jimmy took a deep breath. "This is between you and me."

"You never have to say that," she said. "Silly boy."

"I've got to make a decision," he said.

"About what?"

He paused. "Come here," he said, reaching for her, pulling her to him so her head lay on his chest. He smelled wonderful, clean and wild at the same time, like the wind in the desert.

"What decision?" Lianne said.

"This opportunity's come up."

"Yeah?"

"I can make fifty grand," Jimmy said. "For ten minutes' work."

"What kind of work?"

"Fifty grand," Jimmy said. "In one chunk. Know how much money that is?"

Lianne, not really sure, said nothing.

"Two grand is the most I ever had my hands on at one time in my life," he said.

"When was that?"

Jimmy smiled. "You're something, you know that?" He

rubbed the back of her neck, sending a charge all the way down to her calves, through her butt especially. "It was at the Calgary Stampede," he said. "I took third in the broncos."

"You're a rodeo rider?"

"Was."

"You never told me." She kissed his chest. He was a hero on top of everything. His nipple stiffened. "How come?" she said.

Jimmy shrugged.

"Why'd you stop?"

"No money in it," Jimmy said. "Not for me at least. Not real money. Fifty grand is real money. Thirty-five's the down payment on a ninety-acre spread east of Tubac I know's available, electric in, septic dug, wells all drilled."

"So what's this ten minutes of work?"

He took another deep breath.

"You don't have to hurt anyone or anything?" Lianne said.

"No," Jimmy said. "I'd never do that."

"Then how bad could it be?"

Jimmy turned on his side, facing her, both of them on their sides now. He took her head in his hands, gazed into her eyes. "Why the hell couldn't I have met you ten years ago?"

"I was seven," Lianne said.

Jimmy smiled; those little white teeth. "There's a good reason," he said.

"So it has to be now," Lianne told him.

He nodded. "Supposing a thing's not even real," he said. "How can it be wrong?"

"Is this about Dane?" Lianne said. "And that stupid water company?"

"Sort of," Jimmy said. "But there's no water company, per se. It's more of a . . . I don't know what to call it. Like a conglomerate. They own things."

"What kind of things?"

"A bank in Agua Fría, that's one. Patriot Frontier."

"And?"

He kissed the tip of her nose. "I just thought of a name for the ranch."

"What ranch?"

"The ranch I've been talking about, Lianne, what I need the money for. The ranch where we could live. Aren't you listening?"

"I listen to every word you say. What's the name?"

"Blue Sky Ranch," Jimmy said.

Lianne considered it.

"If you don't like it, we can think of something else."

"No," said Lianne. "I like it. We could paint everything blue—the house, the barn, the fences."

His eyes got a faraway look. "Yeah," he said.

"So tell me about this unreal thing that can't be wrong," she said.

He paused.

"Don't do that sighing thing," she said. "Just tell me."

He nodded, almost like he was obeying her, not possible, Jimmy being a grown man. "They own this bank, Patriot Frontier, like I said, on the main drag in Agua Fría."

"The people Dane works for."

"It's more like this one guy runs everything."

"Is he from Arivaca too, back with you and Dane?"

Jimmy shook his head. "I don't know him personally. Just by reputation. An operator, Lianne, a wheel."

"What does he want you to do, this wheel?"

"Rob the bank," Jimmy said.

"His own bank?"

"That's what makes it unreal. No one loses anything. It's all set up. I go in on a Monday, just before Brinks picks up all the deposits. Monday's when the casino money comes in. Should be five hundred grand, maybe more. I get to keep ten percent."

A million questions popped up in Lianne's mind. She picked one. "What happens to the rest of it?"

"I give it back, of course."

"I don't get it."

"Insurance, Lianne. The bank's insured. The five hundred grand goes right back."

You've got to start learning how the real world works, honey. "So the insurance ends up losing," she said.

"What's the insurance?" Jimmy said. "Nobody."

Lianne couldn't argue with that. "Why you?" she said.

"Got to be someone they can trust," Jimmy said.

"And they trust you because of the bunkhouse."

He nodded.

"What's going on at the bunkhouse?"

"You know."

"Illegal aliens?"

"They're coming anyway, Lianne. Might as well have water, a place to rest for a while."

"So these bank people are smuggling aliens too?"

"I told you—it's like a conglomerate."

"They pay?"

"The Mexicans? Sure. The guy told Dane it's like golf— first you pay the greens fee, then you get to play."

"What guy?"

"The owner."

"What's his name?"

"Samsonov."

"What kind of name is that?"

"Russian."

"I've never met a Russian."

"Me neither," said Jimmy. "So what do you think?"

"How's the robbery supposed to go, exactly?"

"In what way?"

"Will you be safe?"

"Sure. There'll be no resistance or anything like that, no one hitting the alarms, no cops. Plus I'll be wearing a ski mask. It's all timed out. I go in, wave a gun—it's not even going to be loaded—they hand over the money, I'm out of there, van waiting, driver at the wheel, I jump in the back, va-voom."

"Wow."

"Wow good or wow bad?" said Jimmy.

"Both," said Lianne.

"What do you mean?"

Lianne thought, aware of Jimmy's eyes on her waiting, like this was a big moment and her opinion was really important. "These people," she said, "the Russian guy, Dane, the conglomerate, they're kind of criminals, right? Even though they own a bank."

"I wouldn't call them criminals."

"I'm not saying you'd be a criminal," Lianne said. "Since it's all unreal you're not, just like you say. But they are, kind of, anyway."

"Maybe kind of."

"Enough so they really couldn't complain. To the police, for example."

"Complain?" said Jimmy. "About what?"

"If something went wrong with the plan."

"Like what?" Jimmy said. "I don't get it."

Lianne reached down between them, took him in her hand again. Cock, that was the best word for it. Cocky had to come from that, which was just perfect. Why didn't they teach that kind of thing in English? Jimmy's cock grew cockier right away this time: maybe he was starting to think along with her, starting to get it.

"Here's what might go wrong," Lianne said. "You forget to jump in the van."

His heart thumped in his chest. Like a drum: the single beat passing through him and into her breast, the only other place they were touching.

"I climb into something else?" he said.

"Va-voom."

"With the five hundred grand?" Jimmy said. "All of it?"

"Colorado has ranches, Jimmy," Lianne said. "Wyoming, Montana, Nevada, even California. We'll find one on the Internet. Blue Sky."

And now Jimmy was at his very cockiest, like something reinforced with steel. Men came with a handy barometer.

Fifteen

Mackie plucked two tangerines from the tree, her tangerines, her tree. She ate one, left the other on her note for Lianne—*Home by 7. I'll bring dinner. Love, Mom*—drove down to Agua Fría. Her tangerines, her tree: a fortifying thought; thoughts like that could make you stronger. Mackie took only one tiny sip of Stoli as she turned into the employee lot at Buckaroo's. The tangerine taste that had lingered in her mouth the whole drive disappeared.

Mackie went inside. Buckaroo's was all bright and sunny, full of workmen—ripping up the floor, banging down walls, hammering, sawing, welding. Samsonov and Verna sat at the bar, ledgers open in front of them.

"No work today, Red," said Samsonov.

"We'd of let you know if we had your number," said Verna. "Spared you the drive."

"That's okay," Mackie said, keeping her number to herself. Complete separation of work and life the only way: she'd known that from the start. This was temporary. And what if Lianne picked up when they called?

Verna gave her a look, the contrast between the makeup around her eyes—so generous and colorful—and the hard little pale eyes themselves, unsettling.

"Now, now," said Samsonov. "You are Verna, I am Buck, she is Red. This is our M.O. Agreed?" His gaze went to Verna.

"Agreed," said Verna, looking down.

Samsonov smiled. Mackie noticed for the first time that although his top teeth were big, white, and even, the lower ones were yellow and crooked. "You are familiar with this American word M.O.?" he said to her.

"Yes."

"First, you must have a goal," he said. "Then comes M.O. for getting there. Take J. P. Morgan. Goal: financial domination. M.O.: whatever it takes. Example. Today we are closed, to the considerable loss of revenue stream. Why?"

Mackie glanced around. "I don't know."

"Let me ask you a question in the Socratic way," Samsonov said. "If you must describe in one single word Buckaroo's, what would it be?"

Money was the word, but crazily enough Mackie felt there might be something tasteless about saying it. What was he expecting? How about—"Fun?" she said.

Samsonov sat back on his bar stool; Verna watched him carefully. "This is good," he said, "in fact, will make me think a little. But the word I have in mind begins with *c*. Take a stab in it?"

The first *c*-word that came to mind, so obvious, was not a word she was going to utter.

"You are giving up?"

She nodded.

"The word, the magic word," he said, "is classy."

"It was on the tip of my tongue," Mackie said; she felt Verna's hard gaze, but Samsonov seemed pleased.

"Then you should have piped up," he said. "No adventure, no gain."

"So you're making the club classier?" Mackie said.

"Always," said Samsonov.

"How long will you be closed?" She couldn't afford to miss much time, although a little might be nice: if she hurried back right now she could be home when Lianne arrived from school.

"We," said Samsonov. "How long will *we* be closed, if you please."

"We," said Mackie.

"Two days," said Samsonov.

Mackie knew something about construction: it would take more than that just to clean up. "What are the plans, specifically?"

Samsonov paused. "You hear how she talks, Verna?"

"Yeah."

"None of the other girls talks like this."

"No."

"I will tell you what, Red," said Samsonov. "You like shrimp?"

"Well . . ."

"Of course you do," said Samsonov. "Who does not like shrimp? How about a working lunch of shrimp for discussing the plans, the treat all mine?"

"That's very kind of you, Mr. Samsonov, but—"

He was already on his feet. "Lunch with the boss. What could be more American? Am I right, Verna?"

"Oh, yeah."

Lunch with the boss: Mackie couldn't say no.

Samsonov took her to lunch in the Mexican Agua Fría. They walked through the checkpoint with a group of tourists, all waved through without a question, and turned down a narrow street lined with pharmacies and souvenir shops. Hawkers attached themselves to the tourists at once, but they left Samsonov and Mackie alone.

"Everything you are seeing is cheaper on the other side," Samsonov said. "This is the blessing of NAFTA."

He led her across a littered square and into a restaurant called Señor B.'s. Señor B.'s had thick white tablecloths, uniformed waiters, and an elegant maître d' with a flower in his buttonhole: the kind of place Mackie had only been for celebrations.

"Señor Samsonov," said the maître d'. "What a pleasure!"

"How are the shrimp?" said Samsonov.

"Excellent. They came in from Guaymas twenty minutes ago." He smiled at Mackie. "Still flipping and flopping."

"Are they big?" said Samsonov.

"Very big."

"I want big."

"Certainly, Señor Samsonov."

The maître d' led them past the bar, though the main dining room, up a terra-cotta staircase, into a smaller dining room with three or four empty tables surrounding a fountain. They sat by an open window, partly screened by flowering vines. A waiter appeared immediately.

"Dom Perignon," Samsonov said. "Is it cold?"

"Sí, señor."

"I want cold."

"Muy frío, señor." The waiter went off.

"Really, Mr. Samsonov—"

He held up his hand. "Don't disappoint me," he said. "I hate disappointment above all else."

"Disappoint you how?" said Mackie.

"By small thinking. 'Really Mr. Samsonov' is small thinking. There is no room in the organization. And the name is Buck, what everyone calls me. No more reminders, agreed? This is a democracy."

"Agreed."

"Agreed, Buck," he said.

Mackie repeated it.

They drank Dom Perignon, very cold. They ate shrimp, very big. Through the vines Mackie saw that they were overlooking the corrugated steel wall from the other side. No barren strip separated it from the Mexican town: low shanties crowded up against it, laundry flapping in the wind. The fountain made soft splashing sounds.

"Everything is good?" Samsonov said.

"Yes."

"Thank you," said Samsonov. "I am silent partner in this business."

"Not completely silent," Mackie said.

"No?"

"Not if the B's for Buck."

"How quick you are." Samsonov burped, dabbed his mouth with his napkin, dropped it, snapped his fingers. The waiter came running with a new one. Samsonov unfolded it with care, laid it on his lap. "The bodies of women no longer interest me," he said, "except in the professional way, for bringing in the customers."

Mackie, in midbite, felt her stomach close up.

"There is a name for this kind of problem," he said.

"Occupational hazard," said Mackie.

Samsonov laughed. "Oh, so quick." He reached across the table, laid his hand on hers, obscuring it completely. "The minds of most people, not just the women, are worthless to trouble about," he said. "Shit and confusion, pure and simple."

Mackie tried to withdraw her hand, but couldn't, his hand heavily on it even though he didn't seem to be pressing down. "You have not asked if I am married," he said, "or with a girlfriend."

"It's none of my business."

Her hand came free.

They took a different route on the way back, following a street that ran parallel to the steel wall. Buildings, all in need of repair, even the new ones, stood in its shadow: more souvenir shops—figurines, glassware, sombreros, everything in the windows dusty; a drugstore advertising cheap Viagra, no prescription necessary; bars of the kind Mackie would never enter.

"You like Mexico?" Samsonov said.

"I hardly know it at all."

"There is only one thing to know," he said. "The Mexicans want to get out. That is telling all."

Samsonov stopped in front of a windowless two-story building, painted black except for the small pink sign: CLUB GIRLIE. He opened the door. Smoke and music poured out at once, as though under pressure.

"I really should be going," Mackie said.

"Why?" said Samsonov. "This is time you would anyway be working."

Mackie met his gaze. "For you," she said. "Is that your point?"

"Work for me?" said Samsonov. "What a strange idea! You are an independent contractor thanks to the laws of the U.S.A.—an entrepreneur, just like me. Under this best of all possible systems you have choice. Let us go in."

Mackie heard "Maniac" playing inside. "To check out the competition?" she said.

"Competition?" said Samsonov. "This is my little colony. I own Club Girlie, lock and stock. Notice how small and discreet the sign—this is a Catholic country, after all." He put his hand on the small of Mackie's back, guided her inside.

Catholic on the outside, anyway: Mackie's first thought as her eyes adjusted to the dimness. On the inside: porn movies on big screens, the waitresses in thongs and nothing else, the dancer naked, squatting on the stage to pick up balled-up bills in a way Mackie wouldn't have thought possible. The smells: tobacco and marijuana; sweat, male and female. And the floor was a little sticky too. They took a table near the back, a waitress arriving with a bottle of Stoli in an ice bucket, an implant bulging slightly in her breast as she leaned forward to set it down.

"Well?" said Samsonov, filling their glasses. "First impression?"

"No sublimation here," Mackie said.

Samsonov took out his notebook. "This word again?"

She repeated it, spelled it out, raising her voice over the music.

"And the meaning?"

Mackie tried to explain.

"This concept is unfamiliar," said Samsonov.

They sat, drank, watched. Samsonov's face, like those of the customers, grew shiny. Mackie felt hers growing shiny too. Up onstage, the line between the suggestion of self-stimulation and the reality began to blur. To her surprise and discomfort, Mackie found that it was working on her, this performance, exhibition, whatever it was. She put down her glass, looked away, saw that Samsonov's eyes were on her.

"I am reading your mind," he said.

"Oh?" She meant it to sound insouciant, but her mouth was suddenly so dry she hardly got the word out.

"You would like to dance here but are thinking, no visa. Not to worry—no visa necessary."

"You read me wrong," Mackie said.

"I don't think so," said Samsonov. He topped up her glass. "How about this proposal? I will pay you, oh, say a thousand dollars to dance up there like Sola's doing."

"That's Sola?"

"Of course. Is there something wrong with your eyesight? I have had several dancers wearing glasses, all to good effect. There is something about a nude and glasses, so don't be shy of putting them on."

But there was nothing wrong with Mackie's eyesight. The dancer was Sola, all right. The problem was Mackie hadn't looked at her face.

"No," Mackie said.

"Five thousand," he said.

She shook her head.

"You are a good negotiator," said Samsonov.

"I'm not negotiating."

"Ten," he said. "Ten grand, cash in the barrel."

Dane appeared, gave Mackie a little wave. She almost didn't recognize him at first, here in another country; crazy, with the border no more than a few yards from where they sat.

"Cowboy's on the phone," he said to Samsonov.

"Is there some issue?" said Samsonov.

"Just wants to deal with the boss," said Dane.

"The personal touch—very important," said Samsonov. He rose, said, "Think about it," to Mackie, and followed Dane the length of the bar and down some stairs.

Ten grand. The answer was no, but was there a number where it changed to yes? Mackie knew there was, shied away from thinking about how low it might be. She needed money, goddamn it. So easy to judge when you didn't.

Samsonov did not return. Mackie finished her drink. There were many men in Club Girlie, most of them drunk, but no one even seemed to notice her, dressed in sweats and a baseball cap, ponytail pulled through the back. After a while, Mackie rose, not completely steady, and headed for the stairs. As she went down, catching sight of the runwayless stage from this new angle, she realized she'd seen it before, on one of the monitors in Samsonov's office.

Down in the basement, Mackie found herself in a cinderblock hallway, much like the one under Buckaroo's. She followed it to a steel door, knocked.

The door opened. A man in a red T-shirt with ALL-AMERICAN AMUSEMENTS, INC. on the front looked out, a shotgun in his hands. "Señora?" he said.

"I was looking for Mr. Samsonov," she said. "To tell him I'm leaving."

Over his shoulder, Mackie saw a corridor, long and shadowy, with crude wooden beams and dangling naked bulbs, someone pushing a handcart in the distance.

"I will pass along the message," said the man in the red T-shirt, closing the door.

Mackie went upstairs, outside, walked to the border crossing, got waved back through. She drove home. Lianne was at the kitchen table, busy with her homework. Just the sight was soothing.

Sixteen

What are you doing here?" Timothy Bolt said.

"Looking for you, of course," said Athena. She looked fine, except for—shit: that goddamned *looked*, way too close to *looking*, why did that have to happen, had nothing to do with anything, have to fix it later—*one small thing*. And what would that one small wrong thing be, that one telling detail? A tendril of hair out of place? Wretched cliché; and that horrible word *tendril*. A tiny drop of blood on her white collar? The slight tremor in her hand? The paleness of her face? All done and done, writing by the numbers, none of those numbers adding up to a passing grade when it came to knowing women.

In his room at the Crossing Inn, one notch up from its only competition in Agua Fría, a Motel 6, Loeb spoke the words aloud: "She looked fine, except for one thing . . ." No thing came. Maybe the knowing women part of the assignment was beyond him.

Loeb gazed out the window. The Crossing Inn stood at the highest point in Agua Fría, a hilltop at the end of a winding road half a mile west of Oro. He could see over the steel wall to houses on the other side. A woman with dangling earrings leaned from a window and wrung out a red shirt. Water gushed down, red at first, then pinker. A mangy dog ran up and licked the dirt where it fell. Loeb remembered the pariah dogs in *Under the Volcano*, their triumph over the consul at the end. Dog, booze, woman, blood: his fingers moved to the keyboard.

The phone rang.

Harry. "How's it going?"

"Not bad. I'm going to know women if it kills me."

"Just wear a condom," Harry said. "Any progress on the title?"

"Didn't we discuss this? *White Heat,* unless something better crops up."

"I mentioned it to Lucy. She's got some doubts."

"Lucy hasn't even seen the manuscript yet," said Loeb, "how it fits."

"The marketing people don't like it either."

Marketing people: the publisher's doomsday weapon, to which there was no deterrent. "What about *Red and White*?" Loeb said, the idea coming to him in a flash.

"Like the stores?"

"*White and Red,* then."

"*White. And. Red.* Maybe a bit too much like a kids' book, *Go, Dog, Go,* that kind of thing."

"Or *The White and the Red,*" Loeb said. "A little twist on Stendhal."

Pause: and in that pause, Loeb was almost certain that the name was brand new to his literary agent.

"The point is," said Harry, "the marketing people aren't completely sold on this whole white thing."

"Whole white thing?"

"As a concept."

"Aren't we a little past the concept stage?" Loeb said. "Three books already out, a starred review in *PW*—"

"That was nice."

"—the *Tribune* piece—that doesn't happen every day— and the fourth one on the way. Facts on the ground, Harry."

Over in Mexico, the woman appeared at her window again, wrung out another shirt, this one blue. Blue drops fell. If only they could have been red! That was what he wanted, Loeb realized, to wring out blue and turn it red. Magic on the page. No point in passing that on to Harry: all at once, New York seemed very far away.

"There are lots of different facts, Nick," Harry said.

"That sounds ominous."

"It does?" said Harry. "I'm just trying to tell you what I'm hearing."

"Where was it?"

"Where was what?"

"The lunch where you heard this."

"Cité," said Harry. "Cassoulet de veau occitan and the morel soup with lemongrass. Since you're having trouble coming up with a *White* name anyway, I don't see why this is so objectionable."

"But it was their idea in the first place," Loeb said, "to help unify the series, give it a brand."

"True," said Harry. "But those people are gone now."

And some of the people who'd come after were already gone too. "Do they care about the series or not?" Loeb said. "Whoever's calling the shots, I mean."

"Possibly," said Harry. "But not necessarily as a series. Oops. Got to take this call. Something to think about, anyway. And don't forget those condoms, Nick."

Slight tremor in the hands: dumb cliché of detective fiction for sure, but Loeb looked at his own hands and saw it happening in real life. *Not necessarily as a series.* What did that mean?

Loeb's hands went to the keyboard, stilled themselves. He wrote: *Athena looked fine, except for the red tears falling from her eyes, the blue blood pouring from her mouth.* My God: was that the greatest sentence he'd ever written? Loeb soon came to his senses and folded up his laptop. Over on the other side, the woman was no longer at her window; shadows moved behind it, just out of sight.

Seated at the plastic table in his room—319, top floor,

corner next to the vending machines—Loeb turned to the notes he'd made on the Whiskers case. Turned with relief: police procedure was a lot easier than writing. You drove around in nice country, asked a few questions, batted ideas back and forth over Danishes, lived in the outside world.

> *Whiskers Case*
> *Flora Gutierrez Invu—loved cat*
>   *Harvey Dunn red herring*
>   *ain't no justice—tears*
>   *didn't file no complaint*
>   *Ultimate Fighting?*
> *Scene of Crime (14 Frontera St.)—gone*
> *Theme Park Developer Invu (Mr. Samsonov, Buck)—*
>   *ASPCA supporter*
>   *also owns strip club*
>   *free champagne (1)*

Loeb stared at this for a while. It was shaped like a poem, and like a lot of poems demanded interpretation without providing much guidance. Was it trying to tell him something? If so, what? He went back over it, this time from bottom to top. His eyes rested on *didn't file no complaint.* No complaint, despite an attachment to Whiskers so strong she lugged his picture around. She wanted nothing to do with whatever had happened, also didn't want her ex-boyfriend involved: *Keep Harvey out of this.* As soon as the meaning of *this* came up, she'd suddenly found herself running late and terminated the interview.

Loeb wrote: *Therefore a* this *exists.* Someone nailed Whiskers to a tree. Loeb tried to picture the scene. It hit him again how sickening that was. There really were people in the world capable of doing it, not characters but real people. Whiskers nailed to a tree; loved by Flora Gutierrez; who filed no complaint. But where to go from here? What was the next step? He had no idea. Was there anything else he knew? Gazing at *didn't file no complaint,* he realized he'd failed to include one more detail, a connection inspired by the tattoos on the theme park workers: Lonnie Mendez had said the exact same thing.

Connection? Was there any reason to use that word? No. Neither was there a Mendez case, as Clay Krupsha had made clear. But wouldn't it be interesting to find out if Lonnie Mendez knew Flora Gutierrez? Wouldn't that be good police procedure?

The door to room 209 at the Baja Medical Center was open. Loeb looked in. The emaciated old man on oxygen was still there, still on it, but Lonnie Mendez was gone. In his bed lay another emaciated old man, also on oxygen. Pinging sounds came from their monitors, combining in a bouncy little rhythm.

"Checked out," said the nurse at the main floor station.

"Any idea where I can reach him?" Loeb said.

"Not allowed to give that out."

"I'm working with Detective Krupsha." That sentence came so fast, so of its own volition, that it surely revealed something basic about his true nature.

"Oh, yeah?" said the nurse. "Then I guess it's all right." She copied Lonnie's address from the chart: 1256 Kino Road.

Would that have happened back home? Never. Loeb knew he was in the heartland at last, and more, was fitting in beautifully. It felt great.

Kino Road led Loeb out of town, up through some hills, and onto a high plain, the houses growing meaner and farther apart. Twelve fifty-six, about a mile beyond the end of the paved part of Kino Road, was the meanest of all. Loeb parked beside a shiny cluster of motorcycles and got out of the pickup, the wind blowing something gritty in his eye right away. He stepped on the sagging porch, knocked on the door.

A woman answered. She wore a sleeveless T-shirt, had big biceps—LONNIE on the right, MAVERICKS, over what looked like a mushroom cloud, on the left—and a tongue ring that flashed in the sun when she said, "Yeah?"

"Lonnie Mendez?" Loeb said.

"Who are you?"

"Nick Loeb. We've met before."

"Never laid eyes on you in my fuckin' life."

"Lonnie and I met, that is," Loeb said. "At the hospital."

"You a doctor?"

"No."

"Then what?"

"Actually—"

A voice called from within. "Who the fuck is it?"

The woman raised her voice, her gaze remaining on Loeb. "Some guy from the hospital."

"Huh?"

"He'll recognize me once he sees me," Loeb said.

"You're not a cop," the woman said.

"Of course not," he said, an unnecessary reply, maybe, since there hadn't been the slightest question in her tone.

She scanned his body. "Packing anything?"

"No."

"Then I guess it's okay," she said. "You first."

Loeb entered the house, the woman close enough behind him that he felt her hot breath on the back of his neck. It was dark inside, blankets over the windows, but he could make out a pile of dishes in the sink tall enough to qualify for some sort of competition.

"Thataway," said the woman, guiding him with a little push in the back, her nails like razor wire.

They went into a back room, lit only by a big-screen TV and shafts of sunlight, boiling with dust that came through rips in the shade. Lonnie lay on the bed, a towel wrapped around his middle, a beer in his hand, a soap on the screen.

"Hi, Lonnie," Loeb said. "How are you feeling?"

"Who are you?"

"Nick Loeb. I visited you in the hospital."

"The fuck you did."

Loeb felt the skin on his back crawl, anticipating those nails. "Maybe whatever drugs they had you on affected your memory."

"Drugs affect my memory?" said Lonnie. "What's that supposed to mean?"

"Who can remember?" Loeb said, a crazy flight of broad humor he regretted immediately. The razor-wire nails made contact with his back, light but touching.

"Best explain what you're doing here," the woman said.

Loeb turned to her. All her facial features were a little too small, the eyes smallest of all. Was it possible Lonnie really didn't remember, that the cognitive data had gone missing completely? Timothy Bolt, master of improvisation, always rose to this kind of occasion. He might say something that seemed at first to have no bearing on anything, something like, "I'm with the EPA." Loeb said it.

"What's that when it's at home?" the woman said.

Lonnie laughed, one loud bark. Loeb backed up a little so he could keep them both in view. "Environmental Protection Agency," he said. "Anything to do with oil spills ends up on my desk."

"Oil spills?" said Lonnie; he made that puzzled frown of his that brought all his eyebrow piercing rings clinking together.

"Even little ones, like that oil slick on the Old Sonoita Highway," Loeb said.

"Huh?" said Lonnie.

"Where you had your accident," Loeb said.

A light went on in Lonnie's eyes, not bright, but there.

"The thing is," said Loeb, "now there's been a second crash. Does the name Flora Gutierrez mean anything to you?"

"Crash?" said the woman. "What crash?"

Lonnie glared at her. "Take a fuckin' hike," he said.

She glared right back. "Kiss blow jobs good-bye," she said, and left the room.

Kiss blow jobs good-bye: a sentence Loeb knew he'd never heard before, nothing even close. His eyes met Lonnie's.

"What makes her think she's the only one gives me blow jobs?" Lonnie said.

"Good question," said Loeb. He tried to imagine Flora Gutierrez as one of the other providers. "Getting back to Flora Gutierrez," he said.

"Never heard of her," said Lonnie. "But you're fuckin' right it's a good question. How about grabbin' me a beer out of the cooler? And take one for yourself."

"Any openers around?" Loeb said.

"Gimmee," said Lonnie.

He took the bottles, opened them with his teeth, both at once, handed one to Loeb. Loeb suspected they'd reached the high-water mark of their friendship, might never again be this close.

"Here's another one," he said.

"Another what?" said Lonnie.

"Another good question. How come, falling hard enough the way you did to dislocate your hip, there's not a mark on you?"

Lonnie, in midswallow, lowered his bottle. "You calling me a liar?"

"I'm hoping you are," Loeb said.

"Huh?"

"Because if you really wiped out on an oil slick, I'm going to be up to my ears in paperwork for the next year. Plus I'll have to come back here with a crew and tape an interview with you, then we'll need you for the re-creation-of-the-scene video up on the Old Sonoita Highway, after that the Friends of Arizona will be around to get your statement, the Sierra Club will probably want a piece of the action, and that's not the half of it. But if, by some miracle, you didn't hit an oil slick and fall off your bike, even if you understandably thought you had for a while, disoriented in the hospital or for any other reason imaginable, then I can just close the file on this, walk out that door, and you'll never hear from me again."

"I pick that one," Lonnie said.

"That one?"

"Of the choices. You walking out the door."

"Meaning there was no accident on the Old Sonoita Highway."

Lonnie gave him a long look. Then came a slight head movement that Loeb took for yes.

"That's it, then," Loeb said. "Case closed." He went to the cooler. "Another beer?"

"Why not?" said Lonnie.

Loeb handed him the bottle. "Get well soon."

"Thanks."

"I'll be on my way."

"Great."

"But just out of curiosity, Lonnie, how the hell did it happen?"

"You don't want to know."

"Not desperately," Loeb said. "But we've both got a little time to kill."

"Fuckin' say that again. I'm goin' nuts lyin' here all day."

"Then you shouldn't have put those blow jobs at risk."

Dead silence in the room: then Lonnie burst out laughing, beer spewing through those dusty shafts of light; not that barking laugh of his, but something that sounded almost giddy. "You're one funny fuck," he said.

"Thanks."

"Know much about Ultimate Fighting?"

"I've heard of it."

"I ran into a former world champ. Problem is, I didn't know it at the time."

.

"Where was this?"

"In town. Place called Buckaroo's."

"The strip club?"

"You should have seen her, this redhead. I'm as laid-back as the next guy, but there's a limit."

"Meaning?"

"I couldn't help myself."

"I hear you."

"Tit was just hanging there, practically in my face. What the hell am I supposed to do?"

"It's a tough call."

Lonnie sat up a little higher. "Fuckin' right. I—" He winced, reached for a bottle of pills by the bed, popped a couple, washed them down with beer. His eyes glazed over before they hit the back of his mouth.

Loeb showed himself out. There was no sign of the woman, although he heard low male and female sounds coming from behind a closed door down the hall from Lonnie. An hour later he parked in front of Buckaroo's: CLOSED FOR RENOVATIONS. GRAND REOPENING TOMORROW. BIGGER AND BETTER.

Seventeen

Eight hundred fifty-three dollars, seventy-three cents," said Mr. Fertig. "Doable?"

"Per month?" said Mackie.

"Payments due on the fifteenth."

"They like that date."

"The IRS?" said Mr. Fertig. "A world of its own."

"Like the planet in *Alien*," Mackie said, multiplying on a calculator. "Yes, it's doable." If everything kept on just like this, and why wouldn't it? She had taken charge of her own life, as all the checkout counter magazines advised.

"Things seem to be stabilizing a little," said Mr. Fertig. "Have you taken on some help?"

"Help?"

"In your house-cleaning business. I only ask in case incorporating might make sense."

"I don't think it would," Mackie said.

"No?"

"I've been branching into other things."

Pause: where she might have gone into detail, might have explained how incorporating didn't make sense.

"Whatever I can do," Mr. Fertig said.

On the other hand, maybe it did make sense. Was Zazee incorporated? Cocoa? Shasta? Sola—in two countries, perhaps, a multinational in one hard little body?

The front door opened. Lianne came in. "Hi, Mom. You're home early."

"Took the day off."

"Yeah? Feeling okay?"

"Perfect."

Lianne glanced at the paperwork on the kitchen table. "Everything all right?"

"Hanging in," Mackie said. "How was school?"

"Got my report card."

"Give."

Lianne handed her the report card. Mackie opened it. "Wow," she said. "Come here." Lianne walked around the table. Mackie rose and hugged her, her hand touching the back of Lianne's head, her hair like silk, only better; alive. And the brain inside that head: where had it come from? This girl was going places, despite the divorce, all the moving around, the sudden rises and falls in status. One of the lyrics of Mackie's working life came to her: *When Rita leaves, Rita's gone.* She gave Lianne an extra squeeze.

"It's only a midterm, Mom."

Mackie sat down, read all the grades again, luxuriated in the teacher comments. Down at the bottom was a note from the principal. "Congratulations on a fine report. Despite the absences, Lianne has been doing an awesome job. Has she considered college yet? Somewhere like Berkeley might be a nice fit."

Mackie checked the box beside *Absent:* 14. "What are these absences?"

Lianne peered over her shoulder. "Oh, those," she said. "They're not really absences."

"What are they?"

"Nothing. Like if your homeroom teacher doesn't notice you, or you come in two minutes late and he's already filled in the form and doesn't bother fixing it."

"Who's your homeroom teacher?"

"Mr. Grubb. He's been there for fifty years, Mom. He falls asleep and drools. Don't worry—I'll get them cleared."

"I'm not worried." She read the Berkeley part again. "What about college?"

"What about it?"

"This Berkeley idea."

"I don't think I want to go that far," Lianne said.

"It's not really far," Mackie said.

"For me it is."

Mackie glanced at her. Lianne looked determined, about what Mackie wasn't sure. "I'm surprised," Mackie said.

"Why?"

Mackie thought about it. "You're pretty independent."

"Think so?"

"Yes."

"Thanks, Mom. It's a good thing, right?"

"As long as you remember you're not alone."

"Oh, Mom. I never think that."

Right then, Mackie knew for sure that in this area at least she hadn't failed.

"But it doesn't mean I have to go to Berkeley, does it?" Lianne said.

"Of course not."

"Or any other college, for that matter."

"Whoa," said Mackie. "What are you saying?"

"Just floating a trial balloon, Mom."

Mackie made her hand into a gun and shot it down. Lianne laughed. "College is expensive," she said.

"I'll worry about that," said Mackie. First you must have a goal; then an M.O. for getting there. *Whatever it takes* was the M.O. that Samsonov liked. Mackie could do what it took. Hadn't she proved that to herself by now? Lianne would go to the best college she could get into, no matter what.

Bub came to Mackie in the night, along with other men from Buckaroo's. She'd been so careful to face all these men without seeing, to seem to be making eye contact when she wasn't, in the belief that she wouldn't know what they looked like and thus they would never be real. But now they were here, every warped feature of every glistening face sharp and clear.

"We need to see more close up," Bub said, shifting her G-string out of the way. Their faces crowded in. "Closer, closer, don't you understand?" they said, opening her legs, peering inside, their eyes intense. "Not close enough," they said, frantic, almost beside themselves. What were they looking for? That was all; there was no more to see. "We'll have to turn her inside out," Bub said. Their hands, so many, descended on her, all over, and got a firm grip, many many firm grips.

Mackie awoke, in a muck sweat and shaking. The room, her bedroom, was quiet, but in a strange way, as though some powerful sound had just that second passed through, like a scream.

When Lianne got up in the morning, she found her mother in the living room, sleeping on the couch: a first. She was wearing that nightgown she always wore, a beautiful blue like the deep sea. At least, that was the color in Lianne's memory. Now for some reason she noticed how faded the real thing was, hem frayed, one shoulder strap held together with a safety pin. Mom was curled up in a ball, her hands between her knees, her bare feet tucked under one of the end pillows.

"Mom?"

No reply.

Mom sleeping on the couch was a first, but before the divorce there'd been many mornings when Lianne had found her father there. She had a crazy thought, made no sense at all. Lianne knew that right away, but it didn't stop her from going back down the hall and checking Mom's bedroom to see if Dad was there. An empty bed: the sheets all tangled, the mattress bare at one corner. On the bedside table, turned toward the pillow where her mom could see it, sat the framed photograph of Lianne that had been by her parents' bed forever. When had Lianne last looked at it? She looked at it now.

Her seventh birthday: she sat on a pony. This must have been in Albany. She had few memories of Albany. Getting hit in the face with a snowball was one; a nun blowing her nose, another. The pony was black and white and had big eyes. Lianne wore a cowboy hat and a little smile. Her hands were curled in the pony's mane. Gazing at the picture, Lianne thought of her and Jimmy, and that slow ride they took on Clyde's broad back. The girl on the pony didn't look like her at all, could have been another kid. Somewhere between then and now, she'd turned into someone else.

Back in the living room, her mom was still in the same position, still asleep. Lianne went into the kitchen, packed up her books. She saw that her mom had forgotten to sign the report card, wrote *Helen MacIsaac* in the space provided, making no attempt to copy her signature. Nobody cared: the space had to be filled, that was all. On the way out, her backpack knocked Mom's dance bag off the table in the front hall. A huge red wig slipped out. Was she dancing again, rehearsing some role with Angie? That was good. Lianne put the wig back, closed the front door softly, and walked down Buena Vida Circle to the school bus stop.

A freshman or sophomore named Doobie or Doober was already there, sitting on his backpack. Lianne leaned against a tree, her eyes raised over the rooftops to the mountains in the distance.

"Bus hasn't come yet," said Doobie or Doober. Was he talking to her? Lianne turned. "It'll be along soon," he said, removing his glasses. "The bus, to take us to school." What was he talking about? "You at the game Friday?" he said.

"What game?"

"What game? Against Alta Vista. We won."

"What sport is this?" Lianne said. She saw a yellow dot way down the long, flat road.

"Geez. Basketball. We're undefeated."

"Must be nice," Lianne said. The yellow dot grew bigger; then a smaller black blur zipped around it.

"You go to Kolb, right?" said Doobie or Doober.

"Yes."

"You're a junior. And your name's Lianne."

Lianne nodded. A motorcycle, coming fast.

"That's a really cool name," said Doobie or Doober. "In my humble opinion. How do you spell it?"

Lianne spelled it.

"That's funny," he said. "It sounds more like L-E-E-A-N-N. My name's—" But whatever it was got drowned out by Jimmy roaring up.

Lianne went over to him. "Hi, baby," he said, putting his arm around her waist. Did jaw-dropping make a sound? Lianne thought she heard it behind her.

"This is a surprise," she said. "I kind of have to go to school today."

"Yeah?"

"Math test."

"But I need some help with numbers myself," he said, giving her back a little rub. "Big ones."

Lianne hopped on. Jimmy wheeled into one of those breathtaking U-turns of his; Lianne caught a glimpse of Doobie or Doober—yes, mouth open; and felt a tiny little skid down under her, a slip, the slightest loss of control, reasserted in an instant. As they passed the school bus the other way, Lianne put her lips to his ear and said, "Want to see my report card?"

Jimmy laughed. "Don't need to," he said. "I could write it up myself—A-plus in everything there is."

Lianne was in love, knew it for sure. She gave him a squeeze, felt something hard in his pocket.

"Is that a gun?"

"*The* gun," said Jimmy. "I'll show you later."

Her hand wanted to go somewhere else, away from that gun. She forced it to stay right there.

"Don't worry," said Jimmy. "It's not loaded."

Lianne wasn't sure whether that made her feel better or worse.

"Ever been here?" Jimmy said as they drove into Agua Fría.

"No."

"It's a bad town."

"Bad how?"

"Look around," he said.

They left the bike in front of a café, the inside almost invisible beyond the dirty window, and walked down the main street toward the barriers of the border crossing. "That's it," Jimmy said, pointing with his chin to a whitewashed building on the other side: PATRIOT FRONTIER SAVINGS AND LOAN. A woman with platinum hair and enormous breasts came out; people turned to look at her as she went by.

Jimmy took Lianne's hand, started across the street.

"Where are we going?" Lianne said.

"In the bank. Got to know the lay of the land."

Lianne pulled him back.

"What is it?" he said.

"They've got video cameras in there, Jimmy. What if they start going over the old tapes after you . . . after?"

"So? I'll be wearing a ski mask."

"What about the rest of you?"

"The rest of me?"

"The body." She gave him a quick kiss on the cheek. "No disguising that."

"But I need to know what's around me."

"I'll check it out," Lianne said. "Draw you a picture."

"But then you'll be on the tape."

"Who cares?" Lianne said. "They won't be looking for a girl."

"But—"

"Just get me something to drink," she said, halfway across the street already. "Something cold."

Lianne entered the bank. She hadn't been in banks very often—her knowledge of the video cameras came from the movies—but this one seemed pretty insignificant. On the right: three teller positions. On the left, behind a low railing with an open door in the middle: three desks with brass plaques—RECEPTIONIST, ASS'T MGR, MGR. Straight ahead, behind steel bars: the vault, its thick door open, a woman—all the employees were women—kneeling in front of the safe-deposit boxes, taking something out. And up on the walls, video cameras, at least half a dozen. She made an exact count.

Lianne went to the first teller—her brass plaque said TELLER OF THE MONTH—handed her a dollar bill, all she had on her.

"Can I get quarters?"

"Certainly," said the teller. Beside her plaque sat a dish of hard green candies. Lianne's mouth started watering for the taste of lime.

"Can I have a candy?" Lianne said.

"Help yourself," said the teller, handing her four quarters.

"Thanks," said Lianne, taking a handful of hard green candies and walking out; one more video camera, over the door, pointing right at her.

Out on the street, she popped one of the candies into her mouth. Mint, not lime: not bad, but disappointing when her tongue was all geared up for lime.

Jimmy came up, handed her a cold bottle, one of those healthy drinks. *Lemon 'n' Lime Sunshine Splash,* it read. They couldn't go wrong. She gave him a big kiss.

"What's that for?" he said.

They sat in the front booth of the café with dirty windows, she and Jimmy on the same bench, touching. Jimmy had a ham-and-cheese omelet and a side of sausages, Lianne apple pie and ice cream, completely unlike her. She was so hungry when Jimmy was around, like she had to be strong for something. There was only one other customer, a heavy bristly-haired man in a tight suit over at the counter, reading a book with a blood-tipped ski pole on the cover.

Lianne drew a diagram of the bank on her napkin: *c* for camera, *t* for teller, *d* for desk, *$* for safe. Jimmy stared at it, licked his lips.

"There are two plans, right, Jimmy?" she said, keeping her voice low. "Their plan and our plan."

He nodded.

"Tell me about their plan first."

"Don't know exactly where to start," Jimmy said, those three horizontal lines on his forehead deepening just a little.

She found his foot under the table, laid hers on it. "Start with the van."

"The one that'll be waiting outside?" Jimmy said.

Lianne put her finger to her lips. He lowered his voice.

"It's going to be untraceable, from Mexico."

"Is the gun untraceable too?"

"Oh, yeah, I just drop it on the way out."

"So you're wearing gloves."

"I better."

Lianne dipped a piece of the pie in melting ice cream, put it in her mouth, felt heat and cold coming together. On TV she'd seen something about girls marrying guys like their fathers. Did Jimmy remind her of her father? A little bit, like just then with realizing about the gloves. But she loved Jimmy, and disliked her father, if anything, so it had to be one of those pop psychology things, complete bullshit.

"This van," Lianne said. "Who's driving?"

"Not sure," said Jimmy. "Dane, maybe."

"Where's he going to take you?"

"After? To this spot where the bike'll be waiting."

"What happens there?"

"Divide up the money, I guess."

The man at the counter turned a page. Lianne put her finger to her lips.

"Divide up the money," Jimmy said softly. "Then I take off."

"Where's this place?"

"Out on the Anza Wash. Runs right up to the Ruby Road. From there I can circle down the back side of the ranch."

"And then?"

Jimmy shrugged. "I'm right there like I never left. I could have been out on the trail, down at the bunkhouse, anything."

"So that's the plan."

"Yeah."

"Their plan."

"Right."

"The fifty-grand plan."

Jimmy grinned, those perfect little teeth, so white. "What's ours?"

"The five-hundred-grand plan?" That depended on a lot of things. "How are you getting down here?"

"In the van."

"They drive you?"

"Yeah."

"Who leaves the bike at the wash?"

"Me."

"They pick you up there."

"I guess."

"So they'll know where you're headed after."

"That's no good," Jimmy said.

"No, it's all right," Lianne said. "Exactly what we want, in fact. We'll have another bike."

"What bike?"

"The Honda two-fifty at Road Heaven, the blue one."

"What would I want with that bitty thing?"

"It's for me," Lianne said. "When you come out of the bank you jump on the back, and . . ." She could see it happening, could feel the power of that Honda between her legs: this was going to work.

"And what?" Jimmy said.

Lianne smiled. "Va-voom." Maybe she said that a little loud; the guy at the bar turned to look for a second. He had purple lips.

"But you don't know how to drive."

"Teach me," Lianne said. "We've got practically a whole week."

"And where will we go, once you're taught?"

"Far as we can," said Lianne. "Where else?"

Eighteen

Loeb was stuck, horribly stuck, on what came next with Athena. This wasn't a matter of being stuck on a single line of dialogue, like *Death row is a little more than going away*, although he was still stuck there too. This was much bigger, about making Athena a tragic figure, giving Timothy Bolt abiding psychic scars, taking the series to a higher level. He knew the goal, but how to get there?

Loeb watched the cursor blinking in empty space, on the border of the known and the undiscovered in chapter eleven of *White Heat*. He remembered that they didn't like the title anymore; blocked the thought that they might be bailing on the whole series. *Athena looked fine, except for the red tears falling from her eyes, the blue blood pouring from her mouth.* The last sentence he'd written, ridiculous, from some other book, an unpublishable one. So why wasn't he deleting it? He felt the need for music, writing music—specifically "When Rita Leaves," left behind in New York.

Loeb grew aware that there was in fact music playing, over the steel wall in Mexico, something cheerful with trumpets. No woman at the window today, but down in her yard a baby wearing only a T-shirt was crawling toward a chicken. Whenever the baby got close, the chicken flapped away, red wattle quivering. The baby changed direction and went after it, a foot at a time. The metaphor was obvious: the baby, Loeb; chicken, the work.

He reread the red-tears/blue-blood sentence. The funny thing was, he could picture Athena like that. It was just a matter of . . . changing the lighting. Yes! New lighting, a fire or something, to light the end of Athena, a scene to come much later. Therefore, could she still be in the cabin now, when Bolt came in? Permutations and combinations made hard-to-follow patterns in his mind, the plot balling into a black tangle. For the first time in his career, it hit him that he needed help. From where? There was Harry, his agent; Lucy, his editor; and Mary Jane Krupsha, his critic.

He E-mailed Mary Jane. *I'd like to send you what I've done so far and have a discussion after you read it.*

Ping. Her reply came back at once. *No problem. Just as soon as we come to an agreement.*

Agreement?

On the fee.

How much do you want?

How much are you offering?

Name your fucking price.

Fifty bucks.

Jesus Christ. Fine. Do you want me to wire it first?

I'll trust you for the money. Send the screed.

Here it is. Quick question—how come Clay came out here?

Why?

Just wondering.

Loeb waited for a reply. None came. Good time for a break: he really had nothing to do till Mary Jane read the chapters. He pocketed his notes on the Whiskers case and the Mendez noncase, and drove to the police station.

Krupsha wasn't there. "You can find him at the Mariposa," said the desk officer.

"What's that?"

"Café over on Oro." She gave him directions.

The Mariposa Café was deserted except for Krupsha, sitting at the counter and reading—even immersed in— *White Midnight*. Loeb sat on the next stool. Krupsha looked up in surprise. A wonderful moment: not as good as the first book-acceptance call, but close.

"Hey," said Krupsha. "This ain't bad."

"Thanks."

"And the part with Bolt and what's-her-name?"

"Athena?"

"That's how you say it? Him and Athena, when they're stuck in that gondola thing, all alone?"

"Yes?"

"I got a semi-boner out of that."

"We'll tape a Viagra to the page in future editions."

Krupsha laughed. The waitress came over.

"I recommend the apple pie," Krupsha said.

"Okay," said Loeb.

"And another slice for me, sweetheart," said Krupsha. "Best in town, though that's not saying much."

The waitress paused, just for an instant, as she turned to go; as though her heel had caught on something sticky.

Loeb and Krupsha ate apple pie, drank milk, like two kids after school. "Not bad, huh?" said Krupsha.

"Not bad," Loeb said. "Ever heard of Ultimate Fighting?"

"Sure," said Krupsha. "Gonna use it in a book?"

"What is it, exactly?"

"Shit. You never seen Ultimate Fighting?"

"No."

"Then you're in for a treat," Krupsha said. "Eat up. I got a tape over at my place."

Clay Krupsha had a nice place on a hillside north of town: a really nice place, creamy-white adobe, pool out back—empty—and an endless desert view. Krupsha took Loeb into a sunken room with a cool tile floor and a huge plasma screen on the wall.

"I'm beginning to understand why you came out West," Loeb said.

"Oh?" said Krupsha, turning to him.

"Hard to have something like this back home."

"Right about that," Krupsha said. "You like tequila?"

"Not really,"

"You'll like this one." Krupsha filled two shot glasses, handed one to Loeb, then slid a tape into the VCR. "This is from a few years ago," he said, "when there were no rules. Now they got rules."

A boxing ring. Two fighters approached each other from opposite corners, both bare-handed and barefoot, wearing only brief-cut trunks. One was huge and terrifying, with massive brow and jaw, and muscles popping up all over his body. The other was much smaller; fit-looking, but in the way of someone who took brisk walks and didn't ask for seconds. No popping-out muscles, not scary: he even seemed to be squinting a bit.

The big guy got into a crouch, circled the little guy. The big guy moved well for someone his size—or any size—light, quick, balanced, his huge fingers and thumbs quivering very slightly, like antennae on a mantis. The little guy hardly moved at all, turned just enough to keep his opponent in front of him. Suddenly, too sudden for Loeb to even see clearly, the big guy was in midair, his foot a blur, kicking the little guy in the throat. Or maybe not quite in the throat, maybe a little lower, the little guy somehow changing the angle. The little guy sagged against the ropes, hands at his sides, and the big guy hit him with a tremendous uppercut below the belt. Below the belt, but maybe the little guy had shifted slightly just in time, taking the blow on his hip. The big guy fell on him, crushing him against the ropes, his hands on the little guy's throat.

Then—and this was his quickest movement yet—the big guy sprang back, letting go of the little guy completely. Blood came shooting out of the big guy's ear. He glanced at it falling on his enormous shoulder, incredulous.

"Catch that?" said Krupsha.

"No."

Krupsha stopped the tape, backed it up, played the last five or ten seconds in slow motion.

"See it that time?" Krupsha said.

Loeb nodded, his mouth dry. Seen, but barely, it was still so fast: the little guy jamming his stiff middle finger right into the big guy's ear, the first knuckle disappearing. The expression on the little guy's face, there and gone in an instant, was one Loeb had never seen before and had no idea how to describe, even though that was his job.

" 'Nother shot?" said Krupsha, stopping the tape.

Loeb saw that his glass was empty.

"Told you you'd like it." Krupsha refilled their glasses, hit *play*.

The big guy didn't lose his cool; his eyes narrowed just a bit, that was all. The little guy stayed where he was, on the ropes. The big guy approached him, crouched even lower this time, made a motion for him to come out, off the ropes. The little guy stayed where he was, but the motion seemed to distract him, and the next instant the big guy was on him again, got him down this time, flat on his back. They tangled themselves up, the big guy's blood mixing with their sweat and turning pink, and then one big arm came free. The big guy cocked his fist, a foot above the little guy's unprotected face. But he never threw the punch. Instead he lowered his hand quickly to the mat, tapped frantically.

"All she wrote," said Krupsha. "Miss it again?" He reversed the tape, ran it once more in slo-mo. "Right there," he said. "The left shoulder—see where it starts to come out, the ball-and-socket thing?"

Loeb saw, saw too that this time the little guy had no expression at all on his face, as though the match had ended a while back.

The big guy stayed on the mat, trainers rushing through the ropes. The little guy got up, went to his corner, wiped his face with a towel, and put on a pair of glasses, the Buddy Holly kind.

"It's all real?" Loeb said.

"Real as it gets," said Krupsha. "Never be this real again. There's a version on pay-per-view, but they made up some rules, like I said. Don't waste your money."

He refilled their glasses, Loeb finding his empty again.

"Seventy-five years old," said Krupsha.

Loeb tasted it this time. Not like tequila at all, any tequila he'd ever tasted.

"The cactus they used is fuckin' extinct," Krupsha said. "Cheers."

"Where do you buy it?" Loeb said, thinking this might be a good Christmas present for Harry, encourage him to fucking do something.

"Can't say exactly—it was a gift," said Krupsha. "Any of that Ultimate Fighting useable?"

"In my work?" Loeb tried and failed to imagine Timothy Bolt taking on a man like that. "I'd have to know a lot more."

"He's a grappler," said Krupsha. "From some hollow in East Tennessee, but he lives here now, retired. The grapplers always win, once it gets up to a certain level. Boxing, karate, judo, wrestling—don't matter."

"Why?"

"You just saw."

Loeb took a sip of his drink; Krupsha was doing the same thing, and their eyes met over the rims of the shot glasses.

"Did Mary Jane ever see that tape?"

Krupsha shook his head. "We were splitsville by then.

She'd have loved it, though." He put down his glass. "That's kind of a funny question, now I think of it."

"Here's another," said Loeb. "Did he"—jutting his chin at the little guy on the screen, trembling slightly in pause mode—"have anything to do with Lonnie Mendez?"

Krupsha smiled. "Havin' fun out here, huh? With the rubes. What you been up to, Mr. Author?"

Loeb shrugged. "Lonnie not having a mark on him bothered me."

"So you tracked him down?"

"It wasn't hard."

"And he just up and told you?"

"Indicated would be more accurate."

"What else did he indicate?"

"Nothing. He was pretty doped up."

Krupsha's smile had faded; now he revived it, purple lips turning up, and clinked glasses. "Congratulations. You've done real good. Yeah, Lonnie ran into little Turbo over at Buckaroo's, the strip joint, which you probably know all about by now, being smart as you are. What you're wondering is why I didn't do anything about it."

"It crossed my mind."

"The thing is," Krupsha began, refilling his own glass, topping up Loeb's.

"This must be expensive."

"I got a whole case," Krupsha said. "Thing is, on the one hand there's enforcing the law. On the other, there's letting justice take its course. The law says bust Lonnie for disturbing the peace, lewd conduct, assault. Justice says Turbo already took care of it. I'm on the side of justice."

"What about other things?"

"Other things?"

"Like maybe Turbo was guilty of assault, too. Or the club's in violation of safety rules."

"You were on a roll for a while there, Nick," Krupsha said. "Now you're getting too imaginative."

Krupsha was right. Loeb had forgotten what he was doing. Did he actually care about the rights and wrongs of the Mendez case? No. He just wanted to find out how things worked. Police procedure, part of his assignment: and this was good stuff. "You're a big help, Clay," Loeb said, his tongue loose all of a sudden.

"No problemo," said Krupsha. "Whether you and Mary Jane are doin' the boom-boom or not. None of my business."

"That's right."

Pause; then Krupsha laughed. "You're a funny guy."

"You too."

"One more pop?"

Loeb rose. "The trick with drinking," he said, "is knowing when you're blotto enough."

Krupsha held out his hand. Loeb shook it.

"How long'll you be out here?"

"I'm not sure."

"Take all the time in the world," Krupsha said. "I'm at your beck and call."

Loeb drove down the hill from Krupsha's house, on the wrong side of the road for the first half mile or so. How many shots had he had? While he was trying to remember that, he remembered instead that he'd forgotten to ask Krupsha about any connection between the Mendez and Whiskers cases. But how could there be, knowing what he knew now? Much too imaginative. He guided the pickup carefully through Agua Fría and parked in the customers lot at Buckaroo's.

"What's with you and Buck?" said Sola.

"Nothing," said Mackie. They were alone in the dressing room.

"I saw you with him over at Club Girlie," Sola said, sprinkling glitter on her muscular little body. She wasn't a bad dancer, probably second to Mackie among the house girls.

"He was just showing me around," Mackie said.

"He never showed me around," said Sola. "Or anyone else I remember."

"Maybe he's changing," Mackie said.

Sola gave her a hard look, but it gradually softened into a smile. "You're not gay, by any chance?"

"No."

"How about experimenting with it, for political reasons or something?"

Mackie laughed.

"Men are pretty sick—you must know that by now," Sola said.

Mackie stopped laughing.

"Or are you the kind that keeps hoping?"

"Definitely," Mackie said.

"About men?"

"Maybe not that."

Sola laughed. Her eyes met Mackie's in the mirror. "You caught my act over there?"

Mackie nodded.

"What did you think?"

"I didn't know what to think."

"It's still just a show," Sola said. "A performance. Doesn't mean anything."

Maybe; but a performance much too distant from *Swan Lake* for Mackie.

"Can I ask you something?" Mackie said.

"Sure," said Sola. "Name's Cathy, by the way."

"Where do you draw the line?" Mackie said, keeping her real name to herself.

"That's easy," said Sola. "Kissing. I'd rather die than let a man kiss me on the mouth. Does that make sense to you?"

"Yes," Mackie said.

"I've fucked maybe a thousand men," Sola said, "and kissed exactly zero."

It started to make a little less sense.

"Hey, Red, for Christ's sake," called Verna from the bottom of the stairs. "You're on."

Loeb sat at the bar in Buckaroo's, by himself except for someone hunched over a book in the shadows at the other end. It was a nice bar, one of the nicest he'd ever seen, highly polished mahogany with an intricate scrollwork of grapes carved in the facing. The whole place was like that, much nicer than he'd imagined: dark-paneled walls, leather chairs in clusters here and there, Tiffany lamps. Fifteen or twenty customers occupied the tables near the stage, a few more sitting on stools that lined its rim. Up onstage, a tall woman shook her breasts, huge and rock-hard, in a way that made one or two men call out, but that left Loeb cold, actually feeling icy in his chest. He ordered a Coke.

"Eight fifty," said the bartender.

"Eight fifty?"

"Check out the renovations."

Loeb remembered the free-drink card in his wallet, handed it across the bar. The reader at the other end looked up from his book and said, "What's *fungible* mean?"

"Like fungus, maybe?" said the bartender. "Poisonous?"

"Actually," Loeb said, unable to stop himself, "it means interchangeable." At least he didn't go on about their unrelated Latin roots.

"Interchangeable?" said the man at the end of the bar.

"For example," Loeb said, "a debt might be paid in cash or gold. They'd be fungible."

The man glanced down at his book. "Hey! That's exactly it. Thanks, buddy."

"Don't mention it."

"Give the man a drink. What's he drinkin'?"

"Coke," said the bartender.

"I'm all set," Loeb said.

"Then offer him some of those nuts at least."

The bartender filled a bowl with nuts, slid them across the bar. The reader rose, book in hand, came into the light, a small man with Buddy Holly glasses.

"Fungible," he said, sitting on the next stool: Turbo, beyond doubt. He looked harmless, but Loeb knew better, his fight-or-flight reflex activating immediately, minus the fight part. "I'll have to use it in conversation—that's the only way to make it my own," Turbo said. "You agree?"

"One hundred percent," Loeb said.

"Ever read this?" Turbo said, holding up the book: *The Croesus Factor: Seven Steps to Guaranteed Wealth.*

"No."

"I understand while I'm reading it," Turbo said, "but then later it gets all scrambled in my mind. Pisses me off like you wouldn't believe."

"I believe," Loeb said. "Maybe if you try—" He stopped. A run of single notes picked on an acoustic guitar, notes he knew well, notes that had even been sustaining his work lately, came over the sound system: "When Rita Leaves." He looked at the stage, saw a new dancer.

And couldn't take his eyes off her. Was it just the music? The music plus seventy-five-year-old tequila? This dancer looked older than the huge-breasted one, maybe in her thirties, and her breasts weren't big at all, but everything about her was right, except for the wild red hair. When she started moving, even that was okay. Her dance was erotic, even a little pornographic once or twice, but not entirely about sex. Some of it was about "When Rita Leaves" and made him hear the song in a new way; it was deeper than he'd thought, a man's song about a woman he couldn't hold on to, but this was Rita, and she was longing too.

"You like?" said Turbo.

"She can dance."

"Name's Red. We never had one like her."

You should have seen her, this redhead. I'm as laid-back as the next guy, but there's a limit. It was all coming together—Lonnie, Whiskers, Turbo, Krupsha, this woman—a picture of something, the whole town maybe. Loeb felt on the verge of really understanding how things worked for the first time.

"Feel free to tip her," Turbo said.

That hadn't occurred to Loeb.

"The girls don't take to perv types who look but don't tip," Turbo said. "Hell, I don't take to them neither."

"What's a good amount?" Loeb said.

"A C-note is always appreciated," said Turbo.

"I like them too," Loeb said.

"Then dance," said Turbo. A shock of recognition, horrible and revelatory at the same time, shot through Loeb: he and the woman up there, Red, had something in common.

The biggest bill Loeb had on him was a twenty. He approached the stage, squeezing past a man who looked like a 1950s TV granddad except for the wad of cash in his fist. Red, one leg wrapped around the pole, spun slowly around, leaning back, back, and her head was suddenly a foot from Loeb's, upside down. Somehow that allowed him to see past the makeup to her real face: beautiful, and much softer than he'd expected. Her eyes met his, or at least looked right at them. Very hard to read, those eyes: what was she thinking? Perv? He grew aware of the twenty, limp in his outstretched hand.

"Just stick it under her strap," said the TV grandfather behind him. "You're in my view."

Red's eyes changed just a little.

Loeb didn't want to stick it under her strap, wanted to simply hand it to her. Was that okay? Why not ask? Was talking allowed? He was considering all that when Red curled back around the pole, straightening as she did. Her leg rose too, all of these movements in perfect time with each other and with the music, swung toward him, her foot shod in a silver stiletto. But the toes were bare, and as her foot went by, she used them to pluck the twenty out of Loeb's hand.

"Hee hee," said the TV granddad.

She moved away across the stage, toward some tippers on the other side. Loeb went back to the bar, had a shot of something, then another; and couldn't believe this was him. He wanted her.

The customer lot sat alongside Buckaroo's and the employee lot behind it, but nothing separated them. When new dancers came on, Loeb went out, reparked the pickup so he could watch the employee lot. A few minutes later, a woman dressed in a sweat suit, brown ponytail pulled through the back of a baseball cap, came out the back door. Loeb wasn't sure it was her. Was the red hair a wig? Then she started walking and he knew. He got out of the pickup and moved toward her. She heard him coming, stopped, and turned.

He raised his hands, innocent. "I love that song," he said.

" 'When Rita Leaves'? " At that moment, she recognized him; he could see it in the slight relaxing of the way she held her head.

"And the way you interpreted it."

She looked surprised. "*Interpret*'s a little too strong."

"I don't think so," Loeb said. He went closer. "My name's Loeb. Nick Loeb."

"Red," she said.

"Is there some other name?"

"Not here."

"Where?" said Loeb. "I can compartmentalize as well as anybody."

She laughed. The sound gave him real pleasure. The expression in her eyes changed—she actually saw him—and it looked like she was about to say more, maybe even her name, but at that moment the TV granddad came running up, comb-over in disarray.

"Red," he said, stepping between them. "I've got something for you." He tried to hand her a little velvet box.

"I can't accept that, Bub," she said.

"Oh, come on. It's just a bitty thing and I want you to have it."

"Sorry," she said, and walked toward an old compact car at the back of the lot.

Bub walked along beside her, jabbing with the velvet box. "Please," he said. "Don't mean anything, just a token of affection."

She unlocked the car, got in.

"Just do me this one little favor," Bub said. "No strings."

"I can't," she said.

"You can," said Bub, and he thrust the velvet box into the car, trying to stick it under the visor. She blocked him with her hand, knocking the box aside. It fell onto the pavement, along with a pen that had been fastened to the visor with a rubber band. She put the car in reverse, backed up, turned, drove quickly away.

Loeb picked up pen and the velvet box, handed the box to Bub.

"I don't get it," Bub said. "She takes money." He opened the box. "She'd just love this, I know."

Loeb looked at the object inside.

"How much did that cost?"

"It doesn't matter. I want to take care of her."

"Marry her, you mean?"

"I hardly dare dream of that," Bub said.

"And your wife might not be too happy about it either," said Loeb.

Just a wild guess, but Bub got all huffy. "I'll have that pen," he said. He snatched it out of Loeb's hand, his eyes quickly drawn to the writing on its side. Loeb snatched it back, or tried to. A little tug-of-war ensued, fought in a cloud of alcohol fumes. Loeb was the better man.

Bub shot him a red-eyed look. "Happy now?" He went back inside.

Loeb read the writing on the pen, a giveaway pen from a real estate developer in Tucson: *Buena Vida Estates. Call Kevin Larkin, President;* plus phone number and E-mail. Loeb put it in his pocket.

Nineteen

This is so much fun," Lianne said. She had to shout over the noise of the engines, the wind, the blood pounding in her ears, to make herself heard. They rode side by side on an empty desert highway—Lianne didn't know where exactly—Jimmy on his big bike, she on the new blue Honda.

Jimmy turned his head, gave her a big grin. Then he roared off, arms stretched out like wings. Lianne goosed the throttle, went after him, dipping just a little to one side, but totally in control. It was so easy. Up ahead a soda can was rolling across the road. Lianne swerved a foot or two or three and flattened it. Cool sound: *thoomp*.

They had lunch in a bar in Arivaca where the sign read: CHECK ALL GUNS WITH THE BARTENDER. POSITIVELY NO EXCEPTIONS. Maybe it was a joke, because Jimmy's gun stayed in his pocket. The bartender knew him; when Lianne asked for a beer he didn't even card her.

Jimmy ordered a T-bone and onion rings. Lianne had a hamburger and fries for the first time in years.

"How's yours?" said Jimmy.

"Great." A little juice squirted out of her mouth, ran down her chin. Jimmy leaned over and licked it off, too quick for anyone to see.

They sat by themselves at the end of the bar, just touching. "What's blue sky in Spanish?" Jimmy said.

"Cielo azul."

"I like that," Jimmy said. He repeated *cielo azul* a few

times. It sounded great, coming from him. They leaned a little closer into themselves.

A picture of something: the whole town, maybe. That was the missing piece in the Timothy Bolt series, the weaknesses with women and police procedure mere symptoms. Loeb understood the Mendez case and its denouement, had met and talked to all the principal players. But the notion of some connection to the Whiskers case kept nagging at him. At first, there'd only been one tenuous contact point: Lonnie Mendez and Flora Gutierrez both using the identical phrase—*I didn't file no complaint.* Now there was another, Flora's question, *You ever seen Ultimate Fighting?* on the Whiskers side; Turbo the ultimate fighter on the Mendez side. Why had she asked him that?

Loeb drove back up the Arivaca road to Kemp's Mobile Home Village, knocked again on the door of Flora Gutierrez's trailer. A bare-chested man opened it, his skin like deeply tanned leather, covered in short white hairs. The heavy gold letters on the chain around his neck read: HARVEY.

"Hi, Harvey," Loeb said. "Flora around?"

Harvey peered out at him from the gloom inside. "We met somewhere?" he said.

"Not till now," said Loeb.

"Then how do you know my name?"

Loeb smelled marijuana, and looking over Harvey's shoulder saw a joint slowly consuming itself on the arm of a worn easy chair. Harvey moved to block his view. "She ain't here," he said. "And who wants to know?"

"I'm from the ASPCA," Loeb said. "It's about Whiskers."

"She don't care about that no more," said Harvey.

"How come?" said Loeb, but even as he did, felt that characteristic brush, stiff and soft at the same time, against the back of his leg. He glanced down, saw a cat walking between his legs, tail raised high; it jumped into Harvey's arms.

"I picked up this little critter at the pound," Harvey said. "So she could put Whiskers behind her. Get on with life. Move forward." He stroked the cat. "This one's called Whiskers Junior."

"Nice," Loeb said. "But I can't do the same thing."

"What same thing?"

"Put Whiskers behind me. Whiskers Senior."

"Why the hell not?"

"Because of my job."

"Which is?"

"ASPCA," Loeb said. "Stopping cruelty to animals is what I do."

Harvey stroked Whiskers Junior again, very gentle. "That's what the *C* stands for?"

"Yes."

"What happened was cruel, all right." Harvey's eyes, dull so far, grew angry. "Maybe you can answer me a question—did they crucify him before or after he was dead?"

"Good question." And Harvey was the first to raise it.

"How about runnin' some tests?"

"I'll look into that," Loeb said. "But I'm more interested in finding out who did it."

"World's full of sickos," said Harvey. "Poor fuckin' Whiskers."

"You and Flora back together?" Loeb said, the question, clearly wrong, just popping out.

"What do you know about me and Flora?"

"Just from the police report."

"I'm in the police report?"

"Yes."

"Meaning you think I done it?"

Or maybe the Flora question was the right one after all: Harvey was shaking now, shaking with indignation. Loeb was surprised to see it happened in real life. This was a moment for feeling bad or pressing on. Loeb did both. "Then give me a name," he said.

"How the fuck would I know? But that doesn't mean I done it. Besides the fact that I'd cut my own throat first, I was in rehab up in Prescott when it happened."

"Maybe Flora said something."

"How would she know either?"

"She knew enough to mention Ultimate Fighting," Loeb said.

There was a long silence. Whiskers Junior's tail rose, the end twining itself in Harvey's long and stringy nicotine-colored hair. "Must of been in some other . . ." He closed his eyes, thinking hard. Whiskers Junior purred.

"Context?" Loeb said.

"Yeah."

"No," Loeb said. "The context was Whiskers, death of."

Harvey's eyes opened. The dull look was back. "I'm not saying another word."

He didn't have to.

Loeb felt Harvey's eyes on him through the screen door as he walked away, maybe the eyes of Whiskers Junior, as well. Trash barrels were lined up for collection at the entrance to Kemp's Mobile Home Village. Loeb noticed *The Whites of Her Eyes* lying on top of one of them; he salvaged it before driving off.

Evening shadows were spreading across the desert on Loeb's way back to Agua Fría, the distant mountains busy with color experiments at the red end of the spectrum. Loeb tried to come up with an original way to put that, failed to find one he liked.

Standing by the window in his room at the Crossing Inn, Loeb took out the giveaway pen, called the number printed on it. Out of service. He tried information for Buena Vida Estates or Kevin Larkin in Tucson. No listing for either.

Over in Mexico, the woman's hand appeared, rested on her windowsill; she wore a silver bangle on her wrist today. A moment or two later, a man's hand came out of the shadows inside and rested on hers. Both hands withdrew. Loeb sent an E-mail to the address on the pen. It came back undeliverable right away.

Clay Krupsha was still in his office, eating a Luna bar, his feet up on the desk. He wore cowboy boots with CK branded on the sides. "It says these are for women, but they're damn tasty," he said.

"You're working late."

"Not really working," Krupsha said. "Just settling. Sometimes a good idea comes along this time of day."

"About what?"

"My cases," said Krupsha. "What else?"

"I might be able to help you on one of them," Loeb said.

Krupsha bit off a big chunk of Luna bar, talked around it. "Not Lonnie Mendez?"

"I think I've got that one down," Loeb said.

"Maybe there is a God."

"This is about the Whiskers case."

"The cat?"

"The cat that belonged to Flora Gutierrez, formerly of fourteen Frontera Street."

"Oh, yeah. You and Frankie Nuñez were looking into that."

"Frankie went down with food poisoning," Loeb said. "I've kind of been pursuing it on my own."

Krupsha smiled. "Any chance I could hire you on a permanent basis?"

Loeb laughed. But he thought: *What happens if they pull the plug on Timothy Bolt?* "Fourteen Frontera backs onto the parking lot of Buckaroo's."

"Correct."

"Where Turbo works. Former Ultimate Fighting champ."

"All true," said Krupsha, finishing off the Luna bar and tossing the wrapper into his wastebasket. "But I thought you were done with Lonnie."

"I am," said Loeb. "Are there any more ultimate fighters in town?"

"Not that I heard. This going anywhere?"

"I talked to Flora Gutierrez and her ex, maybe present boyfriend Harvey Dunn."

"And what did those two solid pot-dealing citizens tell you?"

"They didn't exactly tell me anything. It was more like indicating."

"How so?"

"Flora brought up Ultimate Fighting first, out of the blue. When I mentioned it to Harvey, he got scared."

"Meaning?"

"I think Turbo killed the cat."

"Little Turbo?" said Krupsha. "He wouldn't hurt a fly."

Loeb laughed.

"That wasn't a joke," Krupsha said. "What you saw on the tape, and the Lonnie Mendez thing, that's just a man doing his job."

"I'm not so sure," Loeb said. He remembered that fleeting expression on Turbo's face as he destroyed the big guy's eardrum.

Krupsha shook his head. "He's not a sicko."

"Maybe it wasn't a sicko thing," Loeb said. "Suppose there was a purpose."

"Like?"

"A man doing his job," Loeb said. "If the job had something to do with the theme park, for example."

"Go on."

"Do you know this Samsonov guy?"

"I know everyone in town, Nick. What about him?"

"Was Flora Gutierrez his tenant at fourteen Frontera?"

"If she was?"

"Maybe she didn't want to leave. Maybe she was holding up the development."

"So you're saying this is a landlord-tenant dispute."

"More or less," said Loeb. "Too imaginative, or not imaginative enough?"

"You're a funny guy, Nick. Actually had me laughing, that scene with Sergeant Falco and the pumpkin."

Loeb was pleased. "Think there's anything to the landlord-tenant idea?"

"Much more likely Flora and her boyfriend are trying to bring a little trouble down on Turbo for reasons of their own. But I'll look into it. Give me a couple days."

"Thanks."

"Anything else I can do for you?"

Loeb remembered the giveaway pen. "Have you got one of those reverse directories, where you can look up an address from a phone number?"

Krupsha tapped the desk monitor with the toe of his boot. "Right here, in theory."

"Will it work if the number's no longer in service?"

"Maybe if there was a lightning strike," Krupsha said. "What's up?"

"I'm trying to find the address of a real estate company in Tucson."

"Thinking of moving out here?"

"Yes," Loeb said. He realized he hadn't smoked a cigarette or even thought about it since stepping off the plane.

"Tucson's nice. And you could buzz down here any time you got lonesome for us hicks." Krupsha opened the bottom desk drawer. "Lots of old phone books in here."

"Can I look through?"

"Be my guest," said Krupsha. "I'm going to take a crap." He rummaged through a pile of magazines on a shelf, chose the J. Crew catalog, and left the room.

Loeb found the address in a two-year-old Tucson phone book almost right away: 4 Buena Vida Circle. Ten minutes later, Krupsha still hadn't returned. Loeb showed himself out.

Twenty

There was something horrible in the velvet box, a long-necked, flexible something with teeth for taking a bite out of her, and Mackie refused to look inside. Turbo held her down while Bub tried to pry open her eyelids with his thumbs. Mackie opened them.

Monday morning, still dark. She got out of bed, the sheets dank with her sweat, went into the bathroom, and splashed cold water on her face. In the mirror, she looked the same as always, a look hard to define in a single word, *wholesome* probably as good as any. How was that possible? She went downstairs, lay on the living-room couch.

Lianne awoke just before her alarm went off. She sat at her desk, everything on it lit gold as the sun rose over the mountains, and wrote a letter.

Dear Mom,
Don't ever worry about me. I won't be home tonight or for a little while more. School and everything seems kind of irrelevant right now. The truth is, I have a boyfriend. He's very special, Mom, I know you'd like him, and I'm sure you'll meet him one day. We need to be alone by ourselves. It's crazy to have someone on your mind all the time and hardly ever be with him. I know you understand. You

understand so much. Don't think I haven't noticed.
And your holding everything together—I'll never
forget it. You're the best. I'll call real soon.

I love you,
Lianne

Mackie had breakfast on the table when Lianne came down: scrambled eggs, whole wheat toast, coffee, two tangerines from the tree. "Morning, sweetheart."

"Hi, Mom."

Lianne came over, gave her a kiss on the cheek, sat down. Lianne's place backed into the window; the sun made a halo of her hair. A kiss on the cheek like that didn't happen every day. Its effect lingered on Mackie's skin.

"You look great," Mackie said.

"So do you," said Lianne. "I hope I got your genes."

"Just the good ones," Mackie said. This new self-assurance in Lianne—maybe not new, maybe she was just starting to notice it—but: whose genes were those?

"Yours are all good, Mom."

Mackie felt herself blushing, got up quickly, brought back the coffeepot, refilled their cups.

"What's on tap for today?" she said, sitting back down, sipping her coffee.

"The usual."

"Anything interesting happening in school?"

"Not really."

"How about *Lord of the Flies*?"

"We finished."

"Did you get your essay back?"

"Yes."

"And?"

"A-plus."

"You're really something," Mackie said. "I'd love to see it."

"It's in my locker."

"Can you bring it home?"

"Bring it home?"

"Your essay."

"Oh," Lianne said, laying down her fork. "I'll try." She looked at Mackie through the steam rising from her cup. "I can tell you a bit about it, if you like."

"That'd be great."

"I called it 'Wanton Boys,' " Lianne said. "I remembered this quote from *King Lear* last term, and it fit perfectly."

"What quote?" Mackie said; unfamiliar with *King Lear*.

" 'As flies to wanton boys are we to the gods,' " Lianne said. " 'They kill us for their sport.' "

"Wow," said Mackie. "That's perfect."

Lianne smiled.

" 'As flies to wanton boys,' " said Mackie. "I'm going to remember that. Have another slice."

"Thanks, Mom, but I've got to get rolling." She rose, put on her backpack, extra-heavy-looking today; a hard worker, on top of being so bright.

"I almost forgot," Mackie said.

Lianne paused. "What?"

Mackie reached into the pocket of her old blue night-gown, took out a twenty-dollar bill. "Lunch money for the week," she said.

"Hang on to it," Lianne said.

"What do you mean?" Mackie went around the table, handed the money to Lianne. "Have you been skipping lunch?"

"No, Mom." Lianne put it in her pocket, gave Mackie a hug, a quick one but tight, surprising Mackie with her strength.

"Bye, Mom."

"See you tonight."

Lianne turned, started walking from the room.

"Wait," said Mackie. Lianne halted. "You didn't eat your

tangerine." She tucked it into one of the side compartments of Lianne's backpack.

Lianne went out the front door, down the flagstone path to the mailboxes. She folded the twenty-dollar bill inside her letter—bad, but keeping it would be worse—and stuck it in the box marked 4, then continued down Buena Vida Circle to the bus stop, not looking back.

The mail truck, a little late, was coming up Buena Vida Circle as Mackie walked down the path to the box. She waited. The driver with the long gray ponytail handed over her mail—all bills—and went off with that cheery *toot-toot*. Mackie opened the envelopes: phone and utilities, almost current; Visa and Mastercard, smaller than the month before. This was working.

Mackie drove down to Agua Fría, stopping on the way for a pint of Stoli. The bottle was still almost completely full by the time she entered the employee lot at Buckaroo's, an inch gone at the very most, or possibly two.

Samsonov appeared out of nowhere, opened the door for her. "I am in such good moods today," he said.

"Why is that?" said Mackie, getting out. Bulldozers were digging big holes at the theme park.

"There is so much to anticipate," he said. "Like the candy store kid."

"You're talking about the theme park?"

"And so much more," said Samsonov. "The concept of diversifying is familiar?"

"Not really."

"It is simple: many eggs, many baskets. And these baskets, that is where the creation comes in. You have heard of derivatives, for example?"

"No."

"Good. This will give us subject matter for discussion on our date."

"What date?"

"Like the shrimp," said Samsonov, "but slightly different this time."

"I can't," said Mackie. "I've got to work."

"Is it the money, your reluctance point? I will pay you, pay you in fact more money than in your wildest dreams."

"I'm not dancing at the Girlie Club, if that's what you're suggesting."

"Club Girlie," said Samsonov, correcting her. "But all the better—what a difference there is between ten thousand dollars and wildest dreams!"

"What are you talking about?"

"Theories," said Samsonov. Mackie could see he was excited about something, face flushed, a vein throbbing in his neck. "Theories of success. Here are my new wheels." He held an open hand toward a shiny convertible, huge and red, as though introducing a celebrity. "Cadillac," he said. "I am affording any car on the open road but I choose Caddy. Why? For patriotic reasons. You will notice the red of the body, the white of the leather, the blue of the trim. Get inside."

"I can't go on a date with you, Mr. Samsonov," Mackie said.

He took her wrist, gently. "Buck."

"Buck."

He smiled. "And what is the meaning of this 'can't'?"

"I'm not dating right now."

"Ah, a personal fact," he said, opening the passenger door of the Cadillac. "We will therefore label this research."

Mackie didn't want to get in the car, might not have if Bub hadn't suddenly poked his head around the corner of the building. She almost didn't recognize him at first, his silver hair now dyed a rusty color; and he had something gift-wrapped in his hands, bigger than the velvet box. Mackie got in the car. Samsonov closed the door; top-of-the-line parts thumped perfectly together. He got in the other side, turned to her. She knew what he was going to say before he said it:

"You are catching the sound of those doors?"

She was on her way to knowing every little thing about him.

They crossed the border, drove quickly through the Mexican town, then west into desert that seemed drier than on the other side. Samsonov stepped on the gas, two fingers of his right hand the only contact with the steering wheel. "I feel free," he said. "Free and at the same time on top of my best behavior." He glanced at her and smiled again. His lower teeth now matched his upper; perfect. He must have had them fixed on the weekend. "This we are calling two-lane blacktop," he said. "Two-lane blacktop and a bright red Caddy—like your song about Rita."

"You like that song?"

"The best of all songs at the club."

He'd surprised her.

"And so fitting of the theme of Buckaroo's," he added. "We are selling a package, a lifestyle. You are the only girl who understands."

"What about Verna?" Mackie said.

"Verna is classic middle management," said Samsonov.

Mackie found herself nodding in agreement. What was happening to her? She shouldn't have been able to get past the image of Verna with the shotgun in her hands; instead she'd almost forgotten it.

A mountain rose in the distance, softly humped. As they drew closer and the angle changed a little, Mackie saw there was a second hump, with a saddle in between. "Where are we going?"

"To my retreat," Samsonov said. "All books for the creative executive make the importance of stepping back from the hurly and burly, like the Jews in the desert."

"Are you Jewish?"

He laughed. "What a question! The whole of my childhood was busy as bees with beating up the sons of the Hebrew neighbors."

Samsonov turned onto a dirt road that led toward the two-humped mountain. A white cube glittered near the top of the saddle. "You are thinking temple, Greek," he said.

The ground began to rise; as though under pressure, the road lost its straightness, curving up the base of the first hump. Samsonov slowed down a little and Mackie felt the heat, the first real heat of the year. It relaxed her.

"Thirsty?" said Samsonov.

"A little."

"Open the compartment."

"Compartment?"

"For gloves."

Mackie opened the glove compartment: tidy inside, nothing there but manual, registration, and a pint of Stoli.

"Help yourself and pass along," Samsonov said.

Mackie did.

Samsonov drank, rested the bottle between his legs. "My English is so much better after a few pops," he said. He wiped his mouth with the back of his hand. "We are fucking rockets, you and I."

"I don't know what you mean."

"Sure you do."

He was right about his English: all at once, the accent was almost gone. Mackie preferred his speech the old way. They rounded a bluff, passed the opening of a cave or abandoned mine in an ochre rock face. Bits of toilet paper clung to spiky bushes at the roadside.

"How is this for a view?" said Samsonov.

"Beautiful," Mackie said. They sat on chaises longues by the pool, an umbrella-shaded table with fruit, glasses, and a silver ice bucket between them, a cliff rising to the top of the saddle at their backs. Away to the south rose an anvil-shaped mesa, floating on a mirage; the silence was complete.

"And the statue?" said Samsonov.

"Nice," said Mackie. A life-sized marble nude stood behind them, an expression of deep, inscrutable thought on her stone face.

"Aphrodite, goddess of love," said Samsonov. "She came with the house. The previous owner was a lover of culture. Also the chief of police in Hermosillo, until his disappearance."

"What happened?" Mackie said.

Samsonov poured from the ice-cold bottle of Stoli. "Who knows?" he said. "This side of the border is just like Russia. A mistake is made. Time passes. Then kaboom. The details never stay in your head." He drank. "I am speaking English today, by God. Kaboom."

"When did you leave Russia?"

"As soon as possible." A reflection from the pool shimmered across his face. "Drink up," he said.

Mackie had a little more. Her head was buzzing now, not unpleasantly.

"In Russia or Mexico," Samsonov said, "you are free to dream, but no dream ever comes true. In America dreams come true."

"Only sometimes," Mackie said, "and not for everyone, only for a few, really."

"Good enough," said Samsonov. "You think we are in heaven already? All I needed was the chance."

"But how did you get started?"

He shrugged. "You start. You do what needs to do. Capital arrives. You make it grow. This is the system."

"My ex-husband and I never understood it."

"Ah," said Samsonov, "perhaps you were hooking up with the wrong guy."

That was evident, but Mackie said nothing.

"But you yourself still have a dream," he said.

Mackie nodded. "Owning a dance studio," she said, taking another drink. "That's what I've always wanted."

"What would be the cost of such a studio?"

"Fifty thousand dollars."

"Oh, boy," said Samsonov. He drained his glass in one gulp, pouring it down his throat, that vein throbbing on the side.

"Oh, boy?"

"I am telling you what," said Samsonov, refilling his glass, clinking it against hers. "Here is your chance to make up for your Club Girlie mistake."

Was he going to raise the Club Girlie offer to fifty thousand dollars? Mackie knew her answer, an answer she wouldn't be able to resist, so why bother trying: take that money and never look back. Her skin was just another costume.

Samsonov rose, gazed down at her, his platinum hair shining in the sunlight, the huge empty sky overhead. "What is your name?" he said. "Now is a moment for reality. First name will do."

"Helen."

Samsonov nodded, as though expecting something like that. "Wait here, Helen." He crossed the pool deck, opened a sliding door, went into the house.

Mackie got up, drank down her glass to the bottom, gazed at her reflection in the pool. Her reflection looked nervous.

Samsonov came out, a plastic bag in one hand, a check in the other. He handed her the check: $50,000, drawn on his account at Patriot Frontier Savings and Loan in Agua Fría, made out to Helen, with space for her to add her last name. "And here is a present," he said, shaking the bag out on her chaise: makeup kit, white minidress, blue platform shoes, and a red wig even more flamboyant than the one she already had. "All clear?" he said.

"No."

"For this fifty grand," said Samsonov, "you must dance."

"At Club Girlie?"

"Nothing so challenging," said Samsonov. "Only right here. Just for me."

"But you've seen me dance dozens of times."

"Not like this," said Samsonov. "What I see is art—you are my best dancer, no question. But what I need now is reality."

"What does that mean?"

"The basic you."

"How am I supposed to do that?"

"Showing the basic?" said Samsonov. "But isn't it obvious? For this, you must arouse yourself."

"I don't understand."

"Oh, I know you do, Helen. I can sense of it down under that wholesome skin. You must dance to orgasm." He laid his hand on her back, as though encouraging a child before some test. "To put it in a not so fancy word, meaning to come for real, right here and now, nothing faked, no art, all honest and open." He took the check from her hand, tucked it under the Stoli bottle. "After that, the money is yours. Even a tip is possible, depending."

Silence. Samsonov watched her, probably wondering what sort of thought process was going on. The actual thinking had been over and done with in a second: it was out of the question.

"Well?" he said.

"I'll do it."

"Very wise," said Samsonov. "How many golden chances come along in one life? While you change, I will go put on music—the outdoor sound is prime."

He went back through the slider, disappeared in the darkness on the other side. Mackie picked up the bottle of Stoli and took a big, big hit, more alcohol in that single harsh swallow than she'd drunk in any one day of her life—until recently. Dealing with this would come later. Now was the time for action. *Make me a little stronger.* She took off all her clothes—jeans, T-shirt, bra, panties, baseball cap—slapped on makeup, put on the white minidress, the blue platforms, the red wig. Her reflection, bent and miniaturized, appeared on the side of the silver ice bucket. The wig was ridiculously huge, covering half her face. This other bent bewigged half-faced person would do it, whatever had to be done.

Samsonov returned with a drink in one hand and a remote in the other, sat at the table about ten feet from where she stood. He was dressed as before—jeans, the belt with the diamond-studded BUCK buckle, a Western shirt—but he'd taken off his boots. His toenails were thick and yellow.

"All set?" he said.

Mackie nodded. Samsonov touched a button on the remote. Aaliyah's voice came from hidden speakers all around, from the cliff, the hills, the sky: "Are You That Somebody." This was all planned out. But what difference did that make? Mackie moved around the statue and started to dance.

At first, until the white dress came off, she danced as she danced at the club, only not as well because of how much she'd had to drink. But then, with the dress off: did it surprise him, even just a little, that she wore nothing underneath? She couldn't tell, his eyes and the expression on his face just beyond interpretation in the shadow of the umbrella. And did she care? This was about pleasing her, not him. That was the thought, a wild one but right, to hold on to.

Mackie ran a hand over her breast. When had she last had an orgasm? Months and months ago, possibly a year, back with Kevin in the period of Jenna's coaching. She moved closer to Samsonov, tried one or two of those tricks. Did his lips part, just a little? Yes. Open up, you son of a bitch. Let's see your honest insides.

Closer still: she put one foot up on the table now, not so he could see better—she didn't give a fuck about that—but so that she could demonstrate better. She could feel her nipples growing, the whole tone of her skin changing, everything taut like a powerful athlete. This was actually working: no need to pretend at all. His mouth was open now, transfixed and sweaty, all self-possession and dignity gone; he was beyond convinced, well on the way to help-lessness. Mackie started to pivot, leg still raised, foot still on the table, intending to bend forward like that, her back to him, to really demonstrate, wilder and righter than ever before; and at that moment, the moment of turning, her eye caught a tiny red light blinking on the other side of the sliding door.

She stopped. "You're taping this?" *A long-necked flexible something with teeth for taking a bite out of her.* She took her foot off the table, faced him.

"What?" he said, his voice thick, as though returning from some dreamland far away. "Oh, the DVD. That is nothing, only for my own records. Don't worry—it is on automatic. We are alone. Continue."

"Records?" Mackie said. Records, meaning this was be-yond two memories, was real, documented, forever. She thrust the table over, dumping it onto him, table, ice bucket, Stoli, glasses, umbrella, Samsonov, all crashing down in a heap. "Records?" And the next thing she knew she was right beside him, foot drawn back to kick him as hard as she could. She got in one kick, or part of one, be-fore he grabbed her leg and flung her effortlessly down.

"This is going to be very good, Helen," he said, rolling on top of her—so much stronger than Kevin or any other man she'd known, like a third sex; his lips were an inch from hers. "First, a kiss." He tried to force his tongue inside her mouth. Mackie clamped her mouth shut, twisted her head to the side. He seized her jaw with one hand, twisted it back; his other hand was busy with his belt buckle: the diamonds cut her pubic skin as he yanked the buckle aside.

Mackie punched him as hard as she could, in the side of his head, the back of his head, to no effect; tried to knee him, but her legs were already apart and he was in between, pushing his way into her; tried to bite, but he squeezed her jaw so hard the muscles went numb. His tongue entered her mouth; she felt it, all hard, dry, bumpy, probing around: hated that probing around more than anything else, and bit on it with all her might.

He cried out, and suddenly she was free. She sprang up. He rolled, blood pouring from his mouth, caught her leg again, his nails digging deep, murder in his eyes, honest and open. Mackie, falling, reached out for the statue, got her hand behind its neck, toppled it onto him. There was a great crash of marble, some of it striking his head, Aphrodite's body parts splashing into the pool, and Mackie's leg came free.

She scooped up the white dress, snatched the check off the table, and started running: away from the pool, through the rock garden, around to the garage. The only car inside was the red Cadillac, keys in the ignition. Mackie jumped in, backed out, smashing into a wall on the first try, something else on the second, wheeled around. There he was, running now down through the rock garden, almost flying, face all red in the middle. Mackie put the pedal to the floor, her foot steady but the rest of her shaking out of control.

Twenty-one

Lianne wasn't the least bit nervous. She lay beside Jimmy in the South End bunkhouse, breathing slow and easy until it was time to get up. They got dressed, went out on the bunkhouse porch, sunshine gleaming on their motorcycles, the two-humped mountain in the distance. Jimmy transferred his big saddlebags to her bike.

"What if they're not big enough?" Lianne said, just to be mischievous.

His head swung quickly toward her. "What do you mean?" Maybe *he* was a little nervous; time enough to go back inside, do something about that?

"How much space does half a million dollars take up, Jimmy?"

He shrugged. "Can't be that much, if their plan has me walking out with it."

She nodded. He was thinking okay; it was going to be fine. But she couldn't keep the wildness completely down, like she was a little high. "What if they had a really big weekend at the casino? Like bags and bags of money."

Jimmy smiled. She couldn't get enough of that little white smile: it said so much about him. "Anything we can't carry goes to charity," he said.

She laughed. "But what if there's more, Jimmy, a lot more?"

"Five hundred grand's an awful lot of money, right there."

"Calling me greedy?"

Jimmy tugged on the saddlebags till they were nice and tight. "Sure," he said. "But it looks real good on you."

He had to be wrong: she was only greedy for him. She took his head in her hands, stroked the back of his neck. "Let's go over it," she said.

"We've been over it a million times."

"Once more."

Jimmy sat beside her on the porch. She put her arm around him, felt muscle and bone, his muscle and bone, and therefore the feeling told her a lot, like how tense he was, for starters. But did that matter? Probably the appropriate mood right about now, even if it was all pretend. Stage plays were all pretend too, and everyone got nervous for them.

"I drive over to the Anza Wash," Jimmy said. "They take me to the bank, wait outside. Meanwhile, you come down on the Honda, keep it revving a little ways up the street. When I walk out, you swoop in. I jump on, we're gone. That it?"

"Got the ski mask?"

"Right here." He patted his back pocket.

"Let's see."

Jimmy put on the ski mask, red with white snowflakes and a logo from Steamboat Springs. "Your money or your life," he said in a scary voice. Lianne laughed. Jimmy took the mask off, put it away, a little grin on his face. He was sweating a bit too: the heat was coming. Lianne gave him a kiss, right on that diamond in his ear, tasted a hint of salt. No resistance, no hitting the alarms, no cops. She could see it all happening, just the way it was supposed to; could also see much farther, all the way to the ranch house at Cielo Azul with its blue trim, and those blue fence posts lined up as far at the eye could see.

Jimmy checked his watch. "Guess this is it."

They rose. "You like that name, Jimmy—Cielo Azul?"

"Love it." He put his arms around her. She was sure he was going to add, "And you too." But he didn't.

"See you soon," she said.

"Yup."

They kissed. Maybe he hadn't added *and you too*, but she could feel it in that kiss, stronger than any words. She was living now, actually doing something real.

Jimmy got on his bike, zoomed in a tight circle in front of the bunkhouse. He pulled the gun from his pocket, fired it at the sky—unloaded of course, so nothing happened— then sped off, like a dangerous gunfighter in the Old West. He could be so funny sometimes.

No power, no heat, the blizzard howling outside like a banshee. Delete *banshee*, find something more original. In fact, the whole howling blizzard thing is kind of . . . *They sat in front of the fire, drinking up the last of Colonel Perry's cabernet. "Why do you keep looking at your watch?" Bolt asked.*

Athena said, "

What did she say? Loeb knew that this was crucial, if he was ever going to get to those red tears and that blue blood. Whatever Athena said now would either make her evil, the easiest to do, or dangerously but believably mixed-up, much harder. And mixed-up in some womanly way, if her ultimate betrayal of Bolt was going to work.

Athena said, "

It wouldn't come. Maybe he could help it by walking around a little, like this, or gazing out the window, letting his mind wander. Loeb looked over the steel wall into Mexico. No baby or chicken in that packed-dirt backyard, no woman at the window; in fact, the window was boarded up. Loeb raised his eyes over the rooftops of the Mexican

town, toward the desert beyond, and the single thin black
road bisecting it to the horizon. A tiny red dot appeared on
that horizon, grew bigger.

Behind him, Loeb's laptop beeped. E-mail.

*Went over the material. You're not as funny as you
used to be—how come? But the police procedure stuff
is way better, nothing in there to make me stop and
say WHOA. AND HEY, whuzzup with Athena? Not
that she's a real woman yet, not gonna be that easy,
Mr. Wordsmith, but something's going on, right?
Forward the fifty bucks to me at the address at the
bottom. As for how come Clay left NY, why don't you
ask him? You're a big boy.*
MJ (waiting for more)

Loeb went back to work, stared for a while at the open
quote and the emptiness beyond. Nothing came except
song lyrics, all Elton John, none helpful. He called Krupsha at the station.

"Howdy, pardner," said Krupsha, sounding more upbeat
than Loeb had ever heard him. "Nothing for you yet on
the—what was it?—cat thing?"

"Specifically the landlord-tenant angle," Loeb said.

Pause. "Right."

"Why don't we grab some lunch anyway?" Loeb said.
"On me."

"Tomorrow okay?" Krupsha said. "Got a busy afternoon
shaping up here."

Loeb watched the blinking cursor for a while longer. It
made him sleepy, like a hypnotist. He lay down, pulled the
threadbare yellow bedspread over him. Writers slept a lot.
The better the writer, the more sleep. He'd read that somewhere, but was in dreamland before he could dredge up the
source.

* * *

Goats were crossing the road as Mackie drove into the Mexican Agua Fría; she stopped to let them pass. The little boy herding them gave her a quick glance, then looked away. Mackie crawled through the narrow streets, past all the souvenir stands, the bars, the donkey cart with smiling tourists having their picture taken, and came to the border crossing. The goats, the donkey, the tourists: all distorted, like figures from a nightmare. As the agent approached her window, Mackie realized she had no ID.

"This Mr. Samsonov's car?" said the agent.

"Yes."

He glanced at the damaged bodywork. "Thought so."

"I . . ."

He bent down, gazed at her through the open window, waiting.

"I work for him." Mackie said; very hard to get those words out.

"Thought so," said the agent. "Have a nice day." He waved her through.

Mackie crossed over, turned right on Pershing, drove along the border to Buckaroo's. It was quiet, both lots almost empty. She left the red Cadillac in the employee lot, driving out in her own car, back down Pershing, then north on Oro. Mackie started angling into a metered space in front of Patriot Frontier Savings and Loan, but a beat-up van backed in ahead of her. She parked around the block.

The check was in her hand, had been in her hand the whole ride; and was now a little dampened with her sweat. But the writing was unsmeared. Mackie opened her glove box, a pint of Stoli falling to the floor. She took out her driver's license, found a pen, wrote *MacIsaac* after Helen in the pay-to line of the check, as steadily as she could. Then she went into the bank to cash it before he could stop payment. She'd earned every penny.

There was one teller on duty, a couple of customers waiting in line, a third customer showing some papers to the assistant manager at her desk behind the low railing, the other two desks vacant. Mackie got in line. Everyone turned to look at her, almost in unison, like a school of fish. It hit her then what she was wearing—platforms, minidress, wig. She glared at them, at all these watchers, did it without thinking. They pretended they'd been looking at something else.

The teller—TELLER OF THE MONTH, read her plaque— took a cash deposit from the first customer, counted it out, $47.25, stamped the slip. The next customer said something in Spanish, too fast for Mackie to understand, except for the word *percento*. The teller handed him a form. The customer took it, helped himself to a hard green candy from a dish beside the plaque, walked away without a glance at Mackie.

Mackie stepped forward. "I'd like to cash this and buy a money order," she said. She laid the check and her license on the counter.

The teller looked at the check, then up at Mackie, quickly back to the check. "Buy a money order with the check?" she said.

"Yes."

The teller's eyes went to Samsonov's signature. She turned the check over. "Could you endorse it, please?"

Mackie endorsed the check. Pulling her glasses down to the end of her nose, the teller copied Mackie's license number beneath the endorsement, slow and neat. She turned the check back over, got out a stamping die, pressed it into a maroon stamp pad, held it poised over the check.

"Oh," she said.

"Is something wrong?"

"The date," said the teller.

Mackie read it upside down. "But that's the date."

The teller bit her lip. "The month is right," she said. "The day is right. But the year. That's a three, not a two, see?" She circled it in red ink. "This check is for a thousand years from now."

A three, not a two: no doubt at all.

"I can't cash this," said the teller. "You'll have to get it reissued."

Or something like that; Mackie wasn't hearing properly. She backed away, the check still in her hand.

"Don't forget this," said the teller, passing her the license.

Mackie just stood there, feeling faint.

"Excuse me," said another customer, moving around her.

Mackie turned, took a few steps over to the stand-up counter with the blank deposit and withdrawal slips and the pens on little chains. She gazed at the check, barely aware of gray-haired people entering the bank, one in a wheelchair, all of them in Audubon T-shirts, binoculars around their necks.

A definite three, impossible to neatly reshape into a two and present to another teller at another bank, even without that bright red circle around it. The check was bad from the start. She tried to absorb everything that meant, had barely begun, when someone screamed, a stifled scream, not loud, quickly cut off. Mackie looked up, saw a man with a silver gun in his hand, just inside the door. He wore faded jeans, a black T-shirt, surgical gloves, and a red ski mask decorated with snowflakes.

"Everyone on the floor," he said. "You"—pointing the gun at the teller—"out here."

Everyone—the Audubon people, other customers, assistant manager—got on the floor, except the teller, who came out from behind the counter, hands over her mouth; the man in the wheelchair; and Mackie.

"Me too?" said the man in the wheelchair; gray-headed, but perhaps prematurely: he had the huge arms of a wheelchair racer.

"No," said the man in the ski mask. "But what's *your* problem?" The gun swept through a short arc, pointed at Mackie. She got down on the floor, near the man in the wheelchair. "That's better," said the man in the ski mask. "No one's going to get hurt. This'll be all over 'fore you know it."

From her angle down on the floor, Mackie saw a little pool of urine spreading out from under an old lady a few yards away. The man in the ski mask said, "Now the safe." The teller made a high-pitched little sound. Her feet—she wore clunky black Steve Madden's; Lianne had a pair just like them—and his—dusty cowboy boots—moved toward the back of the bank, out of Mackie's range of vision.

From the street came a booming bass from the sound system of a passing car. In the bank, silence. Then a metallic squeak. The man in the ski mask said, "That the casino one?"

The teller's reply, a faint whimper, was almost inaudible.

"Don't that one say *casino* too?" said the man in the ski mask.

The man in the wheelchair made a low sound in his throat, almost a growl. Mackie looked over at him; a vein was throbbing in one of those big arms. He had a nose like a hawk.

"Now you get down too," said the man in the ski mask. There was a clank of metal, maybe the barred door of the strong room closing. Then came footsteps, quite light, and the cowboy boots appeared in Mackie's view, followed by the whole man, two big canvas bags held in one arm, the gun in his free hand. He moved well, a graceful stride almost like a trained dancer's, except for slight bowleggedness.

"Now everyone stay just like this," he said as he went by. "You've all done real well."

He walked toward the door, his back to Mackie. She started to raise her head. At that moment, the man in the wheelchair made another growling noise, louder this time, gave one powerful thrust of the wheels, and shot forward. He slammed into the man in the ski mask, hitting him low, crumpling his legs, bending backwards like a bow. The canvas bags went flying as he fell, landing right by Mackie's head. The wheelchair tipped, the man in it, his legs all shriveled, falling out, right onto the man in the ski mask. They rolled around on the floor. There was lots of screaming now, all over the bank. All that was clear to Mackie were the canvas bags, their clarity so fine they might have been stills shot by a great photographer. She picked them up and ran out the door, slipping just a little in those blue platforms.

The beat-up van was still parked out front. The driver had a book propped up on the steering wheel, but he turned as Mackie came out, his eyebrows rising. It was Turbo. Mackie kept going, not running, but walking fast. She rounded the corner, opened her car, threw in the two canvas bags, her license, the bad check, got in, drove off. She didn't have a single thought, just a feeling: it felt right.

A few doors down from the bank, Lianne waited, revving the blue Honda. She'd arrived in time to see Jimmy get out of the van, move toward the entrance, hand going to his back pocket for the ski mask. Then all of a sudden a bunch of old people, one in a wheelchair, came down the sidewalk and went in ahead of him. Jimmy stopped right there. He turned toward the van, a kind of questioning look on his face. From her position, Lianne could see only the back of the van; whoever was inside must have reassured Jimmy: his body got a little straighter and he strode into the bank, pulling on the ski mask as he went through the door.

Lianne checked her watch. How long would it take? Say two minutes to establish control, get everyone down on the floor, maybe a little longer with all those old people in there. Then two more for opening that barred door—the thick vault door had been open already when she'd checked it out—and grabbing the money. After that, thirty seconds to get to the front door. Call it five minutes all together, tops. And ninety seconds were already gone. Everyone inside was probably on the floor by now, Jimmy and some bank employee on their way to the safe. This was happening.

Lianne revved the bike, watched the bank door. No one went in or out. The van, dented and dusty, vibrated slightly from its engine running. Across the street, facing her, sat a big green car, a man in the driver's seat. After ten or twenty seconds, Lianne realized that he was watching the bank door too; a heavy, bristly-haired man in a suit jacket the same color as the car. Another ten or twenty seconds and she recognized him: the man from the counter at the café who'd been reading a book while Lianne drew plans for Jimmy on a napkin. Nothing strange about him being parked there—the café was only a few blocks up the street. He had to be a local doing some local thing. A low-rider went by, rap booming out even though the windows were closed.

Three minutes gone, two to go. They'd be on the way to the safe now for sure, Jimmy and the bank employee, maybe already there, the bank employee reaching in, handing Jimmy bags of money. Cielo Azul: magic. Lianne revved the bike, felt its power. The dusty van, the heavy guy in the green car, this whole crummy town, all so dreary, almost unreal or dead compared to her and Jimmy. Ninety seconds to go. Lianne had a premonition, knew for sure it would happen: Jimmy was going to bring her one of those hard green candies. Her mouth started watering, which was kind of crazy: those candies weren't that good. She almost laughed out loud. Vroom vroom.

Thirty seconds. Twenty. Fifteen. She started letting out

the clutch, holding the bike back with her foot. The bank door opened. A person came out, but not Jimmy. Instead it was a woman, a strange-looking woman in a tiny dress with wild red hair and tall platform shoes. She turned quickly—what was that in her arms?—and headed away, up the street and around the next corner.

Then nothing. No one else came out. Time was up. Lianne inched forward on the bike. At that moment, the back doors of the van popped open and a stringy-haired man jumped out: Dane. He ran to the bank, opened the door, glanced in. Then he backed up real fast, threw open the passenger door of the van, was still climbing in as it sped off.

The bristly-haired man got out of his car, crossed the street with quick little steps that made him look silly. He entered the bank, drawing a gun from inside his jacket just as he disappeared.

Lianne let out the clutch, lurched forward, almost losing her balance, skidded to a stop in the space where the van had been. She ran into the bank.

It was all wrong. Too much noise and Jimmy on the floor with all the others. He wasn't supposed to be there, especially not with his ski mask off, and wrestling with some massive old guy. The bristly-haired man stepped in front of her, his broad back blocking her view for a moment. Then came the flash of Jimmy getting an arm free, whacking the massive guy across the head with his gun. The guy let go. Jimmy bounced up, looking around wildly, his eyes passing right over Lianne.

"Police," said the bristly-haired man, dropping into a crouch. "Drop that gun."

Jimmy turned to him. "It's not even—"

The bristly-haired man fired. One of Jimmy's eyes turned into a red hole. The other one went dead. He toppled backwards and lay still.

"Don't nobody move," said the bristly-haired man, mak-

ing a big motion with the gun. But he couldn't stop the
hysteria from happening, taking over the whole bank.
Lianne backed out the door.

Then she was riding the blue Honda through the middle
of nowhere. She'd caught the hysteria from the bank. Hysteria smelled like piss. It infected every cell.

Twenty-two

Loeb opened his eyes. Sunlight filled his room at the Crossing Inn, but redder than before, meaning time had passed, lots of it. He felt like shit. That was a by-product of afternoon naps, probably also of the writing life in general. Sometimes, though, breakthroughs happened at this, the very moment of waking up, just before the crumbling of the bridge to the unconscious. What was Auden's advice? Go immediately to the desk on awakening, without even stopping to brush your teeth. Disgusting; what other hygienic transgressions had Auden been in thrall to, bad habits that might have hampered him in present-day publishing, supposing W. H. snagged an appearance on *Entertainment Tonight*, for example? But the wrinkled old guy had known what he was talking about; Loeb felt something coming.

He sat down to the laptop, read *"Why do you keep looking at your watch?" Bolt asked. Athena said, "*

And wrote her line: *Sometimes you make me feel like shit."*

Perfect. Full of promise, in character and developing character at the same time, and with the bonus of being slightly off-angle, the kind of effect he hardly ever achieved. It struck him that a new side of Bolt would have to emerge now, as a result of this change in Athena. That was something to think about. Perhaps this was the moment for a walk, maybe even a long one, Dickensian. All of a sudden, he was keeping company with the big boys.

Teeth brushed, showered, hair combed, dressed in the navy-blue shirt he'd worn for his own TV appearances, four so far, none on *Entertainment Tonight* or anything close, Loeb walked down the long hill from the Crossing Inn, looking presentable, certainly presentable enough for Buckaroo's, in case he happened to end up there. He had the Buena Vida Estates pen in his pocket. *Hi, Red, you dropped this.* Then she'd say, *Oh, thanks,* and he'd come up with something clever and she'd see he wasn't some periodontally diseased onanist but a sweet breather worth getting to know.

But on the way, another pass by the theme park site. Krupsha didn't buy the landlord-tenant dispute theory, believed instead that Flora and Harvey might have been trying to stir up trouble for Turbo. The logical question that hadn't occurred to Loeb then but occurred to him now: Who in their right mind would even consider stirring up trouble for Turbo? Police work was mostly about logic, as Sergeant Falco had said many times, perhaps too many.

Loeb came to Oro, turned south, toward the border, stopping at the Mariposa Café for a coffee to go, large, black, no sugar. An order he had to repeat twice: the woman behind the counter couldn't take her eyes off a reporter on the TV in the corner, a reporter with a small-time hairdo, doing a stand-up with yellow police tape for a background. But not bad coffee, burning off any lingering nap fog; with the sun on his face, Loeb began to feel pretty good, even tempted by thoughts of well-being in general. Maybe that was what made him slow to pull together the scene he walked into by Patriot Frontier Savings and Loan: squad cars, police tape, reporter with small-time hairdo. He felt a little lurch in his stomach, as though he'd slipped on ice; a *Twilight Zone* feeling.

The reporter was leaning against a satellite truck, cheeks hollow from sucking on a cigarette.

"What's going on?" Loeb said.

The reporter blew out smoke, some in his face, but not intentional; she was wound up, looking right through him. "Sound fuckup," she said. "Got to reshoot the whole thing."

"I meant what's the story?"

"Story?"

"That you're covering."

She waved her hand in the direction of the bank. A man climbed out of the truck, carrying microphones.

"But what happened, exactly?"

"What does it look like?" said the reporter.

"Mind giving us some space here, bud?" said the soundman. "You can catch it at six."

Loeb moved aside, tried to gaze into the bank from the tape barrier, saw people moving around, most of them in uniform. A man in civilian clothes, badge clipped to his shirt pocket, came out. Loeb said: "Is Detective Krupsha inside?"

"Who's asking?"

"Nick Loeb. I'm a friend of his."

"The author?"

"Writer."

"Hey!" said the cop. "Frankie Nuñez."

They shook hands. "Feeling better?" Loeb said.

"Man oh man," said Frankie Nuñez. "Shitting green for two days. But you know the funny thing?"

"What?"

"I got an idea for a book myself."

"Oh?"

"All I need is someone to kind of help me get started."

"Maybe we can discuss it sometime," Loeb said.

"Yeah? Wow."

"But right now I was hoping to see Clay, if he's not too busy."

"He's not here," Frankie Nuñez said. "Probably still in counseling."

"Counseling?"

"Mandatory, after any lethal firearm discharge."

"He shot someone?" Loeb said.

"Where have you been?" said Frankie. "The guy who was knocking off the bank. Or one of them. It's not too clear."

"How many were there?"

"That's the not-clear part. At least two, including a woman—one of the girls from the tittie bar."

"Not Red?"

"Hey! How did you know? She got away with half a mil."

Loeb found Krupsha sitting alone in the police station cafeteria, hands wrapped around a Coke can, the attitude almost one of prayer.

"This a bad time?" Loeb said.

Krupsha looked up at him. "For what?"

"For me to be here."

"Long as you don't bug me about that fuckin' cat."

Loeb sat in a plastic seat fixed to the table like the seats in the cafeteria at his high school.

"Ever killed a man, Nick?"

Loeb almost said, *Of course not.* "No."

"It's not good," Krupsha said. He drank up the Coke, crumpled the can. " 'Specially with the asshole's gun turning out to be empty. Why did that have to happen?"

"His gun was empty?"

"Doesn't change anything. Guy points a gun at you, you take him down. Even you know that, right? But what kind of bank robber shows up with an unloaded gun? How does that add up?"

"Maybe he was high," Loeb said.

"You keep comin' up with shit, don't you?" said Krupsha. "I don't think you're right on this one, but you can judge for yourself."

"How?"

"Ever been in a bank?" Krupsha tossed the Coke can at a wastebasket, not coming close. Loeb saw that he'd sweated through his green suit jacket between the shoulder blades. "It's all on tape, for Christ's sake."

They sat before a monitor in Krupsha's office. "We got a techie downstairs edited this," Krupsha said, hitting *play,* "but it's mostly from the camera back of the tellers."

The techie knew how to tell a story. It was like a screenplay, three or four of which Loeb had sped through in a single day after a call from Harry about an adaptation gig—Bruce Willis as a film noir detective who ends up fighting an intergalactic crime wave in the distant future— he was going to finalize by dinner, but never did.

INT. BANK. DAY.
A bunch of old-looking CUSTOMERS enter,
one of them in a WHEELCHAIR. They start
lining up in front of the TELLER. The ROBBER
comes in behind them, wearing a SKI MASK
and brandishing a GUN. Everyone gets down on
the floor except the man in the wheelchair and a
RED-HAIRED WOMAN (RED) dressed like a
hooker. The robber waves the gun at her. She gets
down too.
We FOLLOW the robber and the teller into the
VAULT. She hands him TWO CANVAS MONEY
BAGS, lies down on the floor.
CUT TO:
The robber, coming toward us, money bags in hand.
He STEPS CAREFULLY over the people lying on
the floor, is almost at the door, when

CU—the man in the wheelchair, looking apoplectic,
suddenly RAMS him from behind.
SHOT of the robber as he FALLS and the money
bags go FLYING.
NEW ANGLE on the chaos developing in the bank.
The robber and the wheelchair man STRUGGLE on
the floor, people scramble and crawl around
frantically.
ON THE RED-HAIRED WOMAN—as she spots the
money bags, in easy reach. She GRABS them and
hurries out of the bank.
ON THE STRUGGLE—the wheelchair man yanks
off the ski mask, revealing the robber's FACE,
young, handsome, scared. The robber gets an arm
free, WHACKS the wheelchair man in the head with
the gun, jumps up.
ON THE DOOR—KRUPSHA enters, GUN raised. A
TEENAGE CUSTOMER comes in behind him. She
FREEZES.
TWO SHOT—Krupsha and the robber. The robber's
still holding his gun and his arm is in MOTION, but
where he's going with it isn't clear. Krupsha
SHOOTS him in the face.
F/X—BLOOD SPURTS out.
The robber FALLS. Krupsha waves his gun around,
looks FURIOUS. Nobody moves except the teenage
customer, who BACKS OUT the door.
FADE OUT.

Loeb turned to Krupsha. Krupsha was watching him;
Loeb got the funny feeling Krupsha had been watching
him the whole time.
"Look high to you?" Krupsha said.
"No."
"Any other questions?"

"I don't know where to start," Loeb said.

"Usual starting point is IDing the perp."

"Which one?"

"What's that supposed to mean?" Krupsha said. His face went all congested, turning almost as purple as his lips.

"Frankie Nuñez said there were at least two," Loeb said. "The guy in the ski mask and the woman who got away."

The purple faded from Krupsha's face. "Frankie's full of shit," he said, without anger. "She had nothing to do with it."

"What am I missing?" said Loeb. "She ran off with the money."

"Just an impulsive moment," Krupsha said. "She's a stripper from the club—they don't think too good by definition."

"Meaning she just happened to be there and took advantage of the situation?"

"If you call ruining your life taking advantage of the situation, then yeah," said Krupsha.

"You caught her already?"

"No."

"Maybe she'll get away."

"Not a chance. It may take a little while to ID her, that's all. Right now we got nothing but her stage name—Red—which is one hell of a way to run a business."

Loeb could feel the pen in his pocket, possible clue to Red's real identity. This was the moment to bring it up, and Loeb might have, had he been able to watch that shooting scene a few more times, make it work right in his mind. He said: "You're referring to Samsonov?"

"You could say that."

"Tell me about him."

Krupsha shrugged. "Nothing to tell. He's a businessman. This is an up-and-coming town, believe it or not. Population's going to double in the next ten years."

Loeb gazed at the dark screen. "So it's a coincidence, her being there." He also wanted to have another look at Red's face, the moment before she grabbed the money: savage.

"Why not?" Krupsha said. "Coincidence just means things happening at the same time, which you ought to know, being in the word business. Turns out she was trying to get a check cashed, unsuccessfully."

"Why unsuccessfully?"

"Something wrong with the check. Point is, the teller must have seen her real name on the check—even had a look at the goddamn driver's license—and can't even come up with the first fuckin' letter."

"Is she the one who triggered the alarm?" Loeb said.

"What alarm?"

"That brought you there."

"Who said anything about the alarm? Was no alarm. Patriot Frontier's my bank. I was depositing this." He reached into his suit jacket, held up his paycheck.

Timothy Bolt can be funny, but there are too many unbelievable coincidences. Mary Jane had written that, perhaps misspelling unbelievable—Loeb couldn't remember. For a moment, he considered quoting her to Krupsha, ended up just saying, "Oh."

"Exercising the brain cells, Nicky?" Krupsha said.

"There's a lot to process."

"And you haven't even got to the important part yet."

"The guy in the ski mask?"

"Bingo. Name of Jimmy Marz, wrangler at a dude ranch not far from here. Only one prior on his record, not counting the usual juvenile shit."

"What kind of prior?"

"Cattle rustling."

"That still happens?"

"What doesn't?" said Krupsha. "But this might have been more of a prank. He got off with a fine."

"So if he wasn't a criminal, what's the motive?"

"Are you kidding? Five hundred grand."

"Seems like a lot to be in a little bank like that."

"Not on Mondays," said Krupsha. "Monday is when the weekend take comes in from the casino."

"So he just happened to pick the right day?"

"Havin' a little fun with me now, Nick?" Krupsha's eyes went dull for a moment, as though he'd suddenly gone weak. Loeb wouldn't have guessed he could look like that.

"How did the counseling go?" he said.

Krupsha waved the question away. Life came back to his eyes, contempt arriving first. "Fuckin' shrink," he said. "I wanted to beat his head in."

"That's only allowed on the premium plan," Loeb said.

Krupsha laughed, kept laughing. For a horrible moment, Loeb thought his laughter might turn to tears. The phone rang. Krupsha stopped laughing. "You're one funny guy," he said, reaching for the phone. "Anything else? Things are going to get busy tonight."

"Just this," said Loeb: "How was Jimmy planning to get away?

Krupsha paused, covering the mouthpiece with his palm. "Maybe exactly like he did."

Twenty-three

Four or five miles north of Agua Fría, blue lights flashed in Mackie's rearview mirror. She pulled over right away, some generator inside her sparking electric jolts through her body. The two canvas bags lay openly on the passenger seat; was there time to throw them into a ditch or gully? No time; and no ditch or gully: just low scrub and a single black manzanita, like a stick drawing of a tree. She tried to think of something to say, hadn't found word one when three SUVs and a sedan sped past. Border Patrol. They were soon out of sight. Mackie realized she was still wearing the wig. She took it off and drove home, losing herself in heavy traffic as she neared the city.

No one waiting in front of 4 Buena Vida Circle, no one in the driveway. Mackie touched the button on the remote over her visor. The garage door opened. Cost: $750, but Jenna had insisted that the model garage have automatic doors. She drove in, hit the close button, and the door rattled down. Jenna had been looking out for her all along.

Mackie got out of the car. A pair of white painter's pants, the bib kind, hung on a hook at the back of the garage, abandoned by Kevin after a brief attempt to cut costs by handling the trim himself. Mackie took off the minidress and platforms, put on the painter pants, rolled up the legs, opened the side door into the house.

"Lianne? You home?"

No answer, but why would there be? Not even dinner-time. And was this the week for the beginning of after-school SAT prep? Mackie thought so. She felt things breaking her way, as though all the last years of her life, that whole slow downfall, was actually something else, and now made sense. Back in the garage, she gathered up the canvas bags, minidress, platforms, wig, bad check, ran inside to her bedroom, and kicked the door closed.

Mackie dumped the canvas bags out on the bed, a green cascade, like a dream come true. So much of it! She flicked through a bundle of hundreds—a bundle of hundreds!—and felt their little breeze on her face.

She unbanded it all and started counting. It took a long time, a deliciously long time, and her hands were dirty by the end: $587,353. She looked at herself in the mirror, a self with huge eyes and an open mouth, and tried to tone it down. The self in the mirror toned it down a little. *That's me. This is real.* Strange sounds hummed inside her head, the kind they put in movies when they want you to get unbearably excited.

Mackie brought in logs from the garage, turned up the air conditioner—she could run it full blast forever now, without a care—and built a roaring fire in the living-room fireplace, not marble, but a clever synthetic, clever being Jenna's word. She threw in the empty canvas bags, minidress, wig, platforms, bad check, watched it all go up in flames. Red, stripper and bank robber, vanished from the face of the earth, leaving behind the smell of burning plastic. Even that was good. Real marble could be hers now, if she wanted. Which she didn't; knowing it was possible was good enough. The sounds in her head subsided a little.

Mackie glanced down Buena Vida Circle. No sign yet of Lianne. She took off the painter pants and tossed them on the fire too. Then she had a shower that she meant to be long and hot, but turned out to be hot only, because as she soaped herself, her mind started dwelling on the scene by the pool.

Mackie dried herself in the bedroom, eyes on the money, felt better right away. Better and better: almost bursting with it, uncontainable. All of a sudden she couldn't sit still, had to get out. She fought the urge, fought it and fought it for what seemed like hours but might not even have been minutes. And why fight? There was no reason to hide. The perp was gone.

Mackie dressed—jeans, T-shirt, baseball cap—shoved a green handful or two in her pockets, dumped the rest in a suitcase and stuck it under the bed. Then she locked the house, every window and outside door, and went out.

Was it possible to spend $150 on a single bottle of champagne? Mackie learned it was. Would Lianne like a real Kate Spade bag? Why not? How about some nice silk dresses to go along with it, like this creamy one, and yes, the blue as well. And the little gold bracelet—wouldn't it look nice on her?—and the Navajo ring, the old one at the back, and this other one, not too grown-up for a seventeen-year-old? No? Gift-wrapped would be nice.

On the way home, Mackie picked up lobster for dinner, just one but it weighed ten pounds. There was a lot of splashing and laughter around the saltwater tank. They gave her extra lemons.

Back home: all quiet. She parked in the driveway, started unloading. The Thorsens, out for a walk, watched her with all those gaily colored bags. She worked two fingers free and gave them a tiny wave.

"Lianne? You home?"

No answer. Mackie checked the time: just past seven, the sky still blue, but no longer bright. Mackie examined the calendar on the fridge. Yes: the SAT prep course started today, room 116 at the high school, circled in red; pizza afterward. Berkeley, Stanford, the best college Lianne could get into—she could go without worry now, even in style. Mackie laid out Lianne's presents on the kitchen table, stuck the champagne in the fridge, put on her biggest pot to boil for the lobster. She could feel the money in the suitcase under her bed: it changed the whole balance of the house.

Mackie heard a sound, cocked her ear. Was Lianne home after all, in her room the whole time with the headphones on or sleeping? She went down the hall to Lianne's room. The door was open, no one there. And the bed was made! That was a first. In fact, the whole room was tidier than she'd ever seen it, nothing out of place except a single piece of paper balled up under the desk. Mackie smoothed it out, read the one word written on it: "Dear." She dropped it back in the wastebasket, returned to the kitchen, immediately heard the sound again; but identified it this time: the lobster rustling around in his white bag. She dropped him in the pot; probably take a long time to cook one his size— Lianne would be home before he was done.

Mackie put on music, turned it up high. Not "Are You That Somebody," "When Rita Leaves," or "Honky-Tonk Woman," songs she knew she would never listen to again, but Van Morrison: "Into the Mystic." Her school of dance: a reality. Also no more Stoli. From now on, champagne, and lots. She opened the $150 bottle, was pleased to find she'd bought two.

But she couldn't stay away from the bedroom. Mackie brought the bottle with her, pulled out the suitcase, dumped it, sat cross-legged on the bed, counted the money again. This time she got $602,019. She laughed out loud. With the laughing, and Van the Man at the top of his lungs, and those movie sounds still in her head, Mackie didn't really hear the bedroom door opening, just looked up and there was Kevin.

He stopped short, unable to take it all in. This was a look she'd seen on his face before, but never so extreme. Floating on a sea of money, champagne bottle balanced between her legs, Mackie reached for the remote and switched off the music. Nothing else occurred to her.

"What the hell's going on?" he said.

"Nothing much." Idiotic, but no other remark came to mind. Mackie tamped down the laughter rising inside her. She didn't love him anymore, not the least little bit. A thought arrived. "I just got back from Las Vegas."

"Las Vegas?" His gaze tracked across the bed, estimating. He didn't look good, far from his handsome best, face too thin, in need of a shave, his clothes wrinkled, even a little dirty.

"How did you get in the house, Kevin?"

"I rang the bell for five minutes. I could hear the music. Then I happened to remember I had a key."

"And the purpose of your visit?"

"I could use a place to stay for a day or two," he said. "Just temporarily. And see Lianne, of course."

"She's not home yet."

Kevin didn't seem to hear. He hadn't taken his eyes off the money for a second. Approaching the bed, he picked up a bill, held it to the light. "You won all this?" he said, eyes now on her, although he didn't let go of the bill, a crisp new hundred.

"Exactly."

"How?"

"Playing games of chance."

"Like what?"

"Baccarat." She remembered the name from James Bond movies.

"You've never played baccarat in your life."

"I have a new life," she said. "You can put that down now."

He laid the bill on the bed. "Wow," he said. "This is fantastic. How much is there altogether?"

"Not as much as it looks like."

"But how much?"

"I'm not even sure."

"Roughly."

"Hard to say."

"You're acting so cool about this. To the nearest ten thou, say."

Mackie got off the bed, money gliding down after her. "I don't see how it's any of your business," she said.

Kevin stepped back. "That kind of hurts," he said.

"Why?"

"I can't believe I have to explain," he said. She saw how hard he was trying to keep his eyes on her and off the money. "We've been through a lot together. And we have a lovely daughter."

"And therefore?"

"I can't help being happy for you," Kevin said. "There's a relationship. An attachment, whether we want it or not."

"Yes to the Lianne part," Mackie said. "No to all the rest."

One of his eyelids trembled; a new development. "You've changed," he said.

"Thank Christ."

"You're harder now."

"It took too long."

"I think I liked you better before."

"When before? When you were fucking Jenna on the living-room couch? Or later, when you were siccing the IRS on me."

"I never meant that to happen."

"Jenna or the IRS?"

"Neither, if you want the truth," Kevin said. Mackie made a disgusted little sound, like *pah*. "But I was talking about the IRS. I had no idea that was going to come down on you." He was gazing at her now with genuine regret in his eyes; regret, sorrow, affection.

"Makes no difference," Mackie said.

"You mean that?"

"Time bombs wore me out."

He looked abashed. "I'm sorry. And I mean that with all my heart, whether you believe me or not."

Then came a scream. Kevin jumped, and so did she.

"What's that?" he said.

Her first thought was *cops*, and those electric jolts went through her again. Then she got a grip. "The lobster," she said, and started hurrying from the room. But stopped at the door. "Better come with me," she said. He nodded, obedient, eyes averted; everything rebalanced. She let him pass, closed the door behind them.

The pot, boiled dry, was smoking on the stove, triggering the smoke detector and filling the kitchen with an acrid smell. Kevin threw open the windows and the screaming died away. The lobster lay blackened in the pot, the thick rubber bands that had held his claws together melted away by the heat.

"Look at the size of him," Kevin said. "That's a shame." He reached for the oven mitts.

"What are you doing?"

"Cleaning this up."

"That's not necessary," Mackie said.

He turned to her. They were side by side at the oven, the charred lobster in the pot between them, carapace cracked in many places. "Just trying to help," Kevin said. He was going to touch her; Mackie could feel it coming.

"You can't stay here," she said.

"This isn't like you," Kevin said. "You have a forgiving nature."

Mackie wasn't sure about that. "What does that mean, forgive?"

"You know, put it all behind you."

"Then you're forgiven," Mackie said. Everything bad was behind her now. Plus she could make an argument that Kevin had ended up doing her a favor. "But you still can't stay in this house."

Kevin bit his lip; he had beautiful lips, the kind Hollywood people had theirs changed into. "How about till Lianne comes home?" He glanced out the window: dark outside. "Where is she, anyway?"

"SAT prep."

"She's a smart girl."

"She is."

"Going places, right?" His eyes welled up.

"Yes," Mackie said; her very thought, not long ago. "Tell you what I'll do."

"What?"

"Just stay here."

Mackie went into the bedroom, counted out some money; an amount he'd just mentioned, and that seemed right. She stuffed the rest in the suitcase, replaced it under the bed. Back in the kitchen, she found him standing in front of the fridge, door open, eating slices of smoked turkey like he was really hungry.

"Here," she said.

"What's this?"

"Ten thousand dollars," she said. "I don't know what for. Just take it."

He did, chewing his food, saying nothing.

"But that's all," she said.

He nodded.

"And I don't want you mentioning this to anyone."

"You're not reporting it?"

"Correct."

Kevin nodded; he would have done the same. "You can count on me," he said. "But be careful, how you deposit it and everything. The IRS finds out about all that shit."

"I'll be careful," Mackie said. She closed the fridge door. "Thanks for the tip."

He put the money in his pocket. "I guess I should say congratulations."

"Thanks."

"And you know what else? You deserve it."

Mackie said nothing to that, but she didn't disagree. She walked Kevin down to his car—the old BMW, filthy now, and the windshield cracked—not to be polite or to prolong the contact, but to see him get in it and drive away.

"Tell Lianne I stopped by."

"I will."

Kevin drove off; muffler gone too. Her heart lifted, right back up the heights it had commanded before he'd walked in. She felt big and powerful, not on a par with all those stars up there, but at least able to hold her own with them in the universe. The phone rang inside the house. She hurried in to answer it.

"Mackie?"

"Hi, Angie."

"You're there."

"Where else would I be?"

"I know," said Angie. "This is crazy. Did you ever try that stripping thing we talked about?"

"Not yet," Mackie said; the answer came so fast, as though her mind had been suddenly souped up. "Why?"

"So you didn't do it, go down to that club in Agua Fría like we talked about?"

"I'm still working up the nerve. What's up?"

"There was a bank robbery down there this afternoon. It was on the news. One of their dancers got away with half a million dollars. And she called herself Red. Can you believe it?"

"Maybe it's a common stage name," Mackie said.

"I hope she gets away with it," said Angie.

"Me too," Mackie said.

Her hand wasn't steady as she put down the phone; it rattled in its cradle. Angie had slipped her mind. Was there anyone else, even remotely, in a position to connect Helen MacIsaac, living quietly at 4 Buena Vida Circle in Tucson, and Red, formerly a dancer at Buckaroo's in Agua Fría, now incinerated? No.

Mackie turned on the TV, flipped through the channels, caught the tail end of a report on the robbery, the part where they show the composite. Her composite looked nothing like her at all: too thin, too hard, even dangerous—a white trash caricature. Beside it, they put up a black-and-white still from the video camera inside the bank. The wig, in combination with the camera angle, hid half her face. The half that showed was blurred with her heavy makeup, smeared from the encounter by the pool. Luck was with her; she could feel its presence, like a drug. The TV news moved on to a story about a jackknifed tractor-trailer on I-10. News got old fast. In a week or two she'd feel it leaving her behind: in a month she'd be forgotten.

Twenty-four

But Lianne wasn't home. She stayed out late sometimes—she'd be eighteen in May, and her present was going to be a car, Mackie decided that on the spur of the moment, couldn't wait to watch her choose it—but she didn't stay out late on school nights, and it was almost ten. Mackie called the high school, listened to a selection of voice mail choices. Easy to picture her with a bunch of kids somewhere after SAT prep: wasn't there a little coffee place on Catalina Highway they liked to go?

Mackie went into her bedroom, pulled the suitcase out from under the bed. The money couldn't stay there. But where to keep it? Kevin was right. Banks reported big deposits to the IRS—ten thousand? Twenty? She wasn't sure of the threshold. Perhaps she could open several accounts—they wouldn't all have to be in Tucson, or even Arizona—and slowly make smaller deposits in all of them, consolidating later. That would take time, meaning she had to find a safe place for the money now.

Mackie wandered around the house, gazing at walls, cupboards, recessed lights. The whole place felt different, no longer the massive embodiment of a complex nest of problems, just simply hers, but totally. The moment she realized that, the solution came, obvious, funny, right: Jenna's fountain.

More accurately, the spot in the front hall where Jenna's fountain was supposed to have stood. Jenna's fountain, sculpted by a New York artist now living in Tubac, would have cost $1,750, but the money ran out before the delivery date. All that remained of the idea were a few photographs somewhere—polished steel geometries, resembling spiky coral formations from certain angles—and a hole under the tile for the plumbing, a hole patched temporarily with a scrap of plywood and covered by a red-clay planter.

Mackie rolled the planter aside. The scrap of plywood, cut out of the sub-floor, wasn't even nailed down, just rested on the edges of the empty plumbing space in the slab. Mackie raised it, stuffed the money in two shopping bags, dropped them inside. Then she replaced the plywood, rolled back the planter. The plant, a tall ficus, was drooping a little. She gave it half a pitcher of water, drank the rest herself, suddenly thirsty.

Ten-thirty. Mackie opened the front door: the first hot day, but the night still cool, west wind rising, blue TV lights glowing in most of the houses on Buena Vida Circle, no Lianne. She put on a jacket, locked the house, drove to the high school. The dark shapes of the goalposts seemed unsteady as she went by the field, as though they were losing their balance. The school itself was unlit, the parking lot empty.

Mackie drove east on Tanque Verde, turned onto Catalina Highway, found the little strip mall with a coffee place: Nth Degree. She parked outside, could see kids in there, a dozen or more, sprawled on chairs around a big table in the middle. A few of them looked familiar, and one she knew by name, Ashley, a Chinese-American girl who'd once been over to the house. And there, back to the window and slouched so low in her chair that only the top of her head showed—hair in that silver-and-turquoise comb for which there now waited on the kitchen table an antique matching ring: Lianne. Mackie knew that comb—hers, in fact, but Lianne liked to borrow it—knew that hair.

Almost eleven on a school night, but Mackie could re-

member being seventeen, and how intolerable her entrance
would be right now, or even finding her waiting outside.
Lianne didn't have a lot of friends. Mackie put the car in
drive, meaning to go home, be a cool mom about this instead of an embarrassment. At that moment, Lianne rose
slightly and leaned to her right, reaching for a cigarette offered by a blue-haired boy. As soon as she moved—forget
about that first sight of the profile—Mackie knew it wasn't
Lianne; except for the hair and the comb, no resemblance
at all.

She turned off the engine. The girl with the silver comb
resumed her former position, smoke rising above her, doing un-Lianne-like things from time to time. After five or
ten minutes, the kids started coming out, piling into cars.
Ashley appeared last, by herself, keys in hand. Mackie got
out of her car.

"Ashley?"

The girl turned, looked at her without recognition.

"Helen MacIsaac," Mackie said. "Lianne's mother."

"Oh, right. Hi."

"I looked in to see if she needed a ride home, but I guess
she's already gone."

"Lianne?" said Ashley. "She wasn't here."

"She wasn't?"

"Uh-uh. Not tonight."

"You wouldn't know where she went, by any chance?"

"How do you mean?"

"After the SAT prep."

Ashley's eyes went a little vague, under the influence of
some teenage code.

"She's not in trouble or anything," Mackie said. "A ride
home, that's all this is about."

Ashley watched the other kids driving off. "Um," she
said. "I didn't actually see her at SAT prep either."

"You didn't?"

Ashley shook her head. "She wasn't, like, there." She

saw some expression on Mackie's face and added, "But someone as smart as Lianne, it's probably not necessary."

"Is there any way you could have missed her?"

"In room one-one-six?" said Ashley. "Only three kids came tonight, besides me. Our class is great, don't get me wrong, but not the most ambitious, you know?"

Mackie went home. Four Buena Vida Circle was dark. Inside, she called: "Lianne? You home? Lianne?" She listened for the beep of the message machine, heard nothing.

Dark and freezing: the air conditioner left on, full blast. Mackie switched it off, turned on lights. The planter in the front hall looked a little off-center. She moved it, raised the plywood, peered in the hole: shopping bags still there, still full. She put the planter back in place, getting it exactly right this time.

Back in Lianne's room, she ran her gaze over the shelves and the desk, opened the drawers, turned on the computer, saw nothing unusual. But what would be unusual? What was she looking for? Lianne was out late, like thousands of kids across the country tonight, maybe tens of thousands, just trying to hang out with friends, be by themselves, away from adults. Mackie understood: it wasn't that far back.

Her eye went to the crumpled sheet of paper in the wastebasket. She picked it out again, stared at that single word, *Dear*. After a while, its placement on the page—top left—plus that capital *D* began to suggest something.

Mackie returned to the kitchen, found the mail, handed to her that morning by the ponytailed mailman, checked it again: bills, as she remembered, but now meaningless, their dreadful power gone; and nothing for Lianne, who'd been at school when the mail came, in any case. But that *Dear* looked like the beginning of a letter, maybe abandoned, maybe started over on another sheet. Did Lianne know that mail could be left in the box for pickup, as long as you stamped it and raised the little flag for the mailman? Had the mailman looked in the box? No, not with her being right there.

Down at the mailboxes on Buena Vida Circle, the flag to number four wasn't raised, nothing there for pickup. Mackie flipped the box open anyway; and found something inside, a single sheet of paper.

Then she was unfolding it under her front door light. A twenty-dollar bill fell out, fluttered at her feet; more dreadful than any demand that had ever awaited her in that mailbox.

I'll call you real soon. Mackie hurried in, listening for the message beep. Silence. She ran through all the old messages anyway, useless. Then she called Kevin on his cell. He answered after five or six rings. "Yo," he said. Mackie heard laughter in the background, laughter, music, tinkling glasses.

"Kevin—" she began.

"Well, hi there! If it isn't my favorite ex-wife in the whole Wild Wild West." Blues music: he was at that bar on Speedway.

"We've got a problem," Mackie said.

"Nothing we can't solve," Kevin said, "especially now." He added something else, lost in a Doppler effect of passing hilarity.

"Can you come over?" Mackie said. "We need to talk."

"What?"

"I said we need to talk."

"I'm in Scottsdale."

How quick to celebrate: then she realized she'd been about as quick, could still taste $150 champagne at the back of her mouth. "You don't have to come over. We just need to talk."

"About what?"

"Lianne."

"I didn't catch that."

"Lianne," said Mackie, louder this time. When Kevin spoke again, the background wasn't so noisy.

"What about her?"

"She's . . ." How to put it? Run away? Eloped? "She didn't come home today. I found this letter." Mackie read it, skipping only what came between *I know you under-stand* and *I'll call real soon*—the part that said *You under-stand so much. Don't think I haven't noticed. And your holding everything together—I'll never forget it. You're the best.* No point in subjecting him to that.

Kevin was silent for a moment. Then he said: "The little slut."

"What did you say?"

"Lianne. She's so hot to trot for that fucking cowboy she can't see straight."

"I don't understand a word you're saying."

"Her boyfriend, as she calls him, is shit. Thirty-five if he's a day, married, a kid or two."

"You know him?"

"Sure. He's a wrangler down at Ocotillo."

"And you didn't do anything about it?"

"Such as?"

"Telling me, for starters."

"Telling you what, exactly?"

"About him."

"Figured that was up to her."

"If you're right about the details—"

"Trust me."

"—then she's in trouble and I had a right to know."

"She's a big girl," Kevin said.

"And our daughter."

"When are you going to start learning how the world works?" he said.

That enraged her. "You're fucked up," she said.

"Hey! Watch how you—"

Her voice rose over his. "That's why everything you do fucks up."

"Jesus Christ. What's gotten into you?"

"An aversion to fuckups," Mackie said. "Are you going back tonight?"

"Back where?"

"The ranch."

"Why would I do that?"

"Because you work there," Mackie said. "How drunk are you?"

"Just got a little buzz on, that's all. A pleasant one, till you called. Did anyone mention there's not much fun left in you?"

Mackie thought of all her admirers, former admirers, at Buckaroo's: it was almost funny. "I'll be more amusing after you get back there and see what's going on."

A pause. Kevin had pauses of different lengths, signifying different surprises in the works. The longest, three or four seconds like this, meant a big one. "I'm actually between jobs right now. I thought you knew."

"How would I know?"

"From Lianne."

"The little slut, as you call her, didn't say a word."

A silence followed, a silence in which Mackie assumed Kevin felt guilty, while her own mind went back to Lianne walking up Buena Vida Circle on a Sunday night, not dropped off at the door because of how Dad was always in a hurry, she'd said; and she'd been humming to herself. Mackie also remembered the report card: *Absent: 14*.

"When did they fire you?"

"Who said I was fired?"

"When did you leave, then?"

"A while back."

Lianne's not saying a word about that took on a different meaning.

Up in Scottsdale, a woman with a British accent said: "There you are, Kevin." Followed by muffling as he covered the receiver with his hand.

"Kevin?" Mackie said.

He came back on the line. "I wouldn't worry too much about it," he said.

"What are you saying?"

"She'll get sick of him pretty soon, drag her ass back home."

"How can you talk about her that way?" Mackie said.

Kevin laughed, a laugh meant to sound wicked. "I'm not being judgmental," he said. "I remember what seventeen was like."

The British woman said, "I want to hear all about it."

Mackie did not. "What's the boyfriend's name?" she said.

"Jimmy Marz."

She hung up.

Mackie drove across the desert, road map on the seat beside her. At first a car or two went by the other way; then she was alone. She remembered everything about Lianne that morning: what she'd said—*I hope I've got your genes,* and *as flies to wanton boys*; how she hadn't wanted her lunch money for the week; and most of all, that kiss on the cheek. Mackie thought she could still feel it. And that quick tight hug: her daughter wasn't planning to come home anytime soon.

The pavement ended. She flew past a sign: COLDWATER WASH. Dry, of course. All those dry washes, streams, rivers: the irony was starting to wear on her. It got mixed up with the message of the mountains around her, now invisible: nothing you can do will last. She crossed a valley full of tall cacti, a shadowy army in a formation of their own devising. A sign arched over the road: OCOTILLO

RANCH. Lights shone in the distance, a ridge rising behind them, not quite as dark as night. Mackie drove up to the main lodge, shut off the engine.

A dog slept on the porch. The lodge was quiet. Mackie opened the door, heard a horse neighing, not far away. She had one foot on the ground when the front door of the lodge opened and a man appeared. A tall man, bald on top with a long stringy fringe: Dane. Cooling metal under Mackie's hood made popping sounds; like snare drums to her, but Dane didn't seem to hear. He spun a cigarette into the darkness, stepped back in, and closed the door.

Mackie stayed still, foot on the ground, door open. Dane didn't belong here. This ranch lay within the narrowing sliver where her life and Kevin's still overlapped. Dane was from another world, Red's world, down in Agua Fría, a completely separate world that had ceased to exist for her, except in memory. It made no sense. She listened to the wind, felt the remoteness of the place. But Dane was here, inside the overlap. Therefore that feeling of remoteness was somehow false. She pictured Ocotillo on the road map, realized it was roughly equidistant to Tucson and Agua Fría, an equilateral triangle that was actually pretty small. Something slipped deep inside her, like a weight-bearing support starting to give.

Mackie got out of the car, walked softly around the lodge. She smelled a swimming pool nearby, heard the faint sucking of water at a drain. The lodge rose high on the other side. She climbed some stairs, found herself on a balcony. A glass slider looked into a darkened dining room, place settings reflecting a gleam of starlight here and there. Mackie tried the slider; unlocked. Something bumped the back of her legs. She wheeled around: a dog, tail wagging. She patted his head. He walked around in a little circle and lay down with a sigh. Mackie went inside.

She moved silently between the tables, past a bar, a fridge humming somewhere behind it, and into what must

have been the main room of the lodge: high ceiling, Indian
rugs, leather furniture, flowers everywhere, all in shadow.
At the far end, a little fire burned in a huge stone fireplace,
the only light source. Five people sat around the fire—
Dane; an old man; two women of about her own age,
dressed in denim, their faces ruddy from weather; and a
younger man also in denim, also ruddy-faced. A younger
man, but not thirty-five, probably ten years older than that,
silvery glints in his mustache. One of the women had a
guitar in her lap, but she wasn't playing it. The other
woman wiped her eyes on the back of her sleeve. Mackie
watched them for a while. They talked a little. They drank
a lot—some golden drink, like scotch or brandy. The
woman wiped her eyes. Once the old man did too. Dane
took a deep breath, let it out, shook his head. No sign of
Lianne. Mackie waited for something to happen, for Dane
to leave, or one of the others to go somewhere she could
follow. All that happened was a slow fading of the darkness. An alarm buzzed somewhere in the lodge. Mackie
became aware that she was seeing colors. She hurried back
through the dining room, out the slider, down the stairs and
around to her car.

All the way home, the conviction that Lianne would be
there kept growing in her. She drove faster and faster, so
unaware of everything around her that she almost didn't
notice the gas needle, below empty. She filled up at a station on the Ajo Highway, went inside to pay.

The morning papers were just coming in. Mackie bought
the *Arizona Gazette*, found the robbery on an inside page,
no pictures, the article not very long, news getting old even
faster than she'd imagined. She scanned it quickly, then
backed up, read it again. Then went outside, leaning into
the building, and tried once more. Lines of print, ordinary
dull newspaper language, were on the move, writhing
around like snakes. The bank robber had been identified as
Jimmy Marz, 29, assistant wrangler at the Ocotillo Ranch.

He'd been shot dead by Clayton Krupsha, captain of detectives on the Agua Fría force, while resisting arrest.

"You okay, miss?" said the attendant.

Mackie nodded, or said something, or made a gesture.

Back at 4 Buena Vida Circle: no Lianne. She rolled
away the planter, raised the plywood scrap: money still
there. She began to sense some terrible cosmic deal.

Twenty-five

In the middle of the night, Sergeant Falco played a trick on Loeb, jumping out of character without warning, or possibly just growing in an unexpected direction. Loeb awoke, dim orange light leaking into his room from the sodium arcs on the border. He got up, switched on the desk lamp, wrote on a sheet of paper: *Sgt. F. is fucking Athena.* He yawned and added: *has been fucking her for years.* After that, he flipped open the laptop and started writing a scene out of sequence, something he'd never done—the scene where Timothy Bolt's suspicions are first aroused. It began with Bolt looking for the steak knives in the kitchen of Athena's condo at Crested Butte and went quickly after that, about as quickly as he'd ever written, screenful after screenful, all punctuated by the irregular dripping rhythm of a giant melting icicle, big as a broadsword, hanging in front of Athena's bedroom window; a metaphorical effect he'd never before come close to. Then, from out of nowhere, he thought of Mary Jane and what she had said re Falco and Bolt: *That note of mutual distrust could be even stronger.* His hands went still; a well inside drying up, like that. He got a strange feeling, strange and creepy, sensed a shadowy authorial presence somewhere behind his back. Had Mary Jane found her way into the supply room, deep in his subconscious?

The sky lightened. Mexico appeared, a complex awakening on the far side of the steel wall, but Loeb hardly noticed. He doodled for a while—pistols, kites, musical notes. When he tired of that, he just tapped the pen, taking a long time to notice what it was: the pen from Buena Vida Estates.

The newspaper thumped down outside his door. Loeb read the account of the robbery at Patriot Frontier Savings and Loan, learned nothing new. He studied the artist's composite: not close. He was wondering whose descriptions the artist had relied on, when the phone rang.

Harry. "How are things in the heartland?"

"Is this the heartland?" Loeb said. "It's starting not to feel that way."

"How come?"

"Heartland implies stability. This place doesn't have it."

"Hey, that's pretty interesting," said Harry. "Kind of an aperçu, right? I've got a little piece of news."

"Oh?" said Loeb, casual, but thinking right away: movie deal.

"Lucy Pearlstein got fired. Or will be, by the end of the day."

"Lucy?" Loeb suddenly felt as dependent on Lucy as if he were a toddler and she the mother, even though she'd backed away from a new contract, and never given him the impression of even liking Timothy Bolt much.

"Strictly a numbers game," said Harry. "The book business becoming like any other business—the old, old story. No one reads. Didn't I mention that?"

"What's she going to do?"

"Who?"

"Lucy."

"Who knows? The point is, they'll be assigning you someone new."

"And?"

"Looks like it's going to be Benjamin Klein."

"Benjie? Lucy's assistant Benjie?"

"The same."

"Benjie's an intern, Harry. He's still at NYU."

"He's taking the semester off," Harry said.

"This is bad, isn't it?" Loeb said.

"How so?"

"It shows where they peg me."

Harry didn't answer. A rooster crowed on the other side of the wall, harsh and loud. Loeb felt a strong need to hear something promising, no matter how vague or tenuous.

"Any news at all from Hollywood?" he said. A tenth-hand rumor, already discredited, would do.

"Don't even mention Hollywood these days," Harry said. "If Timothy Bolt had started as an action figure, then maybe."

"So we're in trouble."

"I didn't say that."

"Give me some advice, Harry."

"Like what?"

"What to do next."

"Come home. Finish the book. Make it sing on every page."

"And that will be enough?"

"Enough for what?"

"To make them give me a new contract."

Long silence.

"So the answer's no."

"Don't be pessimistic," Harry said. "It's catching. And pessimism never writes checks."

"I'm optimistic," Loeb said. "Wildly."

"Nick?"

"Yes?"

"It sucks that being a good writer isn't enough." The best and worst thing Harry had ever said to him. "If only," he went on, "you had a hook."

"Like what?"

"You know—say you were a DA or a medical examiner, the usual. Something for talk shows to talk about."

Loeb knew some of those writers, had read their books: infuriating. "What about if my plane is hijacked on the way home and I single-handedly subdue the hijackers and bring it smoothly down on the infield at Yankee Stadium?"

"Then you'll be on the bestseller list next Sunday."

Or solve a crime. A major one.

"Late for a meeting," Harry said. "Chin up."

Loeb turned into Buena Vida Circle, went by some brand-new houses all jammed together, parked in front of number four. He'd expected an office, but this was just another hacienda, or whatever they were. An orange tree grew in the front yard, the oranges unreal, too big and bright. A van from Coronado Locksmiths sat in the driveway. Loeb got out of the pickup and walked to the front door.

A workman knelt on the threshold, door open, screwdriver in hand. Loeb heard running water in the house.

"Changing the locks?" he said.

"You writing a book?" said the workman.

An unexpected bit of snappy New York–style sarcasm: Loeb found he didn't miss it at all. "I'm actually looking for Buena Vida Estates," he said. "Kevin Larkin."

The workman glanced up at him, squinting into the sun. "Hey," he called over his shoulder. "Someone at the door."

The water stopped running. Loeb heard footsteps, squeak of sneakers on a tile floor. He readied his little speech: *Sorry to bother you, Mr. Larkin. A woman forgot her purse. No ID in it. Just this. (Hold up pen.) I know it's a long shot but maybe if I described her—*

The footsteps grew louder, light, probably female. A woman moved around a big planter in the front hall, came into view. Speech unnecessary: Red, but in her T-shirt and jeans mode; and no one using that composite would ever find her. But he already had, had solved a major crime, and before breakfast. The smart move right now would be to get back in the truck, drive away, make two calls, the first to Krupsha, so he could come get her; the second to Harry, so he could get started on the press release. MYSTERY WRITER CRACKS REAL-LIFE CASE. And Benjie Klein: he'd have to get those presses rolling, rush truck convoys on the road to Borders, B&N, the independents, stock the shelves to bursting. And those ridiculous cardboard dumps right by the cash register: don't forget them.

That would have been the smart move, dealing with a bank-robbing stripper, guilty as sin. The problem was that while the composite looked the part, the flesh-and-blood woman did not.

Someone at the door; not Lianne, of course, who would have walked right in. Mackie's pulse rose as she moved through the house. Then she saw him: not a cop, not Samsonov, Turbo, Dane; some stranger, his stance unthreatening, polite. He held up a pen, one of the purple-and-gold giveaway pens, the idea Kevin's, the color choice Jenna's. Something about Buena Vida? She started calming down.

"Yes?"

"You left this behind," he said.

"I did? Where?"

"At the Delbert McClinton discussion," he said. "In Agua Fría."

Then she recognized him. The customer who'd wanted to talk about "When Rita Leaves" and also wanted to know her real name: he'd found her, penetrated the overlap. Her pulse got going again. Ferdie, down on his knees—he'd done the locks on all the houses—glanced from her to the customer, back to her.

"Thanks," she said, taking the pen.

"I'm interested in real estate," he said.

Mackie knew that was clever somehow; it scared her. "Sorry, I can't help you," she said, trying to sound businesslike. "I'm not involved with Buena Vida anymore." He was watching her carefully; there was nothing of that

Buckaroo's clientele creepiness about him—he wasn't even bad-looking—but she didn't like that watchfulness. He'd found her. "And all the houses are sold," she added.

None of that even slowed him down. "Maybe there are similar developments nearby," he said. "Mind if I pick your brain for a minute or two?" He gave her a smile; nice, friendly, maybe not even intended to chill. Bub and his stupid gift, a pen falling out of the car: that was all it took.

He waited for an answer. Ferdie waited too. Mrs. Thorsen came out of her house with golf clubs, glanced over.

"I'm in a bit of a hurry," Mackie said.

"On your way to work?"

The smile was still on his face, broader if anything. The word *Buckaroo's* was coming next. "Maybe just for a minute," Mackie said, standing aside to let him in.

"Hey!" said Ferdie. "What about Red Rock Vistas, over on Skyline?"

The man didn't seem to hear. He was already in the kitchen. She followed him. His eyes took in everything—tangerines in the bowl, car keys on the table, lobster pot on the drying rack.

Mackie closed the door, lowered her voice. "I don't get involved with the customers."

"Who could blame you?" he said. "I've seen some of them."

"Meaning you shouldn't have come here."

He turned to her. "I didn't think you'd actually be at this address—that part's pure luck. Who's Kevin Larkin?"

"Why do you want to know?"

"His name's on the pen."

"So? You don't really care about real estate."

Their eyes met. "Then call it filling in the blanks," he said.

Mackie thought: maybe he is a cop, after all. She had to

force herself not to back up a step, not to glance around for some escape route. There was none.

"Blanks in what?" she said. But what kind of cop would have had anything to say about her interpretation of "When Rita Leaves"?

"Your life," he said.

"How is that your business?" she said. And if he was a cop, didn't he have to identify himself? "Who the hell are you?"

"Nick Loeb."

Yes, he'd told her that already, in the parking lot. What else had he said? Something that had made her laugh: *I can compartmentalize as well as anybody*. That didn't sound like a cop either. "I meant what do you do," Mackie said.

"I'm a writer."

"A reporter?"

"No," he said. "Crime fiction."

She didn't like the sound of that. She examined his face, intelligent, alert, judgmental, found nothing there to help her. "I'm not going to go out with you or date you or have sex with you or whatever else is on your mind."

There was a knock at the door. "All set," Ferdie called from the other side.

"Come in," Mackie said, her face reddening a little, so stupidly.

Ferdie handed her a bill: $445. "Those deadbolts are a little pricey," he said, looking at them both with interest.

Mackie turned to block Loeb's view, took the roll of money from her pocket, peeled off what Ferdie wanted. It hit her then: what would happen if Nick Loeb opened today's paper or turned on the TV?

"But when push comes to shove," Ferdie said on his way out, "they're worth every penny."

Now Loeb's eyes were on Mackie's front pocket, where the money was.

Mackie held the door open. Ferdie was driving off.

"You'll have to go now too." She had to get him out. And then what? Get out herself? But what about Lianne? She understood how murder could suddenly seem logical, right, the answer.

"You didn't ask if I've published anything," Loeb said.

"So?"

"Everyone asks that when they hear I'm a writer."

"Why would anyone call themselves a writer if they hadn't published anything?" Mackie said.

He laughed. "Careful where you say that."

"Thanks for the tip," Mackie said. "Good-bye."

He didn't move. The image of Samsonov by the pool came to her and her voice rose. "Get out."

"Why don't you call the police?" he said.

The phone rang as he spoke that last word. They both turned quickly, watched it ring again. Mackie picked it up.

"This is Mrs. Dekker from administration at Kolb High." Mrs. Dekker had one of those loud voices that carried far beyond the receiver. "Lianne's not in school today, and when a student accumulates fifteen absences in a term, the rules say we start calling the home."

"She's not feeling well," Mackie said.

"So she's there?" said Mrs. Dekker.

"Yes."

"Excellent. I hope she's better soon."

Mackie hung up. Loeb had moved over to the fridge, was looking at Lianne's school photo; she wore a little silver chain around her neck and had her hair up. "Who's this?" he said.

"No concern of yours."

"Your daughter? What's her name?"

Mackie said nothing.

"Where is she?" he said, his eyes still on the photo.

"I will call the police," she said.

"Really?" Loeb took the photo off the fridge, held it up. "Even with her being on the video?"

"What video?" Mackie said. She snatched the photo from him. "I don't know what you're talking about." But she got a strange cold feeling on the backs of her shoulders.

"The video Clay Krupsha showed me—captain of detectives in Agua Fría. He thinks you and Jimmy Marz were strangers. I don't. And now I'm sure. Banks tape everything—didn't you know?"

Mackie sat down. She had no choice: her legs went dead beneath her. The adrenaline for running, for flight, surged through her anyway, making her voice unsteady. "Lianne was there?" she said, incriminating herself completely. "In the bank?"

"You're trying to tell me you didn't know?" Loeb said.

"It's not true."

"She comes in at the end, like an ordinary customer—just in time to see Jimmy get shot. Was she too late? Is that what went wrong?"

Mackie felt a sudden pain, deep within her, like a hard contraction. "Did anything happen to her?"

"She backs right out."

Mackie tried to see inside him, couldn't get past the intellect in his eyes. "I don't believe you," she said. "You're making this up."

"I can probably arrange a viewing of the tape," he said.

She started to hate him. "Why are you doing this?"

"That's a good question," Loeb said. "Before you pulled off the bank job, I just wanted to meet you. The way you danced to 'When Rita Leaves,' all that. Now I'd like to hear the whole story."

"Why?"

"Call it my assignment."

"Are you working with the police? Do they know where I am?"

"You'd be locked up already if they did. All they have is a lousy composite and the fact that a dancer named Red got away with half a million dollars."

But Mackie knew she'd gotten away with nothing. The decision wasn't even hard. Could cosmic deals be undone? "Take it," she said. She went into the hall, rolled the planter aside, kicked away the scrap of plywood, bent down for the shopping bags. He watched.

"Do what you want with it, I don't care," she said, handing him the bags. She had to get rid of him, find Lianne, run. Where could she be? In shock, holed up somewhere? Or was it even worse, in some way she couldn't imagine?

Loeb stood in her front hall, the money in his hands. "Just keep you out of it?"

"And my daughter."

The expression on his face changed, appeared for the first time a little unsure. The intelligence and alertness were still there, maybe even more obviously—she could almost feel the pressure of his thinking pushing into her own brain—but the judgmental part was softening: did she see something helpful now?

"I'd have to know a lot more," he said.

Maybe not. "Why?" she said.

He walked back into the kitchen, looked again at Lianne's picture, now on the table.

"Don't you get it?" Mackie said. "The money's yours."

He glanced down at the shopping bags in his hands, put them down. "I don't want it."

"You don't want half a million dollars?"

"Not this way."

"Some other way?"

He didn't answer.

"There's a reward," she said. "You're planning to turn me in."

"I don't know about any reward," he said.

But she was close; she thought she could see it in his eyes, maybe a little like hers after all, not always good at hiding what was inside. A writer of crime fiction, clever, watchful: he was from another world and could have any motive at all. How could she trust him? She couldn't. That was that. "You want the whole story," she said.

"Yes."

"Then why not start with the funniest part?" she said. "The money's not even in there."

"It's not?"

She shook her head. "Take a look."

He bent over the bags. Mackie took one quick step toward the counter, grabbed the lobster pot with both hands, wheeled, and brought the base of it down on the back of Loeb's head; not as hard as she could, but hard enough.

Twenty-six

Lianne didn't like the little blue Honda anymore. Its zippiness, perkiness, hopefulness: all wrong now, in bad taste, heartless. She drove it slowly along the winding gravel cemetery trails. The cemetery was its own world, a patch of country inside the city, and not even desert country, but full of dense, dark green cypresses, and other wetter-weather trees whose names she didn't know. Jimmy wasn't going to like it here.

She glimpsed a little group of people, motionless in the distance, and left the bike behind one of those cypresses. A narrower walking trail led her up a rise and around to the far side of the . . . mourners. Wasn't that the official word? Thirty or forty yards beyond them, Lianne found a bench screened off by round flowering bushes. The whole goddamn place was just bursting with life, all of it vegetable.

Everyone was dressed up, except for the grave diggers in their white coveralls, like golf caddies on TV. They lowered the coffin, brass handles gleaming in the sunlight, down into a rectangular hole. Who had made this decision? All wrong for Jimmy—he should have been turned to ashes, and the ashes scattered off one of those precipices on the Ruby Road. A man in a white collar took off his sunglasses and said a few words, the sound carrying up the rise to Lianne, but not the meaning. The mourners kept their sunglasses on. Lianne recognized some of them—Mr. Croft, Rags, Nadine, Ramon, others from the ranch; and figured out the identity of two more, standing off by themselves, hand in hand—a woman with glossy black hair and a little boy, maybe three or four years old.

For a while the little boy seemed to be listening to the sermon or speech or whatever it was. Then his mind must have wandered, and he started getting restless. The woman with the glossy black hair—Lianne could tell she was beautiful, even from this distance, maybe part Indian—gave him a gentle tug. He shaped right up, went quiet again, but a minute or two later was back to looking around. His gaze swept by Lianne, returned, settled. He saw her, for sure. His face got all interested. Little Jamie.

You fuck her, your ex-wife, while you were up in Phoenix?

Just the once. After a few drinks, when we got the word it wasn't leukemia.

Then they'd laughed about it, just laughed and laughed, sharing the joke and the relief and lots more. He was going to rob the bank anyway, right? So her suggestion, taking it all for themselves, hadn't made any difference in what had happened. But what if she'd said, "Tell them no." Then he'd be alive, making no the right answer. Therefore, instead of making things better for him with her brainy idea, she'd let him down. And then she remembered something awful. A different context and all that, but it made no difference at that moment: Jimmy, the two of them naked in the South End bunkhouse, when they'd both wanted more, more, more, saying: *You're going to kill me.* Lianne started crying; just tears, no sound, so no one heard.

The minister, or whatever he was, stopped talking. One of the grave diggers handed him a shovel, not a special new one with a silver spade, but an old dirty one like the kind in any garage. That bothered Lianne a lot. The minister scooped up some rich brown dirt from a pile by one end of the rectangle and tossed it in. That bothered her too, the way he did it; wasn't there some better way of shoveling at times like this?

He handed the shovel back to the grave digger. The mourners shed their stillness, came alive, started shuffling toward their cars. That was it? They were going to leave him like that, exposed? Little Jamie, waiting as his mother opened the rear door of Mr. Croft's car for him, suddenly turned and looked at Lianne again. This time he said something too, and pointed right at her. His mother took no notice, gave him a little push inside. Everyone drove off.

They weren't even out of sight before a grave digger drove up in an earth-mover, picked up a load of dirt, and dropped it into the rectangular hole. Then came a forklift with a gravestone, dazzling white. The earthmover was digging into the dirt pile for more when one of the grave diggers checked his watch, said something. They all stopped what they were doing, moved off across the perfect landscape, one of them dancing a bit to some music in his head.

That left her alone with Jimmy. Something tangible, like a tendon, connected him down in the partly filled-in hole to her up on the rise, everything else not there. Lianne felt its pull, gave in to it, walking down the rise to the grave site. She examined the stone, still on the forks of the lift: JIMMY MARZ, his dates, so close together, right for some other species, and an inscription: *where the buffalo roam*.

Lianne picked up the shovel, climbed into the grave. She shoveled the dirt off the coffin, a foot or so, then crouched beside it, down at the base of the hole. The lid was clamped shut with brass fittings, but they weren't locked down or anything like that: why would they be? Lianne unfastened them and opened the coffin.

It wasn't him!

But it was.

Jimmy lay on his back, dressed all in white. Tears came again, oceans, and sound too this time, terrible sound from deep inside her. A minute or two passed before she could see him clearly.

Dressed all in white, and his skin was white too, not him at all. Another difference was the patch over one eye; maybe there'd been no way to fix him up. "They hurt you so much," she said; and no one to comfort him. Lianne touched his lips, not cold exactly, just the ambient temperature. From those lips had come things like *She tastes like honey from the bee*. Lianne parted them slightly with her fingertips, wanting one more sight of those perfect little white teeth. The problem was that with all the white around—clothes, skin—his teeth looked yellow.

"Jimmy," she said, just to do something normal, like speak his name when they were close. But this wasn't Jimmy, not with that eyepatch and those yellow teeth. This was some horrible practical joke, or the worst kind of bad dream, and maybe if she closed her eyes and opened them again it would be over.

Lianne closed her eyes and opened them again. They'd left the little diamond stud in Jimmy's ear. Lianne unclipped it very carefully, so as not to pinch him even the least little bit, and put it in her pocket.

"Okay if I hang on to it, Jimmy?" she said. She had nothing else of his, not a single material thing, no hard thing to go into the future with, to remind her how real this was, in case she ever needed reminding. Lianne kissed his lips; could they still be called lips, with that color, that texture? Then, not really knowing what her hands were doing, her mind lagging behind, she was opening his white pants. They were normal white pants, cotton, with snap and zipper, just too-bright white, pants he would never wear.

She looked inside, remembering when he'd been cocky. The funny thing was, this one part of him didn't seem quite as dead as all the rest; maybe because soft cocks weren't fully alive anyway, not as lively as they could be.

Seeing it like this was almost normal. One more kiss, right there. Good-bye.

Lianne closed the coffin, clamped down the brass clamps. Ashes would have been so much better. You could say—he's dead, so what does it matter? But it would have mattered to Jimmy. The steam rising off the horses in the moonlight, the taste of those salted tomato wedges out of his hand, the gray hawk, wings outlined in gold: it mattered. She climbed out of the hole, wishing for a gray hawk now. The sky was empty. She shoveled back in all the dirt she'd shoveled out. Then she shoveled in the rest of it, the whole huge pile, completely filling the hole to ground level, leaving nothing for the grave diggers but the setting of the stone. After that, there was nothing to do but walk back down the gravel path to the blue Honda. It was over. Her muscles suddenly felt weak, as though she'd been sick for a while. She wanted to go home, wanted to have her mom around.

A tall man was sitting on the blue Honda, making it look like a kid's thing beneath him. "Hey," Lianne called; it pissed her off. He turned: a tall man with straggly fringe at the sides and back of his bald head: Dane.

"No offense," he said, getting off the bike. "Just resting my legs."

Lianne went closer. His gaze started at her face, descended slowly, rose in one or two jerks, like a balky elevator.

"My condolences," he said. What were you supposed to say to that? How about: *You got him killed.* But Dane didn't know she knew; best to keep it that way. Lianne just nodded. A shiny new pickup was parked behind a line of cypresses; the lettering on the side read: ALL-AMERICAN AMUSEMENTS, INC. "You doin' okay?"

"Yeah."

"Got flowers in the back," Dane said.

"You're too late," Lianne said.

"Never too late for flowers," Dane said. "Maybe you can help me arrange them right."

"I've got to get going," Lianne said.

"Only take a few minutes," Dane said. "A time like this, they say it helps to talk."

"Who's they?"

"You know," said Dane. "Counselors. The four stages of grief."

"What are those?"

"Maybe it's five," Dane said. "I don't know the actual names. But everything ends up okay."

Then it was bullshit. But flowers couldn't hurt. She walked with Dane to the pickup, the little diamond stud scratching her thigh lightly through her pocket with every step.

"Me and Jimmy go way back," Dane said. "He ever mention that?"

"Yes."

He handed her a bouquet of irises from the bed of the truck, carried the daisies himself. "This was in Arivaca," Dane said as they approached the grave. The grave diggers were back. They'd gotten over any surprise about the grave being filled in, already had the stone in place, and were rolling out sod as green as movie grass. "Everyone rode back then, but Jimmy was always the best," Dane said. "What did he say about me?"

Lianne shrugged. "You were too rough on the ecosystem."

Dane laughed. The grave diggers finished up, rode off on their machines. "How about the daisies over here, and the lilies like so?" Dane said.

"They're irises," Lianne said. "I'll do it."

She bent down, arranged the flowers at the base of Jimmy's stone. They looked all right but she couldn't really tell, the way Dane's shadow was falling on them. Some kind of shiny mineral was embedded here and there in the stone; it made *where the buffalo roam* sparkle.

"Anything else Jimmy told you?" Dane said.

"About what?"

"Me."

"Going way back. Rough on the ecosystem. That was it."

"Nothing else?"

"Oh, yeah. You worked for the water company."

She rose. Dane was shaking his head. "That Jimmy," he said.

"What do you mean?"

"He was a character."

"I don't know about that."

"In a good way," Dane said. "What the hell was the whole bank thing about anyway?"

"I guess he wanted to rob a bank."

"But why?"

"For the money."

She heard Dane taking a deep breath; it whistled a little in his nose. Lianne thought: *coke*. "I meant," Dane said, "why would a guy like Jimmy who'd been straight and narrow most all his life up and do something like that?"

"No idea," Lianne said.

"Doesn't make sense to me," Dane said. "What did he tell you?"

"Nothing." Best to keep it that way, especially since he seemed so interested in knowing.

"Not a word? Like how he came up with the idea in the first place?"

Would Dane believe that, not a word? He'd seen her and Jimmy at the South End bunkhouse; maybe it was asking too much. "He talked about having his own ranch someday."

"And?"

"Maybe once he said something about having to rob a bank to get there, that future. But I took it as a joke."

Dane was gazing at the stone. "He never brought it up again?"

"No."

"So the first you heard about what happened?"

"Was on TV."

"Must have been rough," Dane said, turning to her. "How did he ever get an idea like that?"

"I don't know. Where do ideas come from?"

"It just doesn't seem like him."

"You're saying Jimmy wasn't smart?"

"Hey. Nothing like that." Dane gave her a pat on the back, his long skinny hand covering both shoulder blades. "He was the smartest kid in the class back in third grade."

"Yeah?"

"Sure. The teacher put a gold star on his forehead. Course there were only four of us in the class."

Lianne almost laughed, only didn't because it was way too soon. She could just see Jimmy with that gold star, half-hidden under a lock of hair.

"Come to think of it," Dane said, "I might still have a few pictures from those days kicking around."

"Pictures of Jimmy?"

"Maybe even a few when he was a teenager, getting into rodeo."

"I wouldn't mind seeing them sometime."

"How's now?"

"Now?"

"Why not? I can just throw that bike of yours in the truck. And you can keep any of the pictures you want."

Where the buffalo roam glittered at Lianne in the sunlight. Down below, Jimmy was stuck in a box, teeth and skin the wrong color, all his identity gone. Maybe one day she could dig him up, turn him into ashes, do it right. She wondered about raising the subject with Dane—she might need help. He was waiting for an answer about those photos.

"Thanks," she said.

"Don't mention it," he said, steering her gently toward the path.

Twenty-seven

Loeb was paralyzed. He also had a splitting headache. Everything was dim, reminding him of the recovery room after his ACL repair. For a moment, he got a little confused and imagined that was where he was, in the hospital in Burlington, Vermont, age twenty-one, mediocre collegiate ski racing career over. Then he realized that there were no headaches in the recovery room, all heads still full of anesthetic; headache pain meant no anesthetic, no anesthetic meant no operation, no operation meant he wasn't twenty-one. Too bad: because after they'd moved him to his own room, his girlfriend at the time, also a skier, with the best legs ever, before or since, had stayed past visiting hours, turned off all the lights, pulled down the sheet, and—

And realization number two: The inability to move was not the same as paralysis, not if you were fastened to a bed with duct tape, wound round and round like a cocoon. What were cocoons? Creepy caesuras on the way to some new form of life. That was Loeb's first coherent thought; at least he thought it was a coherent thought. His second coherent thought was that Timothy Bolt had found himself in almost exactly this situation, bound with duct tape, helpless, clock ticking down. But where?

Digression: Clocks didn't tick anymore, except in Hitchcock movies. *Rear Window* was his favorite, Hitchcock more scrupulous than usual about point-of-view, maybe forced by the title alone. Loeb's third possibly coherent thought was a revision of that best-legs-ever judgment, before or since. Red's were better.

Cocoon. Timothy Bolt. Situation like this. Where? It came to him: *White Out,* his first book, and not only that, but the first big scene, fifty or sixty pages in, when Bolt, duct-taped and left for dead in a snow cave, regains consciousness to find he's sharing the cave with a bleary-eyed grizzly bear just emerging from hibernation. The bear, irritable but still in an ursine fog, takes a grouchy swipe at Bolt, clawing through enough duct tape for him to wriggle free and escape. The high he'd felt after that, not Bolt, but he, Loeb, in the middle of the night at his computer: to pull a job like the snow cave scene with nothing but words alone—crime fiction.

Situation like this: on his back in a bedroom, not a cave, the blinds drawn, time of day unclear. No grizzly bear. Ursa Major, Ursa Minor: a scrap of vulgar doggerel created itself instantly in his mind, last word *vagina.*

On his back, in a cocoon. By turning his head to one side, Loeb could make out a framed photograph on a bedside table: girl on a horse. The image led to another—girl, the same girl but older, on the fridge. Recent memory came to order. He was a prisoner at number four Buena Vida Circle, in Red's house. Beautiful legs, and so was the rest of her. Also, he liked her voice. And her taste in music. And how she'd tricked him into bending over the shopping bags: the last thing he'd seen was the money in them, after all.

But she'd robbed a bank, almost certainly in concert with her daughter and Jimmy Marz. And she'd knocked him out. With what? He remembered a little rush of wind, and peripheral silver. Loeb mulled that over for a while before tugging his mind back to the main point: It was possible she didn't like him in return. And she was dangerous. Conclusion: He had to get out. MYSTERY NOVELIST CRACKS CASE was one thing, MYSTERY DEATH OF MYSTERY

NOVELIST another; and a bondage kind of death that would pique the interest of V, S&M neighbor poet, in a way that would be sheer purgatory for him, whether there was an afterlife or not. It occurred to him, perhaps a little late, to test the strength of the duct tape. What if it were merely symbolic, easily rent with one little twist like this? But no. Loeb tested it again, this time with an all-out, muscle-bursting heave that spiked his headache up to another level but had no effect on his confinement.

He raised his head, looked down, checked himself out. Ankles taped together, knees taped together, arms taped to his sides from fingertips to shoulders. What would Bolt do, absent the grizzly bear? Absent? Had he really used the word in that hideous way? Perhaps he had brain damage. He tried and failed to come up with a quick mental test for brain damage, perhaps proving the case right there. A phone rang beside the bed, startling him. He counted the rings: four. Somewhere in the house an answering machine picked up. He heard a man's voice, but could make out none of the words. But: the message machine. He was alone in the house. Now was the time to act.

This was what he did for a living, figuring out ways to get out of situations like this. Plotting, in a word; although Mary Jane considered it one of his weaknesses. Plotting, police procedure, knowing women. Knowing women meant understanding what Red had done inside that bank and why. Police procedure meant finding out what was going on in Krupsha's mind when he'd shot Jimmy Marz. Plotting meant getting out of here, and soon.

My God, he was suddenly thinking clearly indeed. He'd be coming up with something anytime now, for sure. Meanwhile, wouldn't it be nice to consult Mary Jane? He looked around: bedside phone, an arm's length away, if he could free his arm—and what was that? On the bureau, an open laptop that looked like his. Meaning what? That Red had taken it out of the pickup, brought it inside, searched through it. But without the password, what could she find? Even with it?

Loeb's password was *shibboleth*. For no particular reason, he tried to say it aloud. That was when he discovered his mouth was duct-taped too. It hit him: He would have to plot like never before. Maybe some sort of outline would help, but he hated outlines. In fact, and this struck him with the force of a drug-induced satori, he hated doing anything he didn't like. He began to see himself in a new light. But was there time for this sort of self-examination? Probably not; he had to make an outline, soon and without grizzlies.

Proceed from the known to the unknown. What did he know? Turbo crucified Whiskers. Lonnie Mendez's wife or girlfriend was withholding blow jobs and having sex with someone down the hall from Lonnie's room. Buck Samsonov gave him a free-drink coupon. Jimmy Marz robbed a bank with an empty gun. Krupsha shot him anyway, but that happened all the time, a cop thing about assuming all guns are loaded until proven otherwise, and Sergeant Falco would have done the same. Red got away with the money. The daughter was probably in on it too. Why else would she have been there? On the other hand, hadn't the daughter showed up after Red's escape? Simply late, or did it mean something else? Maybe what he needed to know was the original robbery plan. How else to understand what had gone wrong? Unless nothing had gone wrong, but wasn't that impossible, since Jimmy Marz was dead? And what kind of bank robber would have told him to take the money? Was that just a planned step on the way to knocking him out? But why, when he hadn't even known the money was there until she'd taken it from the hiding place?

There: the knowns, except they were full of question marks, like hunchbacks in a petroglyph. His head hurt, and admit it: he was stuck on the outline. Being stuck on the outline: even worse than being stuck in the middle of the story, embarrassing, like a sprinter somehow getting tangled in the starting blocks and falling on his face. The symbolism of the tape over his mouth was not lost on him. Maybe Red was in league with his publisher.

When stuck, Raymond Chandler had advised, have someone enter with a gun. No possibility of that, but the underlying idea was to start some action. Loeb started some action, the only action he could, struggling against his bonds. With all his strength he tried to pry his legs apart, to twist a hand free. He grunted, groaned, thrashed around the bed like a woman in labor; and then he was falling, a very short fall to the floor. That was when he discovered he wasn't actually taped to the bed.

Crash; and a buzzing sound rose in his head, got louder. So loud that after a minute or two he began to doubt the buzzing came from within. He twisted around, saw one of the walls bulge slightly, as though losing its solidity. Then a chainsaw poked through. The sight reminded him of a cartoon, possibly starring Yosemite Sam, but that didn't keep it from scaring him. A big chunk of plaster, Greenland-shaped, fell off the wall. Loeb writhed his way under the bed.

The buzzing stopped. Then came splintering sounds, a grunt, ripping; and a man saying, "Fuck." Footstep, another. The feet padded into view: tennis shoes, size ten or eleven, sprinkled with sawdust. They came closer and closer, stopped inches from Loeb's eyes.

The man's knees bent forward a little. Loeb heard patting sounds on the bed above him, followed by a whoosh of air as the covers were stripped off, flung across the room, landing with a *ploompf*. Hands appeared, strong and tanned. They reached forward; then came a squeak from the box springs, a shifting of weight overhead—the raising of the mattress. The man bent forward to peer under it, his face so close Loeb could see a red vein in one of his eyeballs: a tanned face, handsome, angry, intense. Loeb didn't hold his breath, but only because the timing was wrong—he'd been exhaling when the face appeared. He simply didn't breathe, lungs empty, which was even harder.

"Shit," the man said, letting the mattress go. Thump. Next he would look under the bed. But he didn't, straightening and moving away instead, coming fully into view as he went out the door. Loeb inhaled. He heard a scraping sound, like the foot of a couch on tile, then some banging around, followed by silence.

There was only one thing to look for: the money. Whoever this was would remember to check under the bed eventually. Loeb wriggled an inch of two out from under, noticed a bent nail sticking out of the edge in the hole where Greenland had been. He was formulating a plan when he heard sounds on the other side. Loeb wriggled back into the shadows.

Someone new climbed in through the Greenland hole, possibly two people, but much more quietly than the first explorer, almost silent. Two pairs of feet moved across the floor, one, short and very wide, in sandals, the other in snakeskin cowboy boots. Big snakeskin cowboy boots—Loeb had seen them before. He tried to think where.

The men stopped moving. Loeb sensed some communication passing between them, gestures or facial expressions. They went in different directions, the man in snakeskin boots somewhere out of sight, the man in sandals taking a position behind the open door, where Loeb could see him clearly, although anyone entering the room could not. The man in the sandals yawned. Yawns could mean boredom or nervousness, but since it was Turbo, Loeb ruled out the latter.

From somewhere in the house came a faint crash, possibly a lamp, and the first man saying something with *fuck* in it. His voice grew louder. "I'll turn this place upside down if I have to," he said. "Vegas. Right." He came in the room, quick and athletic, the idea of checking under the bed no doubt on his mind. Turbo slammed the door behind him.

The athletic man jumped at the sound, snapped around toward Turbo. "Who the hell are you?" he said, recovering his composure in seconds. He was much bigger than Turbo, of course. Loeb hoped that didn't give him ideas. Then his eyes shifted: he must have seen the other man, the one in the snakeskin boots, invisible to Loeb. "How did you get in?" he said, backing up just a little.

Voice of the man in snakeskin boots: "This is irony, am I correct?" Samsonov. The lower half of him came into view, with that diamond-studded BUCK buckle.

"Huh?" said the first man.

"Because we could be asking the same precise question, Mr. Loeb," Samsonov said. "But what a waste of time, explaining irony to a writer."

"You guys are making a mistake," said the athlete. "My name's not Loeb and I'm not a writer."

"Save your breathing," Samsonov said. "Bub has told us all about your stalking habit."

"I don't understand a word you're saying."

"Who else but a stalker would break in this way?"

"Are you crazy?" said the athlete. "I'm not a stalker."

"We must have honesty," Samsonov said. "Explain to Mr. Nicholas Loeb, mystery writer, the importance of honesty."

"Me?" said Turbo.

"You," said Samsonov.

Turbo bit his lip. "Well," he said, "they say it's the best policy."

"What the fuck are you guys talking about?" said the athlete. "I'm not a mystery writer. I've never heard of this Loeb guy. Is this a reality TV thing?"

"Explain better," Samsonov said.

Turbo stepped forward as though to give this man, the

Loeb nonpretender, a hug. The man, maybe thinking some touchie-feelie thing was happening—oh, this was going so bad, so fast; Loeb himself would have handled the pacing a lot differently—got angry, pushed Turbo away. Turbo didn't seem to resist, but somehow, without the use of force, induced the man along with him. Then they were indeed in a sort of hug, and Loeb was just starting to steel himself when there was a sharp crack, like good kindling, Georgia fatwood, say, breaking over someone's knee, and the man cried out in agony, one of those unrestrained moments in human life devoid of the ego's mediation. That was one way of putting it. The other: It was sickening. Loeb felt nausea at the back of his throat; not good, with his mouth taped shut. He took a deep breath, very quiet.

The athlete, a golfer or tennis player, was sitting on a chair in front of a makeup mirror, the kind with all the bulbs. It reflected the back of his head: he had a very good haircut. Turbo leaned against the door, polishing his glasses. Samsonov, now in full view, picked up something that had fallen to the floor.

"Well, well," he said. "Look what is falling from his pocket."

"What?" said Turbo, putting on his glasses.

Samsonov held it up. Loeb saw: a purple-and-gold Buena Vida Estates giveaway pen, just like his. "The very pen in question," said Samsonov, "central fact of Bub's story." He read the writing on it, shook his head in wonder. "What a splendid memory Bub has."

"Didn't he use to be a judge?" Turbo said.

"Still is," said Samsonov.

The athlete wasn't listening. "Broke my fucking arm," he said, teeth clenched, left forearm cradled in his lap; bent over in pain, now a hunchback himself.

Samsonov spread his hands. "We are grasping with straws here, Mr. Loeb."

"But I'm not him." The man's lip quivered; he sounded like a little boy.

"Do you know what this behavior means to me?" Samsonov said.

Turbo looked like he was thinking hard, but remained silent. The man on the chair waited, all his attention on Samsonov's face, as though his life depended on the answer.

"Either," Samsonov said, "you are a very foolish man, dumb as beasts, or you have already found Red—Helen is her real name, FYI—and perhaps are in possession of some or all of the misbegotten proceeds yourself."

Turbo nodded.

Samsonov unscrewed one of the little lightbulbs from the makeup mirror. "The female world," he said, "so strange, so vulnerable." He motioned with the lightbulb, not in a threatening way: it might have been an apple. "Your decision is all about how willingly—willingly—can that be right?"

"Sounds good to me," said Turbo.

"How willingly you will help," Samsonov said.

Whatever it is, make it willingly, Loeb thought, *for God's sake.* There was a long pause; maybe the man in the chair didn't understand the sentence.

But he said: "Everyone calls her Mackie."

"Not Helen?" said Samsonov.

The man shook his head, winced. "It's a nickname from grade school. Back in Albany."

"Ah, research," said Samsonov. "You do good work, Mr. Loeb. What of your books would you recommend?"

"Please," the man said.

"Please what?"

"Don't call me that."

"Don't call you what?"

"Mr. Loeb."

Turbo shifted his weight, as though about to come forward.

"Oh, God," said the man. "Look in my wallet. Check my ID. Back pocket."

"Check wallet?" said Samsonov. "Why not?"

Turbo took the man's wallet, gently so as not to jar him at all, almost like a pickpocket, and handed it to Samsonov. Samsonov held the driver's license to the light, glanced at the man, back to the license.

"It says Kevin Larkin," he said. "You look like him."

"I am him," said Kevin Larkin. *Had to be,* thought Loeb: the name on the pen.

Samsonov passed the license to Turbo. "Looks like him," said Turbo. He examined the license more closely. "Hey. This address—that's the ranch."

"The ranch?" said Samsonov.

Kevin Larkin looked from one to the other, a spectator at a game he didn't know but had money riding on anyway.

"Where the wrangler worked," said Turbo.

"You're sure?" said Samsonov.

"Pretty sure."

"This is bad," Samsonov said.

"I've got to get that changed," said Kevin Larkin. "I don't live there anymore."

"But you did," said Samsonov.

"For like a few weeks."

"And you knew the wrangler."

"There were lots of wranglers."

Samsonov tapped the lightbulb on Kevin Larkin's head, like cracking an egg. The bulb popped, leaving one jagged piece in place. "Are you right-handed?" Samsonov said.

Kevin Larkin, eyes on that jagged glass, said nothing. He didn't know the right answer. Loeb knew there wasn't one.

"This is a simple question," Samsonov said.

"Yes, right-handed," said Kevin Larkin, but doubtfully, as though guessing a tough one on the SATs.

"And did my colleague trouble your right arm, even the teensiest bit?"

"No."

"But," said Samsonov, suddenly bringing the tip of the shard right against the inside corner of one of Kevin Larkin's eyes, just resting it there, in the crevice where those little balls of sleep formed at night, "but you are not grateful." He glanced at Turbo. "Explain the M.O."

"Whatever it takes?" said Turbo. "That one?"

Samsonov turned back to Kevin Larkin.

"I am grateful," said Kevin Larkin, his head very still, eyes unblinking.

"Then you knew the wrangler."

"Jimmy Marz? I don't really know him. He was around, that's all." Kevin Larkin breathed in sharply; Samsonov must have pressed a little with the bulb, because a few drops of blood ran down the side of his nose.

"Should I round up some towels?" Turbo said.

Kevin Larkin started crying, tried to keep his face still at the same time. "All right," he said. "I saw the news. But I don't know anything. She had the money here. Now it's gone. She said she won it in Vegas."

"And you believed her?"

"She could never rob a bank. I was married to her for fifteen years. She's gone crazy."

Samsonov stepped back, withdrawing the bulb. "You?" he said. "*You* were married to *her*?"

Loeb's exact thought, at the exact same moment.

More blood flowed from the corner of Kevin Larkin's eye; the bulb must have been holding it in.

"I can show you the divorce certificate. Maybe she has a copy here, or we could drive over to my lawyer's, it's only—"

Samsonov thought about the bulb; didn't look at it or gesture with it, just thought. Loeb could feel the thought, and so could Kevin Larkin. That was all it took.

"I'll help any way I can," Kevin said. "Are you guys cops?"

Samsonov laughed. "This is a good one," he said. "You are looking at the number-one majority shareholder of Patriot Frontier Savings and Loan, duly incorporated under the laws of the great state of Arizona."

"Oh, God," said Kevin Larkin. "And you want the money back."

"Correct."

"But aren't you insured?"

"Who is asking the questions?" Samsonov said. He dropped the bulb. Its remains shattered quietly on the floor.

"You," said Kevin Larkin, relief at its disappearance in every feature.

"Correct again," said Samsonov. He took Kevin Larkin's hand, the left hand, in his. Kevin Larkin's hands were big and strong, but Samsonov's rendered them juvenile. He pulled on Kevin Larkin's left hand, not hard. But it didn't have to be hard. Kevin Larkin cried out, not as agonized as during the actual arm-breaking, but more defeated somehow, perhaps because Samsonov had caught him in that trough of relief. "You must know all the habits of your former wife," Samsonov said.

"So it's true?" said Turbo. "This isn't the writer?"

"I don't know about all," said Kevin Larkin in a small voice.

"But you are willing?" said Samsonov.

"Yes."

"Very willing?"

"Yes."

"How much willing, as percent?"

"One hundred."

Samsonov smiled, was still smiling when the phone rang. He and Turbo both turned to it, then looked at each other, Samsonov thinking, Turbo waiting. At that moment,

Kevin Larkin surprised them, surprised Loeb too, by bolting from the room.

He moved well—very well considering the pain he must have been in—but not quite in Turbo's class. Loeb heard their running feet in the corridor, on the tiles of the front hall. Then came a crash, followed by Kevin Larkin's cry, and another crash, much louder, as something hard and heavy hit the floor.

Silence, except for the echo of the last ring of the phone. Then Turbo called, "Hey, Mr. Samsonov. Check this out."

Twenty-eight

It was hot inside duct tape; a detail Loeb now had in his possession, in case something similar ever happened to Timothy Bolt. Hot: and his headache was getting worse. Somewhere outside the room, Samsonov was saying, "Well, well, well." Then the three of them were back, Samsonov with the shopping bags, Turbo dragging Kevin Larkin across the floor. From that angle, Kevin Larkin could have spotted him with ease, but now both his eyes were closed.

"Count," said Samsonov, dropping the shopping bags on the bed; they thumped down above Loeb's head. A wad of unbanded cash fell to the floor, a foot or so from Loeb's face; and one bill, a fifty—but an old one, before the mint made Grant and all the others androgynous—fluttered underneath the bed, came to rest on his cheek, demanding to be twitched off. Loeb lay still.

"Me?" said Turbo.

"You." One of Samsonov's hands came down, scooped up the money, all except that one fifty; a huge vein throbbed once on the back of his hand.

Turbo counted the money, muttering to himself. Kevin Larkin's eyes opened to slits. He tried to sit up, succeeded after a while.

"What is the word," Samsonov said, "for something that begins unlucky, like you trying to run away, and ends with lucky, such as finding of the money?"

Kevin Larkin didn't answer. Turbo said, "You're making me forget where I am." Loeb thought: *serendipitous,* so often misused as a simple analogue to lucky. Inside the snakeskin boots, Samsonov's toes made little bulges, stretching and curling, the effect very snakelike.

"Five hundred sixty-one thousand, eight hundred ninety-three," said Turbo.

"Then we are short," said Samsonov. "Short by twelve thousand, one hundred forty-one." The number came without a pause. One snakeskin boot shifted, gave Kevin Larkin a little kick on the arm, the broken one. Not much of a kick, and anyone with their eyes open would have seen it coming and shifted that arm out of the way. Kevin Larkin made a hissing sound. Samsonov said, "Where is this missing twelve thousand, one hundred forty-one?"

"I don't know." Kevin forced his slit eyes open a little more; they were fixed on the snakeskin boots. "She must have taken it."

"Now you make sense," said Samsonov. "She is—how slow I have been to see this—a player. We must too be players."

"How do you mean?" said Turbo.

Samsonov turned toward Turbo, his face coming into Loeb's view, and gave him a smile, a fond one—as though Turbo was like a son to him. "Preparation is everything," he said. "Recall how Carnegie handled the coal miners' strike. We must be like pincers—the gentleman and I will try the outside world, you remain here. Make a thorough search while waiting."

"For what?"

"Helpful discoveries," said Samsonov, gently reaching down for Kevin's good arm and helping him to his feet; then leading him out through the Greenland hole, hand on elbow, the way you'd walk an old man.

"Okay if I raid the fridge first?" Turbo called after them. "I'm starving."

No answer. Loeb heard a car driving off.

"I guess it's okay," Turbo said to himself, and left the room. His feet didn't make a sound.

Loeb wriggled out from under the bed. He rolled himself like a log toward the damaged wall, every changing contact with the hardwood floor booming like the soundtrack of an action movie in a brand-new stadium-seating cineplex. Squirming around, he got himself perpendicular to the wall. The nail, about four feet up, still new and shiny, pointed toward the ceiling at a forty-five-degree angle. Loeb raised his duct-taped legs from the waist, did a little peristaltic thing to shorten the distance to the wall, bring his ankles down on the nail. It was like an exercise long abandoned by humane coaches. Down, down, down, and just as his ankles touched the point of the nail, he heard the faint sound of popcorn popping.

Quick and quiet, that was how he had to do it. Loeb pressed down on the nail, got it to poke through the duct tape, right into his skin. But then what? Would he have to make a series of holes? How long would that take? Instead, he raised his ankles—abdominal muscles straining now, perhaps this was the ab-flattener of all time and his fortune was made—raised them almost off the point, but not quite. Like that. Then he jerked his legs down as far as he could, no more than an inch or so. But he heard a ripping sound. How could he have missed it, loud as sailcloth splitting in a gale?

Loeb paused, listened, heard nothing at first, and then the tinkling of ice. He arched his neck, looked backward and upside down at the empty doorway. Turbo was talking to himself again. Loeb caught the phrase "preparation is everything."

Quicker, quieter: he sawed up and down with his ankles. Rip, rip, rip, and they parted; not far, because of the duct tape around his knees, but far enough. He pushed himself away from the wall, rolled over, got his feet beneath him, stood up. Then he shuffled over toward the wall and began rubbing his bound torso against the nail; yes, like a bear. Through the Greenland hole he could see into the garage, chainsaw and plastic gas tank on the floor, shattered window on the other side, Kevin Larkin's own M.O. clear. And so many other blanks now filling in: it would be nice to live long enough to mull them over.

Loeb rubbed himself against the nail. More ripping; one hand free; then the other. He tore at the duct tape, tearing off his shirt too—blood on it, he hardly noticed—yanked the tape from his mouth, was getting the last of it off his legs, almost free to jump through the hole and far away, when he heard a metallic sound, faint but unmistakable: the sliding of a deadbolt. Someone with a key was coming in the front door.

He turned toward the bedroom doorway. It could only be one person. Was it his duty to warn her? No. Did he owe her anything? Certainly not. And hadn't he himself been the one to think: *Who in their right mind would even consider stirring up trouble for Turbo?*

Loeb found himself taking that first step toward the hall anyway, the kind of thing Timothy Bolt would do. But Timothy Bolt, despite his "flaws," "quirks," and "depth" was a "good guy," not a real person. At that moment, Loeb realized he'd been making a huge mistake with the series from the very start. Real people didn't always have motivation for their characters, didn't always have a reason, sometimes acted for no reason at all. What were those layers of the brain? Human, mammalian, reptilian, all piled on each other like the cities of Troy. Who was ever going to understand all that? Not him. All he knew was that Timothy Bolt had to die.

Also at that moment, Turbo flew by down the hall, a silent blur. Turbo: a strange human-reptilian combination, Loeb decided, the mammalian part missing.

Loeb poked his head into the hall, heard sounds of a

struggle he knew would be brief. He turned back to the bedroom, looking for some sort of weapon. A gun was the only possible weapon that would have any effect on Turbo, and there was no gun, no potential weapon at all—except for the chainsaw, horrible cliché of horror entertainment. The struggling sounds ceased.

As it happened, Loeb, from a winter study course in woodlot management, junior year at Middlebury, knew how to use a chainsaw, perhaps making him unique in Brooklyn Heights. He picked it up, a Stihl MS 170, just a little thing, still warm, choke-pulling unnecessary. Plenty of fuel in the tank: he set the switch to on, wrapped one hand around the pull-cord grip, crept out of the bedroom.

Loeb heard Turbo talking, followed the sound of his voice. It led him down the corridor, into the front hall. The planter lay shattered on the floor, dirt all over the place, the plant like a small tree on its side. Loeb crouched behind it, peered through its leaves into the living room.

Mackie—he found himself thinking of her by that name right away, the name that everyone called her in her real life—sat on the couch, bleeding from her mouth. Turbo faced her, sitting on the coffee table, back to Loeb, eating an orange.

"I used to think you were the smartest girl we ever had," Turbo said. "Now I know you're the dumbest."

Mackie said nothing.

"You've pissed him off unbelievably," Turbo said. "Know that expression—too dumb to live?"

"You've got the money," Mackie said. "What else do you want?"

"It's not what I want," said Turbo, taking a cell phone from his pocket. Behind the downed plant, Loeb tried to think of some way to slow this down. His mind froze.

"Does he know you found it?" Mackie said. "You could go somewhere, start a new life."

"Why would I want to do that?" said Turbo. "I have a

great life right here, in on the ground floor, employee number nine. Anyways, he's got it—except what's missing. And that ex-husband of yours."

"Kevin?"

"Quite the dude. He figures you've got the twelve grand somewheres. Might as well cough it up."

Mackie went pale; the contrast between her skin and Turbo's vivid, like a worn-out TV next to state-of-the-art.

"I don't have it," she said.

"Won't really matter in the end," said Turbo. "Recovering the money is only step one."

"Recovering?"

"Don't you get it? Patriot Frontier belongs to All-American Amusements, Inc., and All-American Amusements, Inc., is Mr. Samsonov. If someone like him doesn't deserve respect, who does?"

Loeb watched Mackie's face as she got that, as she began to lose control over the fear inside: her lips parted slightly; blood on her teeth. Turbo raised the cell phone up to eye level. How far away would Samsonov be by now? Ten minutes? Less? Loeb, still waiting for an idea, stepped into the open, yanked the pull-cord. That bloody mouth maddened him.

No response from the saw. Worse than no response: the jangling recoil of the loose cord caught everyone's attention. Turbo was on the move right away, up, turning, eyes going from the chainsaw to Loeb's face. He didn't look the least bit scared of Loeb, but Mackie did. Loeb realized she had no idea whose side he was on, had good reason to believe it wasn't hers, even that Turbo had freed him. Could that work for him in some way?

"I know you," Turbo said, bursting this first idea before Loeb had finished having it. "You're the one who had the hots for . . . Hey! A fast mover, huh?" Then he frowned. "Are you in on this too?"

Loeb pulled the cord again. Zip.

"The choke," Mackie said.

"But it's still warm," said Loeb.

"The mixture's wrong," Mackie said.

"Shut your mouth while you still can," said Turbo.

He started pressing buttons on the cell phone. Loeb glanced down at the chainsaw controls, found the choke, pulled it, tried the cord again. The saw coughed to life, spewed out a cloud of blue smoke, died. But at the instant of the engine firing, Mackie kicked out at Turbo's hand, knocking the cell phone across the room.

A triangle—Turbo, Mackie, himself—and Loeb knew it was important to keep it that way; any two points coming together would be bad. Mackie must have realized that too. She had already vaulted off the back of the couch, so smooth, and was—

Actually, not quite. Somehow Turbo closed the space between them, caught her ankle in midair. She fell face-down, half on, half off the couch, making a stifled little cry, her bloody mouth banging the hard top of the back-rest. Loeb gave a murderous, eviscerating jerk on the pull-cord. It started. He hit the trigger, made it roar, looked up.

Two points together already: Turbo had Mackie in front of him, his forearm under her chin. A ridiculous cliché, the human shield, defining *hack* in one image; an image Loeb would never stoop to. It infuriated him, qua cliché, and so did this demonstration of its elemental power, see-ing it for the first time in real life. How could anything good happen now? Doubly mad, Loeb advanced on the two of them, the saw—screaming like a smoking, over-heating maniac—leading the way. Its mania vibrated through Loeb's body, he and the saw almost becoming one, a gasoline-powered cyborg, mixture wrong, on the edge of explosion. Behind the lenses of those Buddy Holly glasses, Turbo's eyes changed expression, just a lit-tle. Mania as counterploy: hadn't Richard Nixon made it the basis of his foreign policy?

Turbo backed away, dragging Mackie with him. But there was nowhere to go, the wall just a step or two away. Turbo wasn't as tall as Mackie, so not much of him showed behind her. In front of her, though, was that forearm over her throat, and his whole arm up to the shoulder. What had Loeb gotten in woodlot management? A-minus. He jabbed the saw at Turbo's biceps. Turbo yanked his arm away, all his normal grace and fluidity gone, let Mackie go, kicking her forward.

Mackie lost her balance, fell against Loeb. He got the chainsaw up and out of the way, slicing off a lock of her hair—he saw it clearly, just hanging in space for a moment—and then, losing his own balance, threw the saw with both hands, like a basketball player keeping the ball inbounds, over Mackie's head, right at Turbo.

Turbo ducked. The saw hit the wall behind him, conked out. In the silence that followed, everything seemed finally to slow down. There should have been plenty of time for Turbo, Turbo of all people, to avoid the saw, now falling, to shift just a few inches. But because of the sudden silence, or lack of precedent, or mental overload, he did not. It hit him on the head, the heavy base part, containing the motor and fuel tank. He slumped to the floor, glasses knocked off, eyelids fluttering. Loeb jumped up, grabbed the saw, started it up in one rip, hit the trigger, held it inches from Turbo's throat. Turbo's eyes cleared. They got the picture.

There was more duct tape on the roll, enough to wrap two Turbos. They wrapped the one they had—Loeb feeling strangely high at the moment; Timothy Bolt had never done better—Mackie doing the wrapping, he himself standing by, chainsaw on idle. Mackie's mouth had stopped bleeding. Her lips moved. Was she saying something to him?

"What?"

She raised her voice over the saw. "I thought you were going to kill me."

"We were lucky," Loeb shouted. "Maple sugar processing was my first choice."

"What?"

"It was full," he told her, now at the top of his lungs. "I had to settle for woodlot management."

"What?"

They left Turbo wrapped up in the living room, went into the hall. He was visible from there, eyes blank, as though he'd gone into deep meditation. Loeb hung on to the chainsaw, now off. The saw—a cliché for sure, yet he sensed a connectedness here in real life, at once symbolic and deadly, a connectedness that was missing from his work: a woman changes the locks on her house; her ex-husband breaks in using a powerful tool, and loses control of it to another man. Same tool: but the new man has more success with it; at least for now.

Twenty-nine

W e're going to Mexico?" Lianne said.

"That's where the pictures are—at this buddy of mine's," said Dane. "You speak Spanish?"

"No."

Dane opened the window, said, "Howdy."

The Mexican border guard said: *"Me gusta tu camión."*

"Pertenece al parque," Dane said.

The border guard said: *"Cuándo lo van abrir?"*

"Algunos meses," Dane told him.

"Va haber una montaña rusa?" said the guard.

"Hell, yes," said Dane.

"Fantástico," said the border guard. His eyes went to Lianne. *"Quién es esa chica?"*

"Solo otra bailadora," said Dane.

The border guard waved them through.

Dane drove through the junky tourist part, past the junky factory part, out into the desert. "Been to Mexico much?"

"A few times," said Lianne, which was true. The part about not speaking Spanish wasn't quite as true. She didn't consider herself a speaker, but she was at the top of her class in AP Spanish and had understood every word, even the expression *montaña rusa*—Russian mountain, Spanish for roller coaster. Just that last part confused her: Who's the girl? Just another dancer. Some kind of slang? Asking about it now would be embarrassing, and what was the point of pissing Dane off? She wanted those pictures.

"Cool place to live if you've got money," Dane said. The sun glared on the windshield, and on bright things here and there in the distance. Lianne spotted a dark-green line of palo verde, knew it followed a dry wash, the way Jimmy had taught her. She could feel him, right beside her, sharing her thoughts. That wasn't going to stop, was it? *I've been so dumb, Jimmy*.

"What was that?" said Dane.

"I didn't say anything." But had she? That was weird. Dane shot her a funny look. She remembered how Jimmy had treated him, almost with contempt. Dane was nothing to worry about, not with Jimmy looking out for her.

"But if you don't have money, nothing sucks worse," Dane said. "Than living in Mexico, I'm talking about. Maybe that's what Jimmy wanted, to set himself up nice and pretty south of the border."

"No."

He glanced over again. "That sounds kind of definite."

"Yeah."

"Makes me think you two did do some talking about the money after all," Dane said.

"I told you, Dane—he mentioned wanting his own ranch once or twice. That was it." Cielo Azul. It was everywhere today, horizon to horizon. Without hardly trying, she could see the outline of his face in all that blue. As long as there was blue sky, she'd have Jimmy. She started crying again, but silently, so Dane couldn't hear, and turned her face to the side window, so he couldn't see. They were climbing a long hill, zooming at that moment past a claptrappity truck jam-packed with people, so close together it must have been unbearable. A tiny old Indian woman wedged in the back looked right at her, saw those tears; Lianne could tell from a slight upward movement of her eyebrow, still jet-black although her hair was white; one of those expressions of concern.

"There's an example," said Dane. "Might as well be animals."

At the top of the hill, a two-humped mountain came into view. She'd seen it before, but from the other side, the American side.

Can we climb up there, Jimmy?

That's Mexico.

So?

One day, maybe.

Dane turned onto a dirt road that wound toward the two-humped mountain.

"You'll see the house in a few minutes or so," he said.

"That white dot?"

"You got good eyes," said Dane.

The white dot slowly grew. This was the day: she was finally climbing the two-humped mountain, doing it for both of them. And what better place to seek those childhood pictures; as though she were on a quest. They went up and up on switchbacks, then rounded a bluff, caught the first glimpse of the wide plain that must have stretched into Arizona, although she couldn't be sure: Jimmy hadn't finished teaching her directions.

A cliff rose on their right, blocking the view. They passed a dark opening in its side.

"A mine?" Lianne said.

"You could say that," said Dane.

"What sort of mine?"

"Kind of a gold mine."

Lianne saw shadowy people moving around inside.

"They're still working it?"

"Be working that mine forever," Dane said.

Dane parked beside a red Cadillac, same color as the truck and just as shiny new, except for some dents in the rear, and one taillight hanging loose. At the top of a marble staircase rose a white mansion with columns and statues, one of those homes of the rich and famous.

"Your buddy lives here?"

"Yup."

They climbed the stairs, crossed a terrace bordering a swimming pool that reminded her of the weekend school trip to San Simeon. Greek statues stood at three corners of the pool; at the fourth lay only the head of a statue, tipped on its side. An on-purpose effect, maybe? It made her think of that poem "Ozymandias"; pretty cool.

"In here," said Dane, opening a sliding door to the house. He led Lianne into what looked like the office of someone important: dark wooden desk, huge and heavy, with nothing on it; lots of leather furniture; all kinds of electronic equipment, including a video camera on a tripod.

"Take a seat," Dane said.

"Where are the pictures?" said Lianne.

"I'll go get 'em," Dane said. "Be right back."

Dane went out another door; she heard the squeak of his sneakers on a tile floor before it closed. She sat on a leather couch. A flat-screen TV on the opposite wall was tuned silently to one of those financial channels. Lianne watched the stock prices scroll by. The Dow was down eighty-seven points; then ninety-nine. Two talking heads talked at the same time. Lianne heard a voice call out, somewhere in the house.

She got up. This was taking a long time. She wanted to go home, have her mom around. Maybe she should give her a call. Lianne went to the desk, picked up the phone. A man was already on the line. He said: ". . . no writer, but the former husband, of no good use. What is your mental thinking when you—"

A second man on the line interrupted: "What was that?"

Lianne hung up the phone, gently, like an object easily broken. The first man had sounded angry about something.

He also had a funny accent. *These people, the Russian guy, Dane, the conglomerate, they're kind of criminals, right? Even though they own a bank.*

Her glance touched on the desk. Was it possible the pictures were waiting right here? Lianne opened the top drawer: empty, except for a pint of vodka and a gun. She closed the drawer, went to the window.

Dane and a big platinum-haired man appeared on an upstairs gallery in the opposite wing of the house. They walked quickly to a curving outdoor staircase, came quickly down. The sun glittered on the platinum-haired man's belt buckle. Lianne didn't like how fast they were moving. What if Jimmy's pictures weren't even here? She backed away from the window. There were two ways out—the door to the terrace, too late; and the door that Dane had gone through, farther into the house. She opened that one. A man stood on the other side. He wore a red T-shirt with ALL-AMERICAN AMUSEMENTS, INC. on the front, and had a shotgun in his hands.

Nicholas Loeb, writer of mysteries, although Mackie had never heard of him, stood in her front hall, his purpose unclear. All she knew was that he'd saved her from Turbo. "I guess I should apologize," she said.

"For what?"

"What I did to you."

"Perfectly understandable," Loeb said.

"You should do something about those cuts."

"I'm fine."

Mackie went into the bathroom, returned with hydrogen peroxide. "Turn around," she said.

He turned. Over his shoulder, Mackie saw Turbo, still on the living-room floor, still in a trance. She dabbed hydrogen peroxide on Loeb's back. He had a nice back, cool to her touch. His body was shaking a little, and so was hers.

"Is it safe to try again?" he said.

"Try what?"

"Asking if you knew Jimmy Marz."

His back tensed slightly under her fingers; did he really think she'd knock him out again? "The answer's no," she said.

"You just happened to be in the bank," Loeb said.

"It's a little more complicated than that."

"In what way?" He faced her.

Mackie gave him a long look. What did she know about him? Almost nothing. And she remembered Sola's remark: *Men are pretty sick—you must know that by now.* Was she starting to believe it?

"We probably don't have time for a lot of deep thinking," he said.

Mackie knew that, could sense Samsonov out there, restless and seeking. She made a decision, based on very little, other than that word *we.* "I had a motive. Now that I know who owns the bank, it even makes sense."

"You're losing me already," Loeb said.

"Do you believe in cosmic deals?" Mackie said. This one even came with its own music: "When Rita Leaves."

"What are those?" Loeb said.

"Fate or God or something ends up punishing you for everything you get," Mackie said.

"That's crazy talk," said Loeb. He sounded angry. "People do all the punishing."

That anger, so sudden and unexpected, snapped her out of it, knocked her off that wretched self-pitying track.

"Tell me about this motive," he said.

Mackie told Loeb about the motive, told him that, and everything else—beginning with the collapse of Buena Vida and ending with the disappearance of Lianne, two events that suddenly seemed directly connected. That wasn't self-pity or even self-blame: just a fact. The expression in his eyes changed as she told the story. Eager, sympathetic, into it: she would have had trouble describing the change in words; all she knew was it made telling him a little easier.

"Go over the part about the ranch," he said. "Jimmy and Lianne. Is that where he lived?"

"I don't know. I tried to find out, but Dane was there."

"Dane?"

"He works for Samsonov, but it seemed like a wake with all the ranch people, and he was part of it."

"We'll have to risk it," he said. "The ranch is our best bet."

"You think she's there?"

"Doesn't it make sense, if that's where they were to-gether?" he said. "But you're the one who knows her."

Mackie started crying then, a quick burst, stifled right away. "Oh, but I don't," she said, which was worst of all. She reached into her pocket, gave him Lianne's letter.

Reading it seemed to take him just a second or two. "Let's go," he said, handing back the letter.

Their eyes met. "You don't have to do this," she said.

He glanced at Turbo. "Too late," he said.

Loeb backed his pickup into the garage. They carried Turbo through the kitchen doorway, lifted him onto the bed of the truck. He didn't resist at all, didn't even look at them.

"Want some water?" Loeb said to him.

No response. Loeb closed the lid.

"What are we going to do with him?" Mackie said.

"He's our insurance," said Loeb.

They drove out of town, Loeb following Mackie's direc-tions. On an empty stretch of two-lane highway, moun-tains in the distance, a pickup flashed by the other way, the couple in the front close together, woman's head on the driver's shoulder—but otherwise like them—he shirtless, she in a baseball cap. That feeling of belonging out here hit him again. He noticed his headache was gone.

"What's that?" he said. "By those bushes."

"Javelina," said Mackie. "A kind of pig."

Loeb, who cared nothing about animals, couldn't take his eyes off it.

The road curved up through a line of hills, Loeb slowing down behind a tanker truck with lettering on the back: PRIVATE SPRING OWNERS—WE PAY TOP $ FOR H2O. Loeb passed it as they came to the top. To the south lay an endless view, mirages shimmering here and there, everything else a motionless silver-gray under an empty sky. Loeb felt his insignificance, and liked it. He started down the other side.

"Do you think she saw me?" Mackie said.

Loeb knew who she meant. "Couldn't have. She comes in after you were gone."

"What was the expression on her face?"

"I couldn't really tell. She just kind of froze, then backed out. She could have been just another customer."

"What was she doing there?"

"Maybe driving the getaway car."

"She doesn't have her license."

There was a pause. Then she started laughing. Loeb turned to her. Her eyes were all mixed up, amused and full of pain at the same time. He thought about putting his hand on her knee, just in a comforting way, was still going back and forth on it when flashing lights appeared in the rearview mirror.

"Oh, God," Mackie said; and she put *her* hand on *his* knee, nails digging in. Loeb pulled over. Mackie glanced back. "It's just the Border Patrol," she said, her grip relaxing before she took her hand away. Loeb realized she didn't know the drill.

Two agents walked up, one coming to his window, the other stopping at the back of the truck, hand on the butt of his gun. Loeb knew the drill; in fact, he recognized the agents: the same pair had pulled him over on the Arivaca road.

He rolled down the window, gave the agent a smile. "Hi," he said.

She smiled too. "Need you to open up the back," she said.

"But we did this before," he said. "On the Arivaca road."

"Only take a minute," she said.

"And the back was empty, just like now," said Loeb. "Don't you remember?"

"Need you to open up."

"I'm a citizen," Loeb said. "An American citizen, born and bred."

In the side mirror, he saw the second agent taking the radio off his belt. Now the agent by the window had a hand on her gun butt too, and wasn't smiling. "We don't want any trouble," she said.

Loeb opened the door, got out. The agent backed away, drawing her gun. Loeb walked to the back, tried to think of some harmless explanation for Turbo's presence. Practical joke? Scavenger hunt? Maybe he could just act surprised. Mackie's eyes followed him in the rearview mirror. Now she got it. Was she thinking of shifting into the driver's seat, speeding off? A look like that was on her face.

"Crazily enough," he began, as he shifted the lever and raised the top.

Empty; unless you counted the scraps of duct tape, neatly piled.

"Beautiful," said the agent.

Her partner came closer. "Crazily enough what?" he said.

Something out of nothing: quick. "I was going to make a joke," he said, pulse still racing from the shock of Turbo being gone.

"Let's hear it."

A joke: quick. "What if Carmen Miranda popped out?"

"I don't get it."

"Maybe it's not funny."

They gave him a look, as though he were a bit odd, got in their SUV, drove back the way they'd come. Mackie jumped out, crouched, peered under the truck, slowly rose. He hadn't thought of that.

They looked at each other. "Doesn't really change anything," Loeb said. He swept his eyes over the northern landscape; nothing moved except the Border Patrol SUV, already tiny.

"Let's be honest," Mackie said.

The tanker appeared, rounding the last turn. The driver glanced at them as it went by; a Hispanic male, alone in the cab, and no one clinging to the top, hanging off the back, tucked in down below. WE PAY TOP $ FOR H2O.

Mackie closed the lid. "Carmen Miranda?" she said.

"It was the best I could do," said Loeb.

A rider was coming their way as Loeb and Mackie drove under the Ocotillo Ranch sign. Loeb pulled over. The rider trotted up, leaned toward the window.

"You work here?" Loeb said.

"Head wrangler," said the rider, sweat beads on his salt-and-pepper mustache.

Mackie got out of the truck, walked around to him. "I'm Lianne's mother," she said, looking up at him, shading her eyes with her hand. The sun outlined her fingers in gold. And her profile too: imprinting in Loeb's mind a picture of something good—hope, courage, faith, one of them, or a combination. "I'm trying to find her."

"Can't help you," the wrangler said.

Mackie took out the letter, handed it up to him. He found reading glasses in his chest pocket and read. Did his eyes tear up? Loeb couldn't be sure, not with the sun glinting off his glasses.

The wrangler folded the letter with care, passed it back down. "Name's Rags," he said. "What do you want to know?"

"Anything," said Mackie. "Anything at all."

"Haven't actually seen her in a while," said Rags. "But you could try the bunkhouse."

"What's that?"

"The South End bunkhouse," said Rags. "Down on the border. Kind of Jimmy's place." He dismounted, an effortless slide, and crouched on the ground. "I c'n draw you a map." Loeb got out of the truck. They all crouched down together. Rags drew the map in the dirt with his index finger, a squiggly line for some hills, straight line for a wash, X for the bunkhouse. "Don't make sense," he said. "None of this."

"What do you mean?" Loeb said.

"Jimmy doing something like that. Ain't him, I don't care what evidence they got."

"Do you know Dane?" Mackie said.

"Dane from Arivaca?" said Rags. "Can't say knowing— old buddy of Jimmy's, he brung us the news."

The horse snorted.

"Easy, Clyde," said Rags.

Clyde shook himself, then went still.

"Knows he's gone," Rags said.

It was slow going after the dirt road ended. Loeb followed a single tire track, lightly marked in the desert. He could feel Mackie beside him, willing them to go faster. They circled the squiggly line of hills, crossed the straight line of the wash, bumped up the other side. Something slid out from under the seat. Mackie picked it up. "What's this?"

Loeb glanced over. *The Whites of Her Eyes,* the copy he'd salvaged from Flora Gutierrez's trash. "One of mine," he said.

"You don't take very good care of it," she said, removing a teabag stuck inside and tossing it out the window.

Loeb didn't explain. The sun was sinking now—no

more than the width of his hand above distant western mountains—and he tried to go a little faster. "Didn't he say we'd be able to see it from the wash?" he said. No answer. "The bunkhouse, I'm talking about." Silence. He looked over. She was reading. Seen from the side like that, the delicacy of her corneal dome in the red-gold sunlight was beyond his power to describe.

Five or ten minutes later, he spotted the bunkhouse, a dark rectangle on the desert floor, the only straight-lined thing around. The sky sucked up all the light from the land, saturated itself with it, caught fire. He stole another look at Mackie. The book was closed on her lap, and she was silently urging them forward again.

Loeb pulled up in front of the bunkhouse. Mackie was out of the truck before it came to a stop, running onto the porch, throwing the door open. He heard her call, "Lianne." Her posture changed slightly. Not that she slumped: it was more like some inner support had failed and the backup system had clicked on. He followed her inside. "Lianne," she said again, quietly this time.

A simple place: a single bunkbed, with Indian blankets, a heavy round table, carved with initials, a few mismatched wooden chairs, five-gallon water bottles along the wall. An earthenware bowl sat on the table; in it, a tangerine, almost all the color in the room. Mackie picked it up, smelled it.

"She's here."

Loeb glanced into the shadowy corners.

"I know it," Mackie said. She handed him the tangerine, hurried to the window, peered out.

Loeb sniffed at the tangerine, smelled a fresh, orange smell: he believed her. "Then we'll wait," he said.

They sat on the porch. Mackie kicked off her shoes. Weren't dancers' feet supposed to be all deformed? Hers were beautiful. Loeb remembered how she'd plucked that twenty-dollar bill out of his hand with her toes. His mind got stuck there, wouldn't move on.

Mackie watched the sky slowly darken. All the reds and oranges turned purple, like billowing bruises. The mountain beneath it went black. A two-humped mountain: and she, so often, the last to get it.

"That's Mexico," she said, sitting up fast. "His house is on that mountain. The house he took me to."

"Good," Loeb said.

"Good? Why good?"

"Hard to explain," Loeb said. "When things come together, they often come together geographically first."

"I don't understand."

"In my work, anyway," Loeb said.

She thought about coming together geographically, got hit by another one of those horrible contractions. "Are you saying she's over there?"

"Of course not," Loeb said. "How would Samsonov even know she exists?"

"Through Dane," Mackie said. She started to rise.

Loeb took her arm, tried to draw her back down. She resisted. "Besides," he said, looking up at her, "they've got the money back." The last of the purple light faded. His features disappeared. "When things start coming together like this, all the missing pieces get pushed in place."

"That's just in stories—you said so yourself." But Mackie let herself be pulled back down. Night fell. Missing parts, geography, Lianne: she loved those tangerines, would never have left it if she wasn't coming back.

Stars came out.

"Timothy Bolt's pretty funny," Mackie said.

"Thanks."

"Funnier than you," she added.

"The Carmen Miranda thing again so soon?" he said. "What would you have done?"

"Taken off my clothes," she said, the reply just popping out, unrehearsed, unbidden. "The biggest distraction there is."

He laughed. "You handle everything from now on," he said.

A bird flew over. Mackie couldn't see it, but she heard the beating of its wings. Then something rustled in the bushes, not a human sound. The moon rose, hard and silvery, like an anti-sun, lowering the temperature at once. Loeb shivered. He rose, bare chest pale in the moonlight.

"You want the top bunk?" he said.

"Thanks."

"Better get some rest."

"I will."

He went inside. Mackie heard a creaking sound, the flap of a blanket, a sigh. She sat on the porch, listened, watched, waited.

The moon was overhead when Mackie awoke, slumped sideways against one of the posts holding up the porch roof. The desert was bright and cold, the outline of the two-humped mountain distinct. She thought right away of that line Lianne had used for her essay: *As flies to wanton boys are we to the gods.* She gazed out at the desert. Nothing moved. She wanted Loeb to tell her it wasn't true.

Mackie rose, entered the bunkhouse. He was right about getting rest. Staying up all night wouldn't bring Lianne back any faster. She closed the door, picked her way carefully across the floor in the darkness. A wooden floor, old and smooth against her bare feet, and warm from the heat of the day. Her hand touched one of the supports for the top bunk, but couldn't find a ladder. Cowboys wouldn't use a ladder; they'd just hop up. She raised one foot onto the edge of the lower bunk, got her hands on the frame of the upper one, all set to just hop up. Then his hand touched her foot, rested lightly on top of it, so light it might have been an accident of sleep. All set to just hop up, and this invitation, if that was what it was, so gracefully designed to be declinable with no aftereffects: but her foot responded all on its own, made the decision for her. Mackie lowered herself onto the bottom bunk, beside him. Somehow the tangerine from her tree, unseen but only a few feet away, made it right.

Thirty

The man in the red All-American Amusements, Inc. T-shirt said: *"Puedo ayudarte?"* He kept the shotgun pointing safely at the floor.

"I'm leaving," Lianne said, and started to go around him.

He blocked her path in one easy step, the position of the shotgun unchanged.

"What the hell's going on?" she said.

"La seguridad."

Lianne backed into the office, closed the door. Some sort of weird Mexican shit. She'd heard all kinds of stories from other kids, horror stories from south of the border. That gun in the desk: probably wouldn't hurt to—

The door to the terrace opened. Dane held it for the platinum-haired man. They came inside. Dane gave her a big smile.

"Hey, Lianne—this is my buddy I was telling you about."

"Everybody calls me Buck," said the platinum-haired man.

"Have you got the pictures?" Lianne said. "I'm running late."

"Pictures?" said the platinum-haired man, turning to Dane.

"Oh, that," said Dane. "I kind of mentioned these old pictures of Jimmy I might have, going back to when we were kids in Arivaca."

"Those must have been the days," said the platinum-haired man. "These are theoretical pictures?"

"Probably," said Dane. "Although you never know what my mom has kickin' around. A real pack rat as I remember—haven't seen her in ten years or so."

"Are you saying there are no pictures?" Lianne said.

"Don't worry," said the platinum-haired man. "I have pictures to show you. And after, Dane will drive you back across the border."

"That's okay," Lianne said. "I've got my bike."

The platinum-haired man smiled. "The girl is of the spunky kind," he said. "Where is this bike?"

"In the truck," Dane said.

"Unload it."

"Unload it?"

"A bike is heavy. You expect her to do it herself? Where is your breeding?"

Dane left.

"Sit down," said the platinum-haired man, gesturing toward the leather couch.

"I don't have much time," said Lianne.

"How ridiculous," said the platinum-haired man. "At your age, time is on your side, like a big wave." He pulled up a chair, facing the couch. "Sit, and we will have the picture show."

Lianne sat at the far end of the couch.

"What is your age, exactly?"

"Almost eighteen."

"Have you much experience of dancing?"

"What do you mean?"

"Moving to music. This is the art of dance."

"Sure," said Lianne. "I've danced."

"You are reminding me of someone," he said. "When will you be eighteen?"

"May."

"Not so far away," said the platinum-haired man. "Part of my holding is a dancing club."

"What kind of dancing club?"

He handed her a card. *Buckaroo's. Good for one free drink, champagne included.* The Os in *Buckaroo's* had nipples in them. "Perhaps you will come for an audition one day soon."

She tried to give back the card. He didn't take it. "Or just a free drink the first time, Lianne. Your name is Lianne?"

"Yes."

"A nice name. Spell for me, please."

Lianne spelled it.

"Thank you, Lianne. I am still learning this language. You will notice, though, the use of spunky in conversation."

"I noticed."

"Say, 'I noticed, Buck.' "

"Why?" said Lianne.

He looked puzzled. "It's the American way. To call by friendly names."

"I'd like to see the pictures, Buck," Lianne said. "Then I've got to split."

"Split," said Buck. "So natural. You were Jimmy's girlfriend?"

"I still am."

He sat back in his chair. "A thousand condolences," he said. "With stress on *lence*?"

"No."

He repeated the word, getting it right this time. "Somewhat older than you, I believe, this Jimmy?"

"So?"

"So. Of course. So what. I myself never really had this pleasure of getting to know Jimmy. Just once we were speaking on the phone."

"About what?"

"Oh, no more than a little friendly chat. But just from

talking, I would never judge he was the kind of man for doing bank jobs."

"No?"

"But perhaps you know something of his motive."

"I don't."

"He never discussed this?"

"No."

Buck smiled. "Maybe he was planning some surprise for you."

"Like what?"

"Something nice. Diamonds? Gold? SUV?"

"I don't care about things like that." Lianne thought of those blue fence posts stretching away to forever.

"You don't?"

"Not really."

"But I'm certain Jimmy would have had something nice in his mind for such a pretty girl. Or woman. When did you learn about this robbery?"

"After."

"When after?"

"On TV."

"You were all by yourself when you found out?"

"Yes."

"And where was this?"

"At home."

"And this home?"

"In Tucson."

"What part?"

"You know Tucson?"

"I have only now returned from a lovely little home in the Foothills, genuine orange tree in front."

"We've got a tangerine tree," Lianne said.

"This we," said Buck, "it is your nuclear family?"

"Me and my mom."

"Is she as pretty as you?"

Lianne didn't like the way he kept saying *pretty,* wished

she could have met his gaze and said something stinging, but she was suddenly just too uncomfortable. He pulled his chair a little closer.

"And was this pretty mama watching the TV news with you?"

"No," Lianne said; and forced herself to look him in the eye. "Have you got those pictures or not?"

"Pick up that remote," he said.

It lay on the armrest. "You've transferred them to tape?"

"Press video three."

Lianne pressed video three. The two talking heads and the scrolling stock prices vanished from the flat-screen TV on the opposite wall. Then came a fuzzy little jitter and a black-and-white scene stabilized on the screen.

A thin-faced woman enters a room: a big room: a bank. It's her, and proof that pictures don't always tell the story, because there's no indication of how happy she was inside. Lianne looks around, then up, directly into the camera. She walks over to a teller, hands her a dollar bill, gets four quarters in change. She takes a handful of candies from a dish and walks away.

Another fuzzy little jitter, and then the interior of the bank again. A bunch of old people are on the floor, scared shitless. The only ones not on the floor are a wheelchair racer–type guy and Jimmy, wearing the ski mask from Steamboat Springs, money bags in one hand, gun in the other. The wheelchair racer has a real bad expression on his face as Jimmy goes by, but Jimmy doesn't look his way. The moment Jimmy's in front of him, the wheelchair racer rams him in the back. Then comes a big struggle down on the floor, with Jimmy and the wheelchair racer. There's a moment when Jimmy can shoot him, easy, but he doesn't. Then the moment's gone. And what's this? A woman gets up off the floor, real quick, and now she's got the money bags. Is this the woman Lianne caught a glimpse of running away outside? She looks like a hooker—enormous wig, tiny dress, lots of makeup—but there's something about the way she moves, smooth, even in those amazing shoes, and as she passes the camera, the wind from how fast she's going lifts her wig out of the way for just an instant, and—impossible. But: the money coming in, Mom late so often for dinner, the red wig in her dance bag.

The stripper who'd run off with the money: half-formed thoughts boiled through Lianne's mind, much too fast to follow. On the screen, everything now seemed slow. Ski mask off. Jimmy up. Bristly-haired man in. Jimmy's gun moves just the littlest bit in no particular direction. The bristly-haired man aims his own gun in a very particular direction. Behind him stands the thin-faced woman. Jimmy's eyes are looking for something—her, right?—but he doesn't see her. Lianne has a chance to jump on the bristly haired man's back, to knock the gun from his hand, to act; but she doesn't do a fucking thing. The frame freezes right there, her face very clear.

"Any questions?" said Buck.

She looked at him. Even with what happened to Jimmy, and the cemetery and everything, it had never occurred to her that death was in her future too. She knew intellectually, of course, but she'd never felt it. Now she did; and it could come anytime.

"Or maybe amendings of your original story?" Buck said.

Caught, but completely, in a lie. Lianne thought: *The door to the terrace; Buck, even closer now on his chair; the gun in the drawer.*

"Pictures of Jimmy," Buck said. "So glad you asked. So glad you paid this visit. What do you see in this picture show?"

Lianne didn't answer. He was smiling. His teeth were as white as Jimmy's, whiter even, like snow, beyond the human possibility for teeth; and much bigger.

"What if I tell you what I see?" he said. "Then you say where I am wrong. Like a fun game—and I am hoping to lose. With such a pretty girl, who would not want to be wrong? How is the sound of this?"

"All right," she said.

"All right, Buck," he corrected.

"All right, Buck." Up and down her back, where he couldn't see, strange cold sensations were on the loose. Death could happen anytime. She needed that gun.

"First," he said, "I see that you were not at home and watching the news, but inside the bank itself. Am I wrong?"

"No."

"No, Buck," he said.

She didn't answer. He shifted his chair a little closer, leaving almost no room to get around him, run to the desk.

"I see that you knew what Jimmy was doing," he said. "In fact, you helped with planning. Am I wrong?"

"No."

He reached forward, put his hand on her knee; didn't squeeze or anything, just rested it there: a huge hand.

"No, Buck," Lianne said.

"Was the taste of the candy good?"

"Yes, Buck."

He took his hand away. "I see also that you were there at the end for some purpose."

"Like?"

"Like is not following the rules. You must say I am wrong or not."

"I'm not playing this game anymore."

"Yes," he said. "It soon grows boring. We will cut to the chase." He glanced back at the screen—Lianne in the doorway of the bank, behind Jimmy's killer, Jimmy looking for something, not seeing her—then faced her abruptly, leaning forward. She smelled some kind of food on his breath, beets maybe. "How did you and Jimmy make the choice of this bank?" he said.

"Jimmy chose it," she said. "From the yellow pages."

"Yellow pages?"

"In the phone book. He closed his eyes and pointed."

"You saw this with your own eyes?"

"Yes." She didn't like lying about their life together, but Buck was going to keep probing around until she made a mistake, revealed that she knew it was all an insurance scam, with Jimmy just in for ten percent, the dangerous fact that couldn't get out; and this lie seemed like a good one. Wasn't it possible someone like Jimmy would have played a game like that, protecting his girlfriend from knowledge that could hurt her?

"You are a smart girl," he said.

"I'm just telling you what happened."

"What happened," said Buck, "in three parts. This Jimmy wants a ranch. He makes decision to bank rob. He finds his bank in the yellow pages."

"That's about it," Lianne said.

"Okay," said Buck. "Now I understand. I learn more of America every day."

"Great," said Lianne. She rose. "That's where I'm headed."

She stood over him, in the tight little space he'd left for her. He reached out, took her hand, not roughly, but hers was lost in his. "That would be a nice possibility, cheerfulness all around," he said, "if Jimmy was not so dumb."

She jerked her hand free. "Jimmy wasn't dumb."

"Maybe not dumb, but too close to dumb to invent this yellow page mumbo-jumbo. This is right, mumbo-jumbo?"

Lianne didn't answer.

"And another thing I know from my own parents, rest in peacefulness," he said. "When a dumb man finds a smart girl, her brain is the body part he ends up using most of all."

Lianne slapped his face as hard as she could.

It stunned him for a moment. A moment was all she needed to get by him, over to the desk, rip open the drawer, grab the gun. But that was it. Then the room was full of noise, the desk was flipping over, and his face was murderous. Lianne pointed the gun right at him and pulled the trigger. He flinched, but nothing else happened. Lianne tried again. This time there wasn't even a flinch. The murderous look was back in place, a smile now added.

The interior door swung open and the shotgun barrel poked in. Lianne went the other way, whipping open the slider and running across the terrace, headed toward the stairs. Evening shadows were falling now and she didn't see the man in her path, a man in a red T-shirt, until she was almost on top of him. Lianne spun around, ran the other way, around the pool, headed toward a palm tree grove beyond the far wing of the house. But another All-American Amusements man appeared, popping out from behind the pool house, cutting her off. She took the only direction left, back toward the house, up a staircase to the second floor of the far wing, through the first door she found, footsteps behind her. Lianne slammed the door, a door with one of those locks you click. She clicked it, turned into the room.

A room with two men in it. One was Dane, sitting at a card table, dumping banded money from two shopping bags into a thick briefcase. The other man lay on the floor in a bloody heap: her father. She moved toward him. Had he come to rescue her? But—

No time to think it through. Dane was up, slowly backing away. Why? Her father—only one of his eyes was open, and not much—said, "Thank God you're here, baby. Shoot him."

She glanced down at the gun, had forgotten all about it. "It's not working," she said.

"For Christ's sake," he said, sitting up, holding out his

hand. She gave him the gun, got some of his blood on her own hand. At the same moment, Dane came charging across the room. Her father flicked some catch on the gun, pointed it at Dane, shot him in the chest. And then when Dane fell and squirmed around, he shot him once more, a little lower. Dane went still.

"Help me up," her father said. She helped him up, could hardly look at him, his face so bad.

"Oh, Daddy," she said.

He shook his head, kind of angry. "When are you going to start learning how the real world works?" Or something like that: his voice was so croaky. "Throw the rest in that case," he said.

Someone banged on the door.

"Let's just go," Lianne said. "Out the window."

"Can you be a good daughter for once in your goddamn life?" he said.

Lianne threw the rest of the money in the thick briefcase, jammed it shut. More banging at the door. Her father put a bullet into the gun. Then came a shotgun blast the other way, splintering a panel in the door. It made her father angry. He raised his gun.

"Dad," she said, took his hand, drew him toward the window. Down below, not far, lay a little desert garden, the earth brown with watering, soft-looking. Lianne opened the window. "Hang and let go—it's not far," she said. "Can you do it?"

"I'm an athlete, Lianne," he said; one of his front teeth was gone. "Another thing you never appreciated. Drop the case first."

Lianne dropped the briefcase; it landed in the garden with a soft thump.

"Now you," he said.

"You first," she said. "Then if—"

Another shotgun blast at the door, more splintering. Her father gave her a hard push, knocking her against the sill and halfway out. She climbed through, hung, dropped, landed on her feet.

"Dad," she said, looking up at the window. He had his back to it. Shotgun, splintering, the pop of the handgun, her father's voice: "Don't forget the fucking money."

Lianne picked up the briefcase, backed a few steps into the garden. Shotgun, handgun: a crash. Then came yelling, pounding feet, more gunfire, a cry of pain, then another. One more shotgun blast; and silence. Lianne backed a little farther away, to the edge of the palm grove, now in shadow, trying to picture what was going on in that room. Buck's face appeared in the window. Lianne knew; she turned and started running, the briefcase in her hand.

Through the palm grove, down a slope, everything darkening around her, all the greens and yellows fading away, then up: at first running, then walking fast, finally just picking her way up and up one hump of the two-humped mountain, the ground rocky, the bushes spiky, the saguaros like giants. Night fell; or rather, grew up all around her, starting in the deepest gullies, rising to the sky. Lianne looked back. Lights shone from the house on the saddle, so far below it shocked her, like she was leaving planet Earth. A little closer, fainter lights were on the move. Lianne kept going.

She came to a ridge, steep and black above her, followed along the base, hoping for an easy way up, found none. The ridge led her around the face of the mountain, sometimes level, mostly up. Glancing back, she now saw no lights at all. On and on, her mind a blank, no sound but her breathing and sometimes a dislodged rock rolling down the mountain, clacking off other rocks like a billiard ball. What direction was she going? Jimmy hadn't finished teaching her the directions. She checked the sky, saw random stars. One was the North Star, pointing north somehow, but it was hidden up there among the others. She kept going. The next time she looked back, the lights of the house were still visible, but the moving lights were back, and very bright, as though she'd made no progress at all.

Lianne turned to the ridge, still steep and dark, and started climbing, tugging at roots and outcrops with her free hand, sometimes on her knees, dragging the briefcase along. It was getting heavy now, like a bad dog tugging at the leash, trying to get away. That wasn't going to work on her; it just made her angry, made her hold on all the harder. *Don't forget the fucking money.* The good daughter was going to get this right.

The ground flattened out a little. Lianne straightened, moved around a boulder twice her height, and stepped on nothing. Then came a fall, blackness all around and her insides pushing up, and a landing that felt hard but didn't seem to make much sound.

Lianne lay on her back, all the breath knocked out of her body; and couldn't get any in, like she was suffocating. Overhead, she saw a thin slice of starry sky. Then a yellow beam flashed across it, and another. She heard voices. They came closer, went silent. A light beam swept across a rocky wall above her. The voices started up again, moved away.

Lianne's breath came back, first in little gasps, then in deep gulps. She lay there for a long time. A curve of the moon edged into the slice of sky above her. She tried to sit up, found she could. The moon lit everything around her: crevice walls, pebbly floor, the briefcase nearby, battered but still fastened shut. Lianne rose, picked it up, climbed onto a ledge jutting from one wall of the crevice. She raised the briefcase over her head and boosted it up onto level ground. Then she climbed out.

The moon made everything easier. Right away, Lianne found a gully running up the ridge, took it right to the top. She stood on the crest of a long fold of the mountain, gazed all around, saw no lights, moving or still. Far below lay a dark opening in the rock face. Lianne recognized it: the mine that Dane said would be worked forever. People were coming out, forty, fifty, maybe more, shadowy people with shadowy bundles. They set off around the base of the mountain in a group that was straggly from the start and got stragglier. If there was a guide or leader, he'd soon separated himself from all but a few. High above, Lianne followed the stragglers.

They walked all the way around the hump—eastern hump, it must have been; Lianne was learning after all—and started across the plain. She came down on a long curving diagonal, stepped onto the plain herself, fifty yards or so behind the last little group. Lianne made no attempt to join them, just kept them in sight: a family, maybe, man, woman with a baby on her back, two other kids. The baby faced Lianne; she knew because sometimes it opened its eyes, and the moonlight glinted in them.

Was it her fatigue? Or that she started feeling Jimmy's presence, and tried so hard to figure out what was on his mind? Whatever the reason, Lianne's own mind wandered and she didn't pay enough attention to the little family, didn't realize they'd stopped and were sitting down, resting their backs against some rocks on the banks of an arroyo.

"Hola," said the father, making her jump.

"Hola," said Lianne. She'd walked right into them: not just the little family, but others as well, a dozen or so. A cloud covered the moon and they all went fuzzy. Water gurgled from a bottle.

"Es lejos," said the father.

"Sí," said Lianne.

"Siéntate," he said. *"Descansa."*

Lianne sat, back to a rock, briefcase between her legs, felt everyone's eyes on her.

"Es lejos," said the father again.

"Sí." It was long.

"Pero nos acercamos," he said.

He sounded optimistic. Lianne could almost feel his family feeding off it. She thought about her own father, also an optimist. And what he'd done for her: she couldn't let herself think about that—like going down an endless drain.

"Agua?" he said.

Lianne realized how thirsty she was, but said, "No." It was a way of repaying him: why hadn't she called him *Daddy* more often?

"Tenemos bastante."

They had lots. Maybe it was rude to refuse. *"Bueno,"* she said.

The mother got up, handed her a plastic bottle. It said VALVOLINE on the outside. She drank. Water, and good.

"Gracias," she said, handing it back.

"De dónde vienes?" said the mother.

"Guatemala," said Lianne, hoping it would explain how strange she must have seemed to them, alien.

"Es lejos," said the mother.

"Dónde dijo?" said the father.

"Guatemala."

"Lejos," said the father. *"Descansa. Descansaremos cinco minutos."*

A five-minute rest. Someone lay down in the arroyo bed. Even Lianne knew not to do that, on account of the sidewinders. She heard snoring right away. The little family all lay down and closed their eyes, the baby too.

When had she last slept? Lianne couldn't remember. She was safe now, knew where she was going, just not how to get there. The air was cold around her, but the rock at her back felt warm. Lianne closed her eyes, nothing that could really be called closing, more like a long blink.

She sat in Daddy's lap while he drove the bumper car. They shared a huge stick of cotton candy. Then came a big bump and the cotton candy got all over both their faces, sticking them together in a pink cloud.

When the long blink was over, Lianne found the moon, no longer covered, in another part of the sky. The wind had risen, blowing moonlit bits of toilet paper across the desert. The little family and all the others were gone. So was the briefcase. They'd left her the Valvoline bottle, filled to the tip-top with water.

Lianne started walking, much more easily now, without the burden. Direction: away from the silhouette of the two-humped mountain, already not so big against the starry background. She felt Jimmy with her again, but gave up trying to read his mind. It just wasn't going to be like that. Feeling his presence was the best she was going to get.

He was still with her when dawn broke, like paint cans spilled across the sky, the most beautiful thing she'd seen in her whole life. The South End bunkhouse was a short stroll away. The sight would have broken her fucking heart, except for what had happened to her father. Succumbing to heartbreak was self-indulgent. How the world works: she was learning.

Thirty-one

Mackie awoke twice in the night: the first time, when Loeb said, "Sergeant Falco hides in the . . ." She knew who Sergeant Falco was from *The Whites of Her Eyes*, waited to hear his hiding place. But Loeb said nothing.

"Where?" she said.

No answer.

Mackie twisted around—they were sleeping on their sides, his hand resting on her hip, as though this had been going on for a long time, the two of them spending nights together—and saw his eyes were closed. Was his unconscious working out something in the night? She closed her own eyes, but couldn't get back to sleep, more and more aware of his hand on her, sending exploratory sensations on unpredictable routes around her body. Mackie had a vision of a possible future, complete with interesting nights. She rolled on top of him. What happened next was good but a little desperate at the same time. He didn't say a word.

The second time Mackie awoke, she heard soft laughter—the pure, happy kind—not from Loeb, but somewhere outside. She got up, looked out the window. The moonlight wasn't so bright now: were shadows on the move out there in the distance? For a moment, Mackie thought so; then everything went still. She got dressed, walked out on the porch, peered in the darkness. No movement, no laughter.

Mackie stayed on the porch. The moon went down. She leaned against the post, Lianne's letter crinkling in her pocket. For a while it was very dark, as though a black fog had settled on everything. Then a faint milky band appeared in the east, spread slowly across the sky. Pastel colors came first, then fiery ones. Mackie heard a little crunch, saw someone walking over a rise. She started running.

Lianne: she'd known just from the sound of that crunch. Then Mackie had her in her arms, the living, breathing girl.

"Oh, Mom," Lianne said. "They killed him."

"I know," Mackie said. "I've got something to tell you."

Lianne's shoulders gave an impatient shake. "I'm talking about Dad," she said.

The story came out—the words like little islands washed over by crying sounds—true and incomprehensible at once. Mackie held her tight; or they held on to each other. There were Kevin-like things about Lianne's hair, and the straightness of her back. The sky went through more changes above their heads. He'd juggled tennis balls at the wedding party. She could still see it.

The problem with having an imagination was that you could get way ahead of yourself. Sitting at the table in the South End bunkhouse with Mackie and her daughter, Loeb had no trouble picturing a nice familial Arizona future with hiking, horseback riding, pig roasts; this despite the not-quite-dry tear tracks on both their faces, and the fear that came off them in little things to be documented later.

Loeb himself was not afraid. One fact from Lianne—that the bank robbery was unreal, a setup, an insurance scam, an inside job—changed everything. This was like the moment right before the avalanche in *White Out* when Timothy Bolt finds that someone nailed a green-for-beginners sign to a tree at the top of the Banzai Couloir; first big revelation in his first book. Now all that remained was plotting, not his strength, according to Mary Jane, but the next step would have been obvious to the dullest hack.

"We'll go see Clay Krupsha," he said. "Captain of detectives in Agua Fría. He'll arrest Samsonov. Case closed."

"But he'll arrest me too," Mackie said.

"For what?" Loeb said. "We'll say the money wasn't in those bags, never left the bank. And the proof is Samsonov has it and you don't."

"He had it," Lianne said. She explained what had happened to the money.

Loeb laughed. It was perfect, like the end of *The Treasure of the Sierra Madre* only better, because it didn't make the Mexicans, unknowingly watching the gold dust blow away, seem so ignorant. And as for the plan: "It doesn't really make any difference," he said. "Slight adjustment: you found out your daughter's boyfriend was mixed up in this scheme, went to the bank with the intention of stopping it, panicked, and ran, but with the intention of returning the money. Or something similar. We'll improvise. I do this all the time. The point is, no jury would ever convict you, not after they hear about what happened at his house, how he attacked you, the check for a thousand years from now, all that. Krupsha won't even be interested in you. He already assumes you had nothing to do with the original plan, and he prides himself on putting justice before the niceties of the law."

"Krupsha," said Mackie. "Isn't he the one who—" Her gaze went to Lianne.

Loeb turned to the girl. Lianne had dark eyes, not her mother's, with some X factor in there he couldn't identify. "This won't help," Loeb said, "but he feels sick about it."

"He did it on purpose," Lianne said.

"That's how they're trained in weapons situations," Loeb said. "How could he know the gun wasn't loaded?"

"That's not what I meant," Lianne said. "You should have seen the look on his face."

Loeb didn't argue. He had seen the look on Krupsha's

face on the tape, businesslike, and, he now realized, a little afraid. Despite this affair with Jimmy Marz, Lianne was still a kid. "No need for you to see him," he said. "Either of you. I'll go myself."

Frankie Nuñez was working the desk. "Got a few minutes to discuss that book idea?" he said.

"Book idea?"

" 'Member?" said Frankie. "Just to help me get started. That's all I need. It's about this Mafia guy, kind of like the Godfather except he's more ballistic and shaves his head, and—"

"Maybe later," Loeb said. "Is Clay in?"

"Go right on back," said Frankie. "I'm off at four."

Loeb knocked on Krupsha's door.

"Yup."

Loeb went in. Krupsha was at his desk, its top littered with crumpled Coke cans; he had dark patches around his eyes and needed a shave. Sergeant Falco was like that too, overworked and undergroomed; but those crumpled Coke cans were a nice touch he'd have to remember—sugar highs, caffeine jitters, repressed violence, all in one everyday image.

"And presto," Krupsha said, hanging up the phone. "Where you been hiding?"

"I'll get to that," Loeb said, sitting on a hard wooden chair across the desk. "We've got a lot to discuss."

"Not that fuckin' cat?"

"Partly," Loeb said.

"You trying to kill me?" Krupsha said.

Loeb laughed. "I promise not to mention Lonnie Mendez."

"And I'm supposed to be grateful?" Krupsha said.

"He's not part of this."

"Part of what?"

"And you are going to be grateful." Loeb pictured the two of them on *Good Morning America*—one of those oddball crime-busting teams—Diane Sawyer enthralled, books flying out of the stores, a future full of podiums.

"Why is that?" said Krupsha.

"Because I've solved the case," Loeb said. He didn't realize it was one of the proudest moments of his life until the words were out. He was even going to get the girl.

"Which case it that?"

"Which case?" Loeb said. "The bank robbery. What other case is there?"

"Can't exactly call that a case."

"Bigger than that, you mean?" said Loeb. "*The* case?"

"You're one funny guy," Krupsha said. "I'm liking the book, *White Night*—"

"*White Midnight.*"

"And that Athena? She's pretty hot. A blow job's supposed to be happening up there on the chairlift thing, right?"

"Yes." Was he reading the same scene over and over?

"Got my attention," said Krupsha. "But as for real crime, that's a little different."

"Meaning?"

"I'm not saying blow jobs don't happen at unexpected times. That part you got pretty good, better than real life. But in this particular case, there is no case, excuse my own little turn of phrase."

"No case?"

"Course there was a robbery," Krupsha said, "dumbass cowpoke, wheelchair psycho, the rest of it. But no money got taken."

What was this? The no-money-got-taken idea, his own plan for protecting Mackie, but now spinning at him from an unexpected direction?

"Wasn't even there to begin with," Krupsha said.

"I don't understand."

"The stripper—and I hear she's a piece of ass, grade A—got away with two bags of chicken fajita dinner coupons from the casino. Turns out they had some mix-up out there—makes you wonder how Custer lost—and the deposit didn't come in till yesterday afternoon."

"The five hundred grand was still at the casino?"

"You got it."

At that moment, Loeb knew why Krupsha had left the NYPD, was working out here: not smart enough for the big city. True? Or was he letting his annoyance at that piece-of-ass remark think for him? "I've got a question about the casino," he said.

"Shoot."

"Who owns it?"

"The whole damn tribe—there's hundreds of 'em."

"Any silent partners?"

"Silent partners?"

"Such as Buck Samsonov, for example."

Krupsha shrugged. "Not that I know of."

"But you know he owns the bank."

"I heard he had an interest. Where are you going with this?"

"I assume he's your source on the chicken fajita thing."

"Could be. He's the injured party."

Right the first time: Krupsha was much too slow for the big city. "Have you actually seen the money?" Loeb said.

"The money that wasn't stolen? What would be the point? You're losin' me, Nicky."

"Samsonov has a reason for wanting you to believe there was no robbery."

"What would that be?"

"Staying out of jail," Loeb said. How exhilarating, just saying that. "And maybe off death row," he added. "Samsonov planned the whole thing himself. It was an inside job, Clay, an insurance scam. That's why Jimmy's gun was empty. He was in for ten percent."

The dark patches around Krupsha's eyes stayed dark and his purple lips stayed purple, but the rest of his face went pasty. For a moment, Loeb thought he was going to be sick. He knew what was going on inside Krupsha, a sickening epistemological lurch toward the new and horrible knowledge that he'd shot a fake bank robber, not a real one. Krupsha started speaking, had to clear his throat, tried again. "What's your evidence?" he said, voice all raspy.

"Jimmy told his girlfriend."

"And she told you."

"Yes."

"Who's this girlfriend?"

"She's on the tape, toward the end."

"I wondered about that," Krupsha said. "You been busy."

"I had some luck."

"Don't come all over modest," Krupsha said. "I better talk to her."

"She's going to need a little time for that," Loeb said. "With what happened."

The color returned to Krupsha's face. "You questioning my judgment, what went on in the bank?"

Loeb shook his head. Probably more a matter of courage than judgment; it was clear to him now why Krupsha had shot Jimmy: he'd been too scared to wait and see where Jimmy was going with that gun. "As far as you knew, you had an armed bank robber."

"Got it again."

"But it's hard to explain to a kid."

"So I go on just this hearsay, twice removed."

"There's lots more," Loeb said. "More routes into this. Is there anyone you work with in Mexico?"

"Why?"

"Because there's been shooting at Samsonov's place across the border, probably some killing."

"Which is why you made that little death row quip?" Krupsha said.

"I wouldn't call it a quip."

"Then I won't either—you're the word boy," said Krupsha. "Who got killed?"

"I can't say for sure," Loeb said, "but I'm hoping you'll find out. You could also ask to see the money."

"Why?"

"Because Samsonov won't be able to show it to you. The money's gone forever."

"Where?"

"I won't spoil it."

Krupsha opened a drawer, took out his shoulder holster, strapped it on. He rose, slow and heavy. "I got someone I work with in Mexico," he said.

Loeb rose too. "I'm coming, right?" The revision to the death row line that had been eluding him for so long trembled in a corner of his mind.

"Wouldn't be the same without you," Krupsha said.

Thirty-two

Loeb could hardly control his excitement as they drove through the control point, Krupsha's green Crown Vic getting waved right through. It made him talkative, the way he'd been as a little kid.

"Getting back to Whiskers," he said.

"You don't quit," said Krupsha.

"Because Whiskers is the key to this whole thing," Loeb said. "Maybe not the key, more like microcosm." That wasn't right either.

"Words, words, words," said Krupsha.

Krupsha as Hamlet: Loeb had never dreamed. A deliberate quotation, or just an accident? No way to tell from the expression on Krupsha's face. The pastiness was back now; he really did look sick.

"I don't think you understand what Samsonov is all about," Loeb said.

"Don't I?" Krupsha steered through the narrow streets of the Mexican Agua Fría; a hawker waved a Speedy Gonzalez doll in front of the windshield.

"The scope of him," Loeb said. "He owns the strip club, the bank, all the theme-park land that Whiskers died for, God knows what else. He's got an appetite for growth like a nineteenth-century robber baron—even sees himself that way. He's more like a time traveler than an immigrant."

"Losin' me again."

"The America he loves so much doesn't exist anymore," Loeb said. Which was why there had been violence and would be more: misalignment leading to tension leading to breakage. But Loeb didn't get into all that. "How long has he been here?" he asked.

Krupsha turned into a cobblestone square with a restaurant on one side: Señor B.'s. "Maybe two years now," he said.

"Two years?" said Loeb. "He's done all this in two years?"

"Come September, now that I think," said Krupsha.

"Where did the money come from?"

"What money?"

"To finance everything."

"Some people are good at makin' money," Krupsha said. "Don't you know that by now?"

"But the money he needed to make the money—what's the source of that?"

"Have to ask him," Krupsha said.

The door to Señor B.'s opened, and a man in a tuxedo, flower in his buttonhole, spun a cigarette butt into the square. He saw Krupsha and waved.

"Who do you like better?" Loeb said. "Diane Sawyer or Katie Couric?" Diane Sawyer might enjoy Krupsha a little more: he could see the look in her eye.

"Never heard of either of 'em," Krupsha said.

"You don't seem very enthusiastic about what's happening," Loeb said. "Won't it be good for your career?"

Krupsha turned down a dirt alley, the corrugated steel wall rising on their left, spray-painted here and there: soccer players, Che Guevara, an AK-47. "That a big concern of yours, my career?" Krupsha said.

"I assume you've got ambitions," Loeb said. Then he thought of Krupsha's house east of town, almost luxurious, and wasn't sure. Maybe in Krupsha's own mind he'd arrived already, was in semiretirement, with his sunken living room, swimming pool, seventy-five-year-old tequila. "What brought you out here in the first place?" he asked.

"Mary Jane didn't tell you?"

"No."

"But you're hot for the answer?"

"I wouldn't put it that way."

"Forget it, then."

"But I'd like to know." Writers, if not curious, were nothing.

"Make you a deal," Krupsha said. "You come across with the real story on Mary Jane, I'll fess up."

"What real story?"

"I have to spell it out? You and her, tab A, slot B."

"Why do you care so much? You're divorced."

"That's my offer," Krupsha said. His hands were squeezing the steering wheel, knuckles white. Not all the knuckles—important to get these details right—just the first and second, and the color more lemon-yellow than white, but: he was keeping Krupsha in suspense, the white-knuckle kind.

Loeb laughed. "I give up. Nothing happened."

"She says it did."

Loeb stopped laughing. "That's crazy."

Krupsha slowed down, guided the big car into an even narrower alley, almost scraping a wall on the turn. He stopped behind a black windowless building. "Why would she make something like that up?"

"I can think of a hundred reasons."

"Name one." Krupsha got out of the car.

"To make you go through just what you're going through," said Loeb, getting out too.

Krupsha locked the car, used another key to unlock a door in the windowless building. "Why would she want to do that?"

"Maybe it has something to do with your marriage, or why you got divorced," Loeb said.

Krupsha shook his head. "One thing about Mary Jane—she's got this disease of always telling the truth." He held the door open, motioned Loeb inside. "Unlike some others."

"What others?"

"Guys in certain professions."

"Like?"

"Mine and yours," Krupsha said.

Cool air flowed out of the doorway; Loeb saw a brick wall, painted black, and stairs leading down. He paused on the top step. "What's in here?"

Krupsha sighed. "Hell, Nicky, I believe you. Why would a good-looking young guy like you even get a hard-on for an old bag like Mary Jane? Don't know what gets into me sometimes." He held out his hand.

Loeb shook it, unable to find a way of defending his virility or Mary Jane's looks that wouldn't reawaken suspicion. He felt a tremor in Krupsha's hand. "You all right?"

"Must be age," Krupsha said. "Let's get this started."

"What's in here?"

"The guy I work with in Mexico."

"Is this the back of the police station?" Loeb tried to imagine the kind of complex, uncoded, pragmatic relationship that must have evolved between the two forces. This was going to be very useful.

"More or less," Krupsha said. He patted Loeb on the shoulder, guided him through the doorway.

The door closed behind them, shutting out the light. For a moment it was black inside; then Loeb's eyes adjusted, saw faint yellow light at the bottom of the stairs. More cool air, almost cold, came flowing up.

"After you," Krupsha said.

They walked down the stairs and into a long corridor, shadowy and dim, lit by naked bulbs spaced far apart. A crudely built corridor, almost like a tunnel: the walls earth and rock, shored up here and there with wooden beams; and more beams overhead.

"Not much farther," Krupsha said.

They passed an intersecting corridor, this one lined with cinderblocks. Loeb thought he heard music playing some-where above, possibly "Maniac."

"Tell me about this guy," Loeb said.

Krupsha shrugged. "Mexico's Mexico," he said.

A steel door stood at the end of the corridor. Krupsha knocked.

A voice came over a speaker: "Waltz right in."

A familiar voice. Loeb turned to Krupsha as the door opened from the inside. "Thanks again for the book," Krupsha said. "A fun read, plus I sold it on eBay for ten bucks." He gave Loeb a push, just hard enough to send him through the doorway.

Inside: a plutocratic office, Buck Samsonov behind the desk, Turbo behind the door, everything happening fast and Loeb's vision a jumble besides. Turbo banged the door shut, Loeb just catching a glimpse of Krupsha's exit: he looked like he was actually about to start running. Every-thing clarified and locked into place around one central re-alization: once the robbery went bad in such a public way, they didn't trust Jimmy to take the fall on his own, to keep his mouth shut. Krupsha had been stationed there for a rea-son, had shot Jimmy on purpose, as Lianne said. Maybe they'd have killed him after even if things had gone right.

"The worst part," Loeb said, "is that he knew Jimmy's gun wasn't loaded."

"Worst part?" said Samsonov. "What about the money?"

Turbo took off his glasses and put them in his shirt pocket, his movements crisp and professional, like the ges-tures of a trained actor directed to demonstrate *nothing personal*. But there was something horribly unfocused about Turbo's naked eyes.

"What we need to hear," said Samsonov, "is the where-about—this is a word, whereabout?"

"Whereabouts, I think," said Turbo. "But he's the word guy."

"Not word guy," said Samsonov. "Author. But so modest, presenting himself as ASPCA. Whereabouts is right, author?"

Loeb nodded.

Samsonov opened a leather notebook. "All one word?"

"Yes," said Loeb, and considered another word, the proper noun Krupsha: practically a corruption of *corruption*. He should have known. Instead, he'd fooled himself, accepting, for example, that Krupsha's certainty of the spontaneity of Mackie's actions in the bank was based on some kind of deep-in-the-bone cop experience, when in fact he had simply known the plan. Now he understood why Krupsha had threatened Lonnie, why he'd steered him wrong in the Whiskers case, and why Mackie's composite was so bad—he wanted Samsonov, not the police, to find her. And while Bub must have told Samsonov the pen story, sending him to 4 Buena Vida Circle, Krupsha had helped there too: How else would Samsonov have known all about Loeb the mystery writer? And: Why was he asking this now? There would be no revisions.

Samsonov wrote the word down, closed the leather notebook. "The whereabouts, then, of money, Mackie, Lianne. This is our need."

"No idea," Loeb said. Timothy Bolt in a somewhat similar situation in chapter thirty of *White Out* had said, "Fuck you," but Loeb hadn't dreamed up anyone like Turbo for him to deal with.

"Authors should be smart by definition, no?" said Samsonov. He picked up a book from the desk: *The Whites of Her Eyes,* with that disappointing call number on the spine indicating a library copy. "I have been reading in your book," he said. "The whole concept of this skiing detective is foolish to me. This is not what the American people want. He won't be missed."

That annoyed Loeb. "I can tell you about the money," he said. "Gone for good. The migrants stole it from Lianne."

Samsonov, who'd been leafing through the book, went still. "Her whereabouts, then?"

"No idea."

But he'd made a mistake, trapped himself. Loeb glanced at the door, tried to think of some way to get past Turbo, failed. Samsonov was still holding *The Whites of Her Eyes*.

"We could make him eat it," he said.

"Do we have that kind of time?" said Turbo.

"Perhaps only a few chapters," said Samsonov.

He held out the book. Turbo went to get it. Loeb dove for the door, actually got his hand on the knob, or at least touched it, cool and brassy. Then Turbo was on him. Loeb tried to flip him off—did flip him off, Turbo surprisingly light—and darted toward the—

But not quite flipped off: Turbo still had him by the right wrist, his grip not especially strong, almost gentle. Loeb jerked his hand away; or tried to. Then he was twisted all around, and somehow his own pulling force against Turbo got mixed up, as though he were joining the fight against himself, an immense pressure building and building in his shoulder until something snapped, loud as a dried-out wishbone. There was a horrible throaty noise—his own—and he was curled up on the floor, left hand on his right elbow, trying to ease the arm back into its socket. It wouldn't be eased. Turbo gazed down at him, glasses back on, eyes focused now, expressing satisfaction.

Samsonov, behind his desk, said: "Whereabouts, please."

If he had it in him, ever had or ever would, now was the time to say *fuck you*. Loeb said it, or tried to.

"What was that?" said Samsonov.

Loeb said it again, louder this time, although just doing that, adding volume, increased the pain, as if his vocal cords were somehow vibrating in his shoulder.

This time they heard.

"A tough guy," said Samsonov, "like in the book."

Turbo bent over him. "What now?" he said.

"Something not in the book," Samsonov said, getting up. "Something real."

Loeb had one thought: end of story.

The hottest day of the year, air still, nothing moving but jet trails high above, most of them eastbound, and the sun, much more slowly, going the other way. When it got low enough to shine under the porch roof, Mackie and Lianne went inside.

"How long does it take to arrest him?" Lianne said.

"I don't know," said Mackie. The calming force of the South End bunkhouse and the hard beauty all around had leaked away during the afternoon. Now Mackie felt cut-off, unreal.

Lianne opened the wood box, spun the dial on the combination lock of a steel trunk that stood inside.

"What's in there?" Mackie said.

Lianne popped open the top. "My backpack," she said, taking it out.

Mackie glanced in the open trunk. "What's that other stuff?"

"The dynamite."

"Dynamite?"

Lianne pointed out the window, toward the western hills. "Jimmy thinks—" She stopped herself, but there was no sign of tears; Mackie didn't know whether that was good or bad. "Jimmy thought there was gold out there," Lianne said. "From the geology. Once in a while he did some blasting."

"Did he find anything?"

"It was mostly for the fun of it, Mom." Lianne turned away.

Thirty-three

Rags rode up to the South End bunkhouse, his face brick-red from the setting sun, the light also reddening his dusty horse, coating the animal in a shining fuzz.

"Hey, Lianne," he said. "Your mom find you?"

Mom came out on the porch.

Rags nodded to her. "Your friend gone off in the truck?" he said.

"He's coming back."

"Better be soon," Rags said. "It ain't easy in the dark."

"Is that Clyde?" Lianne said.

"Yup."

Lianne came down off the porch, patted Clyde's face, warm to the touch. His ears came forward. "He likes you," Rags said.

Lianne looked into Clyde's big brown eye. "You remember Jimmy?" she said.

"Sure he does," said Rags. "Misses him real bad."

Lianne thought she could see that, an inarticulate deep-brown longing. She stroked Clyde's powerful neck, the feel of it instantly familiar. Was there something wrong with her, how much worse Jimmy's death got to her than her own father's?

"Which kind of reminds me of that old joke," Rags said. "What did the duck say to the horse?"

They didn't know.

" 'Why the long face?' " Rags said.

Lianne could just see them, duck and horse. She started laughing. Laughed and laughed, to the point where she understood the expression about laughing until you cried. But she didn't let that happen.

"Like that one, huh?" said Rags. Something beeped. Clyde's ears shifted back. Rags took a cell phone from his pocket. "Yeah," he said, then, "not yet," "bunkhouse," and "later." He clicked off. "Mr. Croft," he said. "We're checkin' out this weird story. Some crazy talk of money blowin' around out here last night. Actual cash money, I'm talkin' about. Any evidence of that show up?"

They shook their heads.

"See or hear anything strange?"

They shook their heads again. Rags smiled. "Mother and daughter for sure." He gave a little pull on the reins, started turning Clyde around. "Probably nothing to it," he said, and had his boot heels out to give Clyde a kick when Mackie said:

"Can I use your phone?"

Rags checked his watch. "Mind waiting a bit?" he said. "Off-peak starts in three minutes."

Mackie took the phone inside. Lianne followed her. "Who are you calling, Mom?"

"I don't like this waiting," Mackie said.

She got the police number in Agua Fría, called Krupsha's office. He answered on the first ring.

"Krupsha," he said.

"Is Nick Loeb there?" said Mackie.

Pause. "Who's this?"

"I want to speak to him."

"Who's this?" Krupsha said again.

"Is he there?" Mackie said. "Is everything all right?"

"Depends who's calling," Krupsha said.

"If he's there put him on."

"Got to know who I'm talking to first. That's basic."

Mackie tried to picture what was happening inside Krupsha's office, could not. She pressed *off*, went outside, handed the phone up to Rags. It rang before he had it in his pocket.

"Yeah," he said. He looked down at Mackie. "Your name Mackie?" he said.

"Who is it?"

"Don't know." Rags handed her the phone.

"Did you have to make me jump through hoops?" Krupsha said. "Stop worrying. Everything's working out fine here, except for all the paperwork. No charges against you, past, present, or future, goes without saying. Nicky's in with the D.A. right now, but I can swing by and pick you up."

Mackie thought. Lianne, watching, shook her head, just the slightest movement, although she couldn't have heard what he'd said.

"He's got nine-thirty reservations for the three of you at the Cantina Romantica in Amado," Krupsha said. "Supposed to be good."

Mackie had heard of it. "I'll call you back," she said.

"Call me back? But—"

Mackie clicked off, got the number for the Cantina Romantica in Amado, dialed it. The woman who answered put her on hold for thirty seconds or so, came back on the line.

"Is there a reservation for Nick Loeb at nine-thirty?" Mackie said.

"Party of three?" said the woman. "Yes, ma'am."

Mackie called Krupsha. "Okay," she said.

"Just need to know where you are," said Krupsha.

Mackie told him. "It's kind of hard to find, especially in the dark."

"I'm a desert rat," Krupsha said. "Just sit tight."

Mackie turned to Lianne. "Everything's all right," she said.

"You sure?"

"Yes."

* * *

Rags was long gone and night had fallen by the time headlights bobbed up in the northeast. They veered one way, then another, unsteady, restless. Then came engine sounds, first just a little hum.

"All set?" Mackie said.

Lianne put on her backpack. "Thanks, Mom."

Maybe for a lot of things, but Mackie accepted it for what she'd done at Buckaroo's. "You're welcome."

The headlights swept across the side of the bunkhouse, caught their faces. A big dark car stopped in front of the porch. A man leaned out of the driver's side window, smiled at Mackie. She felt Lianne stiffen beside her.

"Sorry to keep you ladies waiting," he said. "Clay Krupsha, at your service."

They got in the car, Mackie in front, Lianne in back.

"Everything all right?" Mackie said.

"Couldn't be better," said Krupsha, rounding the bunkhouse, his headlights finding the track, dust swirling above it from his previous passage. "Nicky's still in with the D.A. but he should be all done by the time we get there." He nodded his head toward Lianne. "Might be some doughnuts left in that box on the floor, in case you're hungry."

"Have you arrested Samsonov yet?" Mackie said.

"Warrant's still being drawn up," said Krupsha. "There's complications, as you can imagine, with two governments involved. But it's only a matter of time. How about some music?"

"You're the one who shot Jimmy," Lianne said from the backseat.

Krupsha twisted around to look at her; the car went over a bump. "Wish I could undo it, young lady. You'da been there when I found out that gun was unloaded, you'd believe me."

Lianne said nothing.

"Practically bawled my eyes out," Krupsha said, straightening around. "Any objection to country?" He stabbed a button on the radio. Dolly Parton. "Ever been to Dollywood?" Krupsha said. "I'm a big fan."

"What about my ex-husband's body?" Mackie said.

"We're workin' on it," said Krupsha. He turned up the volume.

Garth Brooks was singing "Two of a Kind, Workin' on a Full House," when they drove into Agua Fría. A warm night, with lots of people on the street and a long line in the McDonald's drive-thru. Krupsha parked in front of the police station. "I'll just run in and get him," he said.

He went inside. Mackie turned to Lianne. She was rummaging in her backpack. "He wanted to be cremated," Mackie said.

"How do you know?"

"We discussed it once."

"Cremation's better," Lianne said. "Is that what you want too?"

It was, but Mackie didn't say so. Instead, she said: "I want to live." A bit of bravado, maybe, a little posturing, but she felt the truth of it, and more important, was hoping Lianne would say, "Me too." But she didn't, just closed the backpack and fastened the buckles.

"We'll have a ceremony," Mackie said. She wanted to make their lives normal, what they had before now seeming normal; and soon.

"I'll read from *Lord of the Flies*," said Lianne. No streetlights in Agua Fría, and Lianne's face in shadow: Mackie couldn't tell if this was black humor or simply blackness. Her mouth went dry.

Krupsha came out of the station alone, a Styrofoam coffee cup in one hand.

"They've all moved on," he said, getting in, turning the key.

"Where?" said Mackie.

"Buckaroo's."

"Buckaroo's?"

"Course we closed it down hours ago," Krupsha said. "But they're going through the books, and you know Nicky—he wanted to tag along."

"Why?" said Lianne.

Krupsha shrugged. "Writers are curious, got to be. Maybe you'll be a writer too, one day."

Krupsha drove down toward the crossing, took a left on Pershing—chain-link fence on their right and beyond it the white form of a Border Patrol SUV, lights off, parked near the steel wall—and turned into the parking lot at Buckaroo's. The club was dark, the flashing sign switched off, but several cars were in the lot.

"Ladies?" said Krupsha, getting out of the car.

Mackie turned to Lianne. "Why don't you wait here?" she said.

"I want to come." Lianne opened the door, slipped on her backpack.

"Told you," said Krupsha. "A budding writer."

He unlocked a side door of the building, opened it for them. "You've got a key?" Mackie said.

"First thing we do is change the locks," Krupsha said. "After you."

They went inside. The only light came from the exit signs. It glinted on the bottles behind the bar, the glass walls of the music booth, the brass pole onstage. Smells hung in the air—beer, sweat, perfume. For a moment, Mackie felt Lianne's hand on her back, very light; and knew she'd been right about what that thanks was for.

"I think it's this way," said Krupsha, moving past the stage to the door behind the music booth. "Ladies?" he said, opening it and motioning them down the stairs. Dull brown-yellow light shone at the bottom. "Careful now."

They went down the stairs, Mackie, Lianne, Krupsha, down into cooler air, then followed the cinderblock-lined hallway to the steel door at the end.

"All the records got kept in here," Krupsha said, knocking on the door.

A voice came from a speaker: "Waltz right in."

"Run," Mackie said.

Lianne was already moving, but not fast enough. Krupsha stepped back, just a little faster, gun already out of his shoulder holster, and blocked their path.

"Why can't he just get a fucking buzzer?" Krupsha said. His gun on them, sweeping slowly from one to the other, he pushed the door open. "In," he said.

Inside, Samsonov sat at his desk, working on the computer. Turbo lay on the couch, reading a book where all the *S*'s in the title were dollar signs. They barely looked up. Loeb sat propped against a wall, one of his arms at a funny angle, and lots more wrong besides. The wall had bloody patches here and there, as though some artist had smacked patterns with a red mop. Mackie went to him, knelt. He got his eyes open, just a little, opened his mouth too. Blood came out, but not much. He licked his lips, said something that she didn't catch. She wanted to touch him, comfort him in some way, but didn't know where it wouldn't hurt.

He tried again. Mackie could hear the effort of pushing those words out, like some thick liquid forced through gravel. "Tunnel," he said. "The money that makes the money."

She glanced up at one of those monitors on the wall, saw Sola up onstage, one finger in her mouth, Club Girlie–style. Why did understanding always come a beat too late? Dancing was exactly the opposite.

"You get it?" he said. "The meaning?"

"Yes."

"Not the symbolic." He tried to clear his throat; Mackie heard a faint gurgling sound. "The real meaning."

"Yes." Buckaroo's and Club Girlie were connected underground.

He reached for her hand, fumbling like an old man, took it. "I didn't give you up," he said. "Did I?"

"No," Mackie said. "I was stupid, that's all."

He shook his head, one little side-to-side, slow and care-ful. Offering some comfort himself: but it didn't work, not down here, in this subterranean space under the border where there were no laws and whatever was going to hap-pen would never get out.

"Enough of chitchat," said Samsonov, looking up from the screen. Turbo closed the book, sat up. "You are all stu-pid if truth be known," Samsonov said. "Stupidity costs time and time is money." He rose, came across the room. "*Is* means equals, thus time equaling money. You are ask-ing—is fun impossible if this equation is always on the mind? No. I am the perfect example. I will have money. I will have fun." He paused before Lianne, put his hand on the corners of her lips, squeezed them together, making a different female shape that was hard to miss. Lianne tried to jerk her face away but he wouldn't let her. "Five hun-dred seventy-four thousand and thirty-four U.S. dollars— lost in the desert. How will you make this up to me, with so little time remaining?"

He let go of her so she could speak. His fingers had left red circles on her cheeks. Mackie knew what Lianne would do just before she did it, moved toward her, too late. Lianne spat in his face.

A face, spit dripping off the chin, that went red-hot. He threw an enormous punch that caught Mackie—still on the move, stepping between them—in the side, cracking bones and knocking her breath away. She went down, felt Lianne going right over her, throwing herself at Samsonov. Then came another cracking sound, and Lianne was down too. Samsonov bent, took a handful of Lianne's hair, wiped his face with it.

Krupsha and Turbo came over, gazed down at them. "What's the plan?" Krupsha said. "Mexican interment?"

"This is a very good phrase," Samsonov said; he took a deep breath, calmed himself. "Yes, of course, Mexican interment, very soon for the author, a little later for the others."

"Taking them to the mountain house?" Turbo said.

Samsonov nodded. "We will use up their charms, Turbo, myself, some of the other employees. This we call a perk. You too are welcome, Clay."

"The young one, maybe," Krupsha said.

"I love America," Samsonov said, "but American women are still a puzzle to me. Something is going a little wrong with them."

"Tell me about it," said Krupsha.

Samsonov laughed. "Another excellent phrase, so clipped." He gave Mackie a little kick. "Up," he said. "The temperamental daughter too." They got up. "Help the author to his feet."

Mackie and Lianne went to Loeb. Lianne slipped off her backpack. They helped Loeb stand. He swayed back and forth a little. They supported him on either side.

"Everybody ready?" said Samsonov.

Turbo opened the second steel door. A man wearing an All-American Amusements, Inc. T-shirt stood with his shotgun on the other side. Beyond him another man trundled a cart loaded with what looked like soft, brown bricks.

Out the door: Samsonov first, then Mackie and Lianne, holding Loeb up, his feet trying to help but mostly dragging, followed by Krupsha, Turbo last. They walked along the tunnel, naked bulbs hanging far apart, wooden beams supporting the roof, holding back soft spots in the earthen walls. In the distance stood a yellow forklift, half blocking the passage. Mackie tried to think of some way to use it, could not. But what about when they reached the other side, under Club Girlie, full of people?

She spoke in a low voice, hardly a murmur. "When we get to the other side—" Someone swatted the back of her head. She stopped talking.

They came to the forklift. Across Loeb's shoulders, Mackie felt Lianne give her arm a little squeeze.

"Wait a minute," Lianne said. She stopped.

Samsonov turned.

"I'll make a deal," Lianne said.

"You have nothing to deal."

"The money," Lianne said. "The money from the bank."

"But it is gone with the aliens," said Samsonov.

Lianne shook her head. She started to bend her knees. Mackie picked up her movement; they lowered Loeb to the ground, letting him lean against the forklift. "That was just a story," Lianne said. "I was hoping to hang on to it."

"Where is it?" Samsonov said.

"I'll tell you," said Lianne. "But only if you let us go."

Samsonov gazed down at her. "Money first," he said.

A stone dislodged somewhere nearby, landed with a thud.

"You have to promise," Lianne said.

"I promise."

"Shake on it," said Lianne.

Samsonov laughed, a short little bark, and shook her hand.

"It's in the backpack," Lianne said.

"Backpack?"

"My school backpack," said Lianne. "I left it in your office."

"Why?"

"I had a plan."

"What plan?"

"It doesn't matter now, does it?"

"I am not believing you."

Lianne shrugged.

"Turbo," Samsonov said.

"Get the backpack?" said Turbo.

"Yes."

"You trust him with all that money?" Lianne said.

Turbo turned to her, his eyes making that scary change behind his glasses. They changed in a different way when Samsonov said, "Bringing it back unopened, of course."

Turbo walked back down the tunnel, a little slumped, almost disappearing in the shadows between the lightbulbs. The guard opened the steel door. Turbo went inside, came back out in seconds with the backpack in his hands. He headed back, advancing through the pools of gloom, was almost halfway when Lianne bolted toward him.

Krupsha charged after her, Samsonov too, Samsonov overtaking him almost right away. Turbo stopped under one of the lightbulbs, confusion on his face. Mackie saw Lianne take something from her pocket, a plastic thing like a TV remote. Just as Samsonov was about to tackle her from behind, she dove to the ground, rolled behind a wooden side support, pointing the plastic thing at Turbo. Samsonov wheeled around toward her. Krupsha reached for his gun.

Then came a flash, an incandescent glare in which Turbo vanished, and a tremendous boom, a boom with lots of visual components. One was a wooden beam that flew right through Krupsha's chest. That was the last thing Mackie saw before the boom blew her away.

She came to rest far down the tunnel, the air full of dust, the only light coming at first from sparking wires, then from flames that sprang up here and there. One of them burned near Loeb. He hadn't moved at all, safe in the lee of the forklift. Mackie rose. An earthquake started up, knocking her off her feet. She crawled up the tunnel.

"You all right?" she said.

Loeb nodded.

"Stay here."

The ground kept trembling. Ahead of her, toward the American side, the roof had fallen in, was still falling. Mackie crawled over a mound of debris, came to a region where the cave-in was complete, an impassable wall of earth and rock. Through a narrow shaft, she saw stars twinkling above.

"Lianne," she called. "Lianne." And started digging with her hands, throat and lungs clogged with dust.

"Lianne. Lianne." Mackie dug frantically, clawing through the earth. Everything kept shaking, wires sparked, fires grew, marching toward her up the tunnel from the Mexican side. Her fingers touched something human, a nose, a human nose, a human face. She threw the dirt aside, wiped off the face, her hand a blur: Samsonov. Just his face, like a death mask, the rest of him all buried. He choked, gasped, started breathing. His eyes met hers. She covered him back up.

"Lianne. Lianne."

"I think I've got her," Loeb said.

Mackie turned, saw him digging at her side with his good arm. A beam cracked nearby, then another. Earth fell in clumps from above. They dug together in a frenzy, flinging it aside. A hand appeared, the bloodless curve of an arm, another face like a death mask: Lianne.

Mackie brushed the dirt from her eyes, nose, mouth. "She's not breathing." She put her own mouth to Lianne's, blew in air. It came out: she felt it on her face. She blew in again, and again, and once more. Lianne coughed. More beams cracked. Then another boom, and the roof started falling on the Mexican side, cutting them off.

Lianne tried to say something, her voice so weak it was mostly just breath. It sounded like: "I overdid it."

They dug. Lianne's head came free, then her shoulders. Loeb took one arm, Mackie the other. They pulled her free. The ground shook again, the roof giving way completely in a long cascade from the Mexican side, a wall of earth rumbling toward them, smothering the light of the flames and the sparking wires.

"Up," Mackie said. Doing everything by feel, she pushed Lianne up through that little shaft toward the stars, grabbed Loeb, pushed him up too. They were so slow. She found a handhold, a foothold, started up, the solid world crumbling around her. The wave of earth caught her trailing foot, tried to drag her back down. Mackie strained against it, a desperate animal noise deep in her throat, a horrible image of her bones mingled down there forever with the others. Then her foot came free, and she went flinging out into the night.

For a moment they lay together in a little heap. Then people started coming, lots of them. Mackie rose, pulled Lianne and Loeb to their feet. "Death row is gone for good," Loeb said, bleeding from his nose, mouth, ears. "How's that?"

Mackie didn't know what he was talking about. They got lost in the crowd.

A section of the steel wall had fallen, so the crowd came from both sides of the border, mixed together. Everyone gazed down into the hole, saw what remained of the tunnel. Soon there was plenty of light to see by, because Buckaroo's caught fire and then Club Girlie, sending towers of flame high into the sky, not far from each other at all. For the first half hour or so, spectators passed freely through the gap in the wall, most of them going north.

Loeb turned out to be a poor TV interview—jokes labored, references obscure—but by the time word got around, he'd already been on *Good Morning America* and *Today*, arm in a sling, Diane and Katie cooing sympathetically. *White Midnight* took off, hitting number seven on the *New York Times* bestseller list. Benjie Klein was replaced as his editor by the publisher herself.

At the same time, Loeb lost interest in *White Heat,* two-thirds of the way through. All that work—making Timothy Bolt more real, letting Athena go bad, red tears, blue blood, plotting, police procedure—could wait for another time, or never.

"I'm thinking of trying something a little different," he said.

"Oh," said Harry. "Like what?"

Like what? Like this. It started taking shape in Loeb's mind: "A Western, I guess you could say."